The mind is a terrifying thing

TONY
MARTURANO

a Different Angle

Published in the United Kingdom and the rest of the world by a Different Angle 2017

Cambridge, UK

A catalogue record for this book is available from the British Library

ISBN - 978-0-9540137-9-0

Printed and bound in the USA

For my number one fan, Francesca Marturano-Pratt, who believed in this book before it was even written.

(Oh, and Tommy & Bella, without whom... it would have been finished much sooner!).

*** EXCERPT FROM TRANSCRIPT BEGINS ***

Operator: Police. What is your emergency?
Caller: (inaudible) house.
Operator: Caller, you've reached the police. What's your emergency?
Caller: They're in the house.
Operator: Who? Who is in the house?
Caller: (inaudible) kill me.
Operator: Caller, I'm sorry I can't hear you. Can you speak up for me? What's your name? Can you tell me your name?
Caller: They're inside the house now... Oh God. Please send someone. Please help me.
Operator: Can you tell me where you are? Can you tell me exactly where you are in the house?
(indistinguishable sounds)
Operator: Hello, Caller. Are you still there?
Caller: (indistinguishable sounds. Screaming.) They're killing me! They're killing me!
Operator: Hello? Caller! Hello! Are you there? Can you hear me? Hello? Caller? Hello?

*** EXCERPT FROM TRANSCRIPT ENDS ***

PROLOGUE

I'm a dick.

Granted, I'm also many other things. Most of which are not by any stretch of the imagination complimentary.

I know this.

And, there'll come a point in this story where you won't think much of me either, and that's okay. You won't be the first and you certainly won't be the last.

To be perfectly honest, even I've run out of adjectives to describe someone like me, to explain and or justify the things that I've done. You see, I'm like one of those addicts... the kind you feel sorry for, but would much rather not have around. The kind your conscience compels you to help, perhaps even donate money to, and yet, as soon as your back is turned, I'll most likely go back out and do it all over again.

In my defence – if I were in any way putting up a defence – one could argue that, as an addict, I'm not responsible for my actions. I'm sick. I need help, or maybe even a spot of that overused thing, rehabilitation.

If I were so inclined, and I'm not, I could go into that whole psycho evaluation of why I am the way I am and do the things that I do, but that would take way too long and, well, I don't really have the time. You see, I'm late. In fact, I'm what will most likely be perceived as disappointingly late for a very important meeting with a very important person, and I've got to get going.

So, I guess the only alternative is to take you with me – but only as an observer, of course – and only if you promise not to get all judgemental.

Who am I kidding? You're probably already judging me as you read this. Well? Are you?

If you are, save it. I already have enough of that going on in my subconscious, much of which I've skilfully suppressed, and there's a reason for that.

There's also a reason why most of us go about our lives hiding what we don't want to see of ourselves, and the ones we care about. It is, as you may have seen countless times in movies, our self-preservation reflex. And, sometimes, our minds hide those things so well that even we can't see them.

Yet, like an old sewage system, you plug up one leak and another one's only going to spring up and start spewing out excrement.

It's why the world is spawning a whole new legion of therapists, psychoanalysts, and counsellors. They help people see, opening their eyes to things they'd much rather hide – you know… all those things festering in deep, black recesses, yet manifesting themselves elsewhere. Therapists tend to dig deep, all the way to the rotten root of a problem, and dredge all that putridity to the surface so it can be analysed, processed, and sanitised.

I know this because I, too, have a few bloated corpses of my own. Some of them buried not deep enough to stop the odd waft of decay from bubbling to the surface.

Of course, when it does, I find that a few drinks often help to mask the stench. But when I say I drink, I don't mean I do it to obliteration – that would imply I have a problem. I *don't* have a problem.

You believe me, right?

What did I say about being judgemental?

I don't have a problem with alcohol. I just enjoy drinking, socially, like most people. Sometimes, I drink a little more, but so what? I'm not harming anybody. I'm still able to function, do my job. I'm still able to help all of the other wretched fucks-ups like me. Some of them, worse.

Oh, didn't I mention that?

I am a therapist. A counsellor. A psychologist. Basically, one of those people who likes to poke around in your mind and find out why you do the things you do. And by *find out*, of course, I'm talking about helping you reach that conclusion through a series of consultations.

I've been doing this job a few years now. Okay, well… Correction, I was doing the job until a couple of months ago. I can't remember exactly, because it's one of those things I mentioned – one of those days that I'm trying not to think or talk about, and especially not with you because, well, I don't know you.

Similarly, you don't really know me… although, based on what I've just said, you'll probably have already formed an opinion, a profile, because that's what humans do. We sort, categorise, and stereotype.

See how the mind works?

That said, if you could at least try to give me the benefit of the doubt and not write me off as another cliché, I'd appreciate it.

Either way, it's up to you. Just know that I'm not looking to excuse myself. Nor am I seeking absolution from you of all people, and there's one simple reason for that, I can't.

Bad things happen to all of us even though sometimes they don't seem to happen in equal measure.

ELLIE

Friday. 12:03 PM.

London in September – hot, busy, and stifling.

I can't tell if my shirt is sticking to my back because of the meteorological conditions or the fact that Ellie has finally agreed to meet me for lunch.

This is actually the first time I'll be seeing her after what happened, too, and I'm nervous as a fucking teenager on his first date. Which is odd, considering that she's my wife, and we've known each other since we were kids and have pretty much been inseparable since.

Until recently.

The pungent stench of yesterday's sweaty armpits interrupts my thoughts and I turn to tune into a scrawny looking lad with a faded white vest, greasy hair, and grey eyes who's nodding his head at me. I imagine him speaking the word, "*Wassup?*"

I reluctantly return the nod, moments before a tsunami of humanity engulfs me and sweeps me into the elevator that'll take me up and out of here.

"All the way to the back, please. Please move all the way to the back of the lift," a tinny voice orders from the speaker mounted into the cabin wall.

Like I have a choice.

Jesus.

I'm crushed into the warm metal box as it fills rapidly with hot bodies, shuffling and then pinning me to the back of the smudge-stained container. Subconsciously, I hold my breath until my body starts to rebel against imminent death and forces me, surreptitiously and unwillingly, to exhale and then inhale the dank air into my lungs.

That's when I become aware of her. She's the only thing that truly smells good in here. Fresh.

I turn my head like a satellite dish, making the movement seem casual, away from the ingrained smudges, until my gaze locks on her breasts. They're ample. Delicious. And they're peeking out from a white lace dress. Fleshy. Pink. Enticing. The urge to trail my tongue over them is strong, as if I'm the famished and they the food.

Fuck.

I lift my eyes to discover wavy black hair and a slender neck. It's adorned by a tiny mole that seems to move with her pulse beneath the olive skin that's glowing under a fine mist of perspiration. Her eyes are large and brown. Her nose is broad and curved. Her lips are thick, cherry red, and they're smiling at me.

She's exotic. And in shape.

I smile back.

My heart obviously wants to touch her because it's knocking on my rib cage, asking to be set free as I feel a different kind of heat rising to my cheeks, the tickling sensation of sweat in my hair, and that blissfully familiar tightening of arousal in my jeans.

Shit.

Mercifully, the bell sounds and we spill out of the pen towards the turnstiles where I scan my Oyster card and move forward as fast as I can.

The urge to look back at her, to snatch one last look at that golden skin, is strong, but I resist – telling myself that nothing good would come of this, today of all days.

This is exactly why I hate taking the Underground; too much bloody temptation!

I move out of the building and into the street where I gulp in fresh, albeit warm, air.

As always, Covent Garden is bustling with people who are sauntering, lingering, and rushing in all directions. Many oblivious to those following them and most deep in conversations that fill the air with unintelligible sibilance.

I move skilfully through the crowd; I'm already running late, and the last thing I need today is to be held up by a bunch of strangers who are in no hurry to be anywhere.

The pub, a red brick building with delusions of historic importance as well as an identity crisis – as it doesn't seem to know if it wants to be a traditional establishment or a stuck-up wine bar – is just off the main square. The Grapevine is its pretentious name. It's a favourite of Ellie's and, not unlike the rest of London, it's bloody rammed.

It's one of the few buildings that has a large terrace overlooking part of Covent Garden and, to be fair, the view is impressive, but it isn't a patch on the petite blonde I spot sitting at one of the tiny tables at the far end. And, after pretty much elbowing my way towards her, I pause to take a mental snapshot.

My wife is peering into the depths of her wineglass as if it's a crystal ball. She looks sad. Lonely. Her hair is tied into a ponytail, the rest is swept off her face into a fringe. This makes me smile; it's something she does when she's hot, means business, or both. She's wearing a tight, white shirt and a black skirt, along with her school-teacher small spectacles.

She isn't a school teacher, though; far from it. That's just the pet name I give her when she dresses like this. It's one of my favourite looks for her, because she looks as bloody cute as she is sexy, and much younger than her thirty-three years.

God, I'm filled with so much love for her right now.

My heart's at it again, too. This time thumping against my shirt, which is rapidly becoming a second skin.

Somehow sensing my presence, Ellie looks up with a faint smile and blue eyes that twinkle against the haze of the sun reflecting off her shirt.

I wave as I make my way towards her. "Hey," I croak as I emerge from behind a lanky fella with no self-awareness.

All of the small tables here are taken, which means that there's also a crowd of people standing about with drinks in their hands, each occasionally jostling for the best view over the square.

"Hey," Ellie says softly, looking up at me.

"I'm sorry I'm late."

She shrugs and forces a smile, as if to ask, *What else is new?*

"I bought you a water."

"Oh, thanks," I say, grabbing the bottle which is still glistening with sweat, and breaking the seal to drink it down.

Behind me, the lunch crowd is rowdy and loud, and someone is annoyingly kicking against the back of my chair.

Ellie is gazing across the large flower boxes that overlook the hive of tourist activity below us, and I can't help but wonder if she's genuinely interested in what's going on down there or just killing time as I suck down water like I've just returned from a Saharan excursion. Whatever her reason, I watch her profile and am reminded not just of how gorgeous she is, but of our history together. And our son... And I fucking miss them. I don't think I have ever missed anyone as much as I do the two of them right now, in this very moment.

I place the now empty water bottle on the table between us and expel a grateful sigh of satisfaction.

"Phew, I really needed that," I say with a smile. "Thanks."

She nods.

"It's bloody warm, isn't it?" The weather? Really? I have so much to say, and yet, suddenly and inexplicably, I've lost the bloody power to articulate.

"You look well," she says, nodding at me.

"I do?" I glance at myself as my cheeks flush. "Thanks."

Then I look up at her again and our eyes meet. Shit, where have all my words gone?

"I can't stay long," she says suddenly, breaking the silence between us. "I need to get back to work."

"Oh, I thought we were having lunch," I tell her, disappointed.

"Yes, I know. Sorry. Just, things have been really busy. We have a launch in a few weeks and things are hectic."

"Well, I wouldn't worry about it – I know the boss," I say with a wink, which must annoy her, because she snaps.

"You know that doesn't make a difference, right? The job still has to be done."

"Of course. I know. I wasn't implying anything, I was just…" I stop there, taking a breath because I'm so bloody nervous I know my hands are shaking.

It's so bloody hot and the people behind me are so noisy that I can't hear myself think.

I roll my shoulders in an effort to shrug off the tension that's building in them as another thump jolts me forward and the hyena-type laugh of the girl behind me further scratches down my frayed nerves.

"Look, Ellie," I say, loudly because it feels as if the whole world is closing in on me and my words are being drowned out by the inconsiderate shits surrounding us like Indians around a wagon. In hindsight, this probably isn't the best place for us to do this.

I move to turn in my seat, but feel Ellie's hand on mine. It's cool despite the mugginess.

"…Marco," she says, sensing my tension.

I turn to see she's shaking her head slowly at me, but I'm not sure if she's referring to my action or to what I'm about to say.

"Don't say it," she adds.

"Say what? El, you don't even know what I was going to say."

"Whatever it is. Please don't speak."

I frown. "El—"

"No, please, Marco. I just don't want to hear any more of your excuses."

She sounds angry, seemingly exhausted, as if we've just finished a lengthy debate, when in reality I haven't even managed to start the speech I've spent every waking moment assembling, ever since she finally said yes to this meeting. The same bloody speech that's hiding at the back of my mind, right behind my ability to speak to this woman who I adore, with whom I have a son and for whom I would give my life.

A lump forms in my throat. I know my wife is angry at me. She has every right to be – especially after everything that's happened – but there's something else in her gaze that I'm finding particularly unsettling. Something that tells me that this meeting isn't necessarily about reconciliation, but something else, and that there's a good chance I'm not going to like it.

"How's the little man?" I ask, trying a different tack. She just looks at me, saying nothing. "I was really hoping to see him today," I continue. "It's been a long time, El, I miss him."

She swallows hard and I can see that she's fighting back tears, but then she speaks with trembling determination. "There's something we need to talk about."

It feels like she's just punched me in the gut.

"What is it?" I ask, warily. Something about the way she's said that worries me.

She sighs and looks out over the square again.

Shit. She's avoiding eye contact. That's when I know something is very wrong and, in a kneejerk reaction, I try to head it off.

"Ellie, I know I screwed up," I begin quickly. She starts to shake her head. "But, just hear me out, okay? I know I messed up, and I know you're angry right now, but it's that very anger that's blocking you from receiving constructive…"

"…Are you serious?" she snaps, turning to face me. "I'm not one of your fucking clients, Marco." Her voice is a hiss. Her eyes narrow.

And there it is. Shit, I hate this about us. It doesn't matter how I approach these situations; she always assumes that I'm trying to handle her, though that couldn't be any further from the truth. I just want us to be able to connect. I want to be able to communicate with her, talk this through, and I really hate that, when it comes to her, my skills as a therapist are useless.

"I know you're not. I'm just trying to speak to you, El. I just want us to talk."

"We are talking," she says, pursing her lips and retreating into the back of her chair.

"El, I know what I did seems unforgivable," I try again, calmly, but the words choke in my throat so that I have to pause to take a deep breath and recollect my thoughts.

Then, I hold my hands up. "Okay, look, I can't tell you anything here today that you haven't heard before and probably don't believe anyway, but I'm sorry, El. I'm really, truly sorry, so sorry that you wouldn't even believe it. But, please, don't let everything that's good about us be reduced to this. We're more than that," I supplicate. "And…look, I'm not going to insult your intelligence. Just tell me what to do. Tell me what I need to do. Anything, and I'll do it," I say, ignoring yet another thump against my chair.

"You've already done enough," she responds, and her words are razor blade sharp, even if her face is sad.

"Don't' say that. Definitely don't say it *like* that. Come on, El. Come on. Please."

"No, I mean it, Marco."

I smile, delicately. "You don't – come on, babe. It's still me. I'm still me. Yeah, I'm a dick, but then, you know that. And I am still the guy you're in love with, aren't I? The bloke you married? In fact, you once told me that you loved the fact that I wasn't perfect, that I was flawed. Remember? You said it meant that I needed you, and I do need you, El, now more than ever. I need you to forgive me. Please," I say as I reach across the table. "Help me make this better," I say gently.

Well, as gently I can, considering the fucking racket going on around us.

She pushes my hand away. "No, Marco. Not this time. There's no coming back from this." Her voice is tense, determined, and her eyes… they are everywhere and only eventually on me, and now I can see that they're brimming with tears.

"El?"

She looks away again.

"Babe, please."

She doesn't respond. Seconds tick by. People keep talking, the hyena keeps laughing, and I can feel the anger bubbling up through me like a lava flow, and there's no stopping it.

I cock my head. "I'm confused, El. Why am I here?"

Eventually, she turns to face me, catches my gaze and holds it for a very long time. Long enough for me to tune into the rumble of a jet engine overhead and for my thoughts to drift to the passengers on board. Are they flying away from or back to reality? Closer to Earth, music is pumping through speakers mounted high on the wall above us. Ironically, the dance track is some guy wailing about his partner letting him go.

I tune out the caterwauling and focus on my wife's steely gaze. Her lip is quivering and her eyes suddenly narrow with determination.

I swallow, my mouth dry once more. This *is* serious.

"I can't take you back, Marc." She clears her throat and adds, "I'm not taking you back, not this time." The words come out as a tremble, yet they're laden with resolve.

"El, please. I need you. I need Toby! Please. I have nowhere else to go."

She sneers, "Is that all you're worried about? You have nowhere else to stay?"

"You know it isn't that…"

"Then what is it, Marco?"

"It's you, us, our family," I say softly, reaching across the table once more. "I miss you both, a lot."

She watches me for the longest time, her eyes truth-detecting mine.

"Has David kicked you out already?"

"No, you know he hasn't. But I'm ready to leave. I mean I love him and everything, but have you ever had to listen to two gays mating? It's like a David Attenborough wild animals special."

She suppresses a smile.

I often make her laugh. It's actually one of my few redeeming features when it comes to her. That, and how I am with our son, how safe she feels when she's with me, and who I am. Or more specifically, who I've become, despite my past. And still, there's this thing. This one bloody thing that threatens to ruin it all.

She sits back in her chair again. "What about your dad's place?" Her tone is serious, challenging.

"El. I just told you, this isn't just about having somewhere to stay. I want to come home."

"I heard you. But what about your dad's place?"

"Have I mentioned how pretty you look today?"

"Why do you do that?"

"What?"

"Why do you always change the subject when he's mentioned?"

"I didn't change the subject, El. We're talking about important stuff here."

"Your inheritance is important, Marc. It's money we could use right now and I, you, don't want me to ask my parents."

"So now you only want me for my money?" I ask with a grin and a lift of my eyebrows.

"And now you're back to making jokes," she says with a sigh.

Another knock of my chair jolts a sharper than I intend response. "El, what do you want from me exactly? Just tell me."

I immediately regret the outburst, and so want to turn around and kick the arsehole's teeth down his fucking throat, but I swallow my anger and instead hope that my tone hasn't caused more damage.

It has.

My wife glances at the back of the man standing over me, and then looks me in the eyes and says, "Marc, this isn't just about what happened. It's also about the fact that…" the words catch in her throat, and she has to stop before she continues, "that you need help. You need to face what happened."

"I am facing it. Why do you think I'm here?"

"You need to face *what happened*," she repeats slowly, her eyes boring into mine as if she's trying to get a message to me without anybody else knowing. She continues, "I think some time out of the city will do you good."

A ripple of hope runs through me. "You want us to go away? Where? When?"

"Not us, Marc. You."

"What?"

"You've been agonising about your father's house for months now. I think you need to go back and deal with it."

"Are you fucking joking? I'd rather rip my balls off than step foot back in that place."

"Well, it's yours now. You're going to have to deal with it eventually."

I think about this. "No, I'm not going back to that shitty place, El. Not now, anyway. I just want to come home. Just let me come home. Please.

Besides, for all we know, that place might have been condemned, reclaimed by the fucking ocean, for all I care!"

"You don't know that. You haven't been there since you were a child."

"I know," I say, a bitter taste suddenly forming in my mouth, "and there's a reason for that!"

"You told me that you have wonderful childhood memories from there, with your mother."

"Yeah? Well, I also scream 'God' sometimes after sex, but that doesn't make me religious," I say.

Ah, shit.

She glares at me as I try to recover. "My best memories are with you and Toby…"

"No, hold on," she interrupts. "Are you saying that what you told me about your childhood there was a lie?"

I close my eyes for a few seconds and picture a lorry hurtling toward me – lights blazing, horn blaring – and eventually I confess, "I have *a* memory; the rest I may have romanticised a little, because I know you enjoyed hearing about them, and because you said you didn't have that with your parents…"

I watch storm clouds gather in her eyes. "You really are fucking unbelievable," she sneers.

I add quickly, "El, this isn't about what happened then. This is about what could happen now. It isn't about old memories, but about us making new ones, together."

"Don't you dare do that."

"What?"

"You know what. That whole family crap."

"It isn't crap, El. It's how I feel. You know that."

"Then you should have thought about that before unzipping your fucking trousers!"

Her voice was loud enough to make the group next to us pause their chatter and look over. Yeah. Juicy gossip for you, you fucking arseholes!

I glare at them and then look at my wife. "El, I know I screwed up, babe, I do…"

"…Oh, stop it, Marco. Just stop. I've heard it all before, remember? It's exactly what you said last time."

I was about to respond, but stop myself since it suddenly and inexplicably feels like I'm pointlessly rolling a giant boulder up a hill. She's right. I was sorry then. I was grief-stricken with remorse, but saying sorry is just fine as the first step in the plan of atonement – it isn't the key to absolution. I know that. I know that not only because I'm a therapist, but also because, as my wife said, we've been here before, and only this time it's worse – much worse.

"I love you, Marco. I love you more than I have and probably ever will love anyone else, but this has got to stop. You have a problem, a serious problem, that needs fixing. If I take you back, I'll just be enabling you, *again,* and I can't; I won't do that. I can't put myself through that, not anymore."

"What are you saying?"

"I'm saying you're sick!" she whispers loudly, desperately. "You're sick and you need help." The last part of her sentence is delivered much more slowly, almost reluctantly.

Then, with a flourish, she wipes a tear from her cheek and reaches into a bag on the floor from which she withdraws a large manila envelope, then places it on the table.

"What's that?" I ask warily, as if it's a vial of acid.

"Marco." Her blue eyes are full of tears once more, but she goes on, "I can't even imagine what life would be like without you…"

"El…"

She holds up a silencing hand, sniffs back tears, and says, "Fuck, it's only ever been us against the world, but…"

"What's in the envelope, El?"

"You love me, don't you?"

"More than my own life."

"And you'll do anything to get us back together?"

"Anything."

"Then prove it," she says, sliding the envelope towards me without taking her trembling hand off of it, as if to do so would be to release its deadly contents prematurely. Then, she dabs away tears with a napkin as I eye the thing like it might explode in my face at any moment.

After a few nail-bitingly long seconds of eye drying, she shakes her head and the resolve comes back into her face. Then, swallowing hard, my wife speaks words that – despite the claustrophobic stuffiness of the place and the stifling heat of the Indian summer – send an icy boulder rolling down my chest and into my stomach.

"Inside the envelope are divorce papers," she says stoically.

"What? El!"

"…divorce papers and a business card."

I move to open the thing, to verify its contents, but she keeps her hand on it and her eyes on mine. Something she always does with both me and Toby when she wants to make sure we're paying attention to what she's saying, and that, at least in the technical sense, we're *receiving*. "You now have a choice. You can sign those papers…"

"…I'm not signing the papers," I say quickly.

"… You can sign the papers or you can ring the number on that card."

I laugh, nervous. "Fine, I'll do that. What's the number?"

"I did a lot of research. He comes highly recommended."

I eye her and her hand, suspiciously.

"He's a therapist," she says.

I smile, relief spreading through me. Divorce or couple's therapy? No brainer. I'm fine with that. I'm sanguine enough to appreciate the fact that I may well be a therapist, but something like this needs the impartial, cold scrutiny of a stranger. "You want us to go to therapy?" I ask with a smile.

She shakes her head. "Not us, Marco. You," she delivers solemnly.

I lose my smile. "What?"

"I want you to book an appointment."

"El," I laugh, incredulously, "I *am* a therapist."

"Then you'll know just how useful it can be."

"Yeah, if I needed therapy, but I don't."

"You do."

"I don't."

"The fact that you can't keep it in your pants tells me that you do. Why else would you fuck around on the person you purport to love? Why would you do *that*, huh?"

Her words are spoken through gritted teeth, a filter for both the rage and her attempt at discretion.

I'm speechless for a few seconds as I take in both the severity of my wife's words as well as the sting they've inflicted, but I'm not hurt – I'm mortified. She's right, after all. How does anyone inflict this kind of shit on someone they're supposed to care about? I love my wife, I adore our son, and yet…

The thumping against the back of my chair brings me back to the moment, and back to the reality of what I'm being asked to do as well as the fact that this meeting hasn't gone anything like I hoped. In fact, it's turned out far worse.

Then, to add insult to injury, it starts to rain. It's more of a mist, though – a very fine mist made of red sand. Billions and billions of sharp, jagged particles scratching against my skin, making my veins itch, my eyes water, and washing the world with scarlet.

The next thing I know, I'm jumping up from my seat, the action flipping the table in front of me, and I'm spinning around to the bastard who's been knocking at the back of my chair. He barely has a chance to face me before my right fist connects with the side of his jaw, catapulting him into the group of people he was yapping to, knocking a couple of them and their drinks over like skittles.

Then, there's screaming from women, angry hollers from men, and imploring tears from Ellie.

The rest is a blur.

DAVID

Friday. 21.30.

There are no prizes for guessing what type of bar-slash-club Rainbow is. Leave it to the gays to convert a decaying warehouse into something that looks more like a film set.

A massive rainbow dominates one end of the place, at the foot of which is a large LED spectacular of a bar. On the opposite side, the dance floor heaves with bodies while, overhead, a giant half-moon glows in a constellation of glittering stars that flicker an array of colours on rhythm with the beat.

The place is impressive, and while it would be easy to label it a gay bar, I've come to learn that it's more than that – attracting all kinds of clientele, including the odd celebrity.

I'm making my way towards the bar, passing standing tables surrounded by a collection of characters. Most of whom are dressed conservatively. Others... well, not so much. The music is loud. I can feel it vibrating through my trainers. The track is familiar; it's a rhythmic deep house mix of *Cruel Summer*. No shit.

David, my best friend and current landlord, is standing at the bar, talking animatedly to a collection of people, but he breaks off the moment he spots me making my way over.

"Ah, there he is," he says, voice brimming with artificial maternal sympathy. It's just David's way of encouraging me not to sink further into an abyss of abject misery.

Oh, and I use the term 'maternal' loosely by the way; David is far from that. Yes, he's gay, but he's not a femme. He'd be the first person to tell you that. He's from Croydon, a borough of London, and has the accent to prove it. He's also six feet something, wears stubble, and knows how to handle himself. Much of that character build comes from school bullying after one of his experimental indiscretions with a close friend was witnessed by another pupil and the news got out.

Not that David allowed it to keep him from success. The man is a computer programming genius. He designed his first app while still in his teens and sold his second to a Californian tech company when he was still in his twenties. Now, in his early thirties, he owns his own fully staffed game design company with offices both here in London and in San Francisco, and it turns over a fortune.

Many have made the mistake of underestimating him, but it's always been very clear to me that, despite the decade that separates us, this guy has his shit together in ways I can only dream of.

I'm reminded of it yet again as he puts an arm around me. "Rough day, eh, buddy?" He asks with an exaggerated Californian twang.

"You could say that," I reply.

"Come on, let's get some drinks in ya. Make ya feel better."

He gestures at a shirtless barman with rippling muscles and glistening skin, and then he turns to me.

"Seriously, David. After the day I've had, you bring me to a gay club?"

"Um, correction. This used to be a gay club – now it's been overrun by your lot. The straight girls started coming here to avoid getting hit on by blokes like you. Now, the straight blokes have clocked onto that and are coming here because of all the straight girls, so it's just a fucking logistical nightmare. Look – we've even got gorgeous babes in bras behind the bar now! Whatever next, huh?" he asks, smiling at the gorgeous barmaid as she moves past us to serve other waiting drinkers.

I nod, appreciatively.

"Yeah, so thanks for making my point. Besides, after a day like yours, the best place to go is a gay club instead of one of those miserable old grey places where people take themselves and each other way too seriously. And anyway," he begins, turning me to face him as if he's about to set to fixing me and my problems, "What the fuck, dude?"

"Hey, David!" The group of people my friend was talking to before I showed up, all of whom are models from what I can tell, are again trying to get his attention.

"Come on, guys, my boy's here and he needs me. Playtime is over," he says seriously, and then adds with a wink, "For now! Now, shoo, I've got serious business to attend to."

The group reluctantly returns to their own conversation.

"Business?" I ask miserably.

"Yeah, well, between you and me, that's how I deal with all of your dramas. I just approach them all as if they're business problems."

"All of my dramas?"

"Are you planning on repeating everything I say? Because if you are, it's gonna be a bloody long night."

"Well, you know, I'm hearing this stuff for the first time."

"No, you're not. You're *feeling* it for the first time."

"And there's me thinking I was the therapist."

"Yeah, exactly. You'd think that, with all of your so-called experience, you'd have somehow learned how to self-heal."

"Self-heal?"

"Put it on my tab, will ya?" he requests with a wink at a different barman. Only this one's sporting a shaved head, and must have poured himself into his black shirt because his biceps are threatening to rip their way out of the fabric. This isn't lost on David, who only absentmindedly pushes my beer in front me.

"Seriously?"

"What?" he asks.

"I'm in deep crisis here, and you're just thinking about your next shag."

"Oh please, like you didn't clock every bird on your way over here, despite your—" he makes quote marks with his fingers... "crisis."

"I didn't actually."

"No?"

"No."

"Interesting. So, you're telling me you didn't notice your fan club over there either?" He nods at a group of girls at the opposite end of the bar.

I follow his gaze; a duo from the group of twenty-somethings congregated there glance in our direction.

This isn't an uncommon occurrence when David and I are out together. He isn't overtly gay and, despite his sticky-out ears, his short mousy brown hair, brown eyes, and toned six-foot frame, he's always managed to attract the ladies. I'm forever teasing him that the attention he receives has nothing to do with his so-called gift of the gab, and everything to do with that one curl of hair on his forehead that I love to refer to as his Rin Tin flick, just because I know it pisses him off.

"Looks like you've struck again," I say loudly, over the pounding dance track. "You'll probably want to go over there and let them down gently."

He takes a sip from his drink, then shakes his head.

"What?" I ask.

He laughs. "After all this time, you still don't see it, do you?"

"See what?"

"It's not me they're looking at, you fool."

"No? Who are they looking at, then?"

"I know them. They're regulars here. They know I don't swing that way, and, from memory, I don't think they swing yours either, but they're looking at you, you dope."

I glance across at them. They wave at me, and then look at each other and giggle.

"How is it you never see this?"

I shrug.

"Seriously, dude, you've been rockin' the whole Jamie Dornan thing for years now – how are you not seeing that?"

I laugh, take a swig from my glass, and ask, "Who the fuck's Jamie Dornan?"

"Seriously?"

"Well, you'll appreciate that I'm not into all of that American Hollywood shit like you."

"He's actually Irish."

"Okay."

"Do you really not know who I'm talking about?"

"No."

"*The Fall*?"

I shake my head. Pull a face.

"*Fifty Shades of Grey*?"

I think about that one for a few seconds. "Oh, him. I look like him? You been popping pills again?"

He puts his hand on the back of my head and turns it to face the mirror behind the bar's optics. I stare at my reflection. My hair, which I normally keep very short, is looking scraggy, and my eyes, normally hazel green by sunlight, look tar black under the LED lights. And I'm sporting some seriously freakish dark circles.

At least, that's all I can see.

"How exactly do you think you managed to have sex with all those birds over the years?"

I groan, shake my head, and drink from my glass. "Don't remind me."

He slaps my back. "So, what happened anyway?"

I have his attention now.

I sigh. "I don't know. I just lost it when she gave me her *ultimatum.*"

"And you decided to deck some stranger to win her over?"

"I don't know what happened. He'd been thumping my chair the whole time I was there. He'd wound me up and I just saw red."

"Is he going to press charges?"

"I don't think so."

"Really?"

"Yeah, Ellie spoke to him."

"She did? Man, you don't deserve that woman. She's always cleaning up your shit."

"Not anymore," I say, taking another long draft from my pint. "Oh, and thanks for your support by the way."

"Well, you're your own worst enemy, mate. You're there to try and reconcile with your wife, but instead you start a bloody fight. What the fuck's wrong with you?"

I glance at him. "Not helping. Aren't you supposed to be *my* best friend?"

"I am. But I'm hers, too."

"Oh, right."

"Oh no, don't start that rubbish. This has nothing to do with our friendship. This is you, not helping yourself. It took me ages to convince her to meet you, and then you piss all over it. What the hell?"

He seems genuinely annoyed, I realise.

We let the music stomp for a few seconds, during which I feel like I should be apologising, but I've already done enough of that. At least, I have in my head.

Oh, and for the record, I may be many things, but I'm not a violent person. Or at least, let me be specific... I don't smack women around or anything like that. God, no. Not that I have to explain myself, but I don't want you getting the wrong idea about me, either.

That said, along with all my other failings, of which there are many, I can be hot-headed. Some call it passionate because I'm part Italian – namely Ellie, when the mood takes her.

"So, I suppose you knew all about the divorce thing?" I ask my supposed best friend.

"No, I didn't."

"Come on, David."

"Fuck off, Marco. No! I didn't know. My guess – she didn't want to tell me because she knew I would try and talk her out of it."

Yeah, he's definitely miffed.

"What's up with you tonight?" I ask. "You'd think you were the one who just pissed all over his marriage and solicited a bloody police warning in the process."

"It's you. You, Marco. You jump from one bloody disaster to another. You've got a good thing here with your family and it pisses me off that you're not doing more to fix this shit. That and the fact that you always manage to make everything about you," he adds, looking away from me and across the dance floor.

Oh? Where did that come from? I launch countermeasures, "Hold on a sec. I tried."

"By putting your fists in some bloke's face?"

I shake my head, and am about to respond, but there's really not anything I can say. So, I just drink some more, and then a bit more until my glass is almost empty.

We both absentmindedly watch people laughing for a minute or so. Then, David sits down on the stool next to me and touches my arm. "Sorry, dude."

"It's okay. I know I'm an idiot, and I appreciate you putting in a good word. I do."

"So what exactly did she tell you?"

"She handed me papers and an ultimatum. Told me that unless I get my shit together, she's divorcing me."

"What does she mean by getting your shit together?"

I hesitate, finishing my drink and prompting David to summon a refill. "She wants me to go into therapy," I answer.

He stares at me for a few seconds, saying nothing – unusual for him – and then he bursts into laughter, and I'm not talking a chuckle, I'm talking big guffaws of laughter that he accompanies with the dramatic gesture of hanging onto the bar for support.

I let him get it out of his system for what feels like minutes, irked that he should find the whole thing so bloody hilarious. I know exactly why he's laughing, of course; the irony of the whole shitty situation isn't lost on me either, but still.

He must see the look on my face because he finally puts his arm around me again and says with a pout, "Oh, come on, mate, you've got to see the funny side of that."

"Yeah, well, I'm glad the implosion of my marriage is the cause of such hilarity for you."

"Come on, bud. You must have known this day was going to come, eventually."

"What's that supposed to mean?"

"Look, Marco, I love you, but you are a bit of a knob."

"Easy – all of your support is making me queasy."

"You've got a stunning wife and a great kid, if you like that kind of thing, and yet… what do you expect after what happened? And it isn't the first time." He hesitates, and piles right in, "Mate, seriously, I agree with her. I think you might have a problem – with sex, I mean."

I tense up there, slowly pull away, and look him in the face.

"Fucking hell. *Et tu brutus,*" I breathe. "She's spoken to you, hasn't she?"

"Well, she works for me. What do you expect?"

"Some loyalty would be nice."

"Seriously? Mate. Don't start that. I didn't ask you to put me in this situation; you put yourself here. In fact, you keep putting yourself here. Ellie's my friend, too, and like it or not, your little family's important to me because they're part of you. So, you can have my home, my car, the clothes off my back… shit, you can have anything… but don't start questioning my loyalty, because that's really gonna piss me off."

He's really annoyed now. And, again, I want to apologise. I know that's what he's expecting, too, but I can't. The idea that they were both colluding behind my back is fucking annoying, regardless of motive.

And besides, I've never really been one to wear my heart on my sleeve, exhibiting my emotional self. It's just not how I am. Growing up as I did, that was a sure as fuck way to get fucked, and not in a good way.

And yeah, I know how all this must sound; a therapist who doesn't like to share. Hypocritical much? But if you're judging right now, I have this for you: those who can't, teach.

Enough said.

So now there's something in the air. I've obviously pissed my best mate off, but what can I say? I'm going for a hat trick. Questioning my best friend's loyalty, and not humbling myself in any way nor apologising, which I know is only going to annoy him more.

It does. Soon enough, he's returned his attention to the conversation he was having with his groupies before I arrived.

Shit.

In the next moment, a loud cheer rises from the masses as an Erasure remix fills the air and they all start singing, *"Please, give a little respect to me."* Everybody's at it and, as stupid as it might sound, it feels like they're singing it to me.

Bastards.

I take another swig from my newly replenished glass and then glance to my left; those girls are still looking my way. I turn; David is still giving me his back.

I consider tapping him on the shoulder, telling him how sorry I am, but I can't. It feels like that's all I've been doing, or at least trying to do, all day.

I cogitate for a few more seconds. Then…Fuck it. I'm not in the mood right now. I'll sort it later. There is something else all of this has got me in the mood for, though.

And no, I haven't got a problem. I just enjoy sex, a lot.

I grab my glass and stride to the end of the bar. One of the girls blushes – the short one with bobbed hair, a pair of giant brown eyes and a cracking figure – and the fact that my mere presence is having that effect on her is causing an effect on me.

"Evenin', ladies. So, this is where all the fun is?" I ask. Then add, "How's your evenin' been so far?"

"It just got a whole lot better," says the tall blonde, Brown Eyes' companion. She's wearing a skirt, way too short for those long legs of hers.

Now, most blokes would find that stuff a turn-on, and it is, but it's a bit obvious for me. I prefer brown eyes because, well, I've got a bit of a thing for those. And this one, she has a certain innocence in hers, but something tells me that she's far from that. Something tells me that, in the privacy of a hotel room, she'd be everything but, and the thought of ruining her evokes a tightening in my boxers.

"So, where are the lads?" I ask.

Blondie cocks her head, and then asks, in a nasal, Estuary whine, "What do ya mean?"

"Well, what are a couple of babes like you doing here all on your own? I would have thought they'd be a whole squadron of blokes lining up to give you ladies the whole platinum rule treatment."

Blondie giggles. "Oh yeah? And what's that?"

I feign surprise. "What? You mean you haven't experienced it before?"

They look at each other, shake their heads and then burst out laughing.

I slide in closer. "Well, you've heard about the," I make speech marks with my fingers, "*golden* rule, right"? They nod. "The platinum rule is when, as individuals, we don't focus on ourselves, but instead we focus on the needs and wants of others," I say with a wry smile, looking straight into Brown Eye's eyes. Oh, and there it is; her cheeks have switched to a dark shade of crimson. "For example, rather than make small talk with you by,

I don't know, giving you some cheesy line about how gorgeous you look, which you both do by the way, and pretend I'm interested in what you do for a living and all that good stuff, I could instead engage you in more meaningful dialogue, you know, about the things that really matter to you. What makes you happy, unhappy, ecstatic, or deliriously blissful." I lean in closer to Brown Eyes, "and I would pay lingering attention to the things you find pleasurable as opposed to the things you don't."

Blondie giggles, "Why would ya wanna know about all that?"

"Well, you're human beings, aren't you? You have a mind, a brain, thoughts and feelings that go beyond sex and how the female physical orgasm is more than often triggered by and heightened by her mental one, right?"

The duo look at each other and erupt into another bout of bashful giggles and, even in the flashing lights, I can see that Blondie's rouge seems to have spread to the rest of her porcelain face.

"No that," she says, quickly. "We'd rather talk about that!"

Oh well. I tried.

***

It turns out that David was right; the girls are a couple of lesbians. So, you can imagine my surprise when, after a few more drinks at a place I don't remember, they invite me back to their flat. But I'm not in the mood to be traipsing halfway across London. Where's the fun in that?

So, I check all three of us into the nearest hotel I can find. Of course, with it being the English capital and all, the room is a rip-off, but it has a great view of the Thames River and St Paul's Cathedral, if you're into that stuff.

But no, the only good thing about it in my opinion is the fact that the room has a fuck of a giant king-sized bed onto which Brown Eyes doesn't hesitate to shove me as soon as all three of us are locked behind a *Do Not Disturb* hotel room sign.

Now, you're probably wondering why a couple of girls would invite me back to their pad, considering that they're an item and presumably not into men.

Well, that would be because of what they told me over the fourth and fifth Vodkas.

First, they gave me the usual spiel about me being hot. Personally, I still don't see it, but hey, who am I to argue with the majority? Then I get the familiar squeals about me looking like that actor, which, of course, was even more of a turn-on for them, and then they dropped the most interesting part of their proposition; they wanted to experiment with me, as neither of them had been with a man before.

Well, anyone who knows me knows that, generally, I can be an obliging type of guy.

Which is why I'm now lying on the bed with some Radio One club mix blasting out of the sound system and my head swimming from a cocktail of alcohol. By cocktail, I mean that it didn't seem to matter what it was that I was drinking tonight – if it had a percentage of some kind, it ended up down my throat.

I'm propped up on pillows and my black shirt's unbuttoned, revealing the smattering of hair on my chest, and I'm watching the girls kneeling at the foot of the bed, tonguing and fondling each other. It's slow, deliberate, with no urgency, and a fucking turn-on.

Then, after a minute or so of tongue massaging and nipple teasing, they both look at me, at the supercilious grin I must have on my face and then down at my thighs and crotch, where they can't help but notice a substantial mound under my trousers. I'm obviously ready to get on with things, but they, not quite.

Blondie leans over to the beside cabinet and picks up the bottle of Vodka we brought back with us. She takes a swig and then kisses Brown Eyes, while allowing the transparent liquid to dribble down their chins

Their breasts were already bulging out of their thin dresses, so it isn't difficult for Brown Eyes to tease Blondie's nipples out of hers with her tongue. After enjoying this for a while, Blondie reciprocates.

And, like any hot-blooded heterosexual male, I enjoy the show, but I'm now ready to join in. However, Brown Eyes puts restraining painted nails on my chest and pushes me back into the pillows. Then, she deliberately leans over me, dangling her breasts in my face while fishing around in her clutch bag on the bedside table.

I suckle as nipples move to and from my lips until she retreats, followed closely by Blondie.

They're both leaning over me now, each in turn placing a pill on the tongue of the other and then washing it down with a swig from the bottle.

Then, they look at me. Blondie pushes both of my hands under the pillows and then sticks her tongue out at me. I understand and mirror the act, and she places a pill on my tongue. Brown Eyes pours booze over my mouth from a height while laughing. I swallow, and that's when the party really starts.

Brown Eyes unbuttons my shirt the rest of the way, licking and biting every bit of skin, treating the revelation of my torso as a Christmas morning gift. She pauses occasionally to kiss her companion, slowly and deliciously, and then they both giggle about it.

Blondie, stilettos still on her feet, pulls up her skirt and straddles me, rubbing her panties against the tightness of my jeans as Brown Eyes kisses her deeply, sensually.

I move to unzip myself, but feel Blondie's Union Jack painted fingers on mine. Slowly and deliberately, she unzips me, relieving some of the pressure, but not before unbuckling my belt and wrapping it around my hands, which I had liberated from their exile under the pillows so that they could join in on the celebration... only for them to be bound and pushed back towards my head once more.

They turn up the music or I suddenly tune into it. The rhythm is tribal, the percussion intoxicating, as is whatever is rushing around my bloodstream, accelerating the pounding of my heart and the pumping of the blood pressure to all the extremities of my body.

Within seconds, both girls have wriggled out of their dresses and are in their underwear, playing and fondling each other as well as the boxer-clad erection protruding through my unzipped jeans, as if it's a newly acquired toy.

Then they exchange a telepathic glance and Blondie is on me once more, rubbing her panties against my crotch, seemingly enjoying the fabric friction. Once again, there's no haste to the action, but it continues slow and deliberate, with the occasional flick as she teases me and apparently herself with the pleasure that's still to come.

As this is happening, Brown Eyes pulls at my jeans until I watch them magically disappear down my legs, leaving just my encased hardness behind.

Blondie licks her fingers, tweaks her nipples, and then slides her hands down her impressively flat stomach and into her panties. From there, she migrates to my boxers and strokes what's inside as if it's a precious jewel. The glee of anticipation is clear on her face and it makes me want to fuck her, hard.

Now.

And they must have read my mind, because Brown Eyes doesn't even bother pulling off my boxers – instead, she slides me out of the slit in them and places her warm, moist mouth on me. I am so primed, so sensitive, I nearly explode at just her touch, but I can see she's keeping her eyes on me, and I know in that moment that that's the last thing they both want.

Over the next hour, it becomes clear to me that the duo has chosen me as their living, breathing sex toy, and, of course, I'm up for that.

They take it in turns with me, each time bringing me close to climax and then pulling away while all the time kissing and fondling each other until, eventually, once they've fully satisfied themselves, they release me from my tantric torture and allow me to explode with the force of an erupting volcano. The energy finally bursting from my body through loud moans of pleasure until we all collapse into a sweaty, exhausted heap of limbs, gasps, and shudders.

Two hours later, after coming round to a hazy, spinning room, I'm naked, lying on my back, my legs and arms wide apart, a sheet partially draped over me.

I'm alone now. The girls have had their fun and are gone, leaving me to bask in the whirling, multicolour fuzziness of the room, bordering between conscious bliss and unconscious exhaustion. The sensation is fucking sublime, like nestling aching limbs in a hammock of cotton wool.

Fuck. That was the best fuck.

Told you I'm a dick, didn't I?

I mean, I could try and justify it, rationalise it for you, so you'll like me more, but, to be honest, I'm beyond caring. I'm too exhausted to get into all of that shit with you right now.

And yes, if you're wondering, of course I love my wife. I love her and my son more than my own life. I do.

And I know people – generally those twee, sycophantic shits who dispense terms of endearment daily, as a pharmacist does pills – say stuff like that all the time, but I happen to mean it. I love my wife as powerfully and as ardently as the heart that is thumping in my chest. And when I say that I love her and my son more than my own life, I fucking mean it; I mean I would give mine to save theirs. I would. There is no doubt about that. No ifs. No buts.

But... But the moment I saw Brown Eyes, I knew I needed to have sex with her. It was an urge, a compulsion that I could not deny – especially not after the day I've had. I could have done her there and then, on the bar, in front of all those people. I had the urge and I needed the release, but, as you've seen, I at least had the courtesy of bringing her and her companion here, to this hotel room.

So, alright, you can quit your judging. I'll answer your stupid question if it's so important to you: *"If you love your wife, then what the fuck are you doing there?"*

I have no idea.

THE DESCENT

Saturday Evening.

So, turns out that hacking into my wife's calendar isn't that difficult.

You see, I need to talk to Ellie about yesterday's disastrous meet, but she hasn't been taking my calls. And though I went over there, Tracy – our nice enough but bored and therefore nosey next door neighbour – told me that she hasn't really spoken to Ellie, but that she did see her load bags into her car... which I'm guessing means that she's taken Toby and gone to spend the weekend with her parents in the country.

I know there's no point in trying to speak to her there. Her father's a bigshot lawyer, her mother an art dealer. They have money. Lots of it. This means that, if they don't want me to access their three-or-so acre property, then it's highly unlikely I'll be able to. And then, even if I could, I wouldn't be able to talk to Ellie without those two having an opinion.

Ellie's parents weren't particularly enamoured with me in the first place, but after what happened... well, things got understandably worse. There's a very good chance that it was her father who helped her raise those divorce papers in first place.

No, the best way for me to talk to her is either at home, to catch her at work or in between meetings, which means waiting until she gets back to the city.

Home isn't any good as there's a good chance Toby would be around – and if things got heated, as they often have recently, I don't fancy the idea of Tracy overhearing us and then having to deal with the subsequent pained, 'Are you okay, hon?' look on her face every time she sees me.

Apparently, according to my wife, Tracy, has a bit of a crush on me. And no, I'm not flattering myself. If you'd seen Tracy – glass bottle spectacles, social security, let–herself-go, cigarette dangling out of her mouth – you'd know why. No, she actually told Ellie this. Apparently, they were in conversation one day when she just came out with it. "*Ere', your Marco's a bit of alright, ain't he? You lucky bitch. Nothing like a bit of Italian stallion to put a smile on your face, eh?*"

Ellie thought it was hilarious and really enjoyed teasing me with this story one day, back when things were good. It was right after we'd finished making love. I told her that I was glad she'd chosen to share that lovely fable after we had sex, too – since, to me, that news and the image of it was somewhat of a passion killer.

No, I'm not being mean. You haven't met Trace.

Anyway, all things considered, I concluded that the best way to speak to Ellie was to catch her either at the office or on her way to a meeting. Yeah, I know, it's kind of an ambush, which I also know can go one of two ways; she'll be unprepared and in a hurry, so she'll let me say my peace just to get rid of me, or, knowing Ellie, she'll just tell me to fuck off. Given that I have very limited options available to me, I'm prepared to take the risk either way.

Now, since she works for my best friend, David, you'd think it would be relatively easy for me to either enlist his help in putting in a good word, again, or, at least, get him to share details of my wife's whereabouts.

Not so.

As we've already established, Ellie is one of David's most prized account managers. Well, actually she's the only account manager. The two of them are thick as thieves as a result, both in and out of the office.

In fact, some time, when I have more time, I'll tell you all about why, occasionally, their whole relationship has me bent out of shape. No, I'm not saying I resent their friendship because it makes me feel left out. That's a given.

Wait. Let me rephrase that. I do like the fact that my wife and my best friend can be, well, close, but what I don't like is how the two of them gang up on me.

And no, before you start putting on that baby voice and telling me to man up, you should stop for a second to consider how bloody frustrating it would be to have your own wife and your best friend in agreement against you. Regularly. It's bloody annoying, because there's nobody to turn to, nobody to vent with. It's like you've lost an argument before it's even begun.

Anyway, I digress.

The point I'm trying to make is that there's no way he's going to give me the information – especially not after last night. He saw me with those two birds, and I saw the judgemental glare he gave me as we left the building.

I suppose it's hardly surprising. You heard him. He agrees with Ellie. He thinks I have some kind of sex problem. Which is hilarious because, by that standard, all blokes who enjoy sex regularly have a bloody sex problem.

I don't have a sex problem.

Anyway, I haven't got time to explain. I need to finish telling you how I accessed Ellie's calendar because, not unlike the first time you met me, I need to be somewhere else and I'm already running late.

It's surprisingly easy, though.

I can't remember if I told you, but David owns this old red brick building in Camden; he's converted the bottom floor into his company's offices and the top floor, or the penthouse, into his own personal dwelling. The penthouse is kitted out with state of the art technology and shares the same WIFI as the company's network.

The only problem is, I don't have a login to their server, and nor do I have access to their calendar from my machine.

I know that Ellie's appointments are all in there. Even her personal ones. She's often said that she has to make sure that absolutely everything is in the diary – otherwise, people in the office just book her out with little notice, and she hates that.

So, the only way to access the company diary is to sneak downstairs and try to log in via one of the company PCs. That or use David's laptop. Well, the latter is somewhat impossible because my friend has a thing about being hacked. Everything is password protected behind a state of the art firewall.

Which leaves me with only one option.

I slip downstairs after hours, and I move the mouse on each machine until I come across a screensaver that isn't password protected. Eventually, thank God, I find one in the *Creative Zone.*

The Creative Zone is an area of the building that's pretty much been cordoned off and kitted out with giant cubby holes resembling human chrysalises; places where members of the so called creative team can go and brainstorm ideas for the next big game.

It's way too Silicone Valley for me, but David loves it.

Anyway, I pull up the calendar and pause. There's an entry for Ellie at 08:00 PM, Saturday. That's tonight.

Well, that catches my attention because, if Tracy's story means anything, then it means that Ellie packed off Toby to her parents but then returned to the city to go to this thing marked *Private.*

Of course, that could just be Ellie's way of saying she's going to be out of the city, or maybe that she's seeing one of her friends. But then, the people she works with are like a small family. If she was going out with a friend, the entry would have something much more colourful, like *Party time!*

So, yeah, now I'm curious.

A *Private* calendar entry, if we can just place the literal definition of that to one side for a second, means it's something that's not work related – something that commits her time without sharing actual details with the rest of the world. Now, I can understand her not wanting her colleagues to know where she's going and with whom, but what about me? We always make a point of discussing Saturday commitments well in advance, because we always try to keep them open for family time with Toby. This despite what happened. In fact, we've always agreed that, no matter what happens between us, our son will always come first.

So, you can understand why, after that ultimatum she gave me via the divorce papers, and this, I'm starting to get just a tad concerned that there may be something, or someone, else going on here.

And that's when I realise just how bloody worried I am. Not just worried, petrified. And my mind's already working overtime with self-recrimination and fear. Fear of losing Ellie. Fear of losing my family.

Butterflies swarm in the pit of my stomach, my heart starts thumping, and my hands suddenly feel clammy.

The same hands that are now logging this machine off.

You see, the thing about stable and open relationships – and by open, of course, I'm talking about having no secrets, (ironic when you consider everything that's come before this) – is that neither of us is precious about his or her devices since, in theory, neither of us has anything to hide.

Yeah, you'd be forgiven for sneering at that, given what you now know about me, but, understand, I'm talking generally here.

My wife and I don't have any secrets. That's why we're both aware of each other's credentials and passwords. Generally, they don't conform to what security analysts recommend, which is to have a different password for different sites – thus ensuring that, if one thing is compromised, the breach doesn't compromise everything else along with it.

So, I log back onto the network as *EBattista* with a password of *l1ttleman* and the number 1 instead of the I.

'Little man' is the pet name we've assigned Toby, because every single day that little man does or says something that consistently proves that he's much older than his years. Sometimes I forget he's only ten, and God do I love that little boy.

Anyway, *Hang on, logging you in* is the pretentious network notification on screen as I wait.

No, I don't feel bad, and no, I haven't considered that I might see something I actually don't want to see. That's because the very reason I'm logging in as my wife to covertly view her diary is because I want to know. There's an entry in here, marked private, that I don't know about. I need to change that.

So, I'm finally logged back in. This time, the profile to the side of the screen doesn't read *Public*; it reads *Elizabeth Battista*.

I launch the diary once more. The days appear from left to right. All the private entries now contain additional information about participants and locations. I deliberately scan all the bookings for the current month first, excluding today's date; they look innocent enough. Then, I look at today. I scroll down to this evening: 08:00PM *Dinner with A.S. at After Dark*.

Okay, so who the fuck is A.S and what the hell is After Dark, beyond sounding like a bloody sex club?

A quick search on Google tells me that After Dark is a restaurant just off Leicester Square.

I love how these places always describe themselves as *just off*. What they actually mean is that they're hidden down some back alley, and then around the corner.

Apparently, After Dark is the best fine dining in the area. It's a great experience and really expensive, according to the Google reviews. It's also won several gastronomical awards and features a Michelin starred chef. Which to me is just marketing-speak for it being a poncey place where the food may look fabulous, but is often an acquired taste and almost always features miniscule portions.

Subtext: someone in this scenario wants to impress the other person. It's not the kind of place Ellie would go with any of her friends, and this can't be a client because we have our weekend rule; family first, no matter what. Yet… she's packed Toby off for the weekend.

Shit.

Now my inebriated mind is racing like a runaway train. Did I mention that I've had a few drinks? Okay, by a few, what I actually mean is about half a bottle of Jack Daniels, or maybe a bit more.

Well, what do you expect after the news I received yesterday? I just needed a few drinks to knock the edge off.

I'm fine. I can hold my liquor.

Anyway, yeah, so the rational part of my mind is trying to slam on the brakes, but the other part is thinking, *What the hell? This is all looking a bit suss.*

So, I'm thinking, no problem. I'll just go over there. Whoever she's with, I won't encroach, I'll just explain she isn't answering my calls or my messages, and that this has left me with no alternative but to show up there, because we need to talk. We need to arrange for me to see my son.

Okay. So, at this stage, you're probably thinking, what's with the double standard after what I did last night?

All I'm going to say is, I didn't buy those girls dinner beforehand; it was just one thing. Admittedly, it was the wrong thing, I know, and I feel awful about it. I do. No, I really do because, like an addict – shit, I just said that word – I felt like crap this morning, full of remorse. But it's done now. It's done. So, now, I can sit and pointlessly agonise over it or I can try and make amends, but I can't do that while I'm sitting on my arse, shoving booze down my throat, now can I?

Of course, there's probably a perfectly reasonable explanation for all this. Maybe a friend surprised Ellie. A relative, even. Whoever. As long as it's someone insignificant because, truth be told, I don't want and I can't handle anything else right now.

I can't.

So, anyway, now that I know where she is, I consider the most cynical of clichés – buying her flowers, or chocolates. Maybe even having them delivered directly to the restaurant. You know... to surprise her.

But no, that won't work because it'll only prompt a perfectly reasonable, *"What, you fuck two complete strangers and then you buy your wife flowers, and you think that's going to make it okay?"*

Of course, you realise that I'm not talking about my wife here, right? I'm talking about you. My judgemental stranger. Remember, my wife doesn't know about last night. The only people who know about it are those girls, David, and you. And even then, David doesn't know all of the sordid detail like you do.

I guess that makes you some kind of reluctant accomplice. Doesn't it? Right?

The truth of the matter is, my wife presented me with divorce paper, along with her ridiculous therapy ultimatum, for something else. Some other stupid thing I did. And, to be perfectly honest, I have no clue how to atone for that. Only she knows the answer, and she isn't talking to me.

Now, given how much you've already gleaned about me, it only makes sense that I share the details with you, but it's far too complex a thing for me to try to explain right now, as I don't have either the brain capacity or the time. I need to be somewhere, and I'm already running late.

It's gone past eight.

I have no idea what I'm going to say when I actually get to the restaurant, of course, but one thing at a time. I'm a therapist. I should be able to deal with most scenarios.

Although, I have absolutely no experience with this one, so you're just going to have to bear with me.

I catch a cab to Leicester Square, which, as you'll know if you've ever been there on a Saturday evening, is a nightmare. Especially when it's autumnal mild. The streets are crawling with people. Tourists and locals alike. They're like ants, filling roads and back streets, doorways and fast food outlets.

I ask the cab driver to set me down a few blocks away since traffic – shocker – is as a standstill. Unlike me because, to be honest, as soon as I step out of that cab, it feels like I've just stepped from one of those spinning teacups you find at theme parks.

Shit. I have to grab hold of the cab to regain my balance – which, of course, freaks out the driver because he thinks I'm trying to put a dent in it.

"It's fine, it's fine," I say, rubbing the patch with my fingers.

On one corner of Leicester Square, I pass a street artist drawing caricatures for a fiver each. On the other, some kid in jogging bottoms and trainers is busting some serious moves to a track with a heavy bassline. I watch him for a short while until he rounds off his performance by spinning on his jacket, then on his head.

For a second, I consider showing him how it's done, but decide against it since it's getting on to eight forty-five.

I hurry by the M&M store and make my way beyond the lights, the sounds, and the smells of food to a back street with filtered light and the toxic stench of industrial dustbins. I cross a couple of streets, passing a theatre decorated with posters featuring stills from a musical I've never heard of, even though it features quotes from an array of five star reviews from various sources.

Then, I see it. Across the road. My view of the place intermittently obscured by noisy, carbon monoxide belching traffic.

The sign over the door is large and black. It has a gold half-moon logo with matching lettering that reads *After Dark*.

Through the glass front, I can see giant star-shaped lamps hanging from the ceiling like dripping honey, casting pools of light over crisp white linen. Waiters, dressed in black uniforms, buzz to and from tables. They carry themselves with poise. Shirts crisp and white. Ties straightened. Not a slouch, not a shuffle.

The restaurant is busy. Most of the tables are occupied.

It is not the kind of place you can get into without a reservation.

I'm just about to cross the street when I spot Ellie. Well, what I actually see is part of her short blonde head peeking out from behind a threesome sitting at the window table. She's in profile to me, to the street, so I move my position on the pavement to get a better diagonal view. Then, I rock my head from side to side unconsciously as traffic grumbles in front of my line of vision, but I'm only getting glimpses of her. She's wearing a black plunge-neck dress with pearls. The dress I don't recognise. The pearls were a gift from me.

She's looking at someone. Laughing at something they've said, but I can't see who it is because of the trio at the table in front of her. Yet, if I move my head… just so… I can see a broad nose and short hair. It's a man. At least I think it is.

This fucking traffic! Those fucking people sitting in the window are making it impossible for me to see!

So, I step off the pavement and am instantly blasted by a black cab. The driver flashes his lights and gives me the finger. I give him two back until his red lights disappear around the corner. No sooner has that happened than I'm blasted by another car.

I turn, "Alright!" I hold up my hands. "Hold your bloody horses!" They're making my head hurt, and I'm already a bit light on my feet. Jesus!

Despite my near mishaps, I manage to make it across the road. Now I can see my wife's shoulders and the face of a man. He's young. Preppy looking, in a shirt and tie, with short mousey hair. Strong, shaven jawline. *Who the fuck are you? And why the fuck are you making my wife laugh?* Heat rises to my cheeks as my stomach churns. They're drinking wine, and something about their body language disturbs me. The way her fingers fiddle with the stem of her glass. Her other fluttering back and forth from the nape of her neck then back around.

My heart is in my throat.

His arm is on the table now. They're talking animatedly about something. It's obviously a topic that they're both enjoying. He's talking. Smiling at her. I can't see her face, but I can tell from the occasional juddering of her shoulders that she's chuckling. Then, he pauses and looks at her intently while lifting the wine bottle. She nods. He refills her glass.

I'm shaking now. Not because it's cold, but from the battle of wills that's raging inside me. I want to go in, but I don't know what will happen if I do, and I'm afraid – not of them, but of myself. I shouldn't have come here. I glance at the opposite side of the road and then back at the restaurant. My head is swimming.

You're going to burst in there and make a complete tit of yourself. Stay calm. There's bound to be an explanation for why she's behaving so fucking intimately with a complete stranger in the middle of a restaurant. There's an innocent reason why she's fiddling with her hair. There's a completely platonic reason why he's reaching across what is a quite generously sized table to touch Ellie's bare wrist. The bracelet that I bought her.

I barge through that door like I own the place. Instantly, I'm greeted by the soft strings of a guitar, the hum and esses of subdued conversation, and then the maître d'.

He looks me up and down. I'm wearing jeans, a tee shirt, and a jacket. All of the other men inside are in shirts and ties.

"Good evening, sir," he says. He's tall, immaculately turned out, and a skilled interceptor. He stops me just a few feet from my wife's chair. I can actually hear her laughing behind him.

"Evening."

"May I have your name, sir?"

"It's Battista."

"Do you have a reservation with us tonight?"

"No, but my wife is sitting just behind you."

"Oh." The man retains his smile, but I can tell he's conflicted. My wife may be behind him, but I'm not dressed to be here. And, by the way his eyes are flickering all over me, I can tell the robot isn't programmed for this eventuality and is considering his next move.

I save him the trouble. "Look, I just need to have a word with my wife," I say, pushing him aside.

"Of course, but… Sir!"

I'm not listening. I'm standing behind Ellie now, but hesitating, not sure which words to use to open up this conversation.

Her companion spots me lingering and pauses his chattering to look up at me. "Hey, what's up?" he asks, casually, in an American drawl.

Ellie follows his gaze and turns in her chair. She sees me and performs a double-take. Instantly, even in the dim light, I can see that her cheeks are flushing.

"What are you doing here?" she asks, her wide eyes filling her face.

"I could ask you the same thing," I respond with a forced smile.

She stands up, looking around the room and then, after shooting me a glare, says, "You can't be here." Her voice is subdued and offered through clenched teeth.

I gaze at her – her pearls, her cleavage, her body in that dress – and I have no idea why, but I just feel instantly protective. It feels like someone has suddenly reached into my life and stolen my family, right from under my nose.

"Is everything okay?" the American asks, standing up.

"Everything's fine, John Wayne, just sit the fuck down," I bark.

"John Wayne?" he echoes as if he's been insulted.

One of the trio who blocked my view earlier, a bald man from the next-door window table, pauses his noisy conversation and looks over.

"What are you doing here?" Ellie demands again. Her tone is louder this time.

"I came here to talk to you," I say, catching her arm and pulling her close to me so that Johnny boy can't hear what I'm saying. "I miss you."

"This isn't the place," she says, pulling away from our intimacy.

"Where then?" I ask, lifting my hands. "Where exactly is the right place, El? You need to let me talk to you. This is killing me." My voice is loud, slurred, whiney.

She scowls. "My God, have you been drinking?" she asks in loud, incredulous whisper.

"Of course I've been fucking drinking!" I retort. Now several tables have been alerted to my presence. "You don't want me coming round to the house. You haven't answered my texts, and you won't take my calls, El!"

She closes her eyes, as if she's just seen her Louie Vitton's crushed under a truck.

"Sir, please." Maître d' is back, leaning into me.

"You need to go," comes my wife's resolute statement.

"No. I'm not going anywhere until we've talked. El, please! You have to let me talk to you. I miss you! I miss our son."

"Hey, look, I don't know what the deal is here, but I think Ellie has made it clear. She'd like you to leave, now," says the American, standing and stepping closer. I glance at him. He's shorter than me, but ripped, to the point where I can see his biceps bulging from under his tight shirt.

I ignore him.

"Ellie. Five minutes. That's all I ask." My tone is soft, supplicating.

She swallows, hesitates, and looks around at the several pairs of eyes that are watching us, and I think she's about to relent when the American puts his hand on my arm. "Seriously, dude…"

"Get your fucking hand off me," I warn, shooting a glare in his direction.

"Sir, please, or I shall have to call the police," Maître d' interjects.

Ignoring the man, I now turn to the American with all the menace of a rabid dog and growl, "Get your fucking hand off me or I'll snap it!"

"I'll do that as soon as you quit spoiling everybody's evenin," he drawls. His words are calm yet assertive as he puffs out his chest and nods at the tables around the room, as if he's speaking for everyone. As if he's Captain America himself.

I tug my arm away, but he remains attached, like a bloody encrustation. "Get. The. Fuck. Off. Me," I spell out through clenched teeth, struggling to break free, but he won't let go, and instead he just shakes his head.

"Leave," he orders.

"Get off me!"

"Sir, please…"

"Leave!"

"Get the fuck off!"

"Stop it," Ellie pleads, tugging at my arm.

"Get off!"

"Stop it!"

"Then leave!"

"Stop!"

And that's it. I see that red mist again.

In one move, I head-butt Captain America in the nose, knocking his head back, shake Ellie off my right arm, then bring it back while simultaneously making a fist that I smash into the American's face. The impact propels him backward, sailing him through the air until he crumples onto a table to a chorus of gasps, screams, smashing crockery, and breaking glass.

"I said, let go!" I yell.

After a few seconds, I realise that the room has become tomblike still, and it takes a few seconds for that to sink in. Then, I shrug to recompose myself, turn to Ellie, and my face drops.

She's being supported by Bald Man and his crew, who are holding a blood-soaked napkin to her nose. She's trembling, eyes full of tears. "Have you completely lost your mind?" she utters in a quivering voice.

"Oh my God… Ellie."

I move towards my wife, but she shrinks back, as does Bald Man and his cronies.

I must have inadvertently clipped her nose when I yanked my arm from her.

I sense movement behind me so I turn to see that the American is also bleeding from his nose. His white shirt's ripped, and now sporting a red stain down the front. He's slowly getting helped to his feet by the dazed couple whose table he just demolished and now he's staring at me with a face that has become a mask of bewilderment.

"What the fuck is going on 'ere?"

I'd recognise that voice anywhere.

I look over, beyond the American. My best friend, David, dressed in a black suit and tie, is walking towards us from the back of the room. Presumably, from the restroom.

I glance at the table in front of me; it's set for three. I look back at David. "Aaron, what the fuck?" He's gasping, examining the man.

"Sir, I've called the police." Maître d' says with his nasal assertiveness.

David gawps at me, at Ellie, and then back at me again. And that angry scowl that's gradually creasing his face is unmistakable; he's done. He doesn't know exactly what happened, but something tells me that he doesn't care either.

So, I turn to Ellie. She's still shaking. Tears are streaming down her face, and there's something in her gaze that I also recognise. Resolve. Resignation.

This time, even I know I've gone too far.

WRETCHED

Sunday Morning.

So, turns out that Captain America's name is Aaron Sinclair. He's some American bloke who David met in California while promoting one of his games. The two of them, unbeknownst to me, have been in regular contact for a while now. David hadn't told me about Aaron since he didn't think their relationship was going to come to much. Then, as time moved on and things became more serious, he invited Ellie out to that swanky restaurant to meet him.

Apparently, David simply didn't invite me because of the situation between Ellie and I. He didn't want any awkwardness, so the plan was for Aaron to meet us separately. Apparently, David was going to tell me it when we met at the club. But, as you know, I first unloaded on him about Ellie's ultimatum, and then I left with those two girls. So, he didn't get the chance.

Of course, I know this not because David told me, but because the American accosted me as I was being frog marched out of David's place and into a waiting cab by police.

Aaron touched my arm, just before I was about to get into the vehicle, as a sombre cold breeze blew about us.

Unlike a few hours before, I was barely able to look the man in the eye, what with my shame pressing on me like the pressure inside my head.

He told me that he was sorry things had turned out this way, but that I shouldn't worry, as David would come around eventually – he just needed time.

My first reaction to that was to think, *What, now you know him better than I do?* But then I realised that he was only trying to make me feel better, which, of course, made me feel worse.

Then, he went on to tell me about how excited David had been for us to meet, that he'd never stopped talking about me, and that – however dysfunctional our relationship might be sometimes – David talked of us as if we were brothers. And that, like a brother, I was often annoying, but that, regardless, he loved me and wouldn't want me to be any different. David had also told him that, of the many people he knew, I was one of a very few with a genuinely good heart.

The American followed that up with a reassuring smile.

So, of course, by this time, I was choking back tears. Not necessarily because of what he was saying, although that brought a lump to my throat, but because he was saying it at all. He didn't know me! Fuck, I'd punched the guy just hours before. He owed me nothing. *He* was the one with the fucking heart!

I felt wretched. Like scum... No, I wasn't even that, I was worse. Much worse. That's why I was unable to find any words for this man. Anything. I couldn't even say I was sorry. That lump in my throat was like a boulder in my brain, impeding my ability to string words together. I could not fucking articulate! Me, the therapist, was incapable of structuring a sentence for this guy, and I think it was simply because, to me, there were no words. No words could make up for my actions.

So, I just smiled at him. It was probably one of the most pitiful smiles he'd ever seen, but that's all I had.

And besides, there was a cop loitering nearby, pretending he wasn't listening to my every word.

So, I climbed into the cab and told the driver to take me to the nearest hotel.

Oh, and in case you're wondering what the police were doing at David's... He called them. Or to be more precise, the maître d' called them to the restaurant, as you know, and from there, names were taken. Complaints lodged.

Then David told the police that I was a friend, a lodger without any form of a tenancy agreement, and that he wanted me out of the house because he feared for his safety. Of course, he didn't. David could easily kick my arse. He worships the gym mecca nearly every day and has those stereotypically gay abs to prove it. No, he wanted to make a show of getting me out of his house and out of his life, and who could blame him?

The good news is that Ellie's okay. At least physically. I just clipped her in the nose when I pulled back to punch Aaron. When I say *just*, you do realise I use that term loosely, right?

I know I fucked up big-time this time, and not just on an interpersonal level. I'm also being punished financially.

The restaurant said they wouldn't press charges for criminal damage if I was prepared to compensate them for the loss, there and then.

I ended up leaving that place over three thousand pounds lighter, and the debit wasn't made from my current account since I don't even have that much money in there. No, it was charged to my credit card, almost maxing the thing out. But I panicked. All I could think about was that I'm a therapist, that I'm better than this. That I should know better. Know how to recognise the signs and handle my emotions.

How do you think I'm doing so far?

Anyway, for some reason unknown even to me, the thought of having some shitty black mark of a charge against my name terrified me. It was only later, upon reflection – basically during what was left of the night, as I lay staring at the ceiling of my hotel room – that I was able to tell myself that the real reason I didn't want that black mark against my name was because I wanted to erase what had happened.

I actually wanted to be able to travel back in time to some point where I was able to tell myself: *"Don't be a fucking idiot. If you show up at the restaurant uninvited and without a clue of what to expect, what do you think is going to happen? Especially when you've had a skin full of alcohol? What the hell is wrong with you?"*

And on and on. These thoughts just rattled around my head until a fiery glow behind the skyline announced a new day.

And you know, for all the sleeping I didn't do, I could have done without the extra charge to my credit card. As I've already mentioned, hotels in London don't come cheap. Still, at least I managed to get a hot shower out of it, which made my migraine feel marginally better, as have the headache pills I've just swallowed.

Now, as I sit on the train at King's Cross station, waiting for the thing to start moving, you won't be surprised to hear that I'm feeling particularly depressed, and that's for a multitude of reasons. With nothing to do but kill time, each and every one of my mistakes has been parading itself in front of my mind like a grotesque procession of nightmares.

Oh, and in case you're wondering why I'm not driving my way out of depression central, that'll be for that reason I've already mentioned; living in London is not only expensive, but parking space is as rare as hens' teeth. What little parking there is comes at a very high premium, and so, with Ellie and I both working in the city, it's made sense for us to share just one car.

And who do you think is using that right now?

Exactly.

It's okay. I doubt I'm going to need a car where I'm going. And besides, what would I use it for, apart from getting me to purgatory? Well, this train is perfectly capable of doing that – if it ever gets moving, of course. I'm used to travelling by train anyway. The Underground, to be precise. I used to commute to work every day. There's a station not far from our flat. Or at least, I made that commute before everything well and truly hit the fan a couple of months or so back, when I was forced to move into David's. There, the only early morning commute I made was from the bedroom to the kitchen, and the only occasional traffic I came across was the naked arse of some guy he'd picked up at the gym, or through work or through an app. I've lost count of the times I've seen blokes wandering around the place butt naked during early morning raids to the fridge. And, if I'm being perfectly honest, I can't say I enjoy that view first thing – and, me being me, I've told him so. Of course, he could have told me to fuck off. After all, it's his house. Yet, David being David, he'd simply grab me by the head and force a slobbery kiss on my cheek, like one of those annoying uncles, and tell me that I should go have a therapy session with myself because I was obviously repressed and clearly uncomfortable with my sexuality.

Um, no. I just don't enjoy seeing a hairy butt first thing in the morning, or at least not one that isn't my own.

But that's David.

I miss him. Already.

And now I've fucked that up also.

So, let's just have a little recap here, because misery does love company, right?

I lost my job in a spectacularly dramatic way, pushed my wife to the point where she had no choice but to ask me to leave my home and my son. I'm paraphrasing, of course. It was more of a demand, and the language that accompanied it was much more colourful. And then, as if that wasn't bad enough, I added insulted to injury, literally, by head-butting and punching David's significant other as well as my wife, while singlehandedly partly demolishing some stuck-up restaurant that has charged me money I don't have for a poncey meal that never happened, to a card that's already bursting at the seams.

Not bad. Even for me.

Oh, and for the record; I do have other friends, but most are married, with their own children and their own lives. Besides, none of them could put up with my shit like David. He, like Ellie, gets me, the way that nobody else does. I guess that's probably due, in part, to the fact that he's in touch with his so called feminine side. Truth be told, that's been a standing joke between us. Ironic, really. Statistically speaking, because of the similarities in temperament, he and Ellie shouldn't get on at all. They should be bumping heads, trying to outdo each other. Instead, those two are actually good for each other, which means that if they used to gang up on me before, there's no doubt they'll be sticking together through this which only makes this whole shit-fest worse. Much worse.

Actually, no, strike that.

While this may well be catastrophic, it's a distant second to what I'm about to do. What I'm about to do feels like I'm already strapped to a chair, about to have my fingernails pulled, all while a dentist is working on one of my root canals.

Yet, even though I swore I would never do this, it seems that I've successfully managed to back myself into a corner so as to ensure that I no longer have a choice.

THE ARRIVAL

Sunday.

I'm being dragged *by my feet over cold pebbles. The clicking and rattling sound they make is loud in my ears as they vie for the best angle to graze, scratch, and dig into my skin as I inch closer and closer to the fizz and rumble of the surf.*

Closer… waves hiss and I can feel the freeze of the water, biting into my flesh now. Oh God… the ocean is devouring my legs. It's eating me. I can't breathe – the frigid water is like a vice around my chest. I can't breathe! He… lp… help… me! H…elp… me I'm dying! I'm dying!

The boom of a train passing on the opposite track wakes me with a start.

I gulp in air and look around me, expecting the giant yawn of an aquamarine tsunami to swallow me, but instead I'm reassured by the rocking of my carriage and the repetitive clatter of the train on its track.

I'm still panting when I turn to look out of the window to see that we've left London, and that the grim concrete greyness of seventies' tower blocks and the faded signs of industrialism have given way to blue skies, green fields, and trees draped in the multicolour cloak of autumn.

It's odd, because as tragic as all of this is, along with my foreboding of what's to come, it's only as I sit here – rocking gently from side to side, my head resting against the cool glass of the carriage window, watching the green blur by and listening to the rhythmic clank – that I'm starting to feel soothed. It's as if my abusive father – the cosmos, if you believe in that kind of thing – has taken a rest from beating me around the head and is instead seeing fit to give me a metaphorical hug… *Sorry I've made your life one big pile of crap, but here's a natural hug to make you feel better.*

And I am feeling better.

Or, let me rephrase that. I'm feeling more positive now. If only because I've resigned myself to what needs to be done. I am going back to this place, not for a visit, nor a trip down memory lane, but with a purpose. I am going to make sure that property is immaculate, and I'm going to rinse it for as much cash as I can before I return to London, to my family. Then, I am going to do everything and anything to earn Ellie's trust, be a good father to my son, and a friend to David. These are the only people in my universe who truly matter to me, and they are going to know it.

That, and this place is somewhere to lay low, gather my thoughts, and see exactly how I am going to achieve the above without fucking up something else.

Daddy, what have you done to annoy mummy now? I can see Toby rolling his eyes. *You better go and make it up to her. Give her a kiss. No, maybe get her some shoes; she likes shoes.*

I miss my son.

I miss Ellie. I miss how we used to be, but I can't allow myself to think about her that way. It's strange, because I'm able to wallow in how I long to see my son, but missing Ellie just reminds me of how I screwed it all up in the first place, as well as the weight of shame hanging around my neck like an iron collar. I wasn't necessarily directly involved in creating the absence between Toby and I, but I was involved in gouging out the chasm between me and my wife.

I know, it's flawed logic, just as I know all of this is on me, and only me.

These thoughts, like the track beneath me, stretch on. Like, how the hell am I going to subsist? I had very little money left already, and I'm obviously still contributing to household expenses.

We should have moved out of the city ages ago. I should have listened to Ellie. Or, more specifically, her parents, but they were the problem. They wanted us to move out near them, but I was still working in the practice at the time.

Oh, God... the thought of moving near them. If you have nosey in-laws who are always crawling up your backside and in your business, you'll know what I mean.

Laughter draws my attention across the aisle, a few seats down. A ten-or-so year old girl smiles at me as she munches daintily on a sandwich.

I smile and wave back at her as I realise that I too am hungry. Luckily, I had the foresight to stop off at one of the metro grocery stores near the hotel and pick up a few things before boarding the train, and it isn't long before I'm people-watching and munching on my own piece of cardboard cleverly disguised as a chicken salad sandwich.

There's also an old couple a few seats down. She's reading through a pair of tiny round spectacles perched on the tip of a very thin nose. He is snoozing; head lolling back and forth with the motion of the train. A couple of rows in front of me, I can see a mop of black hair and giant headphones erupting out of the headrest, like radio masts, and I can just about make out the tinny sound of a bassline I don't recognise. On the opposite aisle, there's a couple sitting across from each other. She is gazing out of the window. He is gazing at her, and behind them, a Constable-like painting of the countryside morphs and blurs as the train moves forward, taking us from one timestamp to the next.

Life goes on.

I've always found this fascinating, and often end up having this conversation with friends and sometimes clients. The way that sadistic time keeps on ticking, and the world keeps on turning, no matter which element of life we're immersed in. Good or bad, time moves on, and the rest of the five billion or so humans who inhabit this earth will continue to be born, die, laugh, cry, agonise, rejoice, mourn, have sex, and experience life – regardless of what we're going through – and there goes time, without an interest or care.

My life may be a mess right now, but they'll be millions of people around the world, laughing. The day Toby was born was, is, and probably will be the happiest day of my life, yet I remember reading that thousands of people died in an earthquake at the other side of the world on that day. There's an action and counteraction for everything. But, is it really? Isn't it just nature doing its thing? People existing through the smidgeon of time they have on this earth. We all experience positive and negative things, regardless of the polarised lives we project onto social media.

I look at my fellow passengers and I know. I know that behind the outward smiles, the chatty demeanours, the weary shuffling to and from carriages, there is a whole universe of uncertainty, secrets, and fear. Each and every one of these puzzle pieces being a derivative of that person's past. Their experiences, good or bad, shaping the people they are today.

And then it occurs to me; what if I open my own practice? There's nothing stopping me. I'm still a qualified psychotherapist. I may have crapped on everything else, but I still have my degree, as well as years of experience. How many exactly, I can't remember, but enough to be bloody good at my job. At least, I was until that day. And technically, I still am, although that'll probably depend on your point of view.

Now, granted, Porthcove isn't exactly a metropolis. In fact, I don't think it's even a town. But there are still people there, right? People, just like this lot, all of whom could probably use a good therapist. They just don't know it yet, but I can see to that. I just need the opportunity to get them talking, and then I'll let my charm do the rest.

What? You don't think I can be charming?

You don't even know me.

I finish my sandwich and formulate a strategy as forests turn into rolling fields and rolling fields turn into arable land, and, eventually, into the peaks and troughs of the Southwest of England.

Mercifully, the sun continues to shine for the rest of my journey, which works wonders at lifting my spirit and, it seems, my headache.

I spend the rest of the trip thinking about my new venture. Maybe this is the fresh start I need.

Don't get me wrong. I'm in no particular hurry to set up shop away from London, away from my family. This is strictly a temporary arrangement. A means to an end kind of thing.

I wonder what David would think? No doubt, he'd tell me to consider my actions carefully. *Don't do anything impulsive and, most importantly, don't make a fucking tit of yourself!* He'd then follow that up with a cackle of laughter because I don't think he's ever been one to consider his actions carefully. He's more of a *live in the moment* kind of bloke. And I admire that about him. Especially since it's seen him well so far.

I smile.

We're close now. The valley has unveiled a whole stretch of sand that glistens under the afternoon sun, and I watch, mesmerised, as the Atlantic lazily rolls in to caress the shore while the fresh scent of the ocean filters in through vents above the window.

I feel an odd sense of the familiar, and I can't decide if that's genuine recognition or if it's in some way psychosomatic. It just feels like we're close.

So, the housekeeper told me…

Oh. Didn't I mention that?

Yes, apparently, when my father's solicitor contacted me to tell me that my stepmother, brother, and sister had inherited all of my father's wealth – and that's a very healthy bank account and a couple of multimillion pound properties, both in and out of London (that's right, properties plural) – and that my father, who barely had the time for me when he was alive, had left me this dilapidated shack by the ocean, he also informed me that the place came with a housekeeper.

Don't get excited, though. When I first heard the man, I too automatically pictured myself in a smoking jacket, ringing a bell for tea, but I knew it couldn't be that.

It isn't Manderley.

Apparently, an old man and his missus, who live in the village have been responsible for the property's upkeep for years. Thankfully, they don't *live in*. That's the last thing I need.

Anyway, the solicitor – a snooty, up himself, sounding dick, with a terribly posh accent – told me that I was to contact the housekeeper and make all necessary arrangements for key collections directly with them. He then, seemingly begrudgingly, gave me the man's home number, because apparently, and here's the shocker, mobile coverage in the area is awful.

So, after several calls, I managed to get hold of the rather cheery man with a gravelly voice and a strong local accent. He told me to take the train to Newquay in Cornwall and then the local line to Porthcove Station, where he would be waiting for me. He was, to use the solicitor's words, frightfully polite, and stopped just short of calling me 'Squire.'

Damn.

Now, as we pull into Newquay Station, my stomach turns, and it isn't the train, although the stop could be smoother. I don't really know what it is. I think it's just the unknown. I have no idea what to expect when I reach this place. I have no clue what state the shack is going to be in, nor do I have any idea what kind of hideous ghosts I'm going to conjure from my memories while I'm there.

I thought I'd put all that crap behind me and, in case I haven't made it clear already, I have no interest in dredging it all up again.

In fact, I made a declaration to Ellie the day I met her; she and the family we made together were my future from that point on. They still are the only thing that matters to me. Everything else is in the past.

Of course, there are no signs for this so called local line the man spoke of. So, to save time, I ask a young uniformed lad. He just gawps at me as if I've just told him his mother is an alien. So, me, my rucksack, and my holdall wait patiently while he runs over to speak to an older uniformed man who obviously has a clue. Then, I watch as the boy – who couldn't be long out of school, or maybe is still in it – starts to explain my query to the bloke who I assume is his superior, certainly in experience. However, the man shakes his head and then, shortly after, comes over to speak to me directly.

I follow the man's directions and, eventually, I manage to find the rather unimaginatively named platform, *Local,* which may as well be Harry Potter's 9 ¾ for all of how difficult it is to find. I mean, the track isn't even inside the station! It's where the old station used to be before it was demolished. Now, the track emerges from a grass-covered tunnel and appears to just stop here, in what can only be described as a field in the middle of nowhere.

'Weird' doesn't even cover it – unlike the moss, weeds, and shrubbery that extend as far as the track and platform, almost as if the vegetation's afraid to venture any further into the concrete world I'm about to leave behind. There's literally nothing here but the track; a rotted, moss-riddled wooden bench; and a rusty sign mounted onto a Victorian looking lamppost that reads, in faded white, *Local*.

Birds chirp in nearby brambles, and seagulls call overhead.

Surreal.

But then, almost as if the conductor sensed a punter, I hear a mournful echo of a whistle and I turn to see a light flickering inside the tunnel.

"Thank God."

My ride is here and I'm not surprised to see that it, not unlike its docking station, has seen better days. It looks nothing like a modern train, but more like something you'd find in a period novel, though it surprisingly *doesn't* chug large plumes of steam or smoke. In fact, it's relatively quiet, which only emphasises the clang and clatter on the tracks, and the creaks and squeaks of the carriages that are a tired red – almost orange, with faded yellow trim.

I'm half expecting to find a skeleton in the driver's cabin, but no, it's an elderly man in uniform. He pokes his head out of to personally wave off several passengers.

Good. I know it's a bit lame, but I do find the fact that other people use this moving claptrap to be reassuring. Especially when it turns out that I'm the only passenger travelling in the opposite direction, and, for a moment after we enter the dark tunnel, I'm half expecting the thing to turn into a ghost ride come television prank.

It doesn't. What it does turn into is something that is equally jaw dropping.

No sooner do we emerge from the tunnel than half of the grassy verge falls away, revealing a spectacular coastline. Waves reach for the side of the train but break on the rocky shore. Seagulls and blackbirds duck and dive alongside the cabin like something out of a BBC documentary.

This majesty continues for five minutes or so until I feel myself gradually fall back into my seat as the train climbs upward, labouring, rattling, and groaning loudly as we reach the crest of the cliffside to a quick succession of triumphant train whistles.

This makes me smile. I don't even know why. It just feels like I'm on a theme park ride. That, or I'm on some kind of chemical trip, because this can't be real. It can't. It's all too...

...my thoughts are interrupted by a new spectacle that reveals itself as soon as we round the bend to one side of the horseshoe that makes up the harbour and bay. It's unmistakable. Even from this angle, – since, as a child, I don't remember ever taking this route to the village, given that we always travelled by car – through the trees that surround it, I can still see white patches of its façade; La Dolce Vita.

It stands regal, magnificent, like a giant white beacon on the opposite side of the horseshoe, at the edge of the peninsula. Behind it is the village of Porthcove. Beneath it, down in the harbour and bay, multi-coloured fishing boats bob on a glassy emerald ocean.

My face flushes hot. Wings flutter in my gut. I'm excited and yet apprehensive, in awe and yet afraid. And it's the latter emotion that I wrestle with as the train makes its way around the bend of the shoe, through the trees, and toward the old man's... no, my home. At least until I manage to sell it.

God, I feel so foolish. What exactly am I afraid of? This is the beginning of a whole new chapter of my life. I have everything to be excited about and nothing to fear. I repeat this to myself over and over again as we move closer and closer. And it seems as if the track is going to take us right by the house. Does the house have its own stop? I don't remember that.

I shift in my seat, trying to peek around trees, but all I can see now is the occasional red and white blur.

Then, the train snakes under a small bridge and emerges to a clearing.

There it is, the front garden of the house. It's less than thirty feet from me. It's bloody... beautiful! Much bigger than I remember, and in much better shape.

Then, it's gone.

I turn and crane my neck as we gradually leave the building behind.

No! I want to shout at the driver, *Let me off here.*

But, slowly, the house disappears behind trees once more until, eventually, the white dissolves to green.

Reluctantly, I turn and face forward. Wow. What was that all about? I went from dreading the sight of the place to feeling disappointment when we left it behind.

I have to keep reminding myself: *The house is your destination. It's where you're going. You aren't leaving anything behind. ... You just need your ride to stop somewhere so you can get off!*

However, the journey continues for about ten more minutes, and features a new moving canvass of arable land and lush fields.

Eventually, of course, the train does slow, coming to a stop amid a symphony of clanging wheels and screeching brakes.

I eagerly collect my belongings, and step out of my carriage and onto the platform that time forgot.

It isn't so dissimilar to the one where I boarded – only much nicer, and certainly much better maintained. Here, I'm standing on a glistening black cobblestoned platform. The Victorian lamppost gleams polished black, and the sign hanging from it sports crisp white lettering that reads, *Porthcove.*

I look up and down the platform. It's empty, but for my elderly driver, who leans out of his cabin and gives me a gappy smile and a wave. I instinctively wave back and then, feeling silly, I follow the neatly hand-painted sign for the exit.

Unlike the station at the start of this leg of the journey, this one has a building... of sorts. It's actually a stone archway with a wooden canopy and a single green bench.

Stepping through the archway is like going through Narnia's Wardrobe, as I emerge into a countryside of trees, flowers, busy insects, and noisy birds.

Now, I have to say... there's rural, and then there's rural. Here, I feel like I've just been plonked into the middle of nowhere. Like it's some kind of a joke. *Hey, let's abandon this bloke in the middle of a field and see how he manages to find his way home!*

Behind me, there's a loud whistle, and then the thrust, shunt, creak, and groan of the train departing, leaving me here.

Shit.

So, it's just as I'm contemplating how the hell I'm going to get back to civilisation when I hear the growl of an approaching vehicle and then, over the hill, I see a conspicuous looking pickup truck.

It's hurtling towards me.

What the…

I maintain my ground, frozen there not out of bravado, but out of amazement. The thing is electric blue, with massive headlamps and gleaming starburst hubcaps. It looks as out of place here as a dildo in a convent. This is Poldark country, not the college campus of an American soap opera.

Interestingly, the driver who pulls up alongside me *isn't* a preppy lad with designer stubble and branded clothing, but Captain Birdseye himself, with a white beard and a beany hat on his head.

"Marco?" the old man asks out of the open window.

Bags in hand, all I can do is nod.

"Welcome," he says with that gravelly voice and a big grin. "Drop those in the back and hop in," he adds, nodding at the rucksack and holdall in my hands. I comply; I dump the luggage and step up, into the cabin.

The man, who must be in his late sixties, takes a good look at me as I slide into the leather seat next to him. "Blimey, you've grown a bit, 'aven't ya? And handsome, too, just like your father," he says, his country accent strong.

I automatically smile as I feel the heat in my cheeks. "Thanks."

"I'm Harvey," he says, offering me his right hand.

I shake it as he continues to observe me for what feels like the longest time, and it's just as I'm about to say something when he nods, expectantly. "You need to strap yourself in, before we get movin'," he says with mock seriousness, as if I'm still the child he remembers.

"Of course," I comply.

Instantly, he pushes the truck into gear and we're off, bumping down what's left of the tarmac road.

"New truck?" I ask appreciatively. The thing looks like it's just come out of a showroom.

He thinks for a second, then smiles, "Oh no, it ain't mine. It's me nephew's. Mine's being serviced, so he told me to borrow 'is. I reckon he did it so he could have a good laugh at seeing me drive it around. Not unlike yourself," he adds, glancing at me.

I try hard to suppress a laugh, especially when I imagine David's reaction to this. "Well, it's certainly, um, bling," I say. "Beautiful, though. Really beautiful."

"Yeah, that's our Shawn. He restored it pretty much from scratch. I think it's what they call his labour of love."

"It shows."

"Yeah. He's a good lad, and smart, too."

"You sound very proud."

"We are. The missus and I. As proud as your old man was of you. You know, I still can't believe you're that teeny lad running around the beach in ya' shorts. Now all grown up."

He keeps glancing at me with a big grin on his face. "And you're the spittin' image of him," he says, shaking his head wistfully while glancing at the road from time to time.

We are negotiating some particularly windy and narrow roads with unusually high grass verges. It actually feels like we're driving through a very deep trench, which makes it impossible to see oncoming traffic. This means that the full weight of the man's words doesn't sink in for a few seconds or so, but then I realize: Did he just say that my old man was proud of me?

Is he on crack?

If the car were stationery, I'd probably take the point up with him, but given the fact that I'm in perpetual imminent danger, I choose instead to say nothing; and besides, he's talking again.

"So, what is it you do in the city then?"

"I'm a psychotherapist," I say, discreetly gripping the door handle.

"Oh, really? One of those, eh?" he breathes, as if I've just told him I came from outer space. "You do all that 'sit down and tell me your problems' lark?"

"Yes," I nod, eyes intent on the next blind bend, as if it's me in the driver's seat.

"And is that for all types of folk, or do you have a speciality?"

I'm not sure I understand exactly what he means by 'all types of folk', and at the same time I wonder if he'd even understand if I told him that I'm presently hypertensive with an elevated heart rate. He's approaching these bends way too fast, considering he can't see who's coming the other way on a road that barely has room for our pimped-out ride.

"No, no speciality. I had, have, all sorts of clients," I lie.

"So, you can do the whole couple's therapy thing, too?"

I steal a glance at him, but his laugh cuts my thought. "Gawd, no. I've been married to Evie for coming on fifty years now, and yeah, we still get on each other's nerves, but that's just how it is. No, I was thinking more for Shawn and his fiancé."

"Fiancé?" I repeat.

"Yeah, they're getting married in a few months, but they spend most of the time squabbling. If you ask me, I don't think they're suited, but Shawn, well, he's besotted with her."

"Yes, sure, of course," I say quickly. I just want to focus, and I just want him to focus, on the road ahead.

"Look at that. You haven't been here five minutes and I've already found you your first customer. Eh, you'll not be charging those London rates down here, though, will ya?"

He laughs.

I'm still busy recovering from the Mario Kart experience. Mercifully, we've emerged from the trench masquerading as a road, and are on a hill overlooking a tiny hamlet – Porthcove. Beyond that is the peninsula, Dolce Vita, and then the ocean that's an aquamarine shimmer in the afternoon sun.

It's beautiful. I must admit it.

But then, it never is about the place, what we remember or think – it's always about the significance we attach to it. Thoughts. Feelings. Keepsakes and buildings are but inanimate objects, as we're the ones who give them life, personality, and power by attaching or projecting significance onto them.

"It's beautiful," I hear myself say.

"Yeah, it is. I couldn't imagine livin' anywhere else," Harvey replies as we descend into the valley.

"How long have you lived here?"

"All my life."

"Really?"

"Yeah. I was born in the very house we still live in."

"Really? That's incredible."

"Yeah. A lot of those years have been in service to your old man. I've lost count of the amount of times I've picked your parents up at that station, and seeing you standing there today was like seeing a younger version of him."

"Yes, you mentioned," I say tersely, looking out of my window.

We're descending further into the valley. Passing a small church and its graveyard, hidden amongst trees but for its oversized spire, to our right.

"13th century," Harvey offers.

"I'm sorry?"

"The church. Dates back to the 13th Century. Listed building."

"They are gorgeous, aren't they?"

"That's where your parents got married."

"What? Really?"

"Yeah. Happiest day of your father's life. Your mamma looked stunning. Like a princess. You know, pretty much the whole village came to that wedding. Had the reception down at the Smuggler's Inn. Fantastic day. Fantastic."

Okay, so this is news to me. I had no idea my parents married here. I certainly had no clue that they married in that church. I didn't even know it existed until now, and I don't really know how I feel about that. How I feel about this whole reminiscing thing that Harvey seems obsessed with. I want to tell him, too. I want to tell him that I'm not interested in hearing about my father or the past. I just want to get to my destination.

All of this chitter-chatter about my parents is starting to make me feel uncomfortable. In fact, it's making me shift in my seat. It's making me want to buzz down the window and get some fresh air in here. The air conditioning is stuffy and starting to smell. It's starting to smell like a library full of musty old books.

"I couldn't help but notice that I've travelled pretty much in a circle," I say, changing the conversation, "and, if I'm not mistaken, I'm sure the train passed right by the house – is that right?"

"You don't miss much, do ya'? But then, I guess that's what they call an occupational hazard in your business."

I think that was a compliment. I'm not sure.

"Yep. The train does pass right in front of the house, but unfortunately for you, it doesn't stop there. You see, it's a local line. Used to be part of the main line, but then they laid new track for the larger trains, so it was decommissioned. Pretty much left to rot. Now it's run primarily by volunteers. Locals. Enthusiasts who don't want to see it fade into the past like everything else. It's also a vital link between the villages and town. There aren't any buses around here and it's much busier during the summer. Tourists and whatnot. Soon It'll close for winter. Open again in the spring. All thanks to donations from your father. He was such a generous soul."

I bite my lip as we pass the Community Hall to the left. It's a handsome stone building bearing a neatly hand-painted sign and an obligatory noticeboard out front, both of which have been immaculately maintained.

Then, we bump our way over a cobblestone street. It's lined with a neat row of small, quaint stone buildings, as well as perfectly placed, symmetrical hanging baskets, each exploding into a rainbow of flowers.

I've deduced that this is their... my... high street.

Each shop with its own seemingly hand-painted sign; Butcher, Bakery, Grocery Store, Green Grocer, Café, Barber, and Post Office.

There are hardly any cars, and the two I've noted seemed to be there for a reason; the drivers were loading or unloading boxes from vehicles that, at least to my mind, must have been a couple of decades old, yet still in mint condition.

Up ahead, outside the Post Office, there's a trio of middle- aged ladies wearing summer dresses, all with primped hair and perfect makeup, alongside of a few children. They're chatting animatedly to each other until they notice us, and then they burst into synchronised smiles and waves.

Harvey stops and then buzzes down my transparent shield.

"Afternoon, ladies," he says with a big smile.

"Good afternoon, Harvey! How has your day been so far?" asks a heavyset lady with a perfect beehive of red hair.

"All good, thank you, Rosemary. How are these two little rascals?"

He's referring to the nine or maybe ten-year-old girl and boy of a similar age who are by her side. She's wearing a blue polka dot dress and has pigtailed hair with ribbons. He's dressed in shorts, shirt, tie, and patent shoes. The boy looks like he's just returned from or is getting ready to be carted off to boarding school.

"Very well, thank you, Mr. Martin," they reply almost in unison, as if they rehearsed the response earlier.

"Well, you make sure you keep it that way," Harvey says as I subconsciously lean back in my chair to facilitate the discourse that's taking place across me.

"Ooh, and who's this handsome fella, Harvey?" asks a heavily made up fifty-something year old blonde, a screaming cougar, over her sunglasses.

"He's Roberto's son."

"No?" comes the incredulous reply.

"Oh, wow. You've grown up so handsome!" says the cougar, appreciatively.

"Oh, he has," echoes Rosemary.

"And he looks just like him," says the other woman. "Doesn't he?"

The other two chorus their approval.

I'm too embarrassed to be annoyed by the comparison. Especially since this whole exchange is taking place through the passenger window. My window. And these... these ladies... are uninhibited in their scrutiny of my face, which probably looks exhausted and now features the crimson cheeks that I know I'm bloody prone to in such situations.

"Anyway, I best get him home," Harvey says.

Thank you, and, it's not my home.

"So, he's staying at the house?" asks the cougar.

"Yes," says Harvey.

Take out an ad in the paper, why don't you?

"Oh, well, don't be a stranger, will you?" asks the cougar.

"It was a real pleasure to meet you," says Rosemary. "Say goodbye," she adds, nodding at me.

"Goodbye," the Village of Damned children say in unison once more.

"Bye," I respond, waving and smiling. A bit like those newscasters do while waiting for the director to tell them that they're off the air. In this case, I'm waiting for Harvey to push the bloody car into gear and get me out of here.

Eventually, he does.

Thank God.

Embarrassed, much? It feels like I've just stumbled into an episode of *Mad Men* and *Stepford Wives* all at the same time. I actually breathe a sigh of relief when their reflection disappeared from the wing mirror.

Being paraded like a show pony? No, not one of my favourite pastimes.

We drive downhill, through an avenue of trees and houses until we come to a natural left bend and a sign that reads *Harbour*. However, here we turn right onto a side road of hedges and trees and go on until we emerge at another junction. Left will take us over a small stone bridge, right leads to a cobbled street and more cottages.

I recognise where we are now. It's the bridge over the railway line, the one I came in on, and it's as we turn left to cross it that I spot the hand-painted sign of white lettering on blue background; *La Dolce Vita*.

The Sweet Life. Oh, the irony.

A slab of cement falls to the bottom of my stomach, and I give serious consideration to asking my race driver to do a U-turn, to take me right back to the station. *Take me home!*

Then I tell myself: *Stop being an idiot. This is home, for now.*

We drive, slowly, under an archway of trees for less than a minute, gravel crunching loudly under our wheels until the vehicle emerges on a square forecourt.

Harvey stops the truck and kills the engine.

"Here we are," he announces with a smile.

I take a few seconds, opting to peer through the windscreen at the white building. I really wasn't ready to see it in all its glory. In fact, I'd have turned in the opposite direction. Fifteen or so yards away is a hedge, and the railway track beyond it.

"Don't worry," Harvey says. "Trains aren't that noisy. Well, you came in on one! And they don't come round that often out of season – about one every couple of hours. They stop altogether in the winter."

I shake my head. "No, it isn't that." It is, though. At least, that's one of the reasons, but I'm not going to tell him my thoughts.

"Come on then, I'll give you the tour," he says excitedly, and is out of the car before I can say anything more. I just want him to go now.

I mean, I'm grateful and everything, but I feel tired, and, quite literally, emotional. There's a lot in the back of my mind, a lot that I can't quite decipher, like the bile at the back of my throat threatening to make me bring up what little I ate today. And let's not forget that I'm still recovering from a pretty wild night – self-induced, I know, but Harvey's driving hasn't helped.

I follow the old man out of the vehicle, though, and the first thing I hear is absolutely nothing. Silence, when compared to the city. I mean, it's weird, because I can actually hear myself breathe! As well as the blood thumping behind my ears. There are no sirens, no pneumatic drills, no car horns, no engines.

Nothing.

Then, gradually, I tune into a whole new life opera.

It starts with the soprano of seagulls, compelling me to squint upward. They're like demanding children, eager to show me how well they can sail on the breeze in a gloriously blue sky decorated with giant marshmallow-type clouds that are so low I feel I can almost reach up and touch them. Then, I can hear the deep base of the rumbling surf. I can't see it, but the sound is coming from somewhere beyond the house, beyond the cliff face. It feels so close, it sounds like it's in the back garden.

Next, I can hear the tenors that are the crows cawing in nearby trees, along with the contralto of other birds, flapping to and from the area. This is all complimented by the mezzo sopranos of bees droning to and from the multitude of flowers that have taken over the place, filling the air with an intoxicating medley of scents.

Okay. So... I wasn't expecting this.

Harvey must have seen the expression on my face because he says, softly, "Your father wanted this place to be a haven for all of you, especially your mother, God bless her soul."

I feel a twist in my gut. Like someone has just reached in, grabbed a fistful, and turned.

I experience a fair collection of emotions as we approach the house, but the one that seems most potent is irritation. Well... no, not irritation. Anger. Although, despite my attempts to identify it, I'm not able to explain why I feel so angry. I mean, first it was directed at my wife, but since then I've realised it isn't her. So, the anger shifts to my old man, or at least to the memory of him. Or more specifically, how he's perceived by the folk around here. It's like Harvey and his lot knew a completely different person than I did. This bloke Harvey insists on describing to me as handsome, generous, and kind is nothing like my old man, and that's not me projecting – that's a fact. The man I knew wouldn't piss on most people if they were on fire. He certainly didn't give a shit about what happened to *me*. He would never have created this little haven, as Harvey put it, by the beach, for anybody but himself.

Oh, and of course, the bimbo de jour.

Oh God, I want to shout. I want to scream. I want to say, *Shut the fuck up about my dad because you haven't got a clue about him, alright? You only know what he wanted you to know!*

"Are you okay, son?" Harvey's asking. He's obviously seen the look on my face, once again.

I think about it. I think that right here, right now, is the perfect opportunity to tell him. *Do you know what, Harvey, I'm not okay. Quite frankly, I'm feeling hungover and rather shitty, and each and every time you bang on about the old man, I want to punch you. I want to punch you right in the face. Do you hear me? Do you fucking hear me?*

"Yes. I'm fine, thanks. Just a bit tired. It's a lot to take in."

"Of course, I understand. It must be quite difficult coming back here."

"It is," I say quickly.

"Well, if it's any consolation, most folk around here really miss your parents, too. Especially your dad. Never had a bad word to say about anyone. Lovely fella. Really popular in the village. Such a shame."

"You knew him well, then?" I hear myself asking, somewhat caustically. If he's noticed, he doesn't show it.

"Course. Most people around here did. He was always in the village, chatting to folk. He was real social, like. That's when he wasn't down at the Smuggler's Inn. He did love a tipple. Gawd bless his soul. Often put money behind the bar. Say the drinks were on him, and he'd talk to anyone and everyone. Didn't have any airs or graces. Nothing like he was the big-shot from the city or anything. Nothing like that. When he was here, he was just one of us. And always a smile on his face. Especially when he looked at your ma. Oh, those two were really... what do you call it? Soul partners; really in love. My wife used to say, 'When are you gonna' start lookin' at me like that?' I'd say, 'When you start looking like her!'"

He laughs.

I suppress yet another flare of resentment. I'm so close to telling him that he really needs to shut up. He really needs to stop talking. But I don't want to appear ungrateful, and especially not after he's just been so busy extoling the virtues of my father. I can't possibly disabuse him of his notions, and enlighten him to the fact that he was actually a dick... as am I, for that matter. But then, they, whoever they are, do say that the apple doesn't fall far from the old, rotten tree.

"So, how long exactly are you planning on being with us?" I hear him ask.

I hesitate, although I have no idea why – this place, for what it is literally worth, is mine now, and I can do with it as I bloody well please. "Just as long as it takes to sell it, really," I say, masking a tinge of delight in my tone.

The man nods. "Aye, I kind of guessed that would be the case," he says. His tone is the saddest it's been since I arrived here.

I nod, awkwardly.

"Well, I can't say it's much of a surprise. In fact, as soon as we found out, I said to the missus, 'He's gonna' sell up now. He'll have all sorts coming back and forth and, before you know it, the place'll be sold…'"

I don't know if I'm supposed to respond to that. I feel like I should apologise or something, but I don't.

"…So we decided to give the place a deep clean, you know. Edith takes great pride in everything she does, but she wanted to be sure that the house looked its best for ya'. Oh, and you'll need these," he says, producing a jangling chain of keys from his jacket. "Edith also wanted me to ask if you'll come over for supper tonight…"

My brain starts an immediate scan for all possible reasons to decline.

"…but I told her, 'Eedy, the lad's just got 'ere! The last thing he's gonna want to do is spend the night with a couple of old farts,' but she insisted I ask anyway…"

I continue the scan as he continues his verbal rampage.

"…but, in case you didn't fancy it, she prepared a basket for ya. You know, just the basics – bread, milk, and whatnot. All local produce. It's not much, but should be enough to see you through until you can get to the supermarket."

Then, conspiratorially, he adds, "I even put a couple of bottles of me own brew in there for ya. We grow our own grapes here. Not many, mind you, but enough for a dozen or so bottles a year. Eedy doesn't really like it. Do you like wine? Anyway, give it a try and let me know what you think."

He finally stops talking.

"Thank you. That's very kind," I say, and I mean it.

I take the keys from him and look at them curiously.

"We've been taking care of this place for years now, for as long as I can remember," he narrates. "You probably won't remember since you were only a wee lad, but Eedy and I looked after you and your parents when you were out here for the summer. We're kind of a team. She takes care of everything inside the house and I take care of everything outside. Just evenings and weekends, mind. I still had a garage to run up until a short while back. That was before Shawn took over."

I shake my head and force my best smile as the acid builds in my stomach and burns its way to my mouth. I'm sorry. I'm really sorry, but I just can't bear it anymore and I'm unable to stop it from boiling over.

"Wow, you're right," I say. "I don't remember that, but that's probably because I don't remember coming out here that often with my parents. In fact, I think it was just the once, and that was…" I stop myself. I don't want to think about my time here, let alone discuss it with a complete stranger, but he isn't done anyway.

He chuckles. "Well, I may be getting old, son, but I don't think Eedy and I will ever forget those years. They were special to us. Really special. You see, since the wife and I weren't blessed with children of our own, we kind of adopted you and your parents as our extended family. And there's no doubt in our minds that your dad felt the same. Yeah, he'd often check on us, even when he wasn't down here. He'd pick up the phone, you know, just to make sure everything was okay. And your mother, Gawd bless her soul, she…"

"…it wasn't my mother," I say, curtly.

The old man standing in front of me frowns, like I'm talking another language. And that grates. I'm sorry, but who the hell does he think he is, talking about my life, my family, like he's the bloody expert?

Shit, now I've done it. The bloody damns open. I continue, casually, sadistically, enjoying the words, for I know how they're going to be received. "That was his bit on the side, or one of them anyway," I say.

It's odd, because I feel like I want to hurt this cute old man. I want to stomp on his sandcastle of happy memories and expose it for what it really is – an ugly, boot-kicked, mangled mess.

He's staring at me, so I push the point home. "Girlfriends, lovers, mistresses," I say loudly, in that patronizing tone people adopt for the elderly.

He doesn't respond, and for a second I think that my revelation has shocked the old geezer so much that he's going to burst into tears.

But then, "Why would you say such a thing?" he utters, with what appears to be genuine heartbreak.

"Because it's the truth, Harvey," I throw back. I even add a smile for good measure.

"What, you think that after nearly ten years, I wouldn't be able to tell the difference between your mother and some meaningless tart?" he asks bitterly.

I smile. The old man is full of surprises.

"Your mother was like a daughter to us, and your father, our son. Now, I know that after your mother passed, the two of you stopped seeing eye to eye, but that man doted on you. They both did and, quite frankly, to pretend to write off those years as if they'd never happened is not only cruel to us, but it's an insult to their memory."

Well, shit. Now I've really done it. The old man seems genuinely upset. Angry. Hurt, even. His whole demeanour has changed; shoulders tensed, eyes moistened. The sparkle of sweet memories replaced by the drabness of melancholy.

I feel a prick of remorse.

Okay, I feel a lot of remorse.

... But, no – fuck him. Stop pretending. Why does everybody bloody go around pretending all the time? It's like that bloody awkward relative at a family gathering. The one who fucked everything up for everyone else the last time, so this time everybody's like, 'Ooh, don't say anything, don't mention what happened, don't set them off.'

Fuck them!

Fuck that!

On the other hand... what the hell is wrong with me? This man has been nothing but kind, and yet I'm lashing out at him. He's standing right in front me, so I don't have time to try and analyse that.

I sigh. I'm tired. Hungry. Sick. Upset. I didn't really mean what I said, right? Well, yes, I did. Ah, shit. I don't even know anymore. I want to tell him, *Look, just go, let me have some sleep and we'll discuss it some other time.*

"Look, Harvey," I begin, but am interrupted by the scrunching sound of tyres on gravel.

We both turn.

The red Mercedes SLK emerges from the canopy of trees, rolls forward, and eventually stops behind the truck. Then, we watch as the driver's door opens and a heavyset Kathy Bates look-alike climbs out of the vehicle, straightens her bulging navy blue suit, and then reaches back into the car to retrieve her handbag and clipboard.

Then... "Why, hello there," she says in an American twang, sharing a perfect white smile with the both of us before walking up and proffering a manicured hand. "I'm Lucinda, Lucinda Kaye. It's a real pleasure to meet you." She shakes both of our hands, whether we like it or not, and then looks up at the house and draws in a sharp breath. "Oh my, isn't this place chocolate box divine?"

I follow her gaze as it surveys the white-stoned building with rusty red tiles and matching shutters. My first impression is Italian villa. This place looks just like a luxurious slice of Italy. And it's then that I realise that, for the first time since arriving here, I'm allowing myself to really take in the place, and to be perfectly honest, it doesn't look anything like I remember. This place looks completely different – grander.

"It's gorgeous!" Lucinda exclaims, and as much as you'd probably have to torture me to confess to it out loud, I do feel a momentary sense of pride.

"Thanks," I garble.

"Oh, would you look at this?" she breathes, walking by us and up to a white picket fence that fronts and runs the circumference of the building. "I haven't seen anything like this since leaving home," she adds, turning to the both of us with her eyes wide with enthusiasm.

I smile politely. I want to ask, *Who the fuck are you?* But that would be rude, even for me. I've already alienated one person, and I've only just gotten here.

"Well, I best get going," Harvey announces, suddenly. Then, as if justifying his eagerness to get away, he adds, "Otherwise, Eady is going to wonder what the 'eck has happened to me." He forces a smile and, although it isn't obvious, I get the impression that the overenthusiastic American's presence is somehow rubbing salt into the wound I've inflicted. "As I say, everything's been taken care of. You shouldn't want for anything, but if you do, we only live across the way." He nods at the trees. "We're the first cottage, just after the bridge. You can't miss it."

He nods at us both. "Enjoy your tour," he says, and then turns and climbs into the truck.

Oh God. Suddenly, I'm feeling a heavy cloak of remorse press on me, and I feel like I should say something. So, I'm moving to follow him when I hear Lucinda ask, "So, did you say it was your pa who owned this place before you?"

"Yes," I reply, distracted, as Harvey slams the driver door shut and starts the truck's engine.

"And you're from London?"

"Yes."

"Do you know if any improvements have been made on the property recently?"

I watch the truck reverse. "No, I don't think so."

"So, shall we?" my unwanted guest asks.

I don't reply as I watch the truck crawl up the driveway and disappear into the trees, leaving nothing but dust in its wake.

LA DOLCE VITA

Sunday Afternoon.

After watching Harvey leave, I reluctantly turn and join the overenthusiastic American by an immaculately preserved white gate with gleaming chrome hinges and a matching loop handle.

"So," I begin. "You made good time then? You almost got here before I did," I say, much louder than I intended.

"You have no clue who I am, do you?" she asks while frowning at her mobile phone.

I smile, sheepishly. "None…but…"

"…Don't you worry your pretty little head, honey. Happens all the time," she says, flashing me that wide smile of hers. "I'm from Kays and Kays." My face must look blank, because she continues, "I'm your realtor. You know, you guys call us estate agents."

"Oh my God, I'm so sorry. I completely forgot. Did we arrange to meet today? I thought we agreed on Monday."

"No, 3 PM Sunday."

"I'm sorry. It's just, well, I've only just got here, and I don't even…"

"That's no bother, we can explore this beauty together," she says. "Oh, would you look at this! It's Colonial meets Mediterranean. I've never seen anything like it." She assumes a grandiose stance of standing back and taking in the symmetrical building.

It's odd because I'm no agent, or realtor, as Lucinda would put it, but, looking at the place, I kind of get what she means.

"What were you thinking? This is no shack – it's more a governor's retreat. Maybe some Lord's loft; and it appears to be immaculately preserved.

Is this your work?" she asks.

She's referring the manicured lawn, the trimmed ivy that smothers both sides of the house, the red rose bushes that appear to have been drawn around the Georgian-looking square downstairs windows, and the technicolour of flowers neatly packed around the edges of the garden, serviced by a dazzling array of multi-patterned butterflies and assorted insects.

"Um, no, I'm afraid not. It's the handy work of the man who just left."

Yes, I feel a stab of guilt.

"He did this?" she asks incredulously.

I nod.

"Well, he's done an excellent job. Just excellent!"

Another stab.

"How much do you know about the place?"

"Well, my father has owned it for as long as I can remember. We spent a few summers out here."

"Just a few?"

She's looking at me.

When I don't reply, she tactfully adds, "I was referring more to the history of the house – the build, the architecture."

I shake my head, thrusting my hands in my pockets like the clueless child I probably was when I was last here. "Not a clue," I say.

"Right, you thought it was a, what was it, fisherman's cottage? Well, I can tell you, honey, this ain't no cottage. It's much bigger and grander than that. There's an unmistakable craftsmanship to this place. You see those three chimneys, two on either and side one in the centre? They're square, oversized to project strength, wealth, security. Those symmetrical square corners? Load bearing; strength. This place was not only designed and built to withstand the ravages of the Atlantic, but also to project power, virility, and beauty. And, I must say, at least on the outside, it's faired remarkably well. Not unlike yourself," she adds, looking me up and down with a curious smile, and then casually continuing, "Cottages are much smaller, and dare I say it, simpler. Designed for practicality, ease and economy, both in build and affordability. This," she says, taking another step forward, "this is something else."

I don't know what to say. I'm still reeling from being made to feel like a prat for failing basic architecture one second, and to being complimented the next.

Yet, it's in this moment that I know she's the lady for the job at hand. She certainly has me hooked, and if I didn't already own the place, I'd be thinking to buy it.

If I didn't already own it. I'd lost sight of that small detail for a moment, and I suppose that's most likely because I've disassociated myself from it. Not necessarily from the building, but what it represents. The attachments I made. This is, was, and has always been the old man's place. Never, not in a million years, would I have allowed myself even to imagine that one day it would pass to me and, but for my wife's ultimatum, I probably wouldn't even be standing here contemplating the thought. And, interestingly, it isn't until this moment, until I pause to watch the afternoon sun smear the white stone of the building with honey-dripping gold, that I'm able to truly appreciate why the old man always escaped here, to his fortress at the edge of the world, flanked by trees for an army, with the bridge over the railway line, like a drawbridge over a moat, and the white picket fence for barbed wire.

And yes, I have noticed all of the metaphorical symbology, but I'm sure that's purely coincidental and has nothing to do with the fact that I, too, have retreated here to protect myself from something.

"When I think colonial building, I think pillars, porches, America. We're at the edge of England," I speak, eager to steer clear of my own introspection.

"Well, with this kind of white picket fence, I'd say you've inherited your own piece of Americana," the agent responds with a smile. "Your parents American?"

I shake my head, "No, my father was Italian and my mother British."

"Huh."

"How about you?" I find myself asking, keen to introduce other topics for conversation.

"You mean the accent?" She smiles. "My husband's British. We met at a convention. Now, he's an estate agent, and I'm a realtor."

I pull a face. "There's a difference?"

She smiles, wryly. "Let me put it this way, honey; we could both help you sell this beauty, but I am gonna make you a fortune," she says, rubbing her fingers together. "Shall we?"

I usher her forward with an outstretched hand and she doesn't hesitate to turn the handle on the gate, causing it to spring open with a quaint creek and welcome us onto a stone slabbed pathway that slices through a small yet lush green lawn framed by more colour-saturated flowers. I say they're saturated because I don't know if it's because the sun's out or because we're in the countryside, but these flowers look surreal. It's as if someone has turned up the vibrancy dial. And the air, it's thick and heady with perfume. To the point where I think Lucinda's paused for a quick spritz, but she's only rummaging through her bag to produce a digital camera.

"Oooh, can you smell that honeysuckle?" she says, creasing her face into an orgasmic grin and then snapping pictures of the cascades of pink draped over parts of the ivy like exhausted lovers.

"Glorious, just glorious!" she continues, snapping more pictures in quick succession like an overexcited tourist.

Wow.

I can't help but be swept up by her enthusiasm. The place is impressive. Not as big as the fuzzy images in my head. But, I suppose that when you're a kid, you don't often stop to literally smell the flowers – especially when, contrary to what my new neighbour would have me believe, this house wasn't all delicious scents and happy memories.

Far from it.

I put the key in the lock and it springs open with ease as we're both startled by a robotic voice announcing, *Front door open.*

"Ooh, it has a fitted alarm, too, and one of those thingamajigs – zone talkers," Lucinda enthuses. I look at her. "Normally, you have to look on the control panel to work out which zone, door, window is open, but this thing tells you. State of the art," she explains.

No, that's not creepy at all.

We step into a spacious entrance lobby.

It's cool inside and a fresh pine scent hangs heavily in the air, as if someone has just finished mopping the floors, which are made of black and white ceramic squares.

"Oh, my Lord," Lucinda gushes, "would you look at this?"

She's referring to the giant well of light, flooding in through a circle skylight in the roof. Beyond it, giant fluffy clouds wander across that immaculate blue sky.

The oculus is about eight feet wide, and through it a shower of sunshine drops onto the marbled steps of a giant indoor water feature. It's decorated with an assortment of flowers, ferns, plants, and dwarf fruit trees. The feature is almost as tall as me, which makes it about six feet. It's beautiful, and I can't help but smile as I watch the wriggling water reflections dance off of the white walls.

"Oh, my word, look at the light in here!" Lucinda is now referring to the semi-circular balcony, on the second floor, that overlooks us, the water feature and the lounge area. It features one long panoramic window, like the deck of a ship, that presumably looks out to the ocean.

To our left, is the kitchen, the stairs to the second floor, and beyond that, the dining room with views of the back garden and on out to sea. To the right are doors to what I remember to be my mother's photographic studio and my father's study.

"This place is awesome!"

And, once again, I have to agree with the overexcited agent. Just the light in here alone is impressive.

I think of Ellie. She's always going on about how the London flat is dingy, and how she'd love a better view than the street. She would flip if she saw this since, beyond fashion, she loves architecture and is a sucker for house moving shows. And Toby, my little man... he wouldn't know which part of this place to explore first.

Shut up. What a stupid thing to think about. You'll be selling this place soon. I, we, need the money.

Lucinda has moved further into *the den*, as she calls it, and I get the distinct impression that she's no longer looking as a *realtor*, but as an admirer.

There are giant squares, fronted by alternating white glossy and glass doors mounted on both walls of the entrance lobby. I'm not exactly sure what they are until the agent yells an excited, "Storage!"

Very retro. Very sixties.

In the den, there's a large white couch with matching armchairs facing large terrace doors. On the floor, in front of them, is a zebra skin rug, which I assume isn't real. Or is it? I'm not sure. Lucinda doesn't seem to care. She stomps right over and, with a small scuffle with the key that's already in the lock, folds open the gliding terrace doors, revealing a large wall window of flowers and shrubs, as well as a lawn that appears to slope endlessly forward until it reaches the white picket fence in the distance. Beyond that, is the azure sparkle of the Atlantic Ocean.

Fuck, is my stupefied response to that. Luckily, I don't say it out loud. I know, it's a primitive response, even for me, but hey... Did you just see that? Who wouldn't want to live in a place like this? It's bloody awesome!

"Fucking awesome!" Lucinda declares.

I look at her.

"Oh, my. Did I just say that out loud? Oh, I am sorry."

I laugh. "Lucinda!"

"Oh, come on now, you know you were thinking it, too."

"Actually, I was."

We laugh until our reaction is upstaged by a loud hissing sound, and it takes us both a second to identify what it is, at which point we both look over in unison.

"Good Lord," Lucinda utters.

"Wow." I feel a twinge of I don't know what. Humility? Incredulity?

I look up into the gnarled arms of the oak tree. It must reach up to twice as high as the house. The hissing sound is the rustling of its red and gold leaves as handfuls of them fly and flutter around us like falling embers.

Beautiful.

"Uh oh. You may want to get rid of that," Lucinda states, her tone no longer breathless, but bossy.

"It's gorgeous," I say, walking over to the tree and instinctively placing my hand on its trunk.

"These things have been known to cause all kinds of havoc with building foundations. Those roots, they travel everywhere, not to mention the ever-present danger of it falling onto the house. This is just a breeze, but the gale around here can be a fierce son of bitch."

Perhaps. But I realise that I'm grinning as I caress the bark, as if I've been caught up in some kind of rapture. "It isn't going to go anywhere," I say dreamily. "This baby was here when I was a baby. It's about the only real memory I have of this place. Admittedly, the creaking sound it makes at night used to scare the hell out of me, particularly on clear nights when the moon's out, casting shadows of its branches into my bedroom. I used to think they were the long talons of something shifting and growing into some kind of monster. My mother used to tell me that there was nothing to fear – that it was, in fact, a warrior sent by nature to protect me. She loved trees. She'd tell me that nature had embedded its roots right outside of my window to ensure that it would never go anywhere. It would never leave my side, and would always be here to protect me."

I smile fondly at the memory I didn't even know I had until this moment.

But, I don't think Lucinda is impressed by the story, or the tree for that matter, since it's dropped a fresh handful of leaves in her hair, forcing her to hastily pluck and brush at them.

There's a large picnic table and bench under the tree and I take a seat while breathing in the freshness of the ocean breeze. "There's a cliff path down to the beach from there," I say, pointing at the gate in the centre of the fence.

"Perfect!" Lucinda has adopted her enthusiastic tone once more.

Then, she attempts to slide her leg onto the bench part of the table, but it proves awkward, so she opts, instead, to perch herself at one end.

We sit in silence for a few seconds, and then I ask, "So, based on what you've seen so far, do you have any idea of how much we're looking at here?" The words just fall out of my mouth.

This is all so weird. I had an image of this place, but this definitely wasn't it. And, after what I've seen, I'm suddenly taking everything seriously. Much more seriously than I was.

"How much do you think?" my estate agent challenges.

I shake my head. For me, anything over £200,000 profit would be good, because it means we can move out of that shitty rented flat in London and put a deposit down on our own home somewhere. Obviously not in London, though – probably somewhere outside of the city, maybe Richmond or something. I don't care, really. Just anywhere we can start anew, and, most importantly, stick it to Ellie's stuck-up parents who never have taken my profession seriously, especially with me being *just* a therapist and not a bona fide doctor.

"Marco?"

I refocus on Lucinda's plump cheeks, "I don't know. Anything above £200,000 will do me," I say earnestly.

She stares at me and, for a second, I think I may have to lower my expectations, but a lesser value isn't going to get me far on a property anywhere near London. Then, she starts laughing. And, it's quite a long laugh, to the point where I'm just about ready to join her.

Then she stops suddenly and asks, "Are you yanking my chain? Are you testing me?"

"What? No. Of course not."

"Two hundred thousand pounds? Honey, you couldn't even by the land this property is standing on for that! Hell, you couldn't even buy that tree! Strike that. You might have to pay that much to get rid of the damn thing. Have you seen the condition this place is in? It's like new-build, Marco, new-build!" she all but shouts in an accent that is as thick as a Southern preacher's.

"Okay…" I say gingerly. Of course, I've noticed the place. Everything shines like it's brand new, and guess who we have to thank for that?

Yes. And guess who feels like shit every time he's reminded of it?

Exactly.

"We haven't even seen any of the other rooms, or the upstairs. But, I'm telling you, honey, if they're anything like the ground floor, I expect this baby to fetch at least four and a half or five, but don't quote me on that. I really need to take a look at the rest of the building before I can make my recommendation, you understand."

"Wow. That's more than double what I was expecting. Half a million pounds?"

She cocks her head, in that way a mother does when she can't believe what her imbecile child has just done.

"What?" I ask.

"Not thousand, honey. *Million*," she enunciates the last word, slowly and loudly, as if she's trying to get through to a deaf person.

"Oh, right... million," I say with a smile, because she's obviously having me on.

She doesn't share my amusement, though, and that's when it truly hits me. "Oh my God, you're serious. You're estimating this place at four to five *million* pounds?"

She nods. Pearlescent teeth shining once more.

"Five million pounds?"

"Well, I need to see the rest of the house first, but…"

"…Four to five million? Lucinda? Fuck!"

She laughs. We laugh. And, I'm not ashamed to say it. I nearly piss myself. I would have been happy with a fraction of that.

Dolce Vita isn't anything like I remember or, at this stage, have imagined. In my mind's eye, I've always had this image of an old stone house with cloudy windows in rotten wooden frames. Instead, I've inherited the culmination of what appears to be the embodiment of the old man's life's work. He crafted this place into a haven of luxury, the very essence of its name. And I've inherited it. All of it.

Of course, the fact that my step family inherited all of the old man's money in addition to his other properties is still very fresh in my mind. The snub still stings now, as it did when I first found out. But, I don't need to worry about that. I'm going to be rich. No... not just rich, but filthy, stinking, fucking rich! I'll be able to afford to buy a new home and then some. A place with lots of land for Toby. We could get a dog, maybe even a couple. He'd love that. He's always wanted a pet, but they're not allowed in the flat. Quad bikes! We could get quad bikes and go riding together, although I'm sure Ellie would have something to say about that. Christ, I might even be able to redeem myself with her after throwing away a perfectly good career for...

"Marco?" Lucinda's smiling face comes into focus once more. Her eyebrows arched, inquisitively. "Are you okay?"

I chuckle. "Lucinda, you can't drop that kind of news on a guy and not expect his heart to stop."

"I'm sorry, sweety. I can only imagine how overwhelming this must be." I nod. "But good overwhelming, huh?" she adds, knowingly.

"Yes. Very good."

"Okay. Well, wanna show me the rest of the place before you start counting those pounds?"

I smile. "Sure. Oh, and by the way, you can just call me Marc."

"Now, why would I wanna do that? Marco sounds much more sophisticated, and sexy."

She lifts thick eyebrows once more. I know she's flirting. Luckily, or at least I hope so, it's harmless.

So, we go through the rest of the house.

The dining room, featuring uninterrupted views out to sea, open onto the decking via its own set of sash patio doors. The dining table, with ample room for a dozen, is made of oak. Parque flooring throughout.

The kitchen overlooks the front garden through large square windows and features a rustic theme of blue stressed pine, a granite island, and stainless-steel top of the range kitchen appliances, built into the opposite wall. There's also an archway to an adjoining utility room.

During the tour, I spot a basket on the island. It's packed with an assortment of local goodies and produce. A hand-written card sits on top of it, which I open.

"Welcome home. Love, Harvey & Edith."

Everything about that sentence makes my stomach roll.

Yes, I'm a dick, but I've promised myself I'll make it right.

Meanwhile, "The back door features a small portal window offering an appetising view of a delightful self-contained courtyard."

Then there's my father's study and my mother's photo studio, neither of which I choose to enter. I just don't think I'm ready for that particular trip down memory lane, not just yet. So, I tell Lucinda that I have some things I need to check on and stop by the bathroom while I'm at it. She accepts my lame excuse and goes off on her own, scribbling notes as she does.

Meanwhile, I hover, like the emotional coward that I am, in between the kitchen and the den. Waiting. When she's ready to proceed upstairs, I appear as if by magic to accompany her up the timber, creaky staircase that emerges onto that glorious landing with ship deck-styled windows that flood the hallway and den below with a curtain of natural light.

There are four bedrooms upstairs. The master bedroom and three others of equal size. The master bedroom features fantastic views of the garden and the sea. The other two rooms feature views of the countryside. At least they do accordingly to Lucinda, I made a point of not going on there. All are furnished to the highest standard. There's also a family bathroom and a landing annex with a spiral staircase to the attic, which could easily be converted into additional sleeping or office space, thanks to the array of Velux windows.

In all, Lucinda stays at Dolce Vita for about three hours. She snaps numerous photos and takes meticulous notes, some of which she narrates aloud, as reproduced here for you.

Now, I like Lucinda – I like her very much – but I'm glad to see her finally board her Mercedes with the promise that I'll be hearing from her as soon as the promos are ready.

It's been a long journey. I'm tired, hungry, and actually in desperate need of some alone time.

The train journey here wasn't the only rollercoaster I boarded today; there were other personal elements to all of this, most of which I struggled to keep to myself in front of my overzealous American friend.

I'm back. Here of all places. Luckily, much of it has changed from what I remember. In fact, it has completely changed. The only thing that's truly resonated in my memory so far is that oak tree. All of this makes it much easier to walk through the place without having a nervous breakdown. Although, I'm sanguine enough to know that I'm going to be here a while. And so, like it or not, I'm going to have to venture into all of the other rooms and deal with whatever ghosts might be lurking there.

It's only a matter of time.

EPIPHANY

Sunday. 18:03.

So, here I am. Alone at last, and it feels so bloody… awful.

I hate being alone. Have I mentioned that? Which, of course, creates a ridiculous contradiction. Everybody was annoying me today, and yet now that they've gone, I'm thinking that maybe… well, um, no, I don't want them back.

That idea is rubbish.

Truth is, I don't know what I want. Though, I suppose I do, and that isn't an option right now. I've got a lot of rehabilitating to do in that department.

In the meantime, it feels like I've been abandoned here. A little boy left in a haunted house all alone, waiting for night to fall and the ghouls to come.

Will they? I mean... tonight, when it's dark and it's just me here, will I start to hear things, memories mostly, from my past, and will they start crawling out of the walls, down from the attic? Will they scuttle over my skin and bury themselves deep into the back of my brain like termites, invading every crevice to scare out those things I've spent a lifetime suppressing? Like actual feelings and emotions.

Oh fuck, I need a drink.

I need a good stiff drink, and I bet this place is as dry as a desert. Ironic, considering that the old man *enjoyed a good tipple.* Harvey was quick to point that out and remind me, once again, that the old apple hasn't fallen far from that proverbial tree.

I'm nothing like him, though.

The thought disgusts me. So, I hurry into the kitchen and fall upon Harvey's courtesy basket like a vagabond onto a decent meal.

I start pulling things out like a mad person. The wine – which brings a smile to my face –, shortbread, preserves; blackberry and strawberry in homemade frilly jars, bread, tea, coffee, sugar, and more cookies.

I make a point of not looking at the card again. I remember how shitty it made me feel the first time around. I didn't like that feeling, and I've already got enough going through my head without adding more.

So, I discard the card to one side, absolving myself from any guilt with the promise that I will make good. I will. After all, if it wasn't for Harvey, I wouldn't be standing to gain multiple millions of pounds from this place. Millions of pounds.

I pull the cork on the bottle, but not before taking a good look at the label, because I want to savour the moment. I want to savour the anticipation of the tangy, sweet, fruitiness of fermented grapes on my tongue.

The label reads *Harvey's Harvest* under a picture of a bunch of red grapes. Then, *Made in Porthcove.*

I chuckle. Then I take a tentative swig and wait for the reaction in my mouth. Not bad. It's kind of warm, with a hint of violet sweets, and then there's a real tangy aftermath.

It wouldn't go down as my favourite vintage, but I've tasted much worse, and this certainly hits the spot right now.

There are two bottles in the basket. From the picture on the labels, I can tell that one's red and the other white. For a second, I consider opening the white also, but decide against it and instead take another generous swig from the red and sluice it over my pallet like a professional taster. This time the flavour's more intense; violets and cherries. Sweet yet sour. And I can feel it at the back of my throat now, in my belly, and though I don't know if it's my imagination, I can already feel it melting away the edge.

I grin. "Good old Harvey." His brew has already started to have an effect on me, as has the old man himself.

I mean, I know he kept banging on about Dad, but he's actually made a very positive impression on me. Like an old, long lost uncle. And again, apart from his favourite topic of conversation, I felt comfortable around him.

Just stop mentioning that man you're all supposed to love around here because he never said a bad word, was generous, and put money behind the bar. I can't remember the last time that bloke bought me a drink. When was the last time he bought Toby a present? His own grandson?

Prick!

I carry the bottle through to the den and take another sip from it. It's doubly tangy now due to the unspoken vitriol bubbling on my tongue. Then, I stand and admire the space.

It's getting dark, so the area is mostly outlines and shadows, highlighted gold by the setting sun in some spots. It reminds me of one of those retail websites that show you a picture of the product with highlighted areas which you can hover over for additional information. And it looks just like that, too. Probably already is, if Lucinda's had her way.

Not that I can check. I discovered pretty soon after arriving here that there's hardly any cell phone signal, and Wi-Fi speeds are slow enough to rival dial-up. It was Lucinda who pointed that out to me. Even the widgets on my phone have been complaining with a fit of messages screaming that they're *unable to connect.*

Ya think?

I tried calling Ellie earlier and only managed to get one bar by hanging my phone and part of me out of the bedroom window, and even then, the call kept dropping until, eventually, I had to concede defeat.

So, yeah. I'm pretty much marooned here.

Alone. With no phone. No internet.

I take another swig from the bottle.

You know, the space between the entrance hall and the den is so large and high that Lucinda's shoes clicked and echoed when we entered the house earlier?

Now I am barefoot, my hair's damp, and I'm wearing jogging bottoms and a sweater with Cambridge written on the back, a la Americana, after standing under one of *the* most luxuriously powerful cascades of hot water I have ever experienced in my whole life.

Yes, I ventured into the inner sanctum of the master bedroom. Again, I don't remember venturing into that room that much as a child, so it didn't have much effect on me. There were no memories lurking behind the wall-length wardrobe, under the pine dresser – not even the king-sized bed. However, as Lucinda would say, there was a gloriously uninterrupted view of the garden, framed beautifully by branches of the oak tree.

No, I didn't feel up to going into my old bedroom. Not yet. Besides, I'm grown up now, so it only makes sense that I should take the grown-up room along with all the modern comforts that come with it.

So, here I am now, shower fresh, with a homemade brew in my belly fermenting its own kind of magic in my brain. I stop and listen. Everything is supernaturally quiet. There's no incessant drone of traffic, no sirens screaming, no children wailing, no people talking. Nothing. It's so deathly quiet right now that I can actually hear that white noise, which I believe is my blood pumping behind my ears. Oh, and nature, of course. Specifically, the crick and creak of the resting building that sounds more like aching limbs, the lifting and falling of the wind as it whistles eerily through the skylight, and the distant rumble of the tide in the distance.

I'm both entranced and terrified. It feels as if I'm the only person left alive in the world and, ironically, as far as the inhabitants of this house are concerned, I am.

I glance across the room at the two closed doors leading to the study and the photography room. Well, I call it that, but I don't really know what it is now. I just have this vague memory of portraits in that room. They could have been painted, for all I know. Only, in my mind, I see photographs, but I'm having a hard time differentiating them from actual memories. In fact, I have no idea which is which, and nor do I want…

The thought catches in my head.

I look at the door handle in a horror film power-zoom.

Oh, for fuck's sake. Really?

I look at the study door. I do need to go in there. I need to see what state it's in – especially if I'm thinking of starting a practice out here.

As I was travelling to my self-imposed exile, I had a vision of me seeing patients by day and toiling by night to restore this place in some sort of cathartic refurbishment, not only of the building, but also of my mind.

But, from what I've seen, this house needs no such intervention from me. As Lucinda said, It's almost *new-build.*

I am in part relieved, as that means no additional drain on my dwindling finances, but I'm also in part disappointed – like, what the hell am I going to do with myself while I'm stuck out here, on my own?

On my own!

It's ironic really. I'm complaining about being alone, yet I would be the first person to tell clients that being alone is actually the first step to catharsis.

Don't worry. I'm not going to go off on one and start espousing quotes from Facebook posters. They're just a load of crap designed for the temporary relief of lazy people who know something isn't right in their lives, and are happy to acknowledge it by sharing trite declarations, yet feel no compunction to actually do something about it.

Truth be told, in order for me to deal with everything that's happened, and in particular with why it's happened, I need to understand why I do the things that I do. I need to better comprehend my likes and dislikes rather than read how these are projected on the people around me. Just like I need to understand why I crave intimacy and thus, consequently, don't enjoy being alone. What exactly am I afraid of? What is it about me that I don't particularly like?

Shit. Well, how long have you got?

Really? You're making a joke about this, about yourself?

See? It's already started. I haven't been here one day and the introspection is already starting to nag me like an annoying relative.

So, anyway, where was I? Yes, before I go off on a tangent, while I may feel like I need to see that room, I doubt I actually do – because it's bound to be in immaculate condition, just like the rest of the house.

Yeah, that's a good enough excuse for me.

Of course, that raises all sorts of questions for which I would now probably have the answers if I hadn't been such a prick to Harvey. Oh God, and here we go again. Why can't I just be an arsehole and have done with it? Why does it always come with this aftermath of guilt like a fucking hair shirt?

It's exhausting!

I know what I'll do.

I rush over to the door, pull on my Timberland boots – a Christmas gift from Ellie, almost like she knew I was going to find myself in need of them nearly a year later –, grab my jacket and the wine bottle and make my way over to the terrace doors.

Terrace doors open.

Yeah, thanks for that.

Wow. Fresh air. It's delicious even if it does bring the effects of the wine into focus, or should that be fuzziness?

Night falls fast around here. I estimate that I probably have about another half hour or so of light. After that, I run the serious risk of misplacing a step and tumbling down the cliff.

Oh well. Right now, I'm not completely against that conclusion to this particular predicament. At least it'll be fast. Or will it? Knowing my bloody luck, I'll fall and break something, condemning myself to months of Harvey, or his wife for that matter, bed-bathing me.

Ugh. No thanks.

There's a real gale blowing at me now, as I make my way from the house to the back gate. After some finger fumbling and juggling with the bottle, I've stepped out from the perimeter when a familiar sound makes me turn around.

The silhouette of the house stares back at me. Beyond it, I can see the illuminated carriages of the train, snaking through the trees like a chain of fireflies.

And I'll be perfectly honest, as much as I thought I was going to hate that bloody thing being so close to the house, I realise now that I quite like it. It's physically and metaphorically my link back to the outside world, and it's with fondness that I watch the string of lights fade into darkness.

When I turn once more to make my way down the rocky path before me, I see another flicker of light in my peripheral vision and I look up. The light is coming across the body of water, from the peninsula about half a mile away.

A lighthouse. Its beam intermittently slashing the darkness like a laser. A rather magical beacon beneath a clear sky where shimmering stars and a full moon have already announced the onset of night.

Beautiful. Ethereal, even. I don't remember seeing this before, but I love it.

After some careful manoeuvring, I manage to make it safely down the zigzag hillside path to the pebble beach below, and all in one piece.

And I spend some time here, listening to the soothing lullaby of the ocean and watching the mesmerising blink of light reach out to me from across the water.

I think about life in London and even flirt with the fantasy of a life out here with my family, if the circumstances were different. I stray over the prospect that, if I play this next move carefully and considerately, I might, with one big fat dollop of luck, be able to make this right.

I drink from the bottle some more, the wine warming me against the ocean chill, as I contemplate Ellie's ultimatum. Then I drink some more until eventually I find myself concluding that I'm going to do it. I am going to do whatever I must to get my family back, and if that means seeing this therapist in London once a week, and submitting myself for analysis and all of the shit that that entails, then so bloody be it.

I'm ready.

Who knows? It might even do me some good. After all, many therapists have supervisors. Maybe if I'd had one, I wouldn't have lost my job, and none of this other shit would have happened.

Maybe. Perhaps. Could be. Should be.

Fuck!

I sound like one of my bloody clients. Maybe if I did this, perhaps if I did that. *Stop bloody speculating and do something. For God's sake, man! Have you become that paralysed, that you're incapable of taking control of your own life? It seems that you're all too happy to relinquish control rather than assume responsibility, and then you wallow in the bloody consequences. Stop talking about what could happen and get on with making it happen! This is the first stage of the rest of your life.*

A grin creeps across my face. And, well, it's hardly surprising after that interval of self-life coaching.

By the time I've drained the last dregs of Harvey's Brew, I can't help but ask myself how much exactly of my so called epiphany could be attributed to the wine.

Ah, who cares? I'm buzzing, and if I think about it, this probably isn't the best time to go roaming down precarious footpaths, but there you go – I love to live my life dangerously.

Eventually, part walking and part crawling – for safety, of course, not because I need to – I manage to make my way back up the costal path and into the house. And, if I'm perfectly honest, I'm quite happy to lock the gale that I originally found refreshing outside. It was causing havoc with my inebriated brain.

And I know I'm pissed because I was able to make it home with relative ease. That was in part thanks to the full moon, but also because one of the upstairs lights was on. I used this as a beacon and, before long, I was back on the other side of the fence.

Now that I think about it, I think it was actually one of the attic lights.

Yeah, I'm definitely drunk. I haven't even been up to the attic yet and, besides, by the time I reached the terrace doors, looked up, all of the upstairs lights were off.

A NEW DAY

Monday. 07:45.

My flesh, my blood, my heartbreak, my joy. I don't want this moment to end. The warmth of the sun on our faces, the nip of cold on our fingers as we cast and wait for the fish to succumb to our bait. Let's stay here forever by this river, breathing in the scent of mud, moss, and grass. Let me hold you forever and never let go… never let go…

The rush of the river gradually metamorphoses into the rumble of the ocean as I wake up to my first morning in Porthcove.

I don't want to wake up. I was dreaming of Toby and one of our fishing expeditions together, and it felt so bloody real. And yet, I'm forced to consciousness by the overenthusiastic birdsong of what I imagine is most of the bird population of the British Isles, not least the gulls. Still, it's infinitely better than the cacophony of London rush hour.

This is like waking up in a Snow White cartoon.

I open my eyes. The room is flooded with light, yet black clouds hang like grapes from a steely sky and amplify my snugness underneath the covers. It's deliciously warm under here, and I have to consider staying in bed all day.

But that would be a waste.

So, after several minutes, I force myself into a sitting position and run my hands through my hair, which reminds me again that it's longer and wavier than I'd like.

I remember seeing one of those traditional barber shops on the way in. One of those ones with the red and white pole out front. Maybe I'll pay them a visit today.

I smile. Not long ago, I remember Toby asking me, rather excitedly, if

I knew the meaning of 'the red and white twirl', as he put it, outside of a barber's shop. And I had to be honest with the little man; I didn't. So, he proceeded to tell me that it dates back to when barbers were also medical practitioners. Or more *pacifically*, *spendifically*, or more *specifically*, as he eventually put it, when they were expected to perform medical procedures, like taking blood and healing sick people.

"The red means blood and the white means bandages."

I laughed as my heart filled with pride. "Every day's a school day, even for adults," I told him. "Of course, that's when they're not busy doing other things, like sucking blood off of people, like vampires!"

He didn't say anything at first to that, but then he rolled his eyes and complained, "Dad."

"What?"

"You're making fun?"

"Don't be silly. I would never dare do that to you."

He gave me his mother's look. I held up my hands. Surrendering.

"Bet you don't know what bloodletting is."

Another look.

"That's exactly what we were learning."

"It was?"

"Yes. It means taking and giving blood."

His words were said so casually, like he'd been a doctor for many years. Then he went back to swishing through his tablet as I watched him. My heart bursting with pride. I couldn't help myself. I pulled him close, squeezed him tight, and kissed his head, eliciting grumpy but ever so cute complaints.

"I love you, little man."

"I love you too, Dad, when you aren't squeezing me to death."

A seagull squawks outside my window, as if protesting the fact that I'm still in bed.

I'm shirtless and in my boxers, and to be entirely honest, I don't remember getting this way. I must have just passed out. I felt so tired after getting back from the walk, and I don't know what the hell was in Harvey's brew, but it knocked me for six. I mean, it couldn't have been more than a litre's worth of wine, but, bloody hell, that stuff's lethal. But then, I've never been a wine guy.

Anyway, after a taking several more minutes to acclimatise to where the hell I am, I slowly crawl out of the lusciously soft bed. Thankfully, I don't have a headache – I just feel groggy.

I pause by the window to enjoy the wonderful view that had Lucinda all excited, looking out to the ocean. It's wild today. Nothing like yesterday. Today, those giant black clouds are scurrying across that blue sky, drifting over the garden like war ships readying to unleash their payload.

Yet, still awesome. Majestic. Beautiful.

I could stand here all day watching the seascape shift and morph before me, but it's chilly. So, I step out of my shorts and am just about to throw myself under that beautiful shower when I catch sight of my naked body in the full-length mirror, and I'm surprised to see that it's still in fairly good shape. Admittedly, my abs have faded. That happened ages ago, since I stopped going to the gym, but I still look trim. Maybe I could take up running while I'm here. I mean, my legs are straight, my thighs quite defined, and there's still a spark in my morning green eyes, even though I look tired. My beard could do with a trim, though, and… is my nose broader? I broke it when I was a child and now, if you look closely, it leans ever so slightly to one side. I look like a boxer. At least, I think so.

Yeah, I know, this all sounds vain, but I'm actually wondering what the hell the fuss is about me. What David has always told me and what he was trying to say at the club. Try as I may, I just don't see it. Yeah, I *know* I'm supposed to look like this movie star guy, but I don't see it. Then, maybe that's it. Maybe that's why I've been so lucky with the ladies, because I still can't see what it is about me that makes them want to use my body – sexually, passionately, sometimes even kinkily… especially the ones I'm not married to. And why does that make me feel so fucking good and bad in equal measure?

Even the one appendage that the females in my life have often been impressed with seems average to me. I mean, right now, he's looking rather depressed, and quite rightly, too. He's been bloody neglected for what feels like the best part of a year. It hasn't been, as you know, yet it feels like it.

Cold chills slide over my skin and lay goosebumps in their wake, snapping me out of my trance. Hurriedly, I jump under the shower, immensely grateful to the hot water that almost instantly drives the freeze from my bones.

Half an hour later, dressed in jeans and a sweater, I pad down the stairs, socks in hand, and make a beeline for the kitchen. I'm hungry, so I make scrambled eggs and coffee, being particularly careful to sidestep another healthy portion of guilt.

And yes, I know. You don't have to be a therapist to understand that there's only one way to avoid my being knifed with shame every bloody time I use something that Harvey and his wife considerately left behind for me, and that's to make amends.

But then, did I really say anything so terrible?

Well... Don't answer that. I already know that I probably could have at least been more appreciative.

Maybe, after breakfast, I'll walk over there. Maybe.

It's my first day here, though, so it makes sense to go explore. I decide, for my sins, to take a walk into town – I mean, the village. I figure that I can check out the place, get a trim, and maybe buy a few essentials assuming they take cards around here, given that I hardly have any cash left. I could really do with a supermarket run, but, on the other hand, it's just me here. I'm not going to need much.

Oh look, shocker, that thought just made me feel sad.

Get on with it!

I tap and then frisk myself. Shit. I've left my phone upstairs. What's the point, though? I can't get a signal, and on those rare occasions where I do, Ellie doesn't pick up.

Still, it doesn't mean I should stop trying. I need to talk to her. I want her to know that I reached a decision yesterday. I want her to know that I'll do whatever it takes to get her and Toby, my family, back together again.

Half an hour later, I've pulled on my boots and my jacket, and have shoved a beany hat over my washed but unkempt hair in the hopes that I'll manage to wrangle a slot in the barber's shop today.

I leave the house. I don't bother to set the alarm again. Not that I know how to yet. I mean, I do remember Lucinda mentioning the make, but beyond that, I'm clueless how to use the thing. Top of the range, of course. To set it, all you have to do is press *Arm,* then leave the room within thirty seconds; I'm just not sure about the disarming. I remember asking her if she's ever worked for a security firm, and she just laughed and said that, after being to as many houses as she has, you get to know all the alarm systems by heart.

I do lock the door, though. I know the countryside isn't like the city and everything, but, still, there's something about leaving the front door unlocked that feels wrong to me.

So, I step out into the fresh air. It's autumnal fresh, where it isn't cold, but nippy, and the scent of damp leaves and burning wood fills the air.

I would never say this out loud, but I could get used to living here. Of course, it could just be the fact that it's all still new to me and I reason that, if I can steer clear of everything that came before, I could learn to like this place.

Yet, I have a word with myself as I cross the bridge. I know what I'm doing. I'm romanticising, overcompensating for the fact that I've been banished here against my will. Oh, okay, I admit, I sort of banished myself here, unintendedly.

Fine – shit, I exiled myself, to keep it real. And now I'm seeing everything that is good while ignoring everything that is bad. Interestingly, when I challenge myself to list all that is truly bad about being here, I can only come up with the same things I identified yesterday; Ellie and Toby, and my being disconnected from the rest of the world. Oh, and those bloody rooms.

I know. But this morning, I did it again. I glanced at both doors and then averted my gaze.

The thing is, I would be the first person to say that the more I do this, the scarier they are going to become until I reach the point where I'll become paralysed by the thought of them. Maybe I should at least start some kind of systematic desensitisation...

"Morning," a loud, cheerful voice slices through my thoughts.

I look up. A smiling postman is rolling his bike down the cobblestoned hill, just in front of what I believe to be Harvey's cottage.

"Morning," I say, mustering a smile.

"Looks like rain later," he continues cheerily, raising his voice while delivering post to a nearby cottage.

I nod, not really knowing what to say to this stranger. "Yes, it does."

"You're the doctor that's just moved into Dolce Vita, right?"

I momentarily don't know how to respond as I wrestle with a few reactions to that familiarity. First, I feel surprise, obviously, and then annoyance, that this man already knows about me, yet I know nothing about him. I'm already on the back foot. *Did Harvey make a public announcement or something?*

"Yes, that's right," I say.

I can't be bothered to go into the minute detail that I'm not actually a doctor. Not in the conventional sense.

Although, at this rate, I won't need to advertise my services.

"Oh, beautiful place, that is. Absolutely beautiful," the postman says, walking up to me. His breath fogging out in front of him.

He's a lanky fella, early fifties, in full Royal Mail uniform, with tufts of curly black hair escaping from under his cap. He beams a generous smile at me, which includes his small grey eyes shining from behind round spectacles.

"I'm Peter. Pete to me mates."

"Hello, Pete, I'm Marco, or Marc to mine."

"Marco. You don't 'alf look like your dad," he says in amazement.

Seriously?

I force a smile.

"You've already heard that, 'aven't ya?"

"Just a few times," I say. "Along with some movie star I've never heard of."

"Oh yeah, now that you mention it." He studies me intently for a few seconds, then says, "Nah, just kidding," and laughs. "Oh, while I have ya," he adds suddenly, and then starts rummaging through the bundle of post in the satchel on his bike.

He grunts after a few seconds and pulls out three envelopes. "I'm not really supposed to, but…"

"… Oh, no, no problem," I say, taking the letters from him while wondering who the hell could be sending me mail at this address already. "Probably all bills," I say shuffling through them.

"I think a couple are," he responds, helpfully.

I laugh again, not knowing how exactly to respond to the fact that he's made a point of looking through my post. "Oh, thanks, Pete. I haven't even been here a day and you're already bringing me bills."

"Sorry, mate. So, how are you settling in?"

I don't reply straight away, since I'm too busy looking at one of the envelopes. It's thick, embossed on the front with the name of a firm of lawyers that I don't recognise. There's that fairground ride sensation in my belly again.

Divorce.

"Marc?"

"Yes, everything's good. Thank you," I say, forcing another smile.

"Signed anyone up yet? You know, for the sessions," he asks conspiratorially.

"No, not yet."

"Ah, I wouldn't worry. They'll soon come flocking. We're all bonkers here, mate!"

He laughs.

I laugh with him.

"So, where are you off to?"

I glance at Harvey's cottage, but figure that this guy already knows enough about me. "Um, I was thinking of going into the town, village, the shops to get a few things," I stumble over the words because I don't even know myself yet.

"Oh, good, good. Listen, if you're going to the grocery store, you'll meet Deedee, my wife. Just tell her I sent you and she'll take care of ya. Do you know where you're going? Just nip through there – it's a great shortcut – and turn left and you'll be on the high street in no time."

"Great. Thanks." There's a few seconds of silence as a distant cockerel confirms it's time for everybody to be out of bed. "Well," I begin, glancing at the bundle of post in his satchel, "I best let you get on with delivering more bills."

He laughs. "Yeah. Well, it was nice meeting ya, Marc."

"And you, Pete."

We turn in opposite directions as I make for the shortcut that will take me to the high street.

"Hey, Marc!" Pete calls from the opposite side of the street, his voice echoing against the row of houses.

I turn to face him once more.

"We're having a birthday bash for my lad, Timmy, down at the Smuggler's Inn tonight. Pretty much the whole village'll be there. You should come."

"Oh, I," I scramble to find an excuse.

"We'll be there from seven…"

"Well, I was…"

"…Don't be shy. I know the rest of the village'd love to meet ya, and I'm not taking no for an answer!" He looks up and down the cobbled road, makes a money gesture by rubbing his fingers together, and then mouths, "New customers," while widening his eyes and nodding, knowingly.

I barely smile my acknowledgement and he's off, whistling to himself as he goes. "See you there!" he calls back over his shoulder then, making his way to his next delivery.

The rest of my morning carries on pretty much in the same vein. Wherever I go, people smile and greet me as if I grew up in the village.

At first, I find it disconcerting, especially when paranoia starts to settle in; they've all been talking about me, wondering about me, probably comparing me to my bloody dad. But, after the fifth person, I have a word with myself.

This is what you do. This is what you're all about, making strangers feel relaxed around you, to the point of gaining their trust so that they'll then feel comfortable telling you their deepest, darkest truths. If you can do that, then dealing with the locals should be a breeze. Besides, as Pete pointed out, every person you meet is a potential customer.

So, I just relax into it and, before long, it's me initiating the greetings, as well as the small-talk about the weather.

Deedee, of course, is just like her husband; all smiles and leaning-in intimacies, along with conspiratorial hushes. She bombards me with questions, comments, and compliments about the house, my parents. Then she babbles on about the villagers and my profession. She asks about my wife, my son, and when they'll be joining me, to which all I can say is "soon". Eventually, I find myself embellishing the story slightly, explaining that Ellie is an important executive in a London company and that it's about to launch a new product, so she's had to stay in the city until that's all done and dusted.

So then, as soon as my new friend, Deedee, is finished being suitably impressed, she moves on to Toby. She asks how old he is, whether he's in school, and do I have a picture. Which, of course, reminds me that I don't. We both marvel at the thought of our children and we're excited to discover that they're of similar age, and that perhaps they can play together when Toby finally gets here.

I ignore the stomach-punch that statement gives me and instead deploy my new skill of overenthusiasm by declaring what a blessing children are when they aren't getting up to mischief.

By the time we've finished chin wagging, I feel much older than my years but, oddly, I quite like it. There's a certain sense of companionship, comradery. Something that I haven't felt in a while and something I quite clearly needed.

Of course, while she's kept me chained to the grocery store counter with her verbal onslaught, Deedee has made a point of introducing me to each and every customer, as if we're old pals.

I just keep chanting to myself, *Potential customer, potential customer, potential customer*, every time I'm forced to smile at a stranger.

Eventually, I'm released with some complimentary fruit and another invitation to the birthday bash at the inn.

When I told Deedee that I needed to nip next door, to the bakers, she told me to tell Rosie that Deedee had sent me, which results in my receiving some free scones along with the declaration that I'll never have tasted nor will ever taste anything like them. "Oh, and here's some clotted cream to go with those," says a rosy-faced, rotund lady with wily hair and a pixie nose.

"Ooh, and will you be coming to Timmy's birthday bash tonight?" Rosie asks as she wraps up my gifts.

"Of course," I say with a big smile. "I wouldn't miss it for the world."

"Oh goodie," she says, clapping her hands together and then promptly tucking a runaway strand of hair behind her white cap.

It's way past lunchtime by the time I've finished my shopping rounds and my wavy hair has been tamed to a short back and sides once more. The barber even threw in a complimentary beard trim as a welcome to the village.

Now, fully groomed, smelling of shampoo and liberally applied lotion, me and my weighty shopping bags are slowly making our down the cobbled high street when I hear the rumble and rattle of a vehicle pulling up alongside me.

I turn to see that it's a Volvo. It's seen better days but is in still in pretty good nick.

Behind the wheel is a thin looking lady wearing a brown coat and headscarf.

She buzzes down an unhappy electric window and looks across at me. "Are you Marco, the doctor from Dolce Vita?" she asks in a diluted local accent.

I suppress a sigh, give her my well-rehearsed nod and smile. She eyes me, warily, and eventually offers me a lift.

My instinct is to thank her, but tell her that I'm okay since it isn't far. Don't ask me why, I don't know. I think I've just had enough inane banter for one day. But, I can also feel the combined weight of the plastic bags; they're heavy, cutting into my fingers. It makes no sense to refuse the ride.

So, it's with relief that I arrange my shopping bags on the backseat as instructed and then waggle my numb fingers before climbing into the passenger seat.

And no, the thought of being tortured by a serial killer with a death wish doesn't cross my mind. This is Porthcove, remember?

After welcoming me to the village, my secret agent of a driver, who only needs a large pair of dark sunglasses to complete her look, introduces herself as Ava. She's married to a salesman and has two children, one of each, both younger than Toby.

I'm about to reintroduce myself when I notice her polite smile; she already knows all about me.

Of course.

Interestingly, she hasn't been given the full briefing because she goes on to ask about my practice in London. How long have I worked there and how many patients have I seen over the course of my career, along with what type of patients.

I tell her that I've worked there for a few years and have seen a couple of hundred patients about a variety of things, ranging from anxiety to couple's therapy. The last bit I throw in since she's told me she's married and I wonder if that might well be the source of her enquiry.

Hey, you can't blame a boy for trying. Needs must and all that.

Naturally, I leave out the part about how I haven't worked at the practice for a while now due to an incident that I'd rather not talk about. This is one of the upsides, I conclude, of moving down here. While everybody knows of me, they don't really know about me.

Thank God.

So, it isn't long before we're crunching down Dolce Vita's gravelled drive, and Ava is complimenting me on how beautiful the place is. She then goes on to add that it must look gorgeous on the inside, but I stop short of offering her a tour since, well, that would be weird.

And so, it's with my most profuse gratitude, both before and after plastic baggage reclaim, that I watch the Volvo disappear in a plume of diesel fumes, back up the gravelled driveway.

Wow, what a day.

I am exhausted and hungry so I make myself a ham baguette and a couple of those scones which, to be perfectly honest, are truly delicious and unlike anything I have ever tasted before, just like Rosie promised.

Then I take a seat in the love chair by the terrace doors and watch the white peaks of the ocean form and fizz as the waves roll forward before disappearing out of view.

Then, as the sun makes an appearance in a temporary patch of blue sky, warming me like a cat in a spotlight, I'm out for the count.

SHAWN AND JESSICA

Monday. 18:05.

I wake up with a start. Someone's pounding on the door. At least I think they are. Or is it the rain? It's falling in sheets; drumming on the windows and pelting the skylight.

Darkness is already pressing on the glass, which is weird because it feels like I was awake only a few minutes ago.

I'm cold, and this makes me think about my fleece, which is in my bedroom, and I'm just getting up from the couch when there's banging on the front door once more. It's urgent and, in my groggy state, irritating.

I rub my face and eyes rigorously to try and clear the dregs of sleep and glance at my watch; it's just gone six.

Reluctantly, I haul myself to my feet and hurry over to the door, snapping on lamps as I go. Probably not the best idea, because I catch sight of myself in the mirror. It's obvious that I've been asleep.

Good. Then, whoever it is will know they've disturbed me.

The banging on the door continues.

"Okay, okay!" I yell, running fingers through my hair. The distance between sofas and the front door seems interminable today.

I'm really irritated now. This whole communal thing takes some getting used to, and I'm not used to it yet.

I yank the door open with a sigh.

Front door open.

"Oh, there you are. I was starting to wonder if you were even in," says a disgruntled thirty-something year old blonde I don't recognise. Yet, she looks at me expectantly, as if we know each other of old. Hunched against the rain, hand bag over her head, she adds, "It's cold out here, and this rain's playing havoc with my hair."

I want to say, *So?* But instead, "How can I help?"

"I'm Jessica. We had a six o'clock?" she says, slowly, as if feeding me clues. Then, obviously noticing my blank face, she adds, "He didn't call you, did he? We're supposed to have a six o'clock."

I shrug helplessly, and she is getting soaked.

"Look, why don't you come in?"

"Well, there isn't much point now, is there?" she asks irritably, her accent noticeable. She annunciates words, yet it's obvious, at least to me, that what's emerging isn't her natural speaking accent.

I haven't even managed to close the door behind her before she's fishing inside her handbag for her mobile phone, dialling numbers and putting the device to her ear.

As she waits, she has a good look around the place, and I'm just about tell her that service here isn't the best when she frowns and looks at the device's display.

"Shit! Perfect, that's just perfect. Shit!"

Her face is one big scowl, and it isn't much different to how I imagine I must have looked moments earlier.

"Look, Jessica – that's your name, right?" She nods and rivulets of rain water dribble off her nose. "Can I get you a towel? Then maybe you can tell me what happened. Would that be okay?"

She shrugs.

I hurry into the kitchen, only to realise that I have no idea if there are even any towels down here. So, I rifle through drawers until I come across neatly pressed tea towels.

When I return, I can see that my diminutive stranger, who is smartly dressed in a trouser suit and completely impractical high heels, is looking around the house. She has her back to me and I can't help but watch. Her jacket is short, which naturally invites my eyes to rove over her backside that, I conclude, does look good. She isn't slim, but curvaceous, and the fabric of those trousers is stretched tightly over that voluptuous rear.

Oh, come on, it has been a few days now. What do you expect? Although blondes, especially those with shoulder-length hair and dark roots, don't normally do it for me. This one doesn't either, particularly, but the vision of a woman inside this house does. And there's something about her demeanour, especially that spark in her eyes, that tells me she's feisty. Maybe a bit dirty. Sexually speaking, of course.

So, I hesitate in the doorway and allow myself to enjoy the side-to-side undulation of her backside as her heels click further into the den.

Then, my pulse starts to quicken.

Shit.

The moment is broken when she turns to look at me, and it's a double-take. One I recognise because I've seen it on the faces of other women. It's as if they're just noticing me and concluding that I'm something they want after all, and it's normally the prelude to a shy or cheeky smile.

No such thing here.

I offer my visitor the tea towel. She stares at it.

"Sorry." I force an apologetic smile. "I've just moved in."

"So I've heard," she says, taking the cloth and dabbing her face and hair with it.

I watch the wet patches of her blouse tighten over her breasts every time her arm moves and realise that my mouth is dry.

Double shit.

"So, what's this all about then?" I ask quickly, softly, thrusting my hands as casually as I can into my jeans and swallowing, hard, the bark that is my dry throat.

"Well, apparently, Harvey – you know him, right?" I nod. "He's been telling you all our business, and you think that you might be able to help us. So, I was *told* that we had an appointment and to see you here at six. But, it seems that I'm the only person who got the memo, because Shawn, my fiancé, isn't here."

"Shawn being…"

"…Harvey's nephew."

"Right, so that makes sense now," I say thoughtfully.

What the hell? I'm not ready to meet anyone. I haven't prepared. I don't even have anywhere to see them. And, as this thought occurs to me, I involuntarily glace at the study door and my stomach somersaults.

No.

Luckily, my visitor's fiancé hasn't shown anyway; otherwise, I was going to have to send them away. Then, I'd talk to Harvey and tell him that…

…I cut off my own thought as my visitor begins to roam once more, taking a good look at the side units and the couch.

I can't make up my mind if I like that or not.

In the meantime, it occurs to me that this isn't Harvey being inconsiderate. It's the opposite. When we discussed what I did and that I was looking for clients, he must have thought he'd get the ball rolling for me. No, I don't think he was being thoughtless. I think he was looking out for me. Seemingly not unlike he did years ago.

They still have to go, though. She has to go. Even if Shawn had shown, I'm not mentally prepared to see anyone. The way I'm feeling right now, I'm likely to tell her to go fuck herself. Or, on second thought…

The sound of her whistling, appreciatively, draws my attention. She's looking at me and, for a split second, I think that her reaction to me has changed, but instead, "Wow, this place is much nicer on the inside than I thought," she says, casually handing the damp tea towel back to me.

"Have you lived here long?"

"No – as I said, I've just moved in."

"Right. With your wife?" She's still holding my gaze, and even in the subdued lamplight, I can just about make out that her blue eyes are twinkling.

Oh, so you're not immune to me.

Then, given the current situation and the unlikelihood that she's ever going to become a client, I allow myself for a second, just one split second, an image… just one discreet, intimate image of us… and it sends an electrical pulse through my body, warms my cheeks, and ratchets up the beating of my heart.

I savour it, then tease myself with the titillation of fingers touching skin through ripped stockings. I lick the thought, then devour the morsel and all its crumbs like a starving man.

"Yes," I lie. I don't know why, but I do.

She holds my gaze for a short while, as if verifying the information, and smiles, then looks at the front door. "Well, if he isn't coming, I probably should get going," she says, getting back to her irritated self once more.

I step aside, but instead of walking forward, she fishes her phone out of her bag once more and looks at the display. "Oh look," she says in mock excitement, "one bar."

I'm about to tell her that it doesn't mean anything. That if she tries to place a call, it'll just drop after a few seconds, but she's already hitting redial, then putting the phone to her ear.

She waits, then mutters, "Bloody voicemail."

I'm naturally surprised. I tried doing that countless times, but it's never worked for me.

She presses disconnect, promptly followed by redial, and then repeats the process twice over, before actually leaving a message. "Where are you? I'm here, and guess what? You aren't. Call me back as soon as you get this."

She's about to drop the phone into her bag when the thing starts to ring. She snatches it up again and, without checking the display, says, "Hello?" Then, the tone of her voice changes. "Oh, hi." There's a pause. "No, I told him that it wouldn't be shipped until next week, earliest."

Pause.

"I told him. I told him on the phone and confirmed by email."

Pause.

"No, I can't right now. The signal's rubbish. I can just about hear you."

Pause.

"No, I told you I can't right now. I'm in the middle of something. Look, I've got to go. I'll call you as soon as I get a chance."

She disconnects again. "Work. I leave the office for two minutes and the bloody place falls apart," she says, dropping her phone into her bag once more.

Then she tucks her hair behind her ears. I notice that she's done this a few times since arriving here, and I wonder if it's more out of habit than necessity; touching herself as a classical gesture of self-reassurance. She's nervous. But of what? Of the potential session or of me?

I can't help but wonder what she's still doing here. Based on what I've seen so far, I would have expected her to be right out of the door, but not this girl... she's lingering. Drying her hair. Making the call. Taking the call. Something tells me that, despite all the bravado, she wants to be here. She wants this session, but she also wants everybody else to think that she doesn't.

Why?

There's still a clear route to the door, and I wait.

She looks at me. Smiles awkwardly.

It seems I'm right, but she's out of time. Her cover will be blown if she lingers much longer.

I decide to save her. "Are you okay, Jessica?"

"Why do you ask?" she responds distractedly as she folds back her hair once more.

"Nothing in particular. You just seem..." I can't find the words. Well, I can, but I'd just rather choose something appropriate. "Preoccupied."

"I'm fine. Just wondering where my fiancé is, that's all. First, they get me to come over, using time I don't have, and then he doesn't bother to show. Doesn't even have the courtesy of letting you know either."

Now she's projecting, drawing me into her explanation as an ally.

She retrieves the phone from her bag. Looks at the display, swears, and drops it back again.

No bars? Good. It annoyed me that I tried God knows how many times to make calls from this dead zone and never succeeded, yet she comes along and...

"...I must look the pits. Can I use your restroom before I go?"

"There' a downstairs *toilet*," I joke with a smile, pointing to the hallway. She doesn't respond. "Just before you go up the stairs," I add.

I've just watched her disappear around the corner when there's an urgent rap at the door.

Front door open.

The security light illuminates a tall man. Taller than me, so that must be over six feet, and he looks like he's from Highlander stock; fair skin, broad shoulders, blue eyes, short red hair and a trimmed beard to match. He's wearing a black T-shirt with blue overalls tied at the waist.

"Shawn?" I ask.

"Yeah," he says humbly, hunching against the rain.

"Come in," I say quickly.

He steps inside and wipes his feet as I close the door behind him.

"Sorry I'm late. Got caught up at work. Some bloke needed his car. Anyway, yeah, I'm really sorry."

"It's okay. Don't worry."

Like his fiancé before him, he's dripping rain, too. "Wow, it's really chucking it down out there, huh?" I offer.

"Yeah."

"Let me get you something," I say.

This time I opt for a roll of paper towels. Somehow, I can't imagine it being a problem for a bloke dressed as a mechanic. I know that's stereotyping, but come on, let's get real. I hand him the roll.

"Thanks," he says with a big smile, unravelling the paper and dabbing his hair and face, before looking up and around with an appreciative whistle. "Some gaff you've got here."

"Thanks," I say, thrusting my hands into my pockets. "Jessica's here. She's just in the restroom."

"Oh great. I bet she isn't happy."

I rock my head from side to side. "Well, I think she tried to call you a few times."

"I know. I got the message, but I was speeding to actually get here. These are clean overalls, you know," he says, looking down at himself. "I thought it would make sense to just pull on these and a fresh T-shirt rather than waste even more time going home and getting changed."

I nod.

"Where the hell have you been?" Jessica demands, clicking her way across the tiled floor.

"Hey, babe," Shawn responds with a big smile. "Sorry. I got caught up at the shop, and…" He moves to kiss her, but she turns away from him to look at her watch.

"We're half an hour late! That's half the session, isn't it?" she asks, looking up at me.

"Well…"

"… you were the one who wanted us to come here in the first place."

"I know…"

"But then you don't even show up. You don't call. Nothing."

"Yeah, I know, I was just telling the doc that…"

"…Now, we're going to have to reschedule, and I don't know if I have the time to…"

"…Excuse me…"

"…you know my mum wants to come over again, I've got a bloody customer who wants me to get a delivery to him, even though I've already told him …"

"…Excuse me." My voice is much more forceful than I intended, but I'm glad for it.

They both turn to me. "I'm sorry, but I don't actually have an appointment to meet with you today." The words come out before I've even had a chance to think about what I'm saying, yet I realise in the very moment that I've just made things worse.

"What?" Shawn asks.

"He's saying we don't even have an appointment to meet him today, brainchild."

"But, my uncle said he'd had a word with you and that it was all arranged for today at six."

They're both still looking at me, expectantly, and I know I have a choice; I can tell the truth and unleash God knows what kind of tirade from Jessica, or I can lie, get on with whatever is left of the session, and then get them out.

Seconds tick by. Rain drums on the skylight.

"I'm so sorry," I say, faking a pained expression. "I am really sorry. What, with the move and everything, it completely escaped my mind... Harvey did mention it yesterday. I'm really sorry."

Jessica eyes me, suspiciously.

Shawn glances at us both, "Well, no worries. No harm done, eh?"

"Please," I say, gesturing to the couches in the den.

Jessica looks at them and then back at me, "What, here?"

"Is there something wrong?"

"Well, yeah, this is the reception area-slash-lounge. Don't you have a study or something, like most therapists?"

She's testing me, and worse, she's noticed me glance at the study door again.

"What? Is it through there?" she asks, walking forward.

"Well, actually, Jessica, I haven't finished unpacking the study yet," I call after her.

"Oh, don't worry about that. We don't mind," she says, heels clicking rapidly across the floor.

"Jessica…"

She keeps walking.

"Jessica!" Shawn calls. Then he adds, lazily, "Jess, the doc obviously doesn't want us going in there."

I wish he'd stop calling me *doc*, and that was the wrong thing for him to say, because it's only fuelled her curiosity.

She's almost across the room now.

"Jessica!" I yell firmly.

She finally stops and turns, but her hand is already on the door handle. "What?" she asks, seemingly perplexed by the sudden harshness of my voice.

There's a moment – a bit like a Mexican stand-off where we all look at each other, but nobody speaks.

The rain is slowing now. I can hear the ocean again. I don't want to go into the study.

"Doc?" It's Shawn. He's looking at me, curiously. "Are you okay?"

I hesitate, and eventually say, "I'm fine." My response is confident, but he's still looking at me. "Just, call me Marc, okay?"

He nods.

"So, are we going in, or are we waiting for that hour to be up first?" Jessica asks, seemingly bored. All she needs is to be chewing gum and her petulant schoolchild image will be complete.

I nod half-heartedly. "Yes," I say, "please, go through."

"Are you sure, *Marc*?" Shawn asks, a faint smile on his face because he's just said my name with emphasis. He's teasing me.

"Yes. Please." I nod him towards the door and then follow him like a child who's afraid to go into the dark room first.

In the time it takes for us to cross the entrance hall, I tell myself that this is probably for the best. At least I'm going into that room with company. Surely, that's got to make it easier. Right?

From the doorway, I hear Jessica remark that the place looks unpacked. Then, it's a, "Fuck me!" and a gasp from Shawn. "Shit, sorry, excuse my language, but look at this." The words are spoken slowly, as if he's just discovered hidden treasure.

The study doesn't look anything like I remember. Or, I suppose a more accurate statement would be that it doesn't look anything like what I've expected. In my mind's eye, I've always seen a traditional wood panelled room with a battered desk and some books, but this is far from that.

This is a minimalist, almost clinical room. Rectangular, sparse and spacious. Probably due, in part, to the fact that one whole wall is made of thick glass. It, like a giant canvass, frames a picture of the lush, rain drenched garden lit by the occasional gold blaze of the setting sun as it peeps from behind defeated rain clouds that are gradually being smothered by a burgeoning blue and red sky. Into the frame, the oak tree's gilded leaves make patterns on the bookcase standing on the opposite wall. The honeycomb structure is made of dark wood. It runs the length and breadth of the wall, and is loaded with a library of books. At the far end of the room is a matching one-piece staple desk. Behind it, a slimline leather executive chair.

In the middle of the room is a leather black swivel armchair on a chrome base. Next to it, a matching couch with red cushions. Both look out to sea.

Jessica's heels continued to clack loudly across the light marble floor as she walks over to the window and utters, "This is gorgeous."

"I'm told that the walls have been stripped back to reveal the original stone," I say. I don't know why. I think I'm embarrassed, and I probably expect Lucinda's factoid to somehow change this invasion back to a session rather than a tour.

Shawn pauses to the left of the doorway where a wall unit runs from floor to ceiling. Its base, also made of dark wood, consists of two giant doors. Above these are shelves displaying an array of ships marooned inside glass bottles of all different shapes, sizes, and colours. On the top shelf is a collection of schooners. Some of them, remote controlled. I know this because I've remembered that the small one on the right, with a faint scuff Marc to its bow, was mine.

"My father collected them," I offer. It's the only thing I have a vague memory of. Something we actually did together. But nothing else in this room feels familiar.

Interestingly, this place is exquisitely furnished to my taste, and had I not already had a pair of uninvited, overexcited guests to contend with, the sight of all of this would probably conjure up my own collection of oohs and aahs, but they are here, and I have to pretend. I have to pretend that all of this was known to me when, in reality, I've never felt more alienated.

Some, perhaps even you, will think I should be pleased that I've shared tastes with my father since they have, for all intents and purposes, transcended time.

I'm not.

I'm not pleased. For some reason, unbeknownst me, I find it difficult to appreciate this shrine of my father's indulgence.

"So, would you like to take a seat?" I ask, walking into the room casually, as if it's a favourite hangout of mine.

"Here?" Shawn asks, pointing to the couch.

I nod.

He's about to sit, but stops to look himself up and down, and then at me.

"It's okay, Shawn."

"They're clean on, I promise. Just stained from previous jobs."

"You're fine. Don't worry," I say with a smile.

"Are you sure?"

"Yes. Please. Actually…" He stops mid-action. "Could you just help me turn this?" I say, grabbing one side of the couch. "So it's facing that way?" I add with a nod of my head, towards the armchair.

The couch must have micro-wheels on it, though, because it turns effortlessly. Of course, spare no expense.

Shawn takes a seat, as does Jessica next to him. Then, she crosses her legs. Heels hang menacingly in the air.

"So, what exactly made you late tonight?" she demands.

"I told you. I got caught up on a job."

"Which job?"

He laughs. "What do you mean *which* job? Just an urgent job. You wouldn't know if I told you."

"Try me."

"Jess." Shawn glances and then points my way. "What does it matter? I'm here now, so let's just make the most of what's left of our time with Marc."

"Okay, so," I say, taking a seat in the armchair and swivelling towards my two visitors like a bloody character out of a James Bond movie.

"You didn't even change," Jessica is saying, scornfully.

He looks at me.

"It's fine, honestly," I reassure him.

What he doesn't know is that I already checked out what he's wearing as soon as he walked through the door. Yes, I'm not ashamed to admit it. The thought of him sitting down on something in his overalls did worry me, but I long ago worked out that they are old stains, and then, when he confirmed it, I felt satisfied that he isn't going to leave any marks.

Well, I am trying to sell the place, remember?

"I'm sorry about this," Jessica says, shaking her head at her fiancé.

I find that interesting because she appears to have no qualms about doing or saying anything without apology, yet she's more than happy to apologise for Shawn.

"You don't have to apologise for me, Jess," he says, as if he' just read my thoughts.

"Well, I'm sure Marco doesn't want you messing up his lovely couch."

"He's already said he doesn't mind. You don't, do you, mate?"

I shake my head slowly while summoning every last shred of patience I have to avoid yelling, *No, I don't mind about the fucking clothes! Now, for the love of God, could we please just get the fuck on with this?*

"See?" Shawn says.

Jessica glares at him once more, then fiddles with her hair. Shawn, obviously aware of her mood, places a hand on her leg, but she casually pushes it off while smiling at me. "This place is lovely."

"Yes, you said," I respond with a smile.

"You know I've always wondered what this house looked like on the inside," she continues.

"Really?"

"Yes, ever since we were kids. This was always, you know, the old house on the cliff top. We used to come up with all kinds of stories about the people who lived here."

"Really? What kinds of stories?"

"Oh, you know. Witches and goblins. Baby eaters. Whatever fantasy my brother could dream up to scare the shit out of me."

"How many siblings do you have?"

"Just one younger brother. Thank God."

"So, you lived here your whole life? Porthcove born and bred?"

"Not her whole life. You spent some time in London, too, didn't ya?" Shawn interjects.

Jessica glares at him.

"Really? What were you doing in London?"

"Just spent some time there."

"How long?"

"A year or so."

"How old were you?"

"Why are you so interested in London all of a sudden?"

"No reason. Just wondering what the attraction was, that's all," I say with a smile. "But, if you would rather not talk about it…" I let the sentence hang. Seconds drift by. "Okay, so. I've been thinking. Given today's aborted start, why don't we just treat this as a casual chat? A kind of a consultation, if you will. You won't be charged or anything, and we'll be all set for our next session. What do you think?"

Shawn nods. "Sounds good."

"Jessica?"

"That's fine."

"Good."

There's another pause, then, "Do you have any brothers or sisters, Marc?" It's Shawn asking the question. "I'm allowed to ask questions, right?"

"Um, yes, of course. Especially this time, but, for reference, the sessions are more about you. So, I'd rather keep the focus on that rather than bore you with details of my life. But yes, I do have a step-brother and sister, but we're not that close. We didn't' really grow up together."

"Well. You aren't missing much," Jessica throws in.

"Why do you say that?"

"Well, let's just say, things can get a bit tense when my brother doesn't get his way."

"What she means is, he's a bit of a mommy's boy. A spoilt brat," Shawn interjects.

Jessica says nothing. Instead, she asks, "So, how exactly will this work – do you just ask these types of questions, or…?"

I give her my warmest smile. "Well, it works however you want it to. There are no fixed rules. I want you to consider this," I gesture around the room, "a safe place. You know, somewhere that you can say anything you like."

"Anything?"

"Anything."

"Bloody 'ell, you'll never get her to leave," Shawn laughs. "Sorry," he adds, when he sees she's not laughing.

Jessica keeps her gaze on me while subtly jigging her leg back and forth.

"What? I'm only joking, babe. Come on. I said I was sorry."

She looks away from him. She's sulking.

"What's wrong, Jessica?"

"Nothing."

"You seem irritated."

"No, not really."

"Is it about this session?"

"No. Although I am finding it funny that Shawn and his uncle should conspire to book this time with you, and then he doesn't even bother to get here on time."

Shawn rolls his eyes. "I said I was sorry."

"Conspire. That's an interesting choice of word. Is that what you think? That they conspired to get you here?"

"Didn't they? I mean, you've barely moved in, by your own words, and these two already have a session booked. Sounds pretty conspiratorial to me." Her last words have been spoken with a whisper, sarcastically.

"Why would they conspire against you?"

"Oh, I don't know. Maybe because, ever since we've talked about marriage, I've been irritable, withdrawn, and, you know, generally unhappy."

"Have you?"

"I'm fine, but maybe you should ask him – you know, just to be sure."

"We didn't conspire, Jess. Harvey was talking to the doc and thought that it might do us good to come over for a chat."

She snorts.

"What was that, Jessica?"

"A chat? He makes it sound like we've come round to an old friend's for tea and biscuits rather than to a stranger who gets paid to sit here and listen to us whine about our problems."

"Is that how you see me?"

"Why? Am I missing something?"

A few laps of waves go by. The sun has now filled the room in a rusty glow.

"Is something bothering you now, Jessica?"

"No."

"Are you sure? Because you seem quite upset."

She doesn't respond.

"Is it still the fact that Shawn was late?"

She considers this. "Well, I just think it's rude. It doesn't project a good impression."

"Why do you want to make a good impression?"

"Don't flatter yourself," Shawn jumps in. "It wasn't just for you. She's like it all the time."

"That's because you're late all the time."

"I'm not late all the time."

"You are, Shawn. I always have to remind you about stuff, and sometimes I just wish you could do something without me having to nag you about it."

He looks at her, as if he's hearing this for the first time, but she doesn't look back at him. She keeps her gaze straight ahead, at me, like he isn't even there.

Silence reigns, as if we've all paused to listen to the angry squabble of seagulls outside.

"Shawn, you seemed surprised when Jessica mentioned having to wait for you all the time. Didn't you know how she felt?"

"I had no clue."

She glares at him.

"What?" he asks.

"Are you seriously going to pretend you don't know how much it irritates me?"

"Alright, I didn't know it irritated you this much, Jess. Jesus, you've done nothing but gripe since we got here. Now, I've already said, I promise I'll try and be more punctual in the future." For the first time since arriving, Shawn has lost his smile.

"Yeah, and how many times have I heard that?" she mutters.

"What's that supposed to mean?"

"Exactly what I said."

There's another pause. Jessica sits back diagonally into the couch, away from him. Then she crosses her leg and begins to swing it once more. This time, the action is obvious, like someone tapping their toe in frustration.

I give them a moment. Then, "Why don't you tell me why you're here?"

Jessica doesn't respond. She's too busy twitching her leg, so I bat the question over to Shawn.

"We, I, thought it might be a good idea for us to get some support," he says seriously.

"What do you mean by support?"

"Well, with the wedding and everything, things have been a bit tense lately, and I thought it might help for us to talk it through with someone who's, you know, unrelated."

"So, it was your idea to come here to see me?"

"Well, my uncle told me you'd just moved to the village, but we both thought it might help."

Jessica's twitch seems to get worse.

"You don't agree, Jessica?"

"Me? I don't care either way. Although, I'm just thinking that if his uncle is so interested our love life, then maybe we should have him organise the wedding, too."

"He just wants to help, Jess. Make sure we start off on a good footing."

I break in. "Help. Support. Shawn, you keep saying these words. What exactly do you think you're unable to cope with?" I ask.

"Well, he thinks…"

"…I'm asking you, Shawn. In fact, I'm asking both of you. What exactly do *you* feel you need support for?"

"Well, you know, the wedding and everything – things have been strained, haven't they?" Shawn offers.

"Have they?"

"Yeah." He looks to Jessica. "You know they have, Jess, come on."

She doesn't respond. Instead, she shakes her head while Shawn explains. "Jess has been really stressed out. More than usual lately."

"No, I haven't."

"Babe, come on. You have. You had that meltdown just last week when ya mum showed up, unannounced."

"That's because you don't know how she gets about things."

"I bloody do," Shawn throws in with a chortle.

Another glare. "Then, maybe it wouldn't kill you to be more supportive, and while you're at it, you can stop calling me 'Jess'. I told I don't like it.

Shawn loses his smile again, and looks at her. "Since when? You used to love me calling you that."

She avoids his gaze by looking out to the garden.

There's silence, and then I say, "Jessica, tell me about your mother's visit."

She sighs. "I'd rather not."

"Why's that?"

"It's just another of her visits."

"Okay. Tell me about this—" I make speech marks with my fingers, "…meltdown."

"It wasn't exactly a meltdown."

Now it's Shawn's turn to snort.

She ignores him, loops a strand of hair behind her ear, and then looks at me. "She's just got this way of always finding fault with stuff. No matter what it is. Last week, it was the wedding invites. The cards we chose were less than a hundred GSM…"

"GSM?" I ask.

"Grams per inch," she explains.

"Her parents think that stuff is important," Shawn contributes, rubbing his fingers together, suggesting that the family has money and, I'm assuming from the shake of his head, this more than sense.

"Anyway, she starts going on about how wedding invites should be at least a hundred and fifty GSM, and how mortified she was when one of her friends made a comment about it."

"What did she say?"

"I don't know. Obviously nothing good – otherwise, my mother wouldn't have felt compelled to point out my faux pas."

"And was it?"

"Was what?"

"A faux pas. Did you make a mistake or was it simply the card you selected? The one you preferred."

She hesitates. "I suppose so."

"Suppose so?" I prod.

"Well, it must have been," Shawn jumps in. "You know all about your cards, don't you, babe?"

"Don't call me that," she says, quickly.

"What's going on with you?" he asks surreptitiously, as if I weren't sitting across from them.

"I have a name – just call me by my bloody name, Shawn," she says through gritted teeth.

There's a pause, and then he looks at me and asks, suddenly, "You know those shocks that happen *after* an earthquake?"

I cock my head, curiously, and then think about the question for a few seconds, "You mean, aftershocks?"

"Yeah, those. Well, this is what you're seeing – the *after mother-in-law*," he says, making speech marks with his fingers.

"She isn't your mother-in-law," Jessica mumbles.

"What's that?"

"I said, she isn't your mother-in-law."

"Will be soon," he throws back.

"But not yet. And besides, she has a name. Use her name. Why can't you just use people's bloody names?"

Shawn grins. "After mother-in-law," he says, nodding at me as if it's now our own private joke.

Jessica grinds her teeth and looks out of the window once more.

I wait a few seconds, then ask, "What's the matter, Jessica?" Her shoulders tense, but she doesn't speak. I wait a few more seconds.

Eventually, she responds, "She just has such a way of making the simplest things seem catastrophic."

"Your mother?"

"Yes. My mother."

"Has she always been like this?"

"Depends what you mean by *always*. If by always you mean since, I don't know, dinosaurs roamed the earth, then yes. Anyway, isn't this supposed to be couple's therapy?"

I smile. "More than often, these things are related."

She pulls a face. "How?"

"Well, some of the things that affect some facets of our life have a way of affecting others. So, what you may think is unrelated to a problem often actually is."

Shawn grins, crosses his arms, and then nods at her, as if to say 'told you so'.

"So, that's it. You've seen us for, what, quarter of an hour now, and you've concluded that my mother is the reason why we snipe all the time?" she asks.

"She's obviously part of the reason," Shawn jumps in.

"I wasn't asking you."

He looks at her, seemingly surprised by her hostility. She looks at me, though, pointedly, so I answer her question.

"Well, to be perfectly honest, I've seen you for more than quarter of an hour now. Just because we weren't in session, that doesn't necessarily mean that I wasn't getting to know you. And yes, there is a good chance that this, um, tense relationship you have with your mother could be affecting your relationship with Shawn."

I give them a few seconds, and then, "Tell me about how you met?" I ask, settling back in my armchair.

Sean smiles, recalling the memory and then looks at her. Jessica sulkily mumbles, "It's such a cliché. In fact, sometimes I think our whole relationship is a cliché."

"Who's going to tell me about it?" I ask.

She nods at me, and talks to Shawn. "You tell him."

"No, you tell him," he says with a smile. "I like to hear you say it."

She sighs, then, "We actually met by the side of the road. It was raining. My car had broken down, so I called roadside assistance, and then Shawn comes along."

"…her knight in shining armour," he adds, puffing out his chest with a big grin.

"Something like that," she nods.

"They were *your* words," Shawn says to her then, turning to me, adds, "I nearly pissed myself. She was all dressed up, ready for her big meeting – suit, shoes, but her hair and makeup…" He sniggers. "Well, those needed some work, didn't they, babe?"

Jessica looks at me. "My hair was frizzy and my makeup had run; I looked like a goth, and I was late for my meeting, which was really important."

"So, what happened?"

"Well, I called ahead to let them know I was having car trouble. Then Shawn stopped off at some fast food place; I can't remember which one…"

"…Burger King," Shawn helps.

"You had time to stop?"

"Not really, but he insisted a few more minutes meant nothing when compared to the confidence I would gain from knowing that I was looking my best. So, I did what I could with my hair, reapplied makeup, and then Shawn drove me to the meeting, which was two hours away."

She smiles awkwardly, as if embarrassed by the memory. Or maybe it's because she feels guilty for being mean to him after recalling what he did for her. I'm not sure.

"Hey, do you remember the look on that woman's face when we drove up to that place in that muddy, greasy old truck? Shit, I didn't know which look was more priceless; yours or hers."

"I was mortified."

The room is all smiles for a second, and then I ask, "So, Shawn, you drove two hours to Jessica's meeting. Was that all part of the service?"

He looks at her and grins. "Hell, no. We're supposed to drop people at the destination of their choice, but within a thirty-minute radius because, you know, we've got other calls... but, well, she seemed really stressed out, so I called the office and managed to swing some time off."

"Off? I didn't realise you took time off," she says, looking at him.

He shrugs. "Well, you didn't need to know," he says, placing his hand on hers.

There's a pause. Jessica looks at his hand and then at me. We listen to a nightingale signal the onset of darkness. "So, what happened next? Did you start seeing each other?"

They exchange awkward glances.

"No. Well, he was already seeing someone," Jessica explains. "And I had not long broken up with my fiancé."

"You were engaged before?"

"Yes, but it didn't work out, for me."

"Arranged marriage," Shawn contributes.

"It wasn't an arranged marriage," she says quickly. Then, to me, she adds, "He was the son of friends of my parents. The families have known each other since we were kids and so they thought we'd make a good match."

I nod.

"His name was Harry."

Shawn snickers. "And he loved to wear dicky bows."

I cock my head.

Jessica has actually been smiling at their reminiscing, but the expression fades somewhat when she says, "Naturally, my parents weren't happy when we broke up. You know the story. You've heard it before. He's successful, works in the city, and…" she trails off there.

"…And I'm just a grease monkey. It's okay, babe, you can say it."

"So what happened? With Harry?"

She pulls a face. "I don't know, really. It just didn't work out."

"She met me. Stole me away. Said she couldn't resist; especially when I was all dirty."

Jessica forces a smile and nods. "I may have called him a few times after that day, yeah. You know, to thank him. Then, one thing led to another."

"Yeah, you needed to call me a few times to do that, though, didn't ya, babe?" he adds with a wink.

"I guess so," she says, her cheeks flushing a little.

"Seduced me. Told me I looked sexy in my overalls. Like something out of one of those calendars," Shawn continues proudly, manspreading not just his long legs, but also his arms over the back of the couch.

"Yeah, he used to look really sexy in his overalls. I mean, that day he got out of the cab and his hair got wet because of the rain…. Phew."

I can see her recalling the memory and allowing herself to be caught up in it as she stares into the middle distance while tapping her foot and pushing her hair back around both ears.

"I mean, at first I didn't really notice it, because I was stressed and everything, but after, when I replayed the image of him in my mind – all tall, strong, dirty – I remember feeling flushed. My stomach all empty and giddy. The works. Yes, every cliché, but it was beautiful." She fans herself again, before refocussing on my face with a smile, and then she looks at Shawn and places a hand on his thigh.

I've noticed that he was wearing a proud grin when the story started, but that this gradually faded as the story unfolded. I'm still watching him, knowing what's coming, when he asks, "Used to?"

"What?"

"You said, I *used to* look sexy. Does that mean you don't think I do anymore?"

"I didn't say that."

He forces a laugh. "Babe, you did say it."

"I didn't."

"You bloody well did. Marco, didn't she say it?"

I go to speak.

"…Shawn, what's wrong with you? It isn't that important," Jessica jumps in, retaining a forced smile on her face as if to encourage him to follow suit.

"Maybe not for you. It never is for you. Not unless it has something to do with work, your dad, or your mum, or fuck, even your good for nothing brother; then every miniscule detail is important."

For the first time since I've met him, Shawn's whole demeanour has changed. Like the weather around here – it's sunny one minute and tempestuous the next. Gone is the smile and the general light in his face, replaced by controlled frowning and a flexing jaw.

Then, neither is looking at the other. Both are looking to opposite sides of the room as the air thickens with tension.

I let it simmer for a few seconds, waiting for either of them to say something, and when no one speaks, I venture, "Jessica, do you know why you used the past tense in that sentence?"

"I knew it!" Shawn explodes, victorious. "I knew you heard her; you just didn't want to say anything. See? Marco heard it, too, Jess."

"So what? Marco heard it, too. What do you want, Shawn? A gold medal for listening?"

"No, I want to know what you meant by it! Is it because you're not attracted to me anymore or is it because what I do for a living is an embarrassment to you?"

"Oh God, not this again…"

"…Yes this!"

"It doesn't embarrass me, Shawn," she says dismissively.

"Yeah, it does. Tell him."

She folds her arms and avoids his gaze.

"Tell him," he repeats, slowly.

"Oh my God, can we please stop focussing on one stupid word? It was just one stupid word. Of course, I still find you sexy, and of course, I'm not embarrassed by you!"

"No?"

"No."

"Then why do you never ask me out with your friends?"

She scoffs, "Because you think they're boring. You've mentioned it enough times. And, by that token, I could say the same thing about you. You never invite me out with yours."

"That's because you think they're beneath you."

"That's not true. I've never said that."

"You don't need to."

I let the room fill with silence for a while, and then I ask. "Guys, what just happened?"

"What always happens. We turn into this giant... what's the word she used earlier? Oh yeah, a cliché. The rich bitch is embarrassed to be around the poor bastard."

Jessica shakes her head. "You're fucking ridiculous."

"Really? Then why did your mum ask me, politely, to review the guests on—" he makes speech marks in the air again, "...*my side* of the wedding list."

"Because the wedding costs are spiralling out of control! We need to make cuts."

"On my friends."

"On everyone."

"Really?" He turns sideways to her. "My friends are not just friends; they're family. Who exactly have you cut from your list?"

"I've cut plenty of people."

"Who?"

"Stop being stupid."

"Answer the question."

"No."

"Answer the question."

"If I told you, you wouldn't even know who they are."

"Try me."

She holds his gaze for a while, then unfolds her arms and looks around the room as the nervous twitch in her leg worsens.

"Thought so," he says, sitting forward once more.

The ocean rumbles. A fluttering creature screeches.

There's another interlude. Then, suddenly, without looking at him, Jessica grumbles. "You're such a fucking child."

"I'm the child?"

"Yes, you are. I have to measure everything I say and how I say it with you – otherwise, you get the sulks."

"Me? I get the sulks?"

She doesn't respond. I wait. I can see Shawn's jaw clenching. He's looking everywhere *but* at Jessica or me, for that matter. After several seconds, I ask, "Shawn, tell me what's going through your mind right now?"

"Oh, you don't want to know what's going through my mind."

"Actually, Shawn, I do."

But he doesn't respond. I wait, then try a different approach. "Shawn, earlier you said that the reason you're both here is because you felt that you could do with some support. Some guidance. What exactly did you mean by that?"

"Isn't it obvious?" he asks, nodding at his fiancé.

"I would like you to tell me again, in your own words."

He thinks about the question, then shakes his head. "I don't know. Ever since the wedding planning started, she's turned into this demon. Gets stressed over the smallest things."

I look at her and begin to say, "Jessica…"

"…For fuck's sake, just call me 'Jessie'. You say 'Jessica' and you sound like my bloody dad!"

I hold up my hands in surrender. "Okay, Jessie. Why are you here?"

"We've been over this."

"No, Shawn has, but I'm trying to understand why you agreed to be here."

"Well, I didn't exactly agree, did I? I was summoned."

"Jessica, if you don't mind me saying, you don't strike me as the type who does things because others demand it."

She looks at me and says, "I'm here because his uncle thinks we should be here, and he always does what his uncle says."

"Well, makes a change from doing what your parents say," Shawn throws back.

I wait, then ask, "Shawn, I take it you're close with your uncle?"

"I am. He and Aunt Eadie, they pretty much raised me."

"Can I ask what happened to your parents?"

"They just... I don't know. Had better things to do with their life."

"What do you mean?"

"Put it this way – I think they both had plans for their lives and they didn't necessarily include me."

"Must have been a difficult..."

"...It was." His jaw is clenching again, but this time I think it's for an entirely different reason. I want to press him on what he means by saying that about his parents, but I feel it's probably a bit early for that. Maybe next session.

"So, how long have you been with your aunt and uncle?"

He thinks about this. "For as long as I can remember, really. Went to school. Left. Started working for my uncle. Now he's retired, I've taken over the running of the garage."

I can tell that he's being deliberately vague. This is obviously a subject he doesn't particularly enjoy discussing. Yet, like someone who's travelled through a storm and emerged on the other side, the light returns to his face, the moment he starts talking about the present again. He adds, "I now manage five other lads, and we've got a fleet of three trucks."

Jessica snickers.

"What's so funny, Jessie?"

"Five other lads and a *fleet* of trucks? You make it sound like it's the AA or something. When, in reality, it's just a bunch of misfits who can't get any other work."

"Yeah, well, I'd take those boys over the jumped-up pricks you work with any time."

"Well, I wouldn't worry about it. I'm sure they feel exactly the same way about you."

I wait, and then, "Jessie, I'd like to return to the conversation we were having about the support…"

"…Oh my God, we've already been over this! Why is it so bloody complicated?"

"Don't take your frustration out on him. He's just trying to help," Shawn throws in without looking at her.

"Shawn…"

"I'm not."

"Sounds like you are."

"Shawn…"

"…What, you mean you actually noticed?" she demands.

"What's that supposed to mean?" He turns sideways onto her once more.

I jump in, "Jessie, I would like to stay with my original question, if I may."

"You've already had an answer to your question."

"Actually, I don't think I have. I mean, I have in that Shawn has explained it to me, but I'm very much interested in hearing your interpretation."

"If, after what you've heard so far, you feel like you still need to ask that question, then I can't help but wonder if our time here is money well spent." Her words are delivered with a steely gaze.

I accept the challenge and lay it out for her. "Shawn said that you both could probably use some support and guidance. This is code I interpreted as that he would really like you to be able to freely express how you feel about the wedding, amongst other things, and in turn, that he perhaps is concerned about how you feel about getting married."

"I'm sorry. Have we been in any way unclear?" she asks with a fake smile.

I smile back, disarmingly, sit forward in my chair and say, "No, you've been quite specific on most peripheral subjects, but for one."

"Really, and what's that?"

"On whether or not *you* want and-or should be getting married."

There are a few seconds of silence as a bird screeches and flaps in the tree outside.

"Wait a minute, I didn't…" Shawn starts.

Jessica isn't looking at me, and I want to stay in the moment, so I ignore Shawn's interjection and plough on, "…Is that why you agreed to come here, Jessie? To find out whether or not you should marry Shawn?"

Shawn looks at me, then at his fiancé, and then at me again. "Wow. Wow, hold on a sec, that's some hefty conclusion you're jumping to, mate. That isn't the reason, is it, Jess?"

She says nothing.

"Is it?"

Jessica doesn't turn to look at her fiancé, nor does she respond; she simply keeps that gaze locked on mine, and then, suddenly, her foot begins to twitch once more.

THE SMUGGLER'S INN

Monday Evening.

So, my meeting with my first clients-slash-patients didn't go smoothly. Okay, it was a disaster... but hey, I'm feeling optimistic. Although, given the way Shawn ended our session today, I don't think there's much of a chance of them coming back next week.

Oh well. It was a stupid idea anyway. Thinking I could slide back into the therapist's chair after what happened. But then, what happened in London has nothing to do with my ability to treat people, and everything to do with me being an idiot.

I suppose it's just going to take time. I'm in a new place – new house, new people. It's going to take some time to get used to, and some time for people around here to trust me enough to want to see me. And, on the bright side – because I've decided that that's what I'm going to focus on – when I first had the idea of starting a practice down here, I had this whole vision of having to create a website, social media pages and hammering the whole advertising thing. But, it turns out that, thanks to the power of gossip, I don't need to. Everybody knows who I am and what I do.

Thanks to Harvey. Again.

On top of that, the pressure to generate cash isn't weighing on me as heavy as the house itself thanks to Lucinda's reaction to the place.

It's good to go. This house is in such good shape that it doesn't need a thing done to it. There isn't a scuff mark on the floor, not a squeaky door. (If you ignore the gate outside, but I quite like that squeak. I think it's quaint.)

Yay.

And who do I have to thank for all of this? Okay. I think I've well and truly made that point.

Bottom line is, maybe I don't need to see any patients. I can just jack this whole idea in and get a bar job instead. I don't exactly have the experience, but that's what everybody seems to fall back on in times of hardship, right? How difficult can it be? I bet there are plenty of opportunities in the village. I bet there's a whole back alley of clubs and sophisticated wine bars just clambering for new staff.

Okay. So, that whole thinking positive thing may take some practice, too. Baby steps, you know. Baby steps.

I'm in the kitchen now. Leaning on the open fridge door, because I can, while I contemplate exactly what I'm in the mood for, and whether I can be bothered to make it.

I stare at ham, turkey, eggs, and cheese. Pork pies and pasties, fresh from the baker's. I grab a pie, close the fridge door, and walk back into the den.

It's getting dark outside.

I pause in the 'entrance hall come lounge', as Jessica described it.

At night, this place feels a bit like a theatre. Life performances take place down here in the entrance hall and the den, and can be watched from the upstairs balcony, and I can't help but wonder just how many such performances have been played out here, between my mother, my father, and his bitches.

Oh yeah, there's that bitterness in my throat again, making it difficult to swallow this mouthful of pie.

Anyway, moving on.

I concluded earlier today that it must be difficult to warm this space in winter due to its very high ceiling and, of course, that skylight. I wonder. Well, if it doesn't sell quickly, I'm going to find out.

The thought sends a shiver up my spine. Winter is only a few months away. I don't fancy being isolated here in the bleak of that.

It's so bloody quiet here. I think I mentioned that already. And by *quiet*, I mean deathly quiet. And hollow. Yeah, there's furniture and stuff, but there's also such an echo each time someone walks around that it feels like a bloody mausoleum.

I stop chewing and listen.

Nothing.

Not the hum of traffic in the distance, no household appliances, nothing but the sound of nature, sighing wearily after a long day, along with the occasional moan of the wind, the lapping of the waves and the creaking of sleepy timber.

Now, if I were in a movie, this would be the part where I'd stare into the middle distance as dissonant voices of my past gradually fade up. I'd hear laughing and shouting, and blurry images of phantom people would appear in front me.

Um... but I'm not.

The only thing I actually can remember is some blurry image of Mother and I, down at the beach, or at least I think it was my mother, because even this memory is way too fuzzy for me to make any sense of it.

No, this is just an empty space in an empty house. And standing in the empty space is me being reminded of my empty heart. Hollow like the hunger of an empty belly and water. My pain sloshing around it, making me feel queasy.

I want to see my son. I want to see my boy, and I know I've mentioned this before, but I feel that it's pertinent right now. Relevant. Given the fact that I am standing here alone, with moist eyes.

Fuck.

I rub my face in an effort to shake off this overwhelming cloak of misery that's creeping up on me like a bank of fog, when I spot the wall units. Haven't really had the chance to look in these things properly, but they look promising.

I hurry over and pull at each of the doors in turn – wine glasses, champagne flutes, tumblers, napkins. Everything but bloody booze. I pull at bottom drawers; nothing.

Shit. I could really use a drink right now.

Then, the greatest thought, ever, pops into my head, so I hurry back into the kitchen and to the island where the wicker basket is still sitting along with Harvey's bounty.

I pull a face. The only bottle remaining is white, and it's not my favourite. Wine generally agrees with me, but white wine makes me want to vomit.

Oh well; needs must.

I open the bottle and take a good glug from it.

"Hmm, not bad."

I take another swig. Then wait a few minutes for it to kick in like a painkiller.

Yeah, being alone is rubbish. Drinking alone, even worse. I've been told many times – mostly by women, including my wife – that I'm crap about being alone and yet I've never seriously considered the theory. Not until now.

And yes, I can confirm that they're absolutely right. In fact, I'll go one step further; I hate being alone, I hate being in this place, I hate having my life turned upside down, and I really hate being away from my family.

And yes, I'll also concede, as much as it's jarring, that the only person to blame for all of this is me. But, you know, when you're able to stand in front of me and tell me that you've never made a mistake, that you've never fucked anything up – in some cases catastrophically – then I'll welcome your snooty judgement. But, until then.

Shit. Sorry. The sound of my own thoughts is starting to drive me nuts.

Another minute has gone, or at least I think it has, scored by the sound of nothing, and that feels like a bloody hour out here in the pitch black of the country. And, as much as it rankles, I must admit that sitting in the old man's study this afternoon, listening to a dysfunctional couple gripe and snipe about their relationship as they drift inexorably toward a catastrophic marriage, is far more appealing than being here, on my own.

Being back in *the chair* felt good. I felt needed and, in the absence of anything else, that suits me just fine.

At least I had company.

Oh, shut up, that's your depression talking!

I know. Maybe I should go for a walk. It's not like I don't have anywhere to go.

I look out the window. The shadows have grown and metamorphosed into darkness.

What, are you afraid of, vampires?

I leave the bottle on the island, pull on trainers and a jacket, and then I'm at the door, but I've forgotten something, so I hurry across to the study.

Five minutes later, *Front door open* is replaced by the call of a stray seagull making its way home for the night. But me, dirty stop out, I've left my self-imposed prison and am making my way downtown. I might even catch a film, eat fast food at one of the many eateries. Who knows? I might even get lucky with one of the locals. Cor, that cougar bird was a bit of alright, or how about my deliciously, tantalising yummy mummy baker? Oh yeah, I bet she loves a bit of slap and tickle.

The thought teases a grin out of my face, finally.

I'm joking, of course. Just in case you're rolling your eyes and thinking I'm objectifying women or some shit.

I told you, what happened the other night will not happen again. Primarily because, if what I saw today is any indication of what's on offer, then me and the shower are going to become much more intimate, if you know what I mean.

Oh, come on. If you're pulling a face right now, don't. I bet you aren't that innocent. There's a reason why men and women were given the gift of orgasm, you know, and it goes beyond procreation and ventures far deeper into the realms of recreation, and Amen to that.

It's alright. It's okay. I'm just musing here. No, I've decided that this old boy's wild days are behind him. Right now, the only thing that matters to me is getting the house sold, collecting the cash, and reclaiming my family. Everything else, including orgasms, is secondary.

For now.

I crunch to a halt for a second to look back at the house, and I don't know if it's because daylight has been dimmed, but I don't think it looks as pretty as it did when I arrived. Now it's looking dull, a bit like a sepia photograph.

And it's as I'm standing here, considering this, that I find myself ducking, instinctively, to avoid the dive bombing of a pair of creepy, juddery silhouettes, which I can only assume are bats. And, I couldn't say for sure, either, but I'm confident they emerged from the roof of the bloody house!

Looks like I'm not alone after all.

Revulsion ripples over me, like a knot of wriggling maggots, as I picture a close-up of the vampire-toothed creatures.

Eeek.

Vampire? That word again in the space of thirty minutes. It's just a coincidence, I tell myself, and turn to be greeted by the clack and rumble of an approaching train. I watch my lifeline to the outside world trundle by and, for a split second, it puts a smile on my face. I don't even know why. Just, something about it. Reassuring. Calming. Hypnotising. Most of the carriages are empty, but for a sad looking elderly lady in a blue hat and scarf in one carriage and a group of kids in another. One of them pulls a face at me. I pull one back, smile, and guess who I'm reminded of?

I pull the mobile phone out of my pocket; I don't look at the signal, and just dial Ellie's number in the hope that I'll simply be miraculously connected.

There's a beep and then nothing.

I look at the screen. Wow – no signal. Really?

A wave of anger envelopes me. So fucking frustrating!

That reminds me… the letters. That one from the lawyers that I didn't recognise. I passed out when I got home and forgot to open the mail. Maybe I should go back, open it, or not knowing is going to needle me for the rest of the evening.

I look up to see that the train has been swallowed up by the black spectres of the trees. I don't know why, but I'm finding those things bloody creepy tonight. This place is surrounded by them and, at night, they're like harbingers of doom swallowing up the house. The world. God know what really lurks inside there. People, beasts, demons.

Really?

No. I'm not going back to the house. I don't want to be alone. I need some company. Besides, I have an invite to a very important event, and it would be rude not to make an appearance. I might even stay a bit longer if the alcohol is flowing.

So, I crunch forward on the gravel. As I do, I notice the row of lights that, like a runway, illuminate the driveway.

Nice.

It's particularly quiet out here, with nothing but the occasional call of an owl and the ever-present murmur of the ocean, and I quite like it. I like being able to hear the sound of my breath, the beating of my heart. Yeah, I know that might sound a bit poncey, but you know what I mean. In the city, you can't hear yourself think. There's no time to stop and contemplate anything. It feels as though you're constantly being chased by a chaotic, frenetic, and impatient monster that'll trample over you if you dare to stop still long enough to let it, but here... Here is something completely different and, right now, I couldn't tell you if that's a good or bad thing.

I cross the bridge, from the fort that is the house, over the railway track to the rest of the village – or, the mainland as I've come to refer to it.

Before long, I see Harvey's cottage. The lights glow amber behind drawn curtains and, from the outside porchlight, I notice yet another immaculately maintained garden, albeit on a smaller scale than Dolce Vita's, and, if I didn't already know it, it would be easy to identify this as Harvey's home.

I stop outside of his gate and consider knocking. I have no idea what I'm going to say exactly, if I do. Whatever it is, it will have something to do with the fact that I feel so bloody shitty every time I'm reminded of how ungrateful I've been. I wouldn't be in line to have the house sold so soon and at such a price if it weren't for Harvey and his wife. The least I can do is thank the man.

But then, on the other hand, he's so bloody irritating, raking up all that stuff about the old man, and my mum. Like he bloody knows me. He doesn't know me. But then, according to him, he does. According to him, we were like his family.

Fuck!

These bloody thoughts keep turning over and over and over in my head, like a bloody hamster wheel; the guilt, the gratitude, the remorse, the rage.

I've come to terms with my bloody past, however warped it might have been. It took me a very long time. I'm in no hurry to re-examine any of that shit. What's the point? I've moved on with one positive thing – that goldmine back there. So, let's just leave it at that, shall we? I don't want to reminisce, I don't want to be reminded, and I don't want to keep any of those so-called memories alive. I'm sorry, but that time of my life is over. Dead and buried. Now I just want to look to the future, and I don't think that's asking too much.

I walk away from the cottage. I know it's chickening out again, but just going through that thought process right there, it helped. I know what I need to say to Harvey. I do. I just need to find the right time, the right words, and the right mood, so that I don't alienate the man even further.

Seriously. I do want to talk to him. If only because the other day, when he was going on about how he used to take care of us, how he considered us family, I allowed myself the wild fantasy that maybe he'll do it again. Maybe, if there isn't anybody else, he might consider adopting Toby as his metaphorical grandchild. I mean, I know the little man already has a set of those, but those two are so up themselves, it's always more about appearances and manners than it is about having fun and driving around in trucks that clearly don't suit your age.

A smile spreads across my face. I will talk to Harvey; just not tonight.

I walk down a cobblestone street of cottages, some with thatched roofs and others with quaint red shingles, most with curtains already drawn against the world.

If the research I conducted before leaving London is correct, there's only one pub, or inn, in Porthcove, and it is, the Smuggler's Inn.

It's nestled in the bay, or harbour, and serves fresh, homemade food, daily; and according to one Google reviewer: *The chips are gorgeous and the fish is to die for. The portions are massive! Five stars!*

I follow a sign for the harbour, which sees me cut through more stone houses, under the yellow hue of a series of street lanterns that look like they're from the last century, although they don't seem to be running on oil. Then, I descend a long series of stone steps until I finally emerge at the harbour's mouth; a cul-de-sac carved from the cliff face.

Ahead, fishing boats rock gently on the tide as it caresses the harbour walls.

I hear the inn before I see it. It's several yards to my left, perched on the edge of the harbour and seemingly sculpted out of the rock face. It looks smaller than it did in the photos; yet, with its glowing amber lanterns, merry folk music, and raucous laughter, it's fairy tale inviting.

I hesitate at the entrance for two reasons. First, the moon looks supernaturally bloody big. It's spot-lit the sky with a deep shade of blue while draping itself in a veil of clouds. I can't take my eyes off of it as it shimmers on the ocean and glints off the pub sign hanging above me. The sign that, by the way, is an eerie representation of the very vista before me; the inn, the bay, and shifty looking men carrying lanterns to and from caves carved out of the cliff face, all while the scene is lit by a similar supernatural moon.

Seriously?

The second reason I've stopped is because I've had a hideous premonition of walking in there and everything screeching to a halt, prompting dozens of curious eyes to glower at me.

Oh well. I push the door open and step inside.

It's rammed. It looks like the whole village has congregated here for this party.

I search around the bodies and across the sea of faces, for the bar. Yes, dealing with people, personalities, and foibles is what I know, but I'm much better at it when I've got a few drinks inside me.

So, having located the bar, I'm pushing my way toward it as fast as I can in a series of "Excuse me's" and "Sorry's" when I feel a sudden slap on my back that startles me.

"Marc!"

I turn. "Shawn. Hey."

I'm actually relieved to see his familiar and friendly face.

"What are you doing here?" he asks with a big grin.

"Well, I was…"

He doesn't wait for a reply, but encourages me forward with a few more slaps on my back, "Come on, I'll buy you a drink or two," he says, following this up with a wink.

We continue the journey to the bar at the back of the place, and I'm surprised by how many people I recognise. All of whom greet me enthusiastically.

From what I can tell, given that the place is writhing with people, the inn is typically rustic. No, not rustic, as that kind of implies that it was deliberately styled to give such an impression, but this place wasn't. This place, with the wooden beams, stone columns, and hanging lanterns is more like the pub that time forgot. I mean, for a second, I find myself wondering if the place even runs on electricity. There are no slot, video, or cigarette machines of any kind – at least none that are visible. Peering into one of the lanterns, I'm somewhat surprised to find that it contains a lightbulb and no oil. The effect, though, is amazing. I mean, this place, and there's no other way to describe it, smells and even feels old. It has that kind of hessian sack, musty smell mixed with ale, food, and maybe even bodies.

I don't remember a whiff of cologne, nor a waft of perfume. It's all... um, natural.

Eventually, we reach the bar. I say eventually because Shawn has stopped to greet and chat and, where appropriate, introduce me to most of the people along the way.

Finally, he says, "Evenin', Spencer," to a burly barman with thinning strawberry blonde hair.

"Evenin', Shawn, mate. How's it goin'?"

"Ah, you know – another day, another million."

The barman chuckles. "That's what I like to hear, mate, that's what I like to hear." He glances at me and smiles. "Evenin', fella, what'll it be?"

Suddenly, both men are looking at me, expectantly. "Um, Corona?" I ask, much more timidly than I intend, but I know it's the wrong thing to say the moment the words leave my lips.

Both men stare at me for a few seconds.

"Bring us a couple of house brews, will ya?" Shawn asks with what is fast becoming his trademark wink. Then, to me, he adds, "You should have said you were coming down tonight; I could have walked with ya."

"Well, to be honest, I didn't even know myself until about an hour ago," I explain.

"Marco's just moved into Dolce Vita," Shawn says to the barman who's now busy pulling our drinks.

"Is that right? I thought the place was falling down."

"Nah, it's been gutted. Looks like something out of a magazine now."

"Yeah? I've always wanted to see the inside of that place."

"Well, play your cards right and Marco might give you the grand tour," Shawn says with a grin, and then adds with a tease, "I might get one, too."

I look at them both and the words just slip out of my mouth, "Well, you both should just come round, any time."

"Yeah?"

"Of course."

"How about Saturday? Oh, I can't, I have a thing with Jessie. What about next Saturday?"

Like I have a choice. I shrug. "Sure."

"Spence, you bring the missus, I'll bring Jessie, and we'll make a night of it. 'Ere Jack from work was saying that he's never been in there, either. What if I asked him and his missus, too?"

"Yeah. The more the merrier. Just invite whoever you like," I say jokingly, but that isn't quite how it's interpreted.

"Fuck, yeah! That's a fantastic idea. A house warming party!" Shawn shouts, happily.

"No, wait, hang on…"

"…We can sort out the catering and the booze for ya," Spencer chimes in.

"Brilliant. Jack's got all the gear for the tunes. I can have a word with him, if you like."

"Um, well, actually…"

"ERE! EVERYONE! QUIET FOR A SECOND! QUIET! EVERYONE! QUIET DOWN FOR A SECOND!" It's Spencer, yelling at the top of his lungs until he's sure he has the pub's full attention. "NOT THIS SATURDAY, BUT NEXT, HOUSE WARMING PARTY AT DOLCE VITA!"

And just like that, the place explodes into raucous cheers, whistles, and hollers of excitement.

Oh fuck.

Then, once the ear-splitting enthusiasm has died down a bit, my new party organisers return to our general chit-chat, as if that hadn't just invited the whole village to my house for a party, on my behalf!

"Anyway, what made you all important to earn yourself a preview of the place?" Spencer is asking.

"Jess and I were just there. You know, visiting the doc earlier."

"Doc?" The barman's bushy eyebrows lift inquisitively.

"Yeah, Marco's the shrink from London."

"Actually, Shawn, I'm not…"

"…Oh, yeah," the man says, sliding a tankard in front of me, "I heard you'd arrived." Then, leaning in conspiratorially, he adds, "Eh, listen, think you can have a chat with the missus for me? She's been acting real strange like, lately."

"You say that about her all the time, Spence," Shawn throws in with a grin.

"Aye, but I'm sure she's getting worse. You know, the other morning I came downstairs to find her sitting at the kitchen table in just her underwear! I said, 'Joanne, love, why are you sitting at the table with no clothes on?' And, at first, she didn't even answer me! Just sat there, staring out of the piggin' winda. I had to walk up to her and touch her arm before she'd even look at me. She said she heard a noise outside and had come downstairs to investigate. So, I said, said, 'Why the 'ell didn't you wake us like you normally do?'"

"What did she say?" Shawn asks.

"She didn't say anything! She just up and left. Shuffled up the stairs, back to bed. When I asked her about it the next day, she told me I'd lost me marbles! Me, I've lost my marbles? So, anyway, what do you make of that, Doc?" he asks, leaning his bulk into both his hands on the bar.

I shake my head, feigning deep contemplation when Shawn saves me. "Sounds like you need to keep an eye on her, Spence, or she'll be sleep walking her way to another bloke next." Shawn follows the line up with a laugh.

Spencer shakes his head. "'Ere, if she carries on like that, mate, I'll be helping her on her way!"

The two men laugh. I smile with them, until Spencer wrinkles his nose and says, "Put it away." He's referring to the wallet in my hand.

"Hay! I was going to buy the doc a bevvie," Shawn protests.

"Next round. This one's on the house. Welcome to the village, Doc."

I'm about to thank him, but he's already serving someone else with a, "Yes, love."

I take a draft from my tankard. Fuck, it's good. I don't know what it is, but it's delicious. It tastes a bit like cider, but only fuller, richer. Sweet, yet strong.

Shawn notices the look on my face and grins, "Good?"

"Excellent," I nod, looking at it appreciatively.

He clinks my tankard with his and a few seconds drift by as we enjoy our drinks and watch the revellers in front of us. I don't think there's a face without a smile in the place. Everybody seems to be having a brilliant time, including the trio of men performing some kind of folk dance in the limited space – which almost ends up in a pile of bodies on the floor.

"What's that?" Shawn asks, or more like yells over the fracas, nodding at the black bag parcel I carried with me that's now sitting on the bar.

"It's a gift."

"For Timmy?"

"Yes."

"Sweet."

"Is Jessie not here tonight?" I ask.

He forces a laugh. "Here? With the great unwashed, as she calls them. Oh no. She tries to avoid this place if she can."

"Why's that?"

He shrugs. "She's just not into these people," he says, looking around at the jolly crowd, smiling along with them. "Her words. Me, on the other hand.... Well, I grew up with this lot. They're my family. This whole village is my family. This whole village is me," he says, turning to me once more. "Do you know what I mean by that?"

I kind of think do. I nod.

He leans in, "Listen, Doc – Marc," he corrects himself. "About today. I didn't mean to leave like that."

"You don't have to apologise, Shawn. Whatever happens in session…"

"…It's just that; well, I really care about Jess, and, well, hearing that was a bit of a shock."

"Of course…"

"…but I'm committed to this. I'm committed because I want to understand what's happening and, you know, if I'm doing the right thing."

There's conviction in his rapidly inebriated eyes. Interestingly, it's a look that I think I recognise. Kind of the way I must look when I resolve to do something. Probably how I looked when I met Ellie last Friday, which feels so bloody long ago now.

"Well, you're doing the right thing," I say encouragingly.

"You think?"

"Of course. The first part of resolving a problem is recognising that it actually exists."

He thinks about this. "Huh. So, you do think there's a problem?" he asks, looking at me with keen eyes.

Shit.

"Look, Shawn, we're not in session, and I don't normally discuss therapy outside of my office. Also, with couple's therapy, the other…"

He places a strong, reassuring hand on my shoulder. "It's okay, don't sweat it. I'm not asking you to discuss it. I'm just glad you think there's something wrong because, for a while there, I was starting to think it was just me. I mean, Jess has always been a bit fiery – it's one of the things that attracted me to her, but lately, she just hasn't been her usual self, and I need to know if it's wedding jitters or something else. And, guess what, Doc, I'm relying on you to help me find out."

He nods, then clicks my tankard with his, just as the place erupts into a chorus of *"Happy Birthday"* Shawn joins in. And, well, the magical brew is starting to work its magic on me, so, when in Rome, or Porthcove… I join him.

I watch as the sea of people part, allowing Spencer and a woman I don't recognise, presumably his wife, to wheel out a giant cake with burning candles, moving by us and on to a table where a boy around Toby's age, with blonde hair peeking out from a cardboard gold crown, sits with Pete and Deedee.

"Make a wish! Make a wish!" everybody chants before an anticipatory hush falls over the place. Then, the boy makes a dramatic flourish of sucking in a lungful of air before unleashing it on the candles. They're all extinguished with the first blow and the place goes wild. It's like watching a football match when the home team has just scored. Everybody's really excited for the little lad and, I've got to be honest, it makes me a little misty eyed.

You know why.

And I can't help but wonder what it must feel like, as a parent, to see your child become the recipient of such collective love. Such enthusiasm. It makes some of those threesome celebrations we've had with Toby seem ridiculously flat. I mean, I know they weren't. Of course, they weren't. We're his parents. We love him. While this may seem exciting... Ultimately, these people are all just caught in the moment, surely. I don't believe for a second that it can be anywhere near the same kind of love. And yet, to a ten-year-old boy, it must feel very special, and I'm glad for that. I feel glad for Pete, Deedee, and the little fella who's grinning from ear to ear.

They're kissing and hugging him now, and I glance at Shawn, who seems enraptured with the proceedings – grinning, hollering, and whistling along with the rest of the crowd, many of whom are now, not unlike the three wise men, forming an orderly single file line to congratulate the young lad and deliver an array of gifts of all sizes.

This is my cue.

I tell Shawn I'll be right back, grab the black bag parcel, and make my way over to the line of people that, I have to say, is moving forward with the efficiency of a wedding reception line. There are laughs, kisses, hugs, and well-wishes as each and every person hands the little boy their gift, which is received and stored off to one side by his parents.

Meanwhile, the cake has been wheeled to a side table and is being expertly carved and distributed around the room by Spencer and his wife.

"Marc! Hello, thank you so much for coming!" Peter and Deedee chorus when they see me.

"Oh, it's my pleasure. You must be Timmy?" I ask, looking at the rosy-cheeked ten-year-old.

"Yes, he is, our thoroughly spoilt baby!" says Deedee, kissing the boy's cheek and making him squirm.

"I'm sure he deserves it," I say, placing my parcel on the table.

"Oh my, what's this?" Deedee exclaims.

"I'm really sorry about the wrapping bag, but I haven't been able to get out."

"Oh, cheers, mate, you shouldn't have," Pete contributes.

"It's just something that I know I really loved when I was your age and, well, I'm hoping you will, too."

"Can I open it now?" the young lad asks, obviously intrigued by what's effectively a black refuse bag wrap.

"Okay… but you'll need to make it quick because there are other people waiting," Deedee responds discreetly.

The birthday boy claws at the plastic and actually has me worried for a second, but eventually he manages to reveal the boat unscathed.

"Wow!" he exclaims.

"Marc, I'm not an expert, but this looks pretty authentic," Pete says with a serious smile. Code I interpret as, *This thing is really expensive – are you sure you want to give it to my ten year old son?*

I'm sure. I know most would wonder why I'd give away something this sentimentally important to a complete stranger. And my answer would be, it's because I believe this is part of the reason why I'm here, to start anew. I don't think I can do that by fostering one good childhood memory when all it's going to do is remind me of all the bad ones. And nor do I want to pass it onto my son. That, and the fact that when I look at this thing, all I can hear is my dad telling me to *be careful. It's very expensive. Do you know that other kids would kill for something this expensive?* I did know, because I was constantly being told.

"It is authentic," I say. "I think there are only a few like it. The remote control still works. It fits into the bottom here." I point to the stern of the ship where a forceful push opens a trapdoor to reveal a miniature remote control device. "You'll need to put batteries in it," I say with a smile.

"If you're sure," Pete says.

"Absolutely," I nod.

"What do you think, Timmy?" Deedee asks.

"It's awesome! Thanks, mister!"

Both his parents laugh. "His name's Marc, Tim."

"Thanks, Marc."

"You're most welcome."

"Thank you so much, Marc. It's really kind of you," Deedee adds fondly, and then mouths, "He loves boats."

I nod again, delighted that the thing will be put to good use.

Then I glance at the line behind me. "I best get going."

"You'll stay for some cake, though, won't ya?" Pete asks.

"Of course."

With that, I shuffle my way forward and am barely moved out of the line when, slowly, like a film scene where the focus puller blurs out the foreground to bring into sharpness a subject in the background, I see her.

She's gorgeous and sitting on a barstool on the other side of the room. Big, almond shaped eyes, rosy dimples, magnificent smile, and long auburn hair that's smouldering under the lamplight.

Then, someone moves in front of her and my eye's camera refocuses on the crowd in front of me once more.

I crane my neck, looking around people, but she's gone. Gone. Literally, one second she was sitting there and the next the barstool's empty. And I'm disappointed, although I don't have time to ask myself why as I feel Shawn tapping my arm.

When I turn, he introduces me to *the lads.* His mates, best friends from work. Jessie's least favourite people. One of whom hands me another drink. Someone else hands me a paper plate with cake, and then there's another drink, and another.

Finally, things are looking up.

THE INTRUDERS

Monday Night.

I don't really know where the next few hours get to. They're pretty much an alcohol induced blur of faces, names, and general banter. I don't even remember paying for any of my drinks. It's as if I've discovered a village custom; new person arrives in town, and everybody buys him a drink.

I think it's somewhere around midnight when we leave the inn. By *we*, I mean me, Shawn and his band of merry mechanics, who, along with several other members of the birthday party, are some of the last stragglers.

The mechanics ask if I need help getting home. "Fuck off," I slur. "I'm a local now. I know this place like the back of my hand." Albeit one that I have to keep squinting at, because I can't work out if I still have all five fingers or if I've grown an extra one. This, of course, is highly amusing to my new chums, who've erupted in guffaws of laughter.

I just wave them off and begin truly appreciating the term *legless* as I stagger in the general direction of the steps that lead up from the harbour and out of here.

And it's now, as I gingerly make my way through the back-alley shortcut, which is dimly lit by the overspill of street lanterns from the main thoroughfare, that I get the hair-prickling feeling that somebody is following me.

My first thought is that it's one of the lads, so I just wave, absentmindedly, and tell them to bugger off home and that I'm fine. But then, when I don't hear a response, or a chuckle of any kind, I look over my shoulder.

There's nobody there.

Then why does it bloody feel like the very shadows themselves are watching every step I take?

Instinctively, I increase my pace, as much as you can when you've had a skin full of that magic brew, which I have to say has really cast a bloody spell on me. I can feel that I'm well and truly hammered. And, admittedly, it does feel good. It's like I've taken a Valium or something... hence why the streetlights that seem to dim with each and every step I take aren't anywhere as creepy as they otherwise might be.

That said, I'm still relieved to make it out of the alley and out of the shadows, to the sound of laughter. At least, I think it's a group of people laughing – I'm not sure. But then, I must have imagined it because the glistening cobblestones are empty. I am on my own. The only thing accompanying me is the brew in my belly.

Somehow, and I don't know how, I reach the bridge, and linger there for a few seconds. I watch my breath fog out in front of me. The night is chilly and deathly still. The sky is still ablaze with a constellation of stars like jewels on the ice queen's cloak as she readies herself to cover the world in glittering frost.

My footsteps seem particularly loud as they scrunch over the gravel, and the ocean does, too, like it's reached the back garden. Obviously, it hasn't; it's as still as a sheet of black ice in the distance. I'm just so pissed I can't even walk straight. What the hell do they put in that brew anyway?

Jesus, and there's me thinking that last Friday was bad. Last Friday? It seems so long ago now, but it isn't. Just feels that way.

I watch the house's moonlit outline and think about its value, and that thought melts away the chill that's clinging to my clothes, making me feel all warm and tingly.

Millionaire.

Once I sell this place, I am going to be a fucking millionaire!

"Cheers, Dad!" I air-clink a drink at the house.

But then, a thought crosses my mind. One I don't think I would have even entertained when I first arrived here.

Maybe this place isn't so bad after all. The people are friendly enough. Back in London, they'd probably be classed as overfriendly. Nosey. Busybodies who need more in their own lives so that they can stop becoming so involved in everybody else's. But that's in the city. Here... Well, it's a whole different story.

So, maybe that's what I should do. Maybe I should invite Ellie and Toby here. Let them take a look at the place. My wife might even be impressed, like everybody else. Especially when she hears just how much the place is worth.

I think about ringing her again, but that thought always seems to occur to me here, of all places, where there's a rubbish signal. Besides, after everything that's happened, she's not going to be in any hurry to chat. Certainly not at this time of night and with me in this state.

Nah... tomorrow. I'll call her then.

I stumble forward and fondle the latch of the gate until it finally springs open – with that now eerie creak that's deafeningly loud in the still night – and shuffle my way up the path.

At the front door, I frisk myself for keys and, after what can only be described as a game of trying to pin the tail on the donkey, I finally manage to swing the thing open.

Front door open.

"No shit," I giggle like a schoolkid.

I push the door shut behind me.

There's no need to lock it. I discovered earlier in the day that the thing auto-locks when pushed on. I made a mental note of that because I didn't fancy the idea of locking myself out.

Then, I turn to drag my weary, inebriated arse up the stairs, and that's when all hell breaks loose.

I'm barely past the kitchen threshold when I hear something that, even in my haze, makes my blood run cold.

Back Door Open.

The electronic voice is like an alarm bell, as if it's yelling at me, screaming the terrifying news that someone is in my house. That they have opened the kitchen patio door and are now noisily rummaging and rustling around in there.

Oh fuck.

I realise that I've momentarily stopped breathing for fear that the intruders might hear me, yet my heart is rigorously protesting inside my rib cage as a vein throbs in my neck. I suck in air as the adrenaline kicks in, switching my intoxicated body from snooze mode to fight or flight.

I'm ready to fly, get the fuck out of here, and yet it's as I consider this that the ear-splintering cacophony of smashing glass and ringing saucepans reaches me.

I jolt away from the kitchen door and I'm staggering backward when I hear slipping, skidding, and jingling sounds from the kitchen. *Something slipping on the floor, tinkling through broken glass.*

Then, the patio door slams against the wall.

"Shit! Shit!" I mutter as I back up against the opposite wall, bile rising to the back of my throat and tears of terror sprinting to my eyes.

I'm breathing heavily. Noisily. I've gone from holding my breath to bloody hyperventilating.

Then, I notice the light switch on the wall next to me, and I don't know what the hell possesses me, but I impulsively flip it on.

Bright, glorious light from the chandelier fills the room, washing away some of my fear, but this is instantly replaced by irritation, anger, and then rage.

Who the fuck are these people to break into my house? I've only just gotten here myself!

So, I look around the room for a weapon. Anything will do, and I'm lucky enough to find every periled man's cliché; a selection of fire instruments hanging in the fireplace.

I grab the heaviest one, the poker, as well as deep lungs of courage and, presumably emboldened by the river of alcohol running through my veins pickling my brain, I lift the poker high above my head and yell, "I'VE GOT A WEAPON! I'VE GOT A WEAPON AND I'M GOING TO KILL YOU! I'M GOING TO FUCKING KILL YOU!" And I lunge, like I'm possessed, through the kitchen doorway. The motion/heat activating the lights as I go.

I'm not sure how I feel about what I see. I think shock is a good way of describing it, joined very quickly by spine tingling astonishment, and then annoyance... slash, what the fuck?

My kitchen has been devastated.

The pans, hanging over the island, are still swinging, occasionally tinkling an odd tune. The fridge door is open, and its contents, like a slashed belly, are either on the floor or spattered up and over units. The patio doors, which you have come to know as the *back doors*, are wide open, as are all of the cupboard doors.

On the tiled floor, a skirmish of patterns has been carved out of the flood of milk and broken glass. Yes, even the milk that Harvey sourced for me in an unusual glass vintage bottle has been spilled onto the floor, the gorgeous container shattered. Its pieces now scattered and glinting like diamonds under the overhead spotlights.

I stand there for a good minute or so, before picking my way around the island to the patio doors, which I approach cautiously, triggering the security light and illuminating the flagstone square surrounded by flowers and herbs.

I cautiously step into the doorway and look out.

The courtyard is enclosed by a seven-foot-something hedge – I know that thanks to Lucinda's detailed report. This means that whomever or whatever was in the kitchen must have scaled that thing with ease. This realisation, of course, renews the current of fear still buzzing through me and forces to attention additional hairs on the back of my arms and neck.

I don't know why, but somehow, my subconscious reconciled itself to the idea that the devastation in the kitchen was created by some kind of wild animal. My conscious brain, however inebriated, couldn't help but question how an animal would have the dexterity to open the fridge, the kitchen cupboards, and the backdoor. But...

But how would a human get over that fence without some kind of perch?

My thoughts are interrupted by a sound overhead, and it's all I can do not to scream out loud. Something is on the roof. Something that, presumably, has been watching me this whole time, and is now shifting, moving covertly from above one side of the door to the other.

Slowly, despite all instincts begging to the contrary, I tilt my head up, just in time to see something snatch a limb away from the ledge. Then I hear thumping, scuffling and ringing, closely followed by a few seconds of silence and then the loud thud of something heavy hitting the ground beyond the hedge, before the familiar rustle and scrunch of something running over the driveway gravel to, presumably, disappear into the woods, causing a dog to bark somewhere in the distance.

It takes a few seconds for me to tune into myself to see that I'm gawking at the hedge. My breath frozen in my lungs, my mind paralysed with inebriated terror.

Then, I slowly reverse back into the house, still staring at the hedge as if something is going to come crashing through it at any second, before I snatch the door shut and throw the locks behind it.

Then, I turn to get the hell out of here, to safety, to call the police. Only, in my haste, I've completely forgotten that there's a milk slick across the floor, so I skid, trip, head-butt the fridge door, and end up crumpling into a heap on the floor before all the lights go out.

EMILY

Tuesday. 10:35.

I have no idea how, but somehow, I managed to get myself to my bedroom and, by the looks of it, use that old cliché of every horror movie; the dresser to barricade myself in.

Really?

I sit up in bed and stare at it. Yep, the dresser is in front of my bedroom door.

What the…

No, I don't think I ever suggested that I was in any way heroic. Far from it. Well, with one correction: there's no doubt in my mind that, if Ellie or Toby were in danger, I'd maim and kill without hesitation, but when… Well shit, I've just realised… when it comes to my own safety, I'd rather run and hide.

That's not good.

Last night, I must have flown up those stairs, probably bolting every door and, I'm not ashamed to say it, leaving every light on.

At least, that's what it looks like so far. Both the overhead and the lamplights are still burning strong despite the daylight streaming in through the window.

Oh God. I've just remembered something else. In my inebriated state, I managed to call the police and make a complete tit of myself. I can't remember exactly what I said, but there was something in there about intruders, as well as the operator asking if I had been drinking, to which I naturally responded in the affirmative, which prompted her to lecture me about wasting valuable resources and… well, it all went a bit downhill from there.

Or did I dream that?

Hmmm... no, from the ache in my side, I'd say I must have been hanging out of that window for some time. Although, they obviously didn't take me seriously, as I don't remember hearing any sirens nor seeing any flashing lights. At least, none beyond those flashing in front of my eyes right now.

Man, my head is pounding.

My only hope is that Captain Birdseye and his wife's Red Cross basket includes a pack of paracetamol.

Shit. I rub my face gently and sigh. The only problem is that the basket is downstairs and I'm up here. That means I'm going to have to leave this soft, deliciously warm bed, drag myself forward and the dresser from in front of the door, and get downstairs.

I can't be bothered.

So, instead I decide to torture myself by watching the sunshine shimmer off of the crisp white *empty* pillow next to me.

Shit, that hurts more than the roadworks in my head.

I roll over and think of Ellie and Toby. I wonder what they're up to right now. I wonder if my son is missing me. Maybe he's already forgotten about me. *Yep. That's your hangover talking. Idiot.*

I think about Ellie. The woman I adore, the same one who blackmailed me into coming to this house of bloody phantoms and into seeing that shrink in just three days, the prospect of which only increases my gag reflex which, you'll appreciate, is quite sensitive right now.

I should be angry at Ellie, but for some inexplicable reason I'm not. I can't imagine why.

Oh okay, I can. It's because I deserve it.

Meanwhile, my sadistic mind decides to transport me back to last night again, to the pub, the people, the chanting...

The kitchen.

The birthday song...

The alleyway. Was someone following me?

The kitchen.

That woman at the back of the pub. The scuffling on the roof.

Fuck!

I can't get the images out of my head, yet at the same time they're fuzzy, like one of those dreams you can't bloody remember.

But I do remember. Not clearly, but I do remember the state of the kitchen. How I felt. But could I have dreamt that? Hallucinated it? The drilling in my head reminds me that I did drink a lot last night.

There's only one way to find out, and the thought of it makes me shiver.

Interestingly, in the warm rays of the morning sun, if I may use such a poetic line, and through the patch of glorious blue window that is the sky meeting the ocean, everything about last night does seem, does feel, completely different. Certainly different from how it felt in the moment.

What the hell did they put in that stuff? Maybe they drugged me.

Seriously?

I squint at the glare of daylight as I take in the room, as if I'm seeing it for the first time. I look up at the giant photographic print of the cliff and rocky shore.

Oh God, I feel sick.

The picture, snapped by my mother, now hangs over the pine framed bed in which my father would have done God knows what with whom.

Eww. Now I'm feeling really rough, and the thought of that alone propels me up from the pillow. Not the best decision, of course, because the hangover roadworks in my head restart with a vengeance.

I need pills. Lots of them. My only hope is to get downstairs, now.

Okay, I will. But I'm coming back to bed the moment I realise that the basket is bloody empty. It's not like I have anything planned for today, apart from some reminiscing around lunchtime, followed by some self-pity in the afternoon and the meeting I just can't get out of with separation anxiety in the evening. So, I may as well sleep off the rest of my day.

I get out of bed and pad over to the door, but not before catching sight of myself in that bloody mirror.

Shit. I look worse than I thought. A reanimated corpse with those dehydrated squinty eyes people get first thing in the morning. Only worse. I'm naked but for my boxers. At least the short back and sides and neatly trimmed beard I acquired in the village yesterday isn't failing me.

Still, I'm a far cry from the so called 'lady's man' I'm thought to be.

And, wow... Now I'm looking at my navel, and I don't know if it's the fact that my head is swimming or not, but I'm sure there's a sign of a beer belly there. Where did that come from?

I pull at the skin. Yeah, there's enough to pinch, although, to be fair, it does seem to retract satisfactorily, but I should take up running while I'm here. Start exercising again. Get ripped before going back to my wife.

There's an idea; but first, drugs.

I pull the dresser aside slowly and carefully, trying to make the least amount of sound possible, and I eventually liberate myself from the makeshift safe room.

I pause. Maybe I should pull on jogging bottoms. It's a bit chilly. I decide against it, though. I can walk around this house completely starkers for all anybody else is going to care. I'm alone here, remember?

Yet, weirdly, I sill peer over the banister as if there might be someone down there. I have no clue why. Maybe it's force of habit. It isn't because I just discovered my fitness is going to shit, nor the fact that I'm shy – I had that kicked out of me in the first week of boarding school.

No, I realise that it's more than that. It's because I still feel like a bloody visitor here, though I'm not. And, there's nobody down there. The only thing stalking the living room is sunshine, and lots of it, streaming in through the landing and balcony doors, and I must say, glare aside, it's making me feel much better. As if it's recharging my courage batteries, buoying me up for what I am going to have to face in that kitchen.

Exactly! That's what all this procrastinating is about. The bloody kitchen. I don't want to be reminded of last night because I was genuinely scared, and especially when I heard whatever it was moving about above my bloody head. What was that all about?

Shit.

Get on with it!

I take a deep breath and move forward, slowly descending the wooden steps. They creak eerily as I inch my way forward, towards the kitchen.

Now my heart is thumping almost as loudly as the headache in my skull. There was something in the kitchen last night. Someone or something was watching me. It could still be watching me. My head's throbbing. I feel nauseated. I'm going to vomit here and now.

Get a grip. Think of something nice.

Toby.

Milk everywhere.

Toby.

Smashed eggs on the floor.

I smile. No, egg and soldiers. Toby's just like me. He loves eggs. I picture him, feet dangling from one of the stools at the breakfast bar as we tuck into breakfast together. That grin of his as bright as the sun itself.

I miss my little boy. I know I've mentioned that before, but I do. Actually, I don't just miss him. I ache for him. It feels like someone has hacked off one of my appendages and that I'm clumsily learning to function without it. In this case, doing a terrible job because I miss my son like an insomniac misses sleep; desperately, angrily, sadly.

And who's fault is that?

My mouth is dry.

Stop stalling and get in there!

I move towards the door. My heart in my throat, sweat on my forehead.

That's when it comes, echoing around the den, slapping me across the face and rattling inside my skull.

Pounding on the front door. Heavy. Urgent. It's a Gestapo-type military urgency that startles me and then makes me spin on my feet while swearing out loud.

I freeze. I don't know why. Perhaps I'm silently wishing I've just imagined the sound, or, if I haven't, that whoever it is might just go away. I don't want to see anyone right now.

Silence. Just the cry of seagulls and the usual rumble of the surf beyond the terrace doors.

The doorbell clangs a Hammer House of horror kind of clang, startling me again.

"Fuck!" I yell. I didn't even know this place had a doorbell.

"Go away!" I shout angrily. I'm irritated, and the pressure inside my head isn't helping.

There's a pause, and I think they've gotten the message, but then the doorbell sounds again.

I glance at myself, in my skivvies, and I consider running back upstairs to pull some clothes on, but no, fuck it, they're the ones intruding at… shit, is that clock saying it's nearly eleven?

I stomp across the room to the front door, just as more hammering echoes around the den.

"Jesus Christ… Alright, alright," I grumble as I pull back the top and bottom door bolts, turn the key in the lock, and then yank the door open.

I instantly regret the action.

The stupid artificial robotic voice has barely announced *Front door open* when the most deafening alarm squeal I have ever heard explodes around me like a percussion grenade.

"FUCK! FUCK!" is all I can chant as I dance from one side of the door to the other – looking and searching around the room both for my thoughts and for the code that I hope is in some way miraculously and conveniently posted *somewhere* so that I can kill the fucking alarm that I'm sure is boring a hole into my eardrums, making them bleed! "Ahhhhhhhhhhhhhhhhhhhh!" I start yelling, as if I can in some way counteract the assault on my ears and, of course, I'm still doing this when the sound mercifully ceases.

Eventually, what must be several seconds later, I realise that the wailing I can still hear is coming from me as I stand in the open doorway wearing nothing but my boxers, and with my hands over my ears.

The police officer is in the house now, standing next to the alarm control panel. She has her hands thrust into her stab vest and is looking at me expectantly. That's right. *She's* looking at me and, no doubt, suppressing a laugh.

And you won't be surprised to learn that, despite my obvious embarrassment, the first thing I've noticed about her is just how *neat* she looks in her uniform. She's obviously fit underneath all of that wear, and her large, almond-shaped blue eyes are watching me from under her hat with mild amusement.

"The code," she says, holding up a flap on the control panel, "is written on the back here. People often make this mistake. You really should change it to one of your choosing," she adds, letting the flap fall shut.

Her eyes stay on me the whole time and, if I wasn't busy wrestling with the heat in my cheeks, I would conclude that the cop's checking me out.

Really?

"Mr. Battista?" she asks casually.

I nod, slowly willing my body to unfold from its protective scrunch and stand tall. And when I finally reach my full height, I catch her snatching a glance at my legs. Of course, in any other situation, I would have played on that, but I'm standing in the doorway, in my underwear, and she's a cop, which for some obscure reason – presumably to do with the fact that she's the one in authority – makes the rouge of my face another shade deeper. This time it isn't necessarily because I'm semi-naked, but more for the humiliating memory of me squealing like a little girl.

"You called us last night," I hear her continue, "to report a home invasion."

After stammering a few times, like I've suddenly developed an affliction, I manage to say, "I, well, I, it wasn't exactly a home invasion. Well, it was but, just, well, the kitchen…"

"The report we received was that an intruder had entered the property without your permission and... made a bit of a mess?"

"Intruders."

"Sorry?"

"I think there was more than one of them," I say sheepishly, willing myself to remain upstanding and not cross my hands in front of my crotch.

I don't know what's wrong with me. The idea of a lady in uniform would normally get my pulse going, yet here I am, behaving like a bloody kid who's just wet himself. I guess I could attribute part of this to the fact that she's seriously cute, and I swear, behind that professional stance, those beautifully blue eyes are smiling at me.

"So, you think there were two people here last night?" she asks, magically appearing a notepad and pen from her pocket and poising to take notes.

"Well," I clear my throat, "I couldn't really say exactly."

She cocks her head and looks at me, expectantly.

"Look, um, is it okay, if I go pull some clothes on? It's, um... I'm kind of, um…" I motion up the stairs.

"Oh, of course," she replies with a grin. And yes, it is a grin and not a smile. The copper is toying, flirting, with me. What's that all about?

I smile back at her and then scarper up the stairs – in the manliest possible way, of course.

I stop at the bedroom door before entering. Then, and I have no idea why, I creep to and peek over the balustrade.

The policewoman has stepped further into the entrance lobby and is having a good look around.

Cheeky so-and-so.

You would think that, given my reaction to everybody else showing up here, the snooping cop would prove equally as irritating; yet, for some reason, she isn't. For some reason, her flirty, cheeky ways are actually amusing me, even tugging a smile from the corners of my mouth.

First, she checked me out, and now she's checking out the pad. Of course, I could well be imagining this. She's probably just doing her job, inspecting the place for anything untoward, like drugs or alcohol abuse, but I know when a girl is being familiar and, I can tell you, this one is – and, of course, I like it.

Well, you can't blame me. You know I'm a sucker for a pretty girl. Especially one in uniform. Admittedly, it's dark, normally brown eyes that do it for me but, well, she's beautiful and, between you and me, I've never done… I mean, I've never *dated* a cop. The closest I've come to a woman in uniform is a flight attendant, but that's a whole different story.

In the bedroom, I pull on the first thing I can find that doesn't stink of yesterday's booze, and that's black jogging bottoms and a white T-shirt. Then, I give my hair a quick comb with my fingers, although it's still holding well either way, and then, nakedness covered and masculinity restored, I casually stride down the stairs once more.

"Sorry about that," I say confidently, doing my best to hide all previous embarrassments in the bottom drawers of my mind, as one would a mess when confronted by an unexpected guest.

She responds with her own confident, pearly smile.

"Can I get you a drink?" I ask, pointing through to the kitchen.

Shit. That' when I remember the kitchen.

"No, thanks," she says, and I breathe a sigh of relief. But then she adds,

"But you can show me around," as she moves forward.

My first thought is that she wants a tour of the house, which, of course, is a bit weird, but she obviously means she wants to see the kitchen. The so-called *scene of the crime.*

When she notices my hesitation, she adds, "Your report said that that the intruder, or intruders, broke in through the kitchen door."

"I said that?"

She cocks her head again, as if to say, "What, you don't remember?" And the answer to that is no. I don't remember a fucking thing!

Reluctantly, I step aside and gesture for her to go forward. Then I reconsider the move and wonder if it should be me going in there first, but concede that she is a cop, after all, and trained for this kind of thing.

The kitchen is ablaze with sunshine bursting through the window, exploding off of the granite island and gleaming off surfaces.

The cop is standing in front of me, so I can't see the slick on the floor, but I can see that the fridge and cupboard doors are closed. The island is clean.

What the…

I step around her. The floor is spotless, too.

"So, you've already cleaned up?" she asks, turning to me.

I have no idea how to respond. I mean, I open my mouth to speak, but the words just aren't forming in my throat.

Did I clear things up before going to bed last night? I try hard to remember, but I can't recall anything about that.

Now I can feel her eyes on me again.

"Well, um, yeah, there was stuff all over the floor – milk and stuff. I couldn't leave it there," I lie. "And I didn't know when you might come, so…"

She nods and walks forward, toward the back door. "And did you notice any damage to the door?"

"Damage?"

"Yes. Did these intruders forcibly enter the kitchen or did you leave the door unlocked?"

"No. The door was…" I don't know what state the doors were in. I have no idea if they were locked or unlocked. I didn't open them, so I assumed they were locked. I didn't think to check. I was bloody drunk!

My mind's reeling. Not because of the hangover now, but more because I'm trying so hard to remember. I was in here. All of that weird shit happened and then… That's it, I turned to run and I slipped. I must have banged my head!

Instinctively, I touch my forehead, but don't feel any lumps or pain of anything. That's when I realise my headache is easing up. It hasn't gone completely – my thoughts are still fuzzy – but at least I don't feel like an elephant's doing a tap-dance on my skull.

"Mr. Battista?"

She's looking at me. The sunshine sparkling off of those giant blue eyes.

And that's when I find it. A memory. Somewhere, deep in the back of my brain. Familiarity… With her… With the cop?

"So, you received a call from me last night?" The words leave my mouth as I move around her to the fridge where, holding my breath, I pull the door open.

Everything is in there; vintage milk bottle, the groceries I bought yesterday.

Shit.

"Yes," she replies. "From the recording, you seemed quite agitated."

"Did I?" I ask, pulling out a bottle of water.

"Yes."

I can feel her curious eyes on the back of my head, so I quickly close the fridge, turn to her, and hold up the bottle of water. "Sure you don't want one of these?"

She shakes her head. Those eyes, curiously searching mine. "No, thanks. You reported someone on your property. You said they had made a mess of the kitchen." She makes a show of looking around the room.

"I did, huh?"

She cocks her head again, curiously, trying to establish if I might be in some way making fun of her. "Yes, you did."

"And yet you didn't show up until this morning," I say, twisting the cap of my bottle. "It's a good job I wasn't being forced to have my feet tickled by a posse of forest fairies," I say with mock reproach and a smile.

"Yes," she drops her eyes. "It's been a busy night."

"Busy? Around here? What happened, did a pigeon get caught in a tree?"

"Um, no. Actually, we've been busy with a missing person."

"Missing person? Here? Well, you don't exactly have far to look, do you?" I ask with laugh, before taking a swig from the bottle. But, I soon realise that the cop isn't laughing with me.

Shit.

I lose my smile. "Who's missing?" I ask, inserting some seriousness into my tone once more.

She looks at me, as if considering if I can be trusted with the information that's obviously already public knowledge. Not that I would know, of course, being stuck out here in my technological dead zone.

"A local boy. He didn't make it home last night after going to a party."

Now my interest is well and truly piqued. "The birthday party down at the inn?"

"That's right. It was actually his birthday party."

I feel a gut stab of concern. "Oh no. Are you talking about Timmy? Pete's son?"

"Yes. You know Pete?"

"Um, kind of. I met him yesterday morning. He invited me to the party. Shit." I'm genuinely shocked. "He must be out of his mind."

"He's not doing too well, no."

"Do you have any leads or anything yet?"

"Not yet, but we're coordinating with County and will be drafting in more officers to the search today."

"So, what happened exactly? I mean, he was with his parents when I saw him."

"Yes. Then he said he was going to walk straight home with his friends, but he never made it there."

"And what do his friends have to say?"

"They're being interviewed now. Did you see anything unusual, spot anyone hanging around on your way home last night?"

I think about this. Of all things, I do remember that bloody bit in the alleyway. That feeling like someone was watching, following me. But then I thought I heard someone talking and laughing, too. Did I? I can't fucking remember!

"No, not really. The streets were pretty much empty when I walked home."

"And what time was that?"

"Around midnight."

I watch her scribble on her pad.

Silence rules for a few seconds as we both process what's just been said. Suddenly, she adds, "Anyway, I'm here to discuss the report that you made."

I squint at her as I drink from the bottle, since you and I both know that I'm what they call a somewhat unreliable witness.

"The report said that you weren't sure if somebody had actually come onto your property since, quote, *I've had a few, so I'm not sure if I hallucinated it.*"

"I said that?"

She nods.

"Ah," I say, putting the bottle down.

Shit.

"This is just a courtesy call, really. You know... making sure everything's alright and that you're settling in okay."

There's a mischievous twinkle in those gorgeous blue eyes. I examine her, and then the words just come out. "Am I missing something here?"

"You have no idea who I am, do you, Marcy?" she asks with a grin.

Marcy? "No, should I?"

"Well, let's just put it this way – it isn't the first time I've seen you in your underwear," she says, melting her cop demeanour and swapping it for a girly grin.

Oh shit! I don't even know why, but I can feel that warm glow returning to my cheeks, like an unwanted erection.

"I'm Emily. Emmy?"

"Emmy?"

"You don't remember me, do you? Even after I let you look under my skirt!"

"Emmy? Oh my God! Emmy! How are you doing?" I ask with mock familiarity.

But she reads right through it. "You still don't have a clue, do you?" she asks.

I pull a face. "I'm sorry."

"Marco!" she complains. "We used to play together as children. Here! Well, not here – alright, maybe a couple of times, but down by the ocean. My parents used to be friends with yours."

I think about this for a few seconds and slowly but surely some images do push through my fuzzy tired brain, and I strain to tune into them. They're grainy pictures, like a television tuning into a weak signal. It isn't anything specific... just me on the beach, again, building something, probably a sandcastle, but only this time, I'm aware of somebody else. Not my parents nearby, but somebody else, sitting in the sand opposite me, and in my mind's eye I look up and smile at a pair of rosy cheeks, with chestnut hair trailing in the breeze like a fiery comet. Then those eyes – big, blue, almond-shaped eyes!

"Oh, bloody hell, Em," I gasp, surprised by the sudden vividness of the recollection.

"Yes, it's me." She grins, then looks at me sceptically. "Are you seriously remembering?"

"Yes, yes, just now. Just snippets of us playing on the beach, right?" She nods. "I'm sorry. I'm really sorry. Just my mind... I've been trying to... you know, getting old." I feel the heat burning my face once more.

Get a grip, man! What is it with you and this bird anyway?

I don't normally get like this in front of a pretty woman. Alright... she's a stunning woman whose skin, I've just noticed, is like porcelain in the sunshine.

"You were at the party last night too," I declare, pointing a finger at her. She nods.

"I was wondering why you were staring at me."

"Yeah, sorry about that," she says with a shy smile. "I wasn't sure it was you."

"Thank God. I thought you were some creepy stalker. Albeit a gorgeous-looking one."

Shit. Did I just say that out loud? Oh God.

"Did I just say that out loud?" I ask.

She grins. Her smile wrinkling that smooth skin over high cheekbones.

"I'm sorry. Um, oh well. I'm committed now, I suppose. It's true, though. You look great!" I say, lifting my hands and pointing at her in her uniform. "And a cop! Wow."

Easy, Battista, you're making a bloody arse of yourself. Reign in the enthusiasm.

"You've changed, too," she offers. Rescuing me from my ridiculous verbal diarrhoea.

"For the better, I hope," I say.

She nods, appreciatively. "Yeah. Quite a bit from the skinny boy with curly brown locks," she laughs.

"I didn't have curly brown locks."

"You did! And they were cute, and now you're..." she trails off there.

I push, because I'm evil like that, and I've already made a fool of myself, so why not encourage some company? "Now I'm what?"

She hesitates. Her face burning almost as hot as mine. "Now, um... has anybody told you that you look like that actor?"

"Oh, come on, seriously? Not you, too!"

"You do, though. And that's a compliment, by the way. A big one."

"Okay, I'll except it as such, then." I toast the fact with my bottle of water.

There's an interlude of a few seconds, which I elongate with my gulp of water. Yes, I'm a coward that way, but she's cute and, well, to be honest, I don't normally get this flummoxed in front of a girl. Plus, I didn't even know I could be this ridiculous, until now.

"So, I heard you're a therapist," she says.

I nod. "You know, a few days ago, I would've been surprised you already knew that."

"Small village." She shrugs.

"Yes. I am, for my sins. You know what it's like – it's kind of a case of, *those who can't, teach*. Of sorts. You know, I can't sort out my own mental problems, so I try and help others with theirs."

"And how's that working for you?"

"Yeah. It's good."

"I hear you have, had, a practice in the city?"

"Yes. I did, until I, um, we decided to move down here."

Be quiet, you. I know that's two lies in two sentences, but what do you expect? The girl's hot, and she's in uniform, so cut me some slack.

"We? Is that meaning your wife?"

"Yes, Ellie."

"And you have a son?"

"Blimey. You have been doing your research."

She shrugs and smiles.

"Don't tell me. Small village?"

"You learn fast."

"Yes. I have a son, Toby. He's ten."

"Oh, lovely. Do you have a picture?"

"You know, I don't. I've just changed phones and I haven't managed to transfer photos across yet."

Which is true, in case you're wondering. I broke the thing on the same day I lost my job and it's bloody annoying. Not the fact that my phone was smashed to bits, but more that I've lost Toby's pictures in the process. And before you ask, I haven't managed to download any others from the cloud or social media yet because, guess what? Internet connection here is shit.

Have I mentioned that before? I forget.

"Anyway, what about you?" I ask, for some inexplicable reason, happy to steer the conversation away from the fact that I'm married with a son.

"Yes. I'm married. I have a son, too. He's actually the same age as yours."

"Really?"

"Yeah."

"And do you have a picture?"

She squirms, then pulls a face. "Do you know what, I don't. Well, at least not on me. My mobile phone's in my locker at the station."

"Looks like we owe each other pictures then."

She smiles. "Yes, we do."

And then it all goes awkwardly quiet. You know, one of those moments where the small-talk ends and you scrabble around in your brain for something else to sustain the conversation, yet the more you dig around in there, the more the brick walls grow…

"I was really sorry to hear about your parents," she says, suddenly. "It must have been really difficult for you."

"Thanks. It was, but that's in the past now."

She must have sensed something in the way I delivered that line, because she quickly looks around the kitchen. "Now you've inherited this place. It's gorgeous. Changed a bit from when we were kids."

"You think?"

"Absolutely. It's been completely, oh, what do the Americans say? Remodelled." She's spoken the last word with an inflection, which isn't so dissimilar to her local accent that's mildly country. Pretty. Yes, that word again, which is weird because, when I see a good-looking girl, I tend to use modern day vernaculars, such as *fit* or *sexy*. Sometimes, if I've had a bit to drink, I even use cruder expressions, like, "*She'd get it*," or my personal favourite, "*I could ruin her.*"

Yet, from the moment I opened the door to this police woman, the only words that have kept springing to mind are *pretty, attractive, lovely eyes, great smile*. Especially when she laughs. Her lashes flicker in those almond eyes like butterfly wings.

Eh?

"It's funny you should say that because my estate agent, or realtor, as she likes to be called, is American."

"Really?"

"Yeah, she's from Kayes and Kayes."

Emily shakes her head.

"You've never heard of them? They're not local?"

"No. Are they from out of town?"

I think about this. I don't know where they're based. Come to think of It, I can't even remember how I found Lucinda now. I don't think it was me. It might have been Ellie.

"So, you're thinking of selling up then?" she asks, interrupting my thoughts.

"Yeah."

"Oh, that's a shame."

"Why do you say that?"

She lifts her shoulders. "Oh, no reason… just, well, this place holds a lot of memories for me."

"Does it?"

"Of course." She lifts her hands to her hips. "You really don't remember, do you?"

I shake my head. "Sorry."

"Blimey – out of sight, out of mind, eh?"

I don't know how to answer that, nor how to interpret it, and we could have another awkward moment, but it's interrupted by a rumbling, clattering sound outside. We both turn to look out of the window and watch as a train trundles by.

"I love the sound of trains," she says wistfully.

"Me, too. At first, I thought I was going to hate that thing, but now I actually quite like it."

"See? You've only been here a few days and you're already falling in love."

"Well, the views are beautiful," I say sincerely as I turn to look at her. My gaze must be intense, because there's a rosy colour to her cheeks again and, if I'm being perfectly honest, I've already grown to like it.

The radio affixed to her right shoulder crackles to life, shattering the moment like delicate crystal.

She instantly turns the volume down and says, as if suddenly waking from a spell, "We best get back to your report. I've taken up way too much of your time already and, as you can imagine, things are pretty busy at the station right now. It's all hands to the pump."

"Oh, of course."

The rest of our conversation is, for want of a better expression, strictly professional. And it's weird, because it's like she can switch that familiarity on and off at will.

I know which side of her I prefer most, though. Especially as I'm not particularly enjoying the cop asking me a battery of questions about last night. Questions to which I don't really have answers.

Do you know how many intruders there were? No. Can you describe them? No. Did they make any distinctive noises or smells? Not really. And so on. I mean, if you were to base my intruders on my statement and description, you'd be looking for anyone, from flying monkeys to Big Foot.

I feel like an idiot. Especially in front of her.

No, I much prefer us talking about the past I can barely remember and basking in the intimate way she knows things about me that I didn't even know about myself. I like that she knows me, and I'd loved to probe her more about the past.

Yes, I heard that word, too, but I'm choosing to ignore it. Remember – to the pure, all is pure.

Besides, we're both married with children. I can't afford to screw up again. I'm in no way unclear about what brought me here and why I need to make a success of it. The future with my family depends on it, and I can't let anything or anyone, no matter how beautiful or mysterious they might be, jeopardise that.

Would you?

AVA

Wednesday. 14:55.

The room is green, gold, and blue. Shadows dance on walls through the haze of the dazzling sunshine that's being filtered through the leaves of the tree outside. It'll be winter soon. My favourite time of the year.

It's quiet in my study, but for the sound of the ticking clock and the moan of the wind through the gaps in the vents of the glass wall. I haven't noticed this before. The sound is comforting, yet eerily spooky. I both like it and hate it, but I guess that, like me, it belongs here now. It's part of the space. Part of the history imprinted here. Not on the surfaces of the wall, but deep inside, in between the stones.

This is my space now. It's where I take refuge inside this fortress, like a cuckoo inside a nest, but for the few, the uninvited.

I just want to stay here, sitting on the floor, basking like a cat in the vacuous heat of the autumn sun – but I can't, as there's something pulling at me, making me stir like a teenager rousing from school-morning slumber.

And now, a shadow falls over me. Someone. A man, a woman, I can't tell, and suddenly it's cold. Damp. Freezing. I try to climb from the deep, but I can't, I can't surface, I can't... I can't breathe! My heart is pounding like a rock on a mansion door, pumping strength through my body, but I can't help myself, I can't move, something is holding me under the water.

"H… l… p… H… l p M… u… m…"

The liquid freeze is in my nose, in my mouth. Gagging. Suffocating.

BANG! goes the beat of my heart.

BANG! BANG! go the lights in my brain.

"Help!"

I'm dying. I'm choking.

BANG!

"Help! Pl… e… as…"

I wake with a start. Screaming. Gasping. Panting.

There's sweat on my forehead and, even though the sun is up and pouring through the glass wall, I'm cold. I'm freezing cold, as if I've just been lying at the bottom of the ocean.

"Fuck!" I swallow, but my tongue is thick. Abrasive. Dry.

I run hands through my hair while all the time breathing and gasping. The action is reflexive, comforting. Reminding me that I'm still here, that I'm not dead. That I did not die in my dream.

Knock! Knock! Knock!

"Shit!" The sound makes me jump. It's the front door. Someone's knocking at the bloody thing a la Gestapo again. Why do they keep doing that? Why do they always knock like they're fucking coming to arrest me? Just use the bloody bell!

I'm annoyed. Irritated. It seems like a perpetual state of mind these days. Okay. Maybe not every day. Not yesterday. Definitely not yesterday during Emily's visit.

The thought of her brings a smile to my face, but it soon vanishes when there's another knock on the door that demands that I get up, that I rise from my comfortable seat here – not necessarily out of a need to find out who it is, but more to make them bloody stop.

I'm in the study. I fell asleep here.

Reluctantly, I haul myself up, causing papers to flutter to the floor. Well, they're not papers, per se, they're pages of a letter. Notice. Formal notice.

I remember now. I remember what I was reading before I fell asleep in here to the lullaby of nature beyond the glass.

It's the letter I received on Monday. The letter from the London firm of lawyers that I didn't recognise. The letter that first surprised and then irritated me. No, not irritated… that's putting it way too mildly. It angered me. Still not quite descriptive enough…it fucking infuriated me. That's more like it. It left me physically shaking and so bloody exhausted I ended up falling asleep in here.

Now, when I look at that printed letter staring up at me from the floor, I just think of resignation. It's just more shit on top of my pile of shit.

Oh, of course. It seems that the Gestapo's finished pounding on the door and its agents have now discovered the doorbell.

Who knows? If I'm lucky, it might be another gorgeous looking bird – one who will hopefully provoke the usual reaction in me, and not the insipid romantic comedy shit of yesterday. Someone who makes me hard. Makes me want to fuck her, because I could really do with a good fuck right now. When I say that, I'm talking about a no-strings-attached kind of a fuck without the foreplay bullshit – just some dirty, wild fucking sex!

Yep, that letter definitely has me rattled. You can tell by the way I'm being deliberately vulgar. It's my way of saying that I've spent my life being fucked over by people, so why shouldn't I return the favour? And no, I'm not boo-hooing and feeling sorry for myself. I'm way beyond that, trust me.

Anyway, you can relax, given the fact that I don't really have anybody to have sex with here. I suppose I could have a drink instead. On no, wait, I can't do that either on account of everybody in this shitty village being on my case. Watching everything that I do. And so, in my quest to clean my act up, play my part, fit in, and not draw attention to myself, this fucking house is as dry as a pharaoh's sock!

It's not that I didn't have the opportunity to remedy the situation, because I did. I spotted a whole array of top shelf booze in the village store, so somebody around here must enjoy a good tipple, but I just couldn't bring myself to buy any of it. Partly because of the so called *new* me and partly because of the ever-watchful gaze of the Stepford women around here. God forbid any of them – or you, for that matter – should frown upon me.

So, anyway, now that I've gathered the shitty letter, envelope, and some control over the current of rage that has just ripped through me once again, you will not be shocked to learn that I am regretting my new no-booze-in-the-house rule.

After all, who fucking cares what these people think of me? I don't know them. They don't know me. Why should I give a shit what anybody thinks of me? That's how it's always been and, I guess, given current circumstances, how it'll always be.

Oh, and no, I haven't forgotten there's somebody at the front door; I'm making my way there now but, again, I don't give a shit, since I doubt I'll be spending much longer with any of these people – especially if the delightful, greedy, bloody, and most likely cock-sucking step family have anything to do with it.

Oh, right. I didn't tell you.

The letter that, given the luxurious paper and envelope set, comes from a very well–to-do firm of London solicitors, is serving me notice that members of Mr. Roberto Battista's family – namely, Roberto Junior and Samantha, otherwise known as my step-siblings – intend to contest my late father's last will and testament.

Apparently, they're not satisfied with the millions of pounds and various properties they've already inherited, but they now intend to contest my father's decision to give me Dolce Vita, also.

The letter recommends that I retain counsel and that I communicate their details as soon as possible so that this matter may be discussed directly, with a view to reaching a mutually satisfactory settlement, before they begin pursuing all and any legal remedies available to them. Oh, and that I have 21 days from the date of the letter to submit the information requested; otherwise, they'll have no other option but to file relevant actions, regardless.

And there's me thinking that it was my wife's solicitors telling me she wanted shot of me.

Oh, every dark cloud, eh?

Another ring of the doorbell makes me yank the door open so fast that I nearly smack myself in the face with it.

An autumn breeze rushes in to greet me as if its wanting to hide from the chill, bringing with it the scents of honeysuckle and jasmine, and the slender shoulders of a grey coat and knitted hat.

"Hello?" I ask.

The shoulders turn to reveal a face that I recognise. "Um, Ava, isn't it?"

"Hello. Yes. Sorry. I didn't think you were in. I was about to leave, but then I noticed these." She's referring to the bed of flowers by the door. "They're beautiful," she continues thoughtfully. "Such a shame."

"Shame?"

"That they have to die."

I step out, following her gaze. Sure enough, every single flower head has wilted.

They all seemed fine yesterday.

"Right," I find myself saying. "I suppose it was only a matter of time. Winter will be here soon."

She nods, but says nothing. A seagull perched on the roof of the house seems to have more to add to the conversation, in fact.

Eventually, summoning what little is left of my so-called charm while stuffing all negative thoughts of a few seconds before to the back of my head, like dirty laundry in a drawer, I ask, "What can I do for you, Ava?"

She's still looking every which way, but at me. Eventually, eyes still lowered, she squeaks. "Um, well, I was hoping you would be able to see me."

I tilt my head. "See you?"

"As a client," she clarifies, quickly. Then she adds, "I tried to call, but then I don't have your number, so thought I would come over on the off chance that you might be free."

"Oh," I say.

Shit.

"Well, I…"

"… if it's inconvenient, then it's alright, I can come back some other time." Her voice is fast, apologetic.

She seems much shier than the woman who gave me a ride the other day. While that lady rarely made eye contact, she at least made conversation. This one appears to be much more timid. I get the impression that it wasn't easy for her to just show up at my door like this.

"Oh, no, please. Come in." I step aside.

She doesn't hesitate. Like a child who has been out way after her curfew, she hurries inside.

I close the door behind her and then take a few seconds to clear my thoughts, and to generally get a grip of my own emotions.

Then I turn around with one of my best smiles, but she isn't looking at me – she, like others before her, is busy taking in the entrance lobby and beyond.

"It's lovely in here."

"Yes, it is," I say, my voice flat since I'm nowhere near enjoying the compliment after that letter. "Please, come through," I say, gesturing to the study since I'm in no mood to be discussing the house or anything else right now. The only thing I'm really interested in is getting smashed out of my bloody brain. But, you and I both know that this place lacks such amenities.

I watch the scrunched-up woman, who reminds me of a little mouse, enter the study and pause in the middle while I close the door behind us.

Oh, please don't start going on about how fabulous the study is, too.

She doesn't. She just stands there, conspicuously surveying this new, uncharted territory. Her eyes roving like a lens. I imagine her pupils are fully dilated, probably with trepidation, as she takes in the books, desk, armchair, and then, dun-dun-duuuun… the sofa!

Battista, seriously?

Get a grip.

I have no idea what's wrong with me. Strike that. I do. Which means I should probably send this innocent looking bird home, but fuck that. I'm a professional.

Compartmentalise. Isn't that what you tell your clients?

I'm trying, but that letter's just stinging like a bloody… Those fucking greedy bastards! Greedy fucking arseholes!

"Do I sit here?" Ava asks in a voice that's so quiet I can barely hear it.

"Please," I say, with my usual gesture to the sofa and a gigantic smile.

So, given the regular stream of uninvited guests, I've decided to get organised, which means that there's already a tray with glasses and a bottle of water next to the sofa.

"Would you like something to drink, Ava?"

"Just water. Thank you," she says, gingerly taking a seat on the couch, but ignoring the drink right next to her.

I sigh inwardly, which is my way of disarming, despite the fact that I can feel the rectangular rigidity of the envelope stuffed into the pocket of my fleece. Its angular points pressing into me like barbed wire. I walk over to the couch, break the seal on the water, and pour it for my guest.

"Thank you," she says, taking the glass eagerly, like she's just traversed a desert.

She's nervous, and maybe if I stopped being a self-absorbed prick, I would take the time to talk to her, put her at ease.

Okay. So, let's take a look.

I don't want to pre-empt anything, because I would rather talk to her first. But, it's clear that she doesn't want to be here.

Shocker.

Most people don't want to be *here*, submitting themselves to the scrutiny of a stranger. I won't say I'm a complete stranger since, as you know, we've met before.

Most hate the idea of seeing a therapist because the very notion of it makes them think that there's something wrong with them, or that they're damaged in some way, to the point where they need to be *fixed*. Nobody wants to see themselves as *defective*. Be that of mind or body. It's another reason why many hate medical check-ups, for fear of what they might reveal. One minute they're bumping along the path of life, minding their own business, and the next, BAM! Something hits them from out of nowhere. Nobody wants that.

If it just happens, then it's fate, but if we willingly present ourselves to a doctor, asking him or her to check for potentially devastating news, then that's just asking for trouble.

And nobody wants that either.

In this case, presenting yourself at a therapist's house uninvited, for a chat, means that this lady has something to share, and yet is afraid of sharing it.

Of course, while I'm considering all of this, which probably happens over the space of five or so seconds, I'm taking a good look at her. She's dressed plainly; patterned dark brown skirt, white blouse, grey overcoat. The same one she was wearing the other day. From what I can see of her dark hair, it's platted and secured to her scalp under her woollen hat.

She may as well be wearing a burka.

"Can I take your coat for you, Ava?"

She hesitates, and then says quietly, "I'd rather keep it on if that's alright."

"Of course."

"I really like your home. It's pretty."

"Thank you."

"I love the view through that glass wall to the tree and garden. It's beautiful," she says with genuine wonder. "What type of tree is that?"

"It's an oak tree."

"It's huge."

"Yes. It's been here ever since I was a boy."

"How long is that?"

I pause and smile at her, sheepishly. "Um, well, the good part of forty years."

"That's still very young," she says knowingly, obviously sensing my reluctance to talk about my age.

Perceptive.

"And you've been a," she fumbles for the words, "a..."

"...Therapist", I help her out. "Yes, for plenty of that time."

She smiles. "You must get all kinds of people in here?"

"Well, as you know, I did in London. I've only just moved here," I say casually, although I know she's testing me, because we already had this conversation in the car. That or her memory might be failing her, but I get the impression it's the former.

There's a long pause, which I'm just about to break when...

..."So, how does this work?" she asks, somewhat awkwardly.

"Well..." again, I use my best smile, "why don't you start by telling me a bit about yourself?"

The question appears to take her by surprise, as if she hasn't come here to talk to a therapist, but more as if she has just presented herself at her gynaecologist for a problem she would much rather not have examined.

The reality is that, my role, if not handled delicately, can be far more invasive than any physical examination. With the latter, you can grin and bear it but, once the moment is over, you pull up your draws and get the hell out of there with, more than often, an ointment or potion for the problem.

Therapy is far more complex and potentially embarrassing since it's not just a one-off appointment, but a series of sessions that involve ruthless, detailed probing of the most painful thoughts and, sometimes, worse still, no matter how excruciating the process might be, they need to be revisited over and over again, and to the point of desensitisation so that the wound can be cleaned and dressed appropriately.

"I'm bored," she says, suddenly.

"I'm sorry?"

"I'm bored," she repeats confidently.

"Okay."

"Don't get me wrong. I don't need for anything. I have two beautiful children and a really loving husband who works hard and provides for us, but I'm just so…" she trails off here and a hand flutters up to her chest, where I can see that it's heaving inside of her open coat. She's breathing heavily, as if she's just revealed she's not of this world, and she's watching me now. It's as if after unburdening herself of this terrible secret, she's now able to make eye contact. She has chestnut eyes and they're now keenly observing me, which is something I haven't seen her do before.

She continues, "You know, my mother used to tell me that only boring people get bored."

"Do you think you're boring?"

"Yes."

"Why do you think that?"

"I just do. I mean, for years now all I've known is being a wife to my husband and a mother to our son."

"Son?"

"Yes, son." She looks at me, perplexed.

I smile. "In the car, you told me you had two children; a girl and a boy, and you repeated that earlier in this conversation."

She smiles as if she's been caught in a lie, and it's the first time since meeting this woman that I notice a certain twinkle in her eye.

She doesn't say anything, though, so I prompt her, "Did you lie, Ava?"

Her lips, that I'm now noticing may be devoid of lipstick, but are quite full and plump, are curving up into a wry smile.

"I didn't lie. I just withheld the truth."

"Do you think there's a difference?"

"Of course. My son always lies to me, but I don't take it personally. Did you brush your teeth? Yes. Did you pack away all of your things? Of course. Can you keep a secret? You bet. He's always fibbing."

"So, you think lying is acceptable, then?"

She shrugs. "Everybody lies. White lies, black lies, rainbow lies. It's instinctive. It's how we get through life. You lie to your wife, don't you, Marco?"

The question is pointed, and it broadsides me. It's not so much that she's asking the question, but more the way she's asking it. Like she already knows something about me.

"What is it you think you know about me, Ava?" The question leaves my lips unintended, and I'm surprised because I realise that it's not the therapist talking, but me. Which means I took the question personally.

Shit.

"I don't know anything about you," she responds. "The only *truths* I know about you are the ones you shared with me in the car." The emphasis on that word only fuels my paranoia.

Calm down. She doesn't know anything about you.

"Do you think I lied to you, Ava?"

"I don't know. Did you?"

Her once shy eyes are locked on mine and there's an intensity there. Sudden. Palpable.

It feels like she's suddenly playing a game with me. Like we've undergone a kind of teleportation chair swap.

Seconds lap by as we hold each other's gazes. Then, I laugh. She does, too.

"I'm sorry," she says. "See? I get like this. I get so frustrated, and now I'm taking it out on you."

"It's okay," I say, waving a hand. I was actually amused by the change in her personality. It's nothing like the person I met that day in the car or even the mouse that walked in here a few minutes ago.

She shifts in her chair as she struggles with her coat, which is caught underneath her.

"Are you sure you don't want me to take that for you, now?" I ask with a reassuring smile.

She looks at me, considers the question, and then slowly stands up and shakes the thing off.

"Thank you. I'll just place it here, if that's okay," she says, folding the coat and setting it down next to her.

"That's fine." I smile as she smooths out invisible creases from her skirt, pulls a face, and then sits back down.

"Mick, my husband, says that what we wear says a lot about us."

I rock my head from side to side. Weighing up the statement.

"You don't agree?" she asks.

"What do you think?"

"I asked you first," she says with a knit of her thin eyebrows.

I hesitate and try not to bridge my hands, stereotypically. I recall my first impression of her. She completely took me in. I'm a therapist and, as such, would normally notice this stuff. But then, I was too busy dealing with my own rubbish to notice the nuances of a stranger.

"I think it's inevitable that what we wear and how we hold ourselves should project something about who we are, but I don't think it's necessarily an accurate projection."

She smiles and shakes her head, as if she has no idea what I'm talking about, but, I don't know why, I get the impression that she's understood me perfectly. I go along with it. "For example, I could be a labourer and spend most of my time in my overalls, pushing a wheelbarrow, pulling out weeds, fixing things – yet, if I don a tux and buy tickets to the opera, it would be easy for me to be perceived as someone who is wealthy, maybe even famous, though the image I'd be projecting wouldn't necessarily reflect who I am."

Ava cocks here head curiously, as if she's carefully considering what she's just heard, and me, although it might be a little early, I decide to add, "And here's just another example. You mentioned that your husband said that what we wear says a lot about us. I get the impression that he's always been of this opinion?" She nods. "So, you've probably sought to please him, perhaps by dressing conservatively, using minimal makeup, and avoiding anything that's too showy, maybe. You might even use a generic brand of shampoo. Although, sometimes a girl has to have her own kind of exotic secret, right? At least, that is according to their suggestive Marketing campaigns."

She touches her hair, subconsciously, her eyes widening. "How do you…?"

I pretend I'm surprised. "What? You really use that brand? What is it? Herbal Essences?"

"How did you know that?"

I smile. "I use it, too. No, I'm kidding. I'm actually a L'Oréal kind of guy." I wink at her. "No, Ava, I don't think our clothing always reflects who we are."

She's smiling, broadly now, and I think we've made some progress. "So, with that in mind, why don't you tell me why you're here? Maybe start by telling me a bit more about you?"

I smile at her, but she looks down at her hands, which I notice she's been wringing so much that her knuckles are turning white.

"Ava?"

She whispers something, but I don't understand it.

"I'm sorry. Could you say that again?" I ask, subconsciously lowering my head to attempt eye contact with her.

Seconds go by. More hand wringing, and I'm just about to ask her again when she looks up at me, eyes full of something I don't quite understand, and, as if the walls can hear her, whispers once more, "I have a secret to tell you."

I nod. Then, I shuffle in my seat. "I'm listening."

She looks out to the garden and then back at me. She's obviously struggling with something, so I encourage her, "Ava, you should know that anything you say inside this room is strictly confidential and that…" I stop mid-sentence as I'm suddenly distracted by sounds outside of the study door. Subdued voices. Movement; a scuffing of shoes, a rustling of clothes.

What the hell…

Somebody, or more like a group of people, have entered the house and have decided to have a bloody chat right outside the door.

"What's the matter?" Ava asks, noticing my distraction since I am staring, probably glaring, at the door.

I can already feel the anger burning in my chest.

"I'm sorry," I say distractedly. "I seem to have some uninvited guests."

I half-expect whoever it is to knock, but they don't. Instead, they bloody carry on their discourse as if they own the place.

"I'm really sorry. Excuse me," I say, getting up from my seat and stalking over to the door. I yank it open as I consider how to tell this lot to fuck off without making a scene.

But there's nobody there.

I step out into the den; it's empty. All doors closed.

"Is everything okay?" Ava calls from behind me as I survey the empty room.

"Hello?" I call to the empty space, but the only response is my echo and the trickling of the fountain.

I freeze and listen for other sounds. Nothing, but the thump of my angry heart. I look up at the balcony; empty.

Shit. What's that all about? I know what I just heard. I run my hands through my hair while looking around the room once more, as if I could miss a bunch of people. Nothing.

The sound of Ava clearing her throat brings me back. Hesitantly, while keeping my eyes on the empty space, I return to the study and then slowly close the door behind me. I wait and listen for sounds, but hear nothing.

Nothing.

"Is everything okay?" Ava asks again, making me jump as she turns around on the sofa.

"Um, yeah. Sorry," I say, walking back to my seat. "I just thought I heard somebody at the door. You didn't hear anything, did you?" She pulls a face and shakes her head.

"Strange," I say, retaking my seat and glancing at the closed door. "Okay. Well, I'm sorry about that," I say, forcing a smile and looking at her.

I really want to get back into the moment, but I can already tell that that look has gone from her face, and that our conversational intimacy has been diluted.

"It's okay. I'm getting used to it," she says casually.

"Getting used to it?"

"Yes. Mick had a similar moment last night."

"Really?"

"Yes, he frightened me to death. I'd just woken up from a particularly bad dream, and noticed that he wasn't in bed. It's dark in the room, so I call out to him; no answer, but when I go to switch on the lamp, he suddenly speaks, tells me not to. Frightened me to bloody death. He's only standing at the foot of the bed, in the dark, staring out of the window. When I asked him what he was doing, he told me he thought he heard noises. So, I asked where, downstairs? He said no, outside the window."

"Did he tell you what kind of noise?"

She nods. "I asked him – was it a bird, an owl or something? He said no. He said it sounded like someone was scratching on the window, outside."

"You live in a bungalow?"

She shakes her head. "No, we don't, and that's just it. I told him to stop being daft, because we were upstairs and our house is just a stone building; there's no ivy or anything for anyone to climb."

"What did he say?"

"He said he knew that. That's why it scared him."

"Did he actually use the word *scared*?"

She shakes her head. "No, he didn't. He actually used the word *terrified*."

UNINVITED GUESTS

Wednesday Night.

Note to self. When in the middle of a session, try not to lose it by hearing imaginary voices right when a client is about to tell you something important.

Shit.

I don't know what that was all about, but I never did manage to get Ava back to that moment. She clammed up right after she told me the disturbing story about her husband, which is obviously something I wanted to hear more about – especially after the episode in my kitchen.

If I'm being perfectly honest, I felt unsettled for the rest of the afternoon and evening, which were interminable.

You see, it's true what they say; you don't really know what you've got until it's gone. In this case, I'm not talking about my family, for once, but online streaming services.

I can't remember if I've mentioned this before, or if you've guessed it, but there is no entertainment whatsoever in this house. No television, books, or radio of any kind, and I'm not talking about the fact that they don't work in this dead zone, I'm talking about the fact that they don't exist.

Which isn't altogether surprising. The old man came to this place to escape life, so the last thing he would have wanted was to bring it here with him. He would have wiled away the time drinking, eating good food and... eww, well, you know... I can't think about it too much because the thought makes me want to heave.

So, anyway, it's just me, myself, and I, staring at the four walls. There isn't so much as a magazine here. Not that I'm a big reader, but still, what I'd give for something to read right now...

And I'm not even going to talk about internet because, well, I'll just lose my mind.

So, anyway, with nothing else to do, I decide to swap listening to the creepy, creaky sounds of the wind in the skylight for the creepy, scratchy, flappy sound of the creatures in the attic, but not before performing security detail – twice. I check that all doors and windows are locked and that the alarm system is armed while imagining the film score to *The Shining* following me about the place.

I don't know what kind of party is taking place in that attic, but whatever creatures are lurking up there, presumably the bats, it seems like they're trying to burrow their way through the ceiling to get to me. At one point, they even dislodge some small flakes of plaster.

Are you fucking kidding me? Plaster. How big are these bloody things, anyway?

Yeah, so, I'm going to have to go and investigate. Um, well... not now, though. I'm many things, but I'm definitely not the stupid hero who decides to investigate the unknown in the dead of night with a flashlight.

No, that stuff can wait until the safe light of day. Besides, I wouldn't be able to see much in the dark anyway, would I? It makes perfect sense to go up there in the daytime.

So then, I'm tossing and turning. I've lost count of the amount of times I've plumped the pillows, shifted positions, and cast unwanted thoughts from my mind. Then, I take to counting the amount of times the lighthouse beam sweeps around the room while I suppress spontaneous images of my breaking out from this prison and being pursued by searchlights.

Anyway, as odd as it may seem, I highly recommend it because, somewhere within an hour, I finally close my eyes.

Sunshine. Summer breeze. The smell of the ocean. Fried onions. A hot dog stand. Laughing. I'm laughing. I'm happy. I'm blessed. I love. I turn to feel the sun on my face. It's warm, like soft fingers on my skin. But then it disappears. It's cold. I look up, and there's a shadow standing over me.

There are people in my room. Standing by my bed!

I open my eyes. Bolt upright.

I'm panting. Sweating. Wheezing.

I remain that way, one hand on my damp chest as if to still the pummelling of my heart. But that isn't the reason. I dreamt that somebody was touching me. Somebody with cold hands placed something on my chest.

I look down, as if I can see in the gloom. I can't. There's nothing there. My fingers feel nothing, and yet I *felt* it. It was ice cold.

I take a deep breath. There's nobody here. It was just a dream. A bad dream that felt real. I take another breath.

Calm yourself. Calm down.

And yet, my anxious heart continues to flutter like a trapped bird. I run my hand through my hair as I conclude that, not unlike Jessy's tucking of the hair behind her ears, I seem to have developed a similar self-assuring move.

Another lighthouse beam licks around the room like a security light. It's empty. There's nobody in here, but me and the shadows, and yet it felt so real. It felt like there were people in here, standing over the bed – standing over me!

Get a grip, Battista! Your mind is lacking stimulus, distraction, so it's conjuring things from nothing.

I'm right. I know I'm right, but still…

I reach for my phone and tap it. It's 02:03. The nights seem so long here. "Jesus."

I'm so tired. First, I couldn't get to sleep, and now I'm bloody exhausted.

I rearrange the pillows, allow myself to fall back onto them, and stare at the ceiling. At least the neighbours have quietened down, which means I can now hear the surf once more. Hypnotic. Calming.

I roll onto my side so that I can gaze out the window at the starry sky, and that's when terror knifes me in the gut as my limbs instantly turn to stone. I'm paralysed. No matter how hard I search my brain for a reaction to what I am seeing beyond the glass, all I can do is stare as my body begins to shake with horror.

I can see them – not one, but two humanoid, moonlit silhouettes. I can't make out their faces, but I can feel their eyes crawling all over me. Observing me as I cower beneath these sheets.

Another turn of the lighthouse beam licks around the room. Shadows grow and shift…and then they're gone!

I lunge for the light, snap it on, and instantly regret the action because now all I can see is my own reflection in the black glass, which itself makes me yelp with fright.

"Fuck!"

I snap the light off once more.

Nothing. There's nothing there! But I saw them. I saw them. I felt them, watching, scrutinising me!

Get a fucking grip!

It's true! They were there!

Get a grip! Think about it. You heard Ava's story, you dreamt there were people in the room, and then you hallucinated people hovering outside of your window. It's classic autosuggestion. You know this, Marco. You know this. Think about it.

Perhaps, but it doesn't stop me sliding out of bed, creeping over to the window, and cautiously peering out.

Stars twinkle like gems in a clear sky ruled by the full moon that spotlights the empty garden while shimmering on a glassy ocean.

I squint into another sweep of the lighthouse's beam as I press my nose against the cold glass to get a better look at the wall. There's nothing there. All I can see are the veiny stretches of thin vine that's presumably ivy, but there's no way that could have sustained any weight. Nobody could have got up here without a ladder.

And yet, I'm still afraid.

RYAN

Thursday. 10:03.

So, after last night's truly terrifying parasomnia, you won't be surprised to learn that I slept like crap, whatever that's supposed to mean, for what was left of the night. And that's only when I did manage to fall back to sleep, because after my *encounter,* the house seemed to come alive with all sorts of strange sounds I hadn't heard before. Sounds that I had previously attributed to the gale that now appears to be relentless around this place.

So, now I'm lying in bed, staring at the ceiling again. There's no sunshine dazzling the room this morning – just the filtered remains of the grey slate sky.

When I first arrived here, I thought the so called creak and groan of the house was endearing. Now, it's just become part of my environment, an ever-present paranoia-inducing characteristic that, given the oddities around here lately, has got me expecting a tsunami to burst through the windows at any moment. That, or my beloved tree. Speaking of which, this, too, appears to be nothing like I remember it. I used to find it comforting. Now the leaves hiss and the branches moan at night, like some demon I've unwittingly conjured from the pit of the earth.

Shit.

Now I'm wide awake, yet tired.

Oh, and I'm losing it.

Did you just read all the crap I've just told you? What the hell? It doesn't even sound anything like me. Paranoia, snakes, demons. I'm supposed to be a therapist, for crying out loud; I'm supposed to rationalise flights of bloody fantasy – not conceive them because of one shitty nightmare.

But, I know what this is about. This is all about that letter. The rage that I felt and the repression that I had to go through thanks to my unexpected client.

Deep inside, I must be worried that those bastards are going to take the house away from me. That I'll be left with nothing, and that all of this will have been for nothing. That I won't have the money to buy a new home and, in some perverse way, my marriage back.

I'm such an idiot.

If there's one thing Ellie and I have always talked about, it's the fact that money doesn't make you happy. Well, she says that, of course, because her parents are loaded. Extremely wealthy. My opinion? Money can bring happiness, albeit temporarily.

God, though. I'm losing my mind! Being here on my own involves way too much introspection, even for me.

So, pull it together. Have a shower. Get productive. You're back in London tomorrow. Civilisation. Admittedly, you've got to endure an hour with the shrink. But you'll be reconnected again. Able to make telephone calls again. So, take control. Stop whining.

I sit up and reflexively run my hands through hair that has been cut far shorter than I'd normally like. But still, at least my beard is neat and I no longer resemble someone out of ancient scripture.

I'm looking forward to getting out of here tomorrow. I mean, I know it's not the house. It is just a building, but I can't help but think that this place is getting me down for all new reasons. And to think that…

What the fuck?

What's that smell? I sniff the air. What is that? Smells like… antiseptic cream. Or is that disinfectant? It must be drifting up the stairs, under the door. God knows there's a bloody draft underneath that thing. It was howling all last night like the brainchild of an overzealous special effects artist. In fact, I'd go as far as saying that this place is a natural setting for anything that would be supernatural. And to think that those are, were, my favourite types of movies. Oddly, I haven't felt the urge to watch any of them since starring in my own. Not that I could in this place.

I slide out of bed. I'm in my shorts, so I pull on a T-shirt. It's chilly in here today. Too chilly, even for me, so I pull on a fleece, too. It's an odd combination, but who cares? It's just you and me here.

I move around the bed. The smell is stronger now. It's filled the room like someone is mopping floors just outside of the door, if not in the room.

What the hell?

I fall to my knees and sniff the planks of wood, which creak at me as if protesting the intimacy.

What a sight this must be. Me on all fours now, sniffing the fucking bedroom floor.

Seriously?

But there's nothing here. Just faint wood, dust, must.

I sniff near the door. Nothing. Yet the smell still lingers in the air. It must be coming from downstairs.

I pull the door open and it greets me with a loud creak. Did I mention that before? No, I didn't, because it's new. I don't remember it doing that when I arrived.

Yeah, like I said – film set.

"Hello?"

No, I don't know why I called out either. Or actually, I do. It's because I'm half expecting to find some old lady in an apron, with a duster in her hand and an overenthusiastic smile on her face. But I know that shouldn't be possible, because even if Harvey still had a spare set of keys, he and his wife wouldn't have been able to enter the house because of the bolts I threw across the door last night.

Well, I did tell you that paranoia was creeping up on me.

"Is anybody here?"

You can hardly blame me for asking, can you? I haven't had a day's peace since arriving here.

Then, right on cue, the clang of the doorbell startles me.

This has got to be a joke. It's barely gone ten in the bloody morning – not to mention that I was just thinking about it, however sarcastically!

Maybe it's the cop.

Now, of all the visitors that have shown up at my door, why would she be the first person I think of?

No comment.

I look at myself. I'm beyond caring. And besides, if it is her, she's seen me wearing less.

Reluctantly, I make my way down the stairs, sniffing as I go.

There's no disinfectant smell down here.

I snatch a glimpse of myself as I pass the mirror. Oh, okay. Right, I look worse than I thought. Okay.

I pull the bolts back and, in what has become a traditional flourish, I yank the door open.

To find a young bloke. Shorter than me. Jeans, black T-shirt, brown leather coat, and aviator glasses. A celebrity on my doorstep, first thing in the morning. He's tapping something out on his phone and doesn't bother to look up.

"Hi," I say. The who-the-fuck-are-you-and-what-are-you-doing-here question is clear in my tone.

Eventually, he glances up at me. "Doctor Bat, Bat…"

"…Battista, yes," I help him, begrudgingly.

"Battista. Italian, huh?" he asks, eyes still on his phone.

"Yes. Can I help you?"

"Yeah, I've got a meetin' with you this morning." I squint at him, equivocally, so he pulls a face. "You weren't expecting me, were ya?"

"Should I have been?"

"Yeah. Your pal said he was going to send you a text."

"My pal?"

"Yeah, gay dude. David."

My ears prick up. "David sent you here?"

"Yeah, kind of. Well, he kind of knows my agent, and he sent me here." The boy, because he must still be in his teens, looks me up and down and, suddenly, I don't know why, I wish I had pulled on some jeans, since I'm feeling exposed figuratively and literally. "You haven't got the foggiest who I am, have ya?"

"Haven't we already established that?" I ask.

"Oh well. If that's the case, it's no problem. I've got other stuff I could be doing today anyway."

He turns and, interestingly, limps away.

"Hey, hold on."

He stops.

"Did David really send you to me?"

He turns back to me, shifting his weight on his feet. "Haven't we already established that?" he asks, mimicking my previous statement, and I want to slap him.

Smart arse. You showed up on my doorstep. The mood I'm in, it won't take much for me to follow through, but only it'll be a punch in the mouth, not a slap.

I force a smile. "Come in."

The cheeky shit rolls his eyes and then skilfully limps by me, into the house.

I glance at the driveway. A gleaming black Range Rover SUV shines back at me.

Like I said. Celebrity.

"Wow, nice gaff," my visitor is saying appreciatively as I walk into the house and close the door behind us. He's from London. Tottenham, by the sounds of it.

"Thanks," I say. "I didn't catch your name."

"That'll be because I didn't tell ya, mate."

"Right. Mr Anonymous, what exactly can I do for you?" I say sharply. I'm in no mood for this shit.

"I take it you're not a footy fan then?" my visitor asks, his eyes roaming around the room.

"Not really," I say, crossing my arms.

He nods, and I get the impression that he's happy with the news since his shoulders had been up, squared, like he was spoiling for a fight, and now they seem to drop.

The phone in his hand beeps and he looks at it. "Shit. My tweet didn't post. There's no signal."

Inside, I'm grinning. "Yes, unfortunately, It's a bit of a dead spot here," I say. The artificial sadness is thick in my voice.

Only after satisfying himself that there really is no signal does he finally push the phone into his pocket and look up. Then, as if he's posing for a close-up, he removes his shades, revealing deep blue eyes.

"You're a footballer then?"

"So, you do know me?"

"No. You mentioned footy. You're driving a brand spanking new Range Rover and you take yourself seriously. it isn't much of a leap," I say. He looks at me, obviously trying to work out if that was a dig. It was. I don't even know this spoiled brat and he's already getting on my nerves. He's still observing me, though, so I repeat, "What can I do for you?"

"How old are you?" he asks, limping a couple of steps closer to me.

Okay, so at this stage, you might be wondering, and thus by association you're expecting me to be wondering, why this bundle of joy, with short blonde hair, is limping around the place. Probably from a football injury.

Either way, unlike you, I don't care. In fact, I don't think I'd be unduly concerned if he limped the fuck out.

That said, arms still folded, I reply, "Forty-two. You?"

"Nineteen. You're not as old as I thought. I mean, you're old – just not *as* old," he explains.

"Well, I'm sorry to disappoint you."

"Oh no, I'm not disappointed."

"Were you expecting a sixty-year-old fella with a beard and an over-worn jacket?"

"Yeah, something like that. I'm Ryan, by the way, Ryan James." He keeps his eyes on me, presumably to see if his James Bond pronouncement means anything to me. It doesn't.

"What can I do for you, Ryan?"

"Don't you have an office, a study or something?"

I consider the question. "I do, but it's normally reserved for me and my clients."

"What do you think I'm doing here?"

"That's what I've been trying to find out."

"How much do you make an hour anyway? Fifty, hundred quid? Do I pay now for my chat or after?"

I know he's testing me. Just like I know this is a defence mechanism. He's a young lad with a potentially embarrassing problem, and he's been asked to drive out here to see me, but, shit, he chose the wrong time to push my buttons. Anyway...

"Is money important to you, Ryan?"

"Isn't it to everyone?"

"Well, I suppose it is. Just different people view its importance differently."

"Is that right? So, it's probably really important to you since you need to be able to pay the mortgage on this place."

"Actually, I own it."

"Fuck me, Doc! You own this pad? You must be much more expensive than I thought. Either way, it doesn't matter – I probably make more in a week than you do in a year anyway." His voice is casual as he plucks out his phone, glances at the screen, frowns, pushes it back into his pocket, and then smiles at me.

Yeah, he's a prick. But young.

"Probably," I say with a smile. "So, who do you play for?"

"If you don't know, Doc, then there's no point telling ya. If you're interested, you can easily Google me. 1st division, five million Twitter followers... kind of speaks for itself."

"Does it?"

He looks at me and eventually smiles. "I get it. With your age, and then being stuck out here, you're probably falling a bit behind on the times."

I shake my head. Silly boy. "The study's through there," I say.

We walk. Or, more specifically, I walk after Hoppalong and suppress the urge to kick him up the arse.

I close the study door behind us, but the kid has stopped by the bottled boats collection. "Fucking 'ell, look at this shit?" he whispers incredulously. "Do you collect these?"

"My dad did."

"They're fucking mental."

"You like them?"

"That's what mental means, Doc," he says, turning around.

"So, where are you from?" he asks. "You obviously aren't from around here."

"I'm from London. East End, originally."

"Fuck off! You're not from the East End," he says with a disbelieving sneer.

I smile. "I am. I moved about a bit in my teens, but yeah."

"You sound like you come from Chelsea."

I laugh. "You think?"

"That, or you went to school somewhere else."

I smile. "You've got me. I did spend some time at boarding school, yes."

"Still, you're managing to hide the old accent quite good."

"You think I'm hiding it?"

"Course. Otherwise, you'd be sounding more like me."

"What do you think you sound like?"

"You know. All common-like," he emphasises the vowels to demonstrate.

"Do you think how someone speaks makes a difference to who they are, Ryan? How they're perceived?"

He looks at me and cocks his head. "Doc, come on, I'm not even officially a patient and you're already trying to get inside my head."

There's a pause.

"So, you said that your agent knows David?"

"Yeah."

"And that you were sent here. Do you want to tell me why?"

"What, no foreplay, Doc?"

"It's a reasonable question. I can't really help you if I don't even know why you're here."

"Well, isn't that all part of your training? Isn't that what you lot do? Examine words, mannerisms – analyse all of that subtext shit?"

I laugh. "I don't know if I'm that skilled, Ryan. I'm just an old therapist, remember? I'm not a spook."

"You're not? Fuck, well, that's boring then," he says with mock disappointment.

He limps across the room, looks out onto the garden, and releases an appreciative whistle. Then, he turns and gestures at the couch, inquisitively.

I nod.

He sits, spreading his arms out over the back of it. "Hey, this thing's comfy."

"I'm glad you like it. So, I'm assuming you play professionally, right?" I ask, since I'm tiring very quickly of the cloak and dagger rubbish. And I know I'm not going to get much more out of him about David. Like when and where did he recommend me. Was it before or after last Saturday? No, I have a choice. I can throw this jumped-up tosser out of my house or I can play along.

Now, the tired me wants to do the former, to tell the little shit to sling his hook and guide him out of the house with my own footie flourish. The other, the more rational me, the psychotherapist, is telling me that everything the teenager is exhibiting is typical. He's obviously successful out there, in the real world, and yet here, on my couch, he's way out of his comfort zone, and he's testing me, to see if I'm trustworthy.

Oh, and I said that I had two choices, but I mean three. The third one is much more practical. If that letter comes to anything, I'm going to need all the money I can get. This kid, sitting on the couch in front of me, examining his phone for a signal for what feels like the hundredth time since he got here, most likely has plenty of it.

Enough said.

"Yeah. That's what 1st division means, Doc. I play professionally. I'm what they call a rising star. Just signed with a major club, which is why my manager is having a shit-fit about what happened."

"Right. So, what happened?"

"Do you go out much, Doc? I mean, you can't see much action stuck here in these four walls, can ya?"

Don't remind me.

"Well, I'm here for the quiet."

"Quiet? What, you writing a book or something?"

"No, but there's an idea."

"Don't do it. A lot of work for little in return."

"Why, have you written a book?"

"Nah, but I know people who have. So, what do you do for fun around here? Bet you must have some mental parties here in the summer."

"Well, you know us *old* folk; when you reach my age, it's all slippers and pipe tobacco," I say with a smile.

"Ah, you're taking the piss now, aren't ya?"

"So, what do *you* do for fun, Ryan?"

"Nah, I think the question you're looking for, Doc, is, what do I not do?"

"Okay. Well, if I asked what you didn't do, that would be boring, surely. So, why don't you give me a flavour. What is it like to be Ryan James? For example, why don't you tell me about your day yesterday? Did you play?"

"Fuck me. You really do live in a bubble, don't ya? Yeah we played, against those idiots at Plymouth, and we thrashed em. Lads were buzzing, because not only did we win, but Arnie – we call him that because he's built like a shithouse – won the bucket challenge."

I squint, curiously.

"Of course, you being old and all, you wouldn't know, would ya?" The question's obviously rhetorical. "So, the bucket challenge's when one of us stands in the middle of the locker room and has to field headers from the rest of the team, all 10 of 'em, or all of the lads that happen to be there at the time. He then has to successfully *head* the ball into a bucket in the centre of the room. It's kind of a ritual. We take it in turns at each of the games."

"What happens if you don't manage to head all of the balls?"

"The game ends until next time. Anyway, we decided to go out to celebrate. Ali, my best mate, decides to invite a few of his friends from work, too. You know, meet the stars kind of thing."

"How did you feel about that?"

He shrugs. "No skin off my nose. The more, the merrier. I was only interested in one thing – getting smashed and sex, of course. It'd been a couple of days.

"So, first we end up at one of those poncey wine bars. You know the type, right? One of those minimalist places with electronic optics and LED lights everywhere. I can't remember what the bloody place was called. Was it Breathe? Air? I don't know. Anyway, this place is just off Piccadilly. The music's good, loud. None of that garage shit. It's more house. Deep house. You know what that is, right?"

I nod and smile.

"Check you. There's me thinking you might be a bit too old for that shit."

"I'm still in my forties, Ryan. We pretty much invented that," I make air quotations with my fingers, "shit."

He looks at me, curiously, "Yeah, as I said, old. Anyway, Ali got the first round – shots, you know, to get the wheels greased, before settling into the usual stuff."

"And what is the usual stuff?"

"Do you wanna hear this story or not?"

I hold my hands up.

"So, we start with shots. I don't know exactly what they were, I just know that those things were on fire, literally. So, as we're knocking them back, a group of birds come in, and that's when the party really starts. It was their last night in London. They were heading back the next day. Swedish, I think. You know – blonde hair, fit as fuck. So, they didn't have the foggiest about who we were and, in their own words, they were wanting to make the most of their last night.

"So, by this time, Nathan and the rest of Ali's mates arrive with their groupies. They'd already been to one of the clubs down the road and had their fill, which meant we had some serious catching up to do. So we ordered a couple of Hurly Burly's and King Konobos. Do you know what they are?"

I shake my head.

"They're fruit, generally watermelons and pineapples, with their insides carved out and loads of booze poured in. Vodka, Grey Goose, orange juice, and fuck knows what else. Anyway, this thing is filled, straws shoved in, and then it's a fucking free-for-all. We ordered a couple and, to be honest, I wasn't that keen at first, because while I can drink anyone under the table, I'm not a good mixer. It's not that I can't handle it. It's just that that shit doesn't agree with me. Do you know what I mean? Anyway, I didn't want to look like a pussy in front of all these birds. Especially this blonde; she was as fit, massive blue eyes, wearing denim hot-pants and a bra. Just my bag."

He suddenly and finally pauses and takes a breath, and then he looks at me curiously. "What about you, Doc? Do you have a type?"

I nod. "Sure."

"And?"

"Well, I wouldn't say I have a type, per se, although I do prefer brunettes, sometimes even redheads... but then, my wife is blonde, so."

Fuck. Did I just say that out loud? To him?

"Sometimes you prefer redheads?" the cocky bastard repeats with a grin as he raises his eyebrows.

"Figure of speech, Ryan," I say as casually as I can, and even throw in my own smile.

He watches me, as if he can read my face. Then, "You been married long?"

"Yes, a few years now."

"You happy?"

Shit. What a rookie bloody mistake. I got so wrapped up in his story, which, by the way, sounded bloody awesome to me. Especially right now.

I realise that I'm automatically rocking my head from side to side, making a mock show of my deliberation, when I'm pissed off for letting my guard down. Now, I'm weighing up whether I even want to go down the whole wife path. The last thing I want to think about during a session is Ellie, and Toby. But, hey, guess what? I already am.

I swallow the lump in my throat, smile and deal a cliché, "Oh, you know, like most relationships, it has its ups and downs."

"Huh." He observes me in that freakish way of his – direct eye contact, hardly blinking – and for a second it looks like he knows I'm talking rubbish, but suddenly he adds, "I couldn't get married."

"Why not?"

"What's the point? Seems like just an expensive excuse to get smashed."

"Is that really how you see it?"

"Don't most people?"

"Well, many see it as a very important way of expressing their affection for their partner, of showing their love and commitment."

"Hypocrites. You're the doctor. You tell me, but last I looked, over forty percent of marriages end in divorce. You can't ignore odds like that, mate."

"You looked?"

"What?"

"You said, last time you looked."

"Figure of speech, Doc, don't get excited."

"So, your parents are divorced?"

"Not yet."

"Not yet?"

"Are you going to repeat everything I say? Because this is going to get boring much faster than I thought."

"Sorry." I hold up my hands again in a *mea culpa* gesture. Then, I restructure my question. "What made you say that?"

"Well, they can only go on pretending for so long."

"You think your parents are pretending to be married?"

"No, I think they're pretending to be *happily* married. Well, my mum does; my step-dad just does whatever the fuck he wants."

"What do you mean?"

He shoots me a wry look. "Doc, come on."

I nod. "So, you think your step-father is having an affair?"

He laughs, then guffaws, and then he laughs some more. Eventually, he says, "'Having an affair?' What is this, daytime soap opera?" He chuckles some more. "Having an affair? Who the fuck talks like that? No, my step-dad is not" – and now it's his turn to make speech marks with his fingers –" having an affair, or sleeping with them; he's fucking them, banging them." He pauses, then follows the thought with, "Where the fuck did that expression even come from? Sleeping with someone. Let's face it – the last thing you do, at least for me, is get some kip, right?"

I nod, then allow some welcome silence to fill the room. Then, "You've mentioned your step-dad a couple of times. Where, if you don't mind me asking, is your father?"

He hesitates, as if the question has surprised him, and then he says quickly, "He's dead. He died a long time ago."

"How long?"

"What, you want details?"

"I'm just interested in knowing how recent your loss was. I'm sorry to hear it, though. Can I ask what happened?"

"Cancer."

"That must have been difficult for you. How old were you?"

He's staring at me again. Actually no, it's more of a scowl this time. I hesitate, "What's the matter?"

"Doc, I'm not a fucking idiot. Just because I talk all common-like, it doesn't mean I'm an idiot." His last words were pointed.

"I don't understand."

"You asked how long ago. I said I didn't want to say, so then you asked how old I was at the time, so you can work out how long ago it actually was."

"I can honestly say that wasn't my intention, but Ryan, you came to me, remember? You obviously want or need to talk to me about something. So, we're talking. But if you don't want to talk, then you don't have to." My voice is firm – not quite an accurate reflection of how I'm really feeling, although I have calmed down quite a bit now. I've switched to psychotherapist mode, which automatically dampens most of my emotive triggers.

That, and I don't know... there's something about this arsehole that I can relate to, although, presently, I have no idea why.

"I was thirteen," I hear him say, suddenly.

"That must have been rough."

"Yeah," he says, solemnly. It's the first sign of vulnerability. This, obviously, tells me a lot about his relationship with his biological father.

Then, he grins, and is back to his usual prick self. "Still, Mum got over it fast enough, though."

Yet, I can tell that his smile is forced. With his lips. Not his eyes. "Was your father a supporter?"

"He loved it. He's the whole reason I started playing."

"It's obvious you love it. How old were you when you first started?"

He blows air over his lips as he recalls, "No idea. Probably seven, eight."

"You must miss the fact that he isn't here to witness your success." Shit. I know the moment the words leave my lips that it's the wrong thing to say.

He's glaring at me. "What do you think?" he asks acidly.

Shit. I'm really off my game, if you excuse the pun. I should have just sent this lad home. I'm in no fit state to be dealing with something like this right now.

There's a very long pause, during which the footballer pulls out his phone once more and checks the display. I can tell that this may well be a habit, but it's also an avoidance tactic.

"Fucking hell! How the 'ell do you survive out here with no bloody phone signal?"

"You get used to it after a while," I say calmly, but am of course reminded of how annoying it bloody is.

Thanks for that.

"Still, I suppose it's not really a problem if you don't have that many people who want to hear from you. Right?" He taps his Nike trainers on the floor, impatiently, as if he's waiting for a bus. They look brand new. Probably part of some extravagant sponsorship deal.

I ignore the obvious dig even though it needles me. "So, how was the rest of your evening? You told me about the match, the girls, the booze, but you didn't finish the story. What else happened?"

He laughs. "What, you need the details, Doc? Are things that dull around here?"

"Well, I thought you were telling me about that particular evening for a reason. Did something else happen that you wanted me to know about?"

He looks at me as if he's going to continue, but instead he turns and looks out the window.

I take my cue. "Okay, why don't you tell me about the rest of your week? What else happened?"

"Seriously? Just like that. You're just gonna ask me how my week was?"

"Why not?"

"Fuck, Doc." He's shaking his head again, forcing a laugh.

"What?"

"You just get straight down to the nitty gritty, don't ya? I mean, where's the preamble? Where's the foreplay? You're not gonna get far, just shooting your load like that, mate."

"I don't understand."

"Yes, you do. You understand alright. So don't give me that shit. I mean, I want this to be over and done with, but even I know that this, this therapy –" there go those speech marks again –"isn't going to be done in a day."

"Okay. How long do you expect it to take?"

He hesitates. "I don't know, a couple of weeks, a month. I don't really give a shit. The sooner the better. I just want to get back to playing."

"I just asked about your week, Ryan."

"You weren't asking about me about my week, Doc."

"What was I asking about?"

"You weren't asking about my week," he says, seriously, catching my gaze and holding it for a few seconds.

And that's when I see something in there. I don't know what exactly, but something. After everything he's told me, there's something about what I just said that touched a nerve, sparked anger.

So, what do I do? I get my revenge by doing my job. I prod him some more. "What was I asking about, Ryan?" I push.

"You were asking about what happened right after you were trying to establish if I had daddy issues."

I nod. Accepting the accusation. "Do you want to talk about it?"

"Well, isn't that why I'm here?" he returns, standing up and turning to the window. "To talk, to spill my guts so you can get all psycho on my ass, spout some shit about why I feel the way I feel, dream the things I dream." I watch him limp over to glass and look out of it. "Hey, sick view, Doc."

"Yeah, I like it."

"I bet it set you back a few. You must make a killing out of listening to nutcases share all of their shit about their lives."

"Are you interested in buying property, Ryan?"

"Are you selling?"

"Actually, I am."

"I would. It's a seller's market right now."

"Really?"

"Yeah."

"You're into property?"

"No, I listen to the news."

He finally turns to face me. He's smiling, but I can tell it's just for my benefit.

He's holding my gaze again. He's good at doing that. Only now he looks younger. The cocky young man, now a little boy, dreading *the talk*. At least that's what I see behind those blue eyes. I see it and recognise it. It's me, each and every time Ellie or anybody hovers around the subject of my youth. For me, that's in the past. There's no point talking about it, I tell them.

Oh, the irony.

I know that makes me a hypocrite. Of course. I never told you otherwise, did I? Believe me, I'm much happier repressing, and you're much better off not knowing.

"Do you not want to talk about what happened, Ryan?" I ask.

He shrugs as if he doesn't care. "Well, we can, but I doubt there's much you haven't already read online. Fuck, it was trending on Facebook for days."

"Well, as you've pointed out. Reception here isn't very good…"

"…what, no Wi-Fi either?"

"…and I'd rather hear it from you."

"What, you don't believe everything you read, Doc? Or in your case, don't read."

"Should I?"

"Fuck! That gets really annoying after a while."

"What does?"

"You! Always answering a question with a question. Does it? Should it? Should I? Do I? Jesus! You must drive your missus fucking nuts with that shit," he says, perching himself back on the couch.

I don't say anything.

He nods, knowingly. "You do, don't ya?"

I cock my head. "Occupational hazard. With you, it's demanding fans; with me, it's questions."

There's a long pause. Then, "It's quiet in this place. Peaceful."

"Yes. It isn't London, but you get used to it after a while."

He sighs and lowers his head, but lifts his gaze so he's looking at me once more. "What do you want me to say, Doc? I wrapped the Range Rover around a lamppost. But then, loads of people have accidents every day. Insurance companies make a killing off that very thing... This is fucking ridiculous. I don't even know why I'm here!" His frustration propels him off the couch once more and he starts limping and then hobbling around the room, as if forcing his leg into recovery, as one does when trying to bring life back to a numbed leg that stubbornly refuses to work.

I give him a few seconds. Then, "Ryan, please. You're not doing your injury any good by applying pressure to it like that. Please," I say softly, motioning to the couch. "Take a seat."

He stares at me, but then reluctantly complies.

I wait, and then, "My guess is, Ryan, that if you're here... Or, more specifically, if your agent recommended that you come and see me, it's probably because he or she thinks there's much more to the accident than you've told me so far. That, or it's one of a series of things that you've done which are of concern."

He says nothing. He's staring at his shiny new trainers.

"Ryan?"

No answer.

"What else has been happening with you?"

Still no answer. Silence, but for the gale whistling around the house.

"Have there been a lot of accidents lately?"

No answer.

"Were they all accidents? How did you hurt your leg?"

He looks up, suddenly. "Jesus, Doc! What's with the questions?"

His eyes are darting everywhere but at me, which is an obvious change to how we've been interacting up until this moment. But I know I'm onto something. I keep going. "Ryan, you are here for a reason. You are here because your agent, and maybe even you, think something is wrong. If you don't talk to me, I can't help you."

"How the fuck would *you*, or *them* know it wasn't an accident?" he spits.

"Them? Insurance company? Your management team? Your family?"

"Everyone. Including the fucking press. Everybody, including you – you all think you know it all when really you don't know shit!"

"Were you drinking at the time?"

His glare gives me my answer.

"Is drinking a problem for you, Ryan?"

"Depends what you mean by problem."

"You know what I mean. Do you drink to help yourself relax? Help you fall asleep?"

He shakes his head. "Fuck, you really haven't got the foggiest about what it's like in this industry, do you?"

"No, Ryan, I don't. I'm just an old therapist who's about ready to claim his bus pass. I wouldn't have a clue. So, why don't you enlighten me?" My tone is much more forceful than I've intended.

He thinks about this for a few seconds, and then says, "Actually, I've got an idea – why don't you go fuck yourself!" he yells the last part of the sentence, his wide blue eyes now narrow and burning. He's angry, but I find that I'm actually grateful he's still in his seat.

"I knew this was a mistake," he says next, standing up.

Shit.

"Why don't you want to be here, Ryan?" I throw after him as he limps towards the door.

He pauses and laughs again. Dry. Incredulous. "Why the fuck do you think? Only yanks, queers, and people who are up themselves are into this whole self-analysis shit."

"Says who?"

"Says me!"

"Why don't you want to be here, Ryan?" I repeat, calmly.

He turns and gawks at me as if I'm an idiot. "You're fucking mental, you are. You're in the wrong job."

"Why's that?"

"Because you obviously don't know what the fuck you're doing."

He makes for the door once more.

"It's a simple question, Ryan," I say loudly.

He whirls around and yells, "I just don't!" His tone is petulant, childish. He pulls the door open.

"I know how it feels, Ryan," I call after him.

"You don't know shit," he hisses without turning to me.

"I do. I know what it's like to have to be somewhere you don't want to be, at the same time knowing that it's the only way to get to the one thing you really want. In your case, it's getting back to playing."

He freezes. There's a long pause broken by the call of a wood pigeon. Then, slowly, he turns to me, the vibrancy gone from his eyes, replaced by a dark veil of something. I can't work out what.

I know now that this is serious. Much more serious than a rich kid gone wrong.

"And in yours?" he croaks.

I rock my head, thoughtfully, and I realise that I'm breathing heavily, that my heart is working overtime.

Shit.

"I'm sorry?" I ask, but I'm stalling. I know what he's asking.

"You said that in my case it's getting back to playing. What's it in yours?"

It's my turn to avoid his gaze, but it's too late to hide. Besides, this is the best opportunity I have to gain some trust credits with this guy, despite the fact that it isn't protocol.

"In my case," I say slowly, "in my case, it's getting my family back."

He nods, as if he was expecting me to reveal this very thing. Then he follows that up with, "I just want to play football."

"What's stopping you?"

"Everything."

I'm about to ask another question, but I stop myself and instead say, "Ryan. I know this is difficult for you, but you need to trust. I'm not your enemy. I really do want to help." My words are soft, sincere, soothing like the muffled sound of the ocean behind the glass.

"Do you?"

"If I can."

"Then sign me off." The light has returned to his eyes, and he limps forward. "Tell them that I've seen you, we had a chat, and you don't think there's anything wrong with me."

I shake my head.

"Come on, Doc. It won't cost you anything. In fact, you'll earn from it. I'll pay ya double, triple your usual rate."

"It doesn't work that way, Ryan."

"It can, though. You know it can."

"It can't. Injury aside, assuming that I'm correct in filling in the blanks here. There's something that's really troubling you, and it's affecting your lifestyle choices and your profession. The profession that you and no doubt your father worked really hard for."

Tears build in his eyes like angry storm clouds, and then he spits, "Fuck you!"

"Ryan…"

"Fuck you! You condescending prick! You know fuck-all about me. You don't know nothing about my dad. Who the fuck do you think you are?"

"Ryan…"

"I should knock your fucking teeth to the back of your throat!" he snarls through clenched teeth as he moves towards me, aggressively. I don't move. I don't even flinch. I've seen this before.

In me.

He's bearing down on me now. Fist raised. Breath thick and fast. Face contorted and hot with rage.

I continue, slowly, meeting his gaze. "Ryan, even if it was within my gift to sign you off, as you put it, I can't do that. Injury and actual details aside, it would be negligent of me. Unethical. The way you're behaving in this very moment only proves that." I glance at his fist, then persevere. "But I am prepared to do you a deal, though. If you sit down and tell me exactly what happened, and then promise to come and see me for at least two more sessions, I promise to review your progress at that time and, all being well, I'll recommend you go back to supervised training, as long as you keep talking to me." The words were spoken fast. I pause to swallow, and then, "What do you say?"

He's so close I can feel his breath on my face. The heat of his body.

Seconds tick by as he processes my proposal. Then, suddenly, slowly, he lets his fist fall by his side.

DOCTOR ETHAN HOLMES

Friday. 09:31.

So here it is. The day we've all been waiting for.

I don't know how I feel about being back in London. On the one hand, I'm happy, relieved, since it feels like a return to humanity. On the other, I'm finding the place particularly noisy, grimy, and smelly even, after the quiet and freshness of the coast. And, as much as I don't want to acknowledge it, I consider doing an about-face and catching the next train back.

All this, and it's barely been a week since I left.

Don't get excited. I don't think it's because I've fallen in love with that place by the ocean; I think it's more to do with the fact that London's noise, and the city's air pollution is jarring after a few days of nothing but nature's symphony.

This, as well as the fact that I'm in no hurry to spend an hour in the office of some jumped-up, overpaid, pretentious prick that I've been coerced into seeing.

Sound familiar?

Yes, I realise that there's much about that young footballer that reminds me of me, and it's bloody uncomfortable viewing. Mostly, I suppose, because it's underscored by the fact that maybe, just maybe, this session that I'm in no mood for might just end up doing me some good.

Don't get me wrong. Especially after what I saw yesterday, I am in no way excited by the prospect of submitting to therapy, to excavating those rotting corpses from my past, but even I have to admit, and I've had a lot of time to think about this, there's got to be a reason for my temper, and I mean beyond the whole stereotypical Italian passionate temperament rubbish.

If I were to be completely honest with myself, I would indeed have to concede that there's a good chance that my quick temper is symptomatic of something else.

On the bright side, when I boarded the train this morning, it wasn't bloody rammed – yay – which meant that I was able to choose my seat rather than having to be grateful that there actually was one at all.

Also, I'm pleased to report that I chose to sit in a part of the train where there were no females. At least, none I'd be interested in, despite the drought.

It's odd, because it was this choice that got me thinking, and actually had me looking forward to this session, despite my superficial misgivings. It reminded me that the fact that I think about sex more than most average men – which, of course, you'd stereotypically find hard to believe – is probably something that I might want to look into... especially when my partners are not my wife, whom, again, as much as you probably don't believe it, I happen to love.

Yes, I'm able and ready to admit to it now. I have a problem. How good are you at admitting to yours?

No, wait, you probably think you have none, that you are purer than pure... but most of us have something to hide and, generally, it's motivated by other life factors, either here in the present or deep in the past.

I take the elevator down, into the bowels of the Underground, but I'm sure to keep my gaze lowered where possible. Similarly, I generally avoid making eye contact with anyone.

Occasionally, when my face starts to contort, I'm reminded that I'm holding my breath. And there are two reasons for this. The first is because the city air tastes tainted. Acrid. Artificial. It's like synthetically flavoured water with that bitter aftertaste. The second reason I'm holding my breath is because I'm trying not to inhale the clouds of perfume hovering above the escalator.

You see, between you and I, this used to be a favourite pastime of mine on my morning commute. I'd willingly file in behind a good-looking woman and breathe in her perfume. It was a hit or miss game, of course.

Mostly hit, rarely miss, but such a turn-on. For me, it was tantric. I could do it the whole day, breathing in these different scents and imagining what the warm skin, from which they'd emanated, felt like to touch, to kiss, to…

Fuck.

Yeah. So, I'm trying to avoid all of that shit, which I promise sounds much more perverse than it is.

I'm nearly there now. I've left the tube. It was its usual hot and claustrophobic, self-absorbed self. A bunch of automatons making their way to work while pretending not to see the faces rocking to and from their armpits, which, by the way, is what it occasionally smelt like down there today.

See what I'm doing here? I'm projecting my bad mood. Well, not completely. The Underground was hideous, and made worse, much worse, when I emerged to a newsstand featuring a sea of headlines – but which one do you think yelled at me the most from the pile of newspapers?

That's right.

"10-YEAR-OLD BOY STILL MISSING." "WHAT HAPPENED TO *TIMMY?*" "POLICE FEAR FOR 10-YEAR-OLD" … and so on.

Each includes a large picture of Tim. One of them is recent, from the birthday party. How do I know that? Because he's standing in front of a mound of presents. And which one do you think is just peeking out from the corner of the photograph? That's right. Mine.

Shit.

My heart aches for Pete and Deedee. I wonder if maybe I should go around there, show some support, but I'm not sure. I don't really know them that well.

I keep my gaze mostly on the pavement in front of me as I hurry forward – dodging, passing shoes, handbags, coats.

I'm just not in the mood for this session right now. Which is odd because, technically, this is probably the best time to see a therapist, since he or she can help me deal with the disappearance of this little boy that so reminds me of my own different type of loss. I know it isn't the same, but I just can't help but compare this to how I would feel if it were Toby who'd gone missing. At least I know that he's alive and well.

Thank God.

So yes, it's one thing to confer, and another to submit for analysis. Worse, I don't remember ever being supervised, which is itself odd because, in my profession, you normally study, graduate, do some kind of tenure, and then get released into the big, bad world... but me, I aced my exams, got my degree, and was pretty much top of my class. I've never had somebody look at how I work, or at me for that matter, and, well, now I know how my patients feel.

Although, I know this isn't just about the therapy per se, but the outcome. I'm scared. No, I'm terrified. I need this to work because, right now, this feels like the only way I'm ever going to get my family back.

I'm nearly there. The hustle of the city has calmed. Concrete is giving way to cobblestones, modern buildings to red bricks and, in some cases, stone. I'm in a leafy suburb of Southwest London where the bumbling drone of a passenger jet overhead, and the hum of traffic in the distance, are the only reminders that I'm back in the British capital and not at my sanctuary by the sea.

Did I just say that?

My gaze is still lowered, which means I hear the footsteps first, clicking towards me. It's a woman. I can tell from the sound and, given the impracticality of those heels, I'd guess that she's relatively young.

I don't look up, but start to hold my breath. She's getting closer now, but she isn't moving fast enough. I want to breath and my lungs are screaming at me, my body fighting against the intentional act of denying it oxygen. The tension's building in my cheeks, behind my eyes.

Closer…

I'm starting to shake.

Closer…

I can't hold it anymore! My lips explode open and suck in air just as the clicking footsteps walk by me. I hear the rhythmic tap and scuffle of her shoes as she hesitates and then steps around me, but I don't look. I can't look.

Fuck.

I can see stockings, black, heels high, thighs, and a long coat, and I instinctively snatch some of the air as she breezes by me, with the fact that I'm not looking at her face making the whole encounter, ironically, even more fucking seductive!

Shit.

I can feel my pulse quicken. Already? What the hell's that all about?

I suppose it's been a while. I need it like an addict needs to score. My heart is thudding. Oh God, I'm contemplating turning around and following her, like a bloody sexual predator.

Shit. I hate that expression. It conjures up a whole different image. That isn't who I am. Is it? I just like sex. Don't I?

What the fuck is wrong with me?

I stop and gulp in the shitty air as I hold on to some conveniently placed black metal railings.

Someone else walks by. It's a suited man. His brisk pace doesn't stop, nor does it hesitate, despite the fact that I'm leaning over and holding onto these metal bars, as if I'm about to throw up.

Cheers, mate!

You'll be pleased to know I'm not. You won't be pleased to know that I'm thinking about rotting flesh and wriggling maggots. Faces of old women with craped skin. And it's working. The thumping inside of my chest is subsiding, the pulse behind my ears slowing, and the tingle in my extremities slacking.

Oh, bloody hell. I breathe deeply. That was a whole new panic attack. Thank God I don't live here right now; I couldn't do that on a regular basis.

I look up, still breathing heavily, and I realise that the iron railing encloses a pretty garden with tall trees, a lawn, and a couple of benches. It's part of the red brick apartment building I've been heading for.

Dr Ethan Holmes' office is on the 4th floor, and I can tell you, climbing the concrete stairs is nowhere near as picturesque an act as making my way up the rocky coastal path from the beach to Dolce Vita.

And, side note: you would have thought that someone who charges nearly two hundred pounds an hour could at least afford a place with a lift.

The antechamber to the doctor's inner sanctum – for there is no other way to describe the waiting room – is a small box, with an equally boxy two-seater leather couch which is probably something he picked up at IKEA. Black framed diplomas hang in a prominent position; Doctor Ethan Holmes MD and Doctor Ethan Holmes PhD. Blimey, this guy has been around the block. There's an obligatory floor plant in the corner, and it is real, too. I know this because, when I pull at the leaves, one of them comes away in my fingers.

I glance around and surreptitiously push it into my pocket.

A square window overlooks the communal garden where a couple are enjoying an early morning chat while clutching Starbucks cups.

Nice. I could use one of those right now.

The other side of the uninspiring pastel-coloured wall features splodges of colour inside a black frame, which is presumably some kind of modern art. Not my bag, but I'm guessing my doctor's deliberate choice is designed to put his 'patients' in a relaxed, if not catatonic, state before they venture inside – which, by the way, is to be found via a clinically white glossy door.

On cue, it opens.

"Good morning," says a young bloke who surely can't be long out of his twenties. He has short, wavy blonde hair and wears square spectacles on a broad nose. I'm expecting him to speak with an American accent because he looks all-American, in a Ryan O'Neal kind of way. Preppy. Fit.

"Morning," I say. If he's noticed the surprised look I must have on my face, he doesn't show it.

"Please, come in," he says in a measured Cambridge articulation.

I accept the invite with a smile, if only to get away from his gaze. I mean, I know the importance of making eye contact with patients and everything, but this guy takes that to a whole new level.

"Please, take a seat," he tells me, gesturing to a low-slung modern piece of furniture, which I'm assuming is an armchair – although I'm not sure whether to sit or lie down on the thing. I sit, backing into it. It isn't optional. That's what the design demands, along with involuntary manspreading. Oh, what the hell.

"Quite a decent set-up for someone so young," I say with a nod as I survey the room.

It's odd. I mean, I've been a therapist for years, yet, being in here right now, it feels awkward. I guess part of it's because I, unlike most, have some kind of idea of what's coming next, to the point where I need to have a word with myself, because I can feel my guard's going up, and I'm already locking filing cabinets to subjects that I'm designating as being off limits. Top secret. I know I'm doing it, and I know that it isn't conducive to therapy, but, oh, I don't seem to give a shit. I just want to skip to the part where he tells me how to deal with what just happened out there and which has been happening for as long as I can remember, when indulged.

"Thanks," he says, sitting in an armchair opposite me.

"Have you been here long?" I ask.

"Um, a few years now," he replies with a nod, while making a show of picking up a journal and a pen.

Notes? Who the hell takes notes in sessions anymore? I don't. I keep all the details in my head. Once I'm in the session, I've recorded it all automatically.

"Lease?"

"No, owned."

"Nice," I nod, appreciatively. I'm not surprised. This place must be a goldmine. Which, of course, gets me thinking. Once I sell the house, I could set up a practice like this. On my own, like this bloke. I mean, if he can do it, I can. I'm just not sure if I want to move back to the city, though – especially after what happened. I think it's time for a change.

And no, I haven't forgotten about my arsehole step siblings and that shitty letter, but this morning, as I was riding the train, I decided that

I'm going to behave as if I never received that letter. More specifically, I'm going to behave like I'm still selling Dolce Vita and getting that money because, today, while I'm back in civilisation, I've already lined up a meet with my own lawyer. I've decided that those greedy fuckers have already stolen enough from me, including my dad, and they aren't going to get this, too. I'd sooner demolish the place.

"…Have you travelled far today, Marco?" my *therapist* is asking.

"You really own this place? It must be worth quite a bit, and you can't have been in practice that long."

He smiles at me. "That's twice you've made reference to my age since arriving here, Marco. Does my age concern you?"

I laugh. It's a hollow laugh, of course. "Not really. I'm just surprised."

"Were you expecting someone older?"

"Yeah. Much older."

"Are you disappointed?"

"Why don't you ask me that question in about half an hour or so?" I patronise. I let the statement hang in the air for a while, then continue, "Oh, and you asked if I had travelled far. Yeah, quite far. I've just come from my place on the Southwest coast," I lie. Well, it isn't exactly a lie, is it? Whether or not I own it in addition to other properties, I'll let him wonder.

"Really? Did you come in by train or by car?"

"Train."

"And how was the journey?"

"Long," I say flatly.

"Yes, always a bit of a shock coming back into the city after the quiet of the countryside."

"Do you live in the country?"

"No, I live in London, but I've got a place in the New Forest."

Of course you do.

I grimace a smile.

There's another long silence, during which he insists on maintaining eye contact with me, and it's really starting to grate.

Then, as if he's read my mind, he asks, "You don't remember me, do you?"

I pull a face. "Should I?"

"We went to school together."

"Did we?"

"Well, not in the same class, but the same school. I think I was a few years below you."

I make a show of racking my brains, then shake my head, "No, I don't remember you." And, as infantile as this may sound, I derive some pleasure from that statement. A kind of, you're-not-important-enough-for-me-to-remember-you bit of pleasure.

"So, you were at Cambridge?"

"No, Compton Fields."

"No, really? Compton Fields. Wow. Now that was a long time ago. I guess I was about fifteen."

"Sixteen. I was about twelve or thirteen at the time."

I hesitate. Okay. So, in the space of a minute, I went from a fuck-you to feeling that this is bloody awkward. This guy remembers what age we were. I can't even remember who the hell he is. And, I have to say, of all the things I expected today, this wasn't one of them.

"So, we weren't friends then," I say. It was meant as a statement, but it sounded more like a question.

"No, we weren't."

"But you knew me?"

"Yes, I knew of you."

He spoke those words with a smile and a nod of the head. The kind of smile that curls the lips, but fails to garner any real traction with the rest of the face. A smile that, in a schoolground singsong, says, *I know something you don't know.*

And this annoys me. No, it doesn't annoy me – it irks me. It's as if the guy has something on me and the session hasn't even started yet. Or has it? What does this bloke know about me and my time at boarding school that I don't even know about myself? Admittedly, it is a period that I've actively tried to forget.

Don't start second-guessing yourself. He's already got you on the defensive. Which, by the way, is not a sign of a good therapist.

Remember your training.

But that's it... I can't remember my training. Right now, I'm feeling like one of his hapless patients, and I don't like it. I don't like it one bit.

Okay, now hold on. Hold your bloody horses. You need to get a grip. You need this guy on your side, remember? That's why you're here.

But, he isn't offering anything to the conversation, which only compounds the awkwardness between us.

So much for putting the client at ease.

Anyway, I wait a few seconds, roll my shoulders, take a deep breath, and decide to put his I-know-something-you-don't attitude to the back of my mind, for now, and comfort myself with the fact that he isn't as young as I first thought.

Yeah, but he looks it.

Oh, shut up!

"So, how does this work?" I ask, stealing a popular line from one of my clients. "Do you ask questions or…" I trail off here and hand the rest of the sentence to him.

He picks up. "Why don't you start by telling me about yourself, Marco?"

"Well, you probably already know most of it," I say with a forced smile. He looks at me, inquisitively, so I continue, "the profile application I had to fill out before coming here."

There's a subtle tone in my voice, which he obviously picks up on, because next he says, "You didn't like filling out the profile?"

"Not particularly."

"Why not?"

I cross my legs, and then instantly regret the move since this bloody armchair makes the action look much more uncomfortable than it really is. I hastily uncross my legs once more.

That was way too obvious. I want to scream at him. I want to say, *Don't go reading anything into that. I'm not feeling uncomfortable; your shitty chair is. This shitty chair which probably costs more than I make in a week.*

I know I'm coming across as being defensive, but I'm not. I don't have anything to defend. I'm pissed off. I'm somewhere I don't want to be, and I've done a crappy job of hiding it.

"Marco?"

He's still observing me from behind those neat spectacles of his. Designer, no doubt. Armani or some shit.

I've used the word "neat" because everything about this guy is neat. His combed hair, his Marks and Spencer blue pullover, the pristine white T-shirt beneath it. The corduroy trousers, not casual jeans, and those brown brogues at the ends of his short legs. This guy takes himself way too seriously. And there's me thinking that I was bad.

Yeah, I'm pissed off. What's that all about?

"No, I loved filling out the form," I say.

He smiles at my sarcasm, "What did you really think? Please. I'm interested in your opinion."

"I just think it's impersonal."

"Don't you keep a dossier on your patients?"

I laugh. This time it's real.

He cocks his head to one side, as if to ask, *What's funny?*

So, I elaborate. "Dossier? Really? It's therapy, not an MI6 interview. Oh, wait, you're not, are you?" I add, seriously.

He just smiles. Yeah, that's getting on my nerves too.

Seconds tick by. He scribbles notes. Traffic drones. A siren blares in the distance.

I take a moment to have a good look around the room. A floating book case, brimming with books, lines one of the walls. A frosted glass desk sits opposite. There's a Mac Book standing on it, but not just any one – this is one of those ones with a fuck-off big flat-screen. There's a chair behind it. Leather, of course, with chrome fittings…

"…Marco."

I look at him.

"Where were you?"

"Oh, I was just taking in the room. Seeing how well you've done for yourself."

"Is wealth important to you?"

"No, I'm more of an as-long-as-you're-happy kind of guy. My father, on the other hand – well, he was more like you."

"How so?"

"Well, he was into the whole image thing, but then again, he was stereotypically in advertising and Marketing."

"Why stereotypically?"

"Well, everybody's in Marketing these days. They cobble together a Word document poster with some clip-art and suddenly they know all about Marketing."

"And I take it your father wasn't like that?"

I snort, "My father? He was ambitious, fanatical about his job, and money."

"Tell me about him."

Wow, straight in there, eh? Alright.

"He left Italy for London in the sixties, without a penny to his name. He was forced to take work wherever he could, but he knew that, to make the best money, he needed to get the best jobs. He had to promote himself. And that included marketing and selling skills and services to potential employers that he didn't possess. This meant learning on the job, on their time. Yet, in the typical trend of commercialism, they bought marketing and advertising services from him, ones that they didn't know they needed.

He started out by selling his so-called services to bars and clubs that he was already working in. These people literally bought the belief that he was elevating their profile when, in reality, he was elevating his own. And, when each competitor saw what the other was doing, they started soliciting his services. So, by day, he was a waiter, by night he was a barman, and by lunch hour, or in any spare time he could lay his hands on, he was a Marketer. He grafted, honed his craft, and before long, he was being hired not for his ability to serve food or pull pints, but for his ability to peddle people stuff they didn't need. Now, he owns several buildings like this all-around London. One of them not too far from here."

Now shove that up your arse, you condescending little boy.

"You must be very proud."

I don't respond.

"What about your mother? You didn't mention her."

"What would you like me to say, Doctor?"

"Well, what does she do?"

"Not much. Like him, she's dead. She used to be a model. That's how they met. On a photoshoot. The old man always did have a soft spot for beautiful ladies."

"Sounds glamourous."

"Oh yeah, very." The bitter taste of disdain is smothering my words, so I add, cheerfully, "There you have it, my mother and father rolled up in one neat little package for you."

He flips his pen, casually. "Am I sensing some cynicism?"

"Not really. I just imagined that you'd want to explore the whole parents thing, so I thought I'd save you the trouble."

"Don't you want to talk about your parents?"

"Not particularly."

"Only, you started talking about them. I assumed it's a subject you wanted to discuss."

"I did, so now that we've covered that off, we can move on."

"What would you like to discuss?"

"Oh, I don't know. Why don't you tell me a little about you?" I ask sarcastically.

He thinks about this, and then nods. "Okay. What would you like to know?"

"I don't know." I nod at his hand. "You're wearing a ring. How long have you been married?"

"A couple of years."

"Right. What does she do?"

"*He* works in marketing."

A noise escapes from me like a bubble does to the surface. I think it's a chuckle, I'm not sure, but it's accompanied by an awkward smile. I straighten in my chair, then shake my head. "As Jack Nicholson once said, 'Don't I feel like the asshole.'"

"I don't know. Do you?" He's smiling.

I return the smile.

"Which part of that made you feel like," he holds up speech mark fingers, "an asshole?"

"All of it. What I said about people who work in marketing."

"So, which part?"

"Sorry?"

"You said that you felt like an asshole because of what you said about people in marketing, but you started out by saying, and I'm paraphrasing, that all of what you said made you feel that way. Does that include the part where I told you I have a husband?"

I expel air through curled lips. "Please. You want to convert what I said into a homophobic slur?"

"No, I was just asking a question. Was it?"

"No, it was not. Come on. We're therapists. It's not for us to judge how others conduct their lives."

"No, but I assume that you do have an opinion on the matter?"

"Hey, man, if that's what floats your boat, that's entirely up to you. Besides, my best friend's gay."

"He is?"

"Yes."

"Is he married?"

"No."

He nods. Muses for a few seconds, then says, "I'm curious. So, we've talked about your parents' marriage, and mine, but we haven't talked about yours." Now it's his turn to nod at the ring on my finger. Is that subject off-limits, too?"

"No, not really. In fact, she's the reason I'm here."

"How so?"

I shift in my seat, looking around the room some more. I'm not actually in the mood to talk about Ellie, but I guess I don't really have a choice – especially since there's a good chance she's already spoken to this guy and told him everything. After all, she's the one who gave me his card. "I'm here because I received an ultimatum," I declare, like I've just won the lottery.

"Want to tell me about it?" His question's casual, as if people receive ultimatums all the time.

"The kind that says that if I don't spend an hour with you each week, my marriage is over. But then, you probably already know that."

"Why would I know?"

"You telling me that my wife hasn't called you?"

TONY MARTURANO

He shakes his head. I hold his gaze, but he isn't giving anything away. He's just projecting one of those poker, makes-you want-to-punch-it, faces.

"What made your wife resort to an ultimatum?"

I laugh, and wag a finger at him. "Come on, Ethan. Can I call you that, or should I call you Doctor?"

"You can call me whatever you like."

I give him a look, as if to say, *Don't tempt me.* He just bats it back with another one of those smiles.

"That was sneaky," I continue. "And, if you don't mind me saying, a bit obvious. If you want to know what happened, why don't you just ask?"

"I thought I had."

"No, you asked a related question on a different subject."

He shakes his head. "I don't follow."

"Instead of just asking what happened, you pitched a leading question about what disagreeable action or actions I may have repetitively and consistently performed that eventually drove my wife to issue an ultimatum."

"You think I was trying to trick you?"

"Weren't you?"

"Why would I try to trick you?"

"I don't know. You tell me."

"I have absolutely no reason to try and trick you. I'm here to help."

"Right. Help."

"You don't believe me?"

"I've only just met you. Oh, apart from all those years ago that I can't even remember."

He thinks about what I've said for a few seconds, and then, "Did my bringing up school irritate you?"

"A bit."

"Why?

"I don't know. It just felt you were trying to get one over on me."

"Why would I try to do that?"

"I don't know, Ethan, *why would you?*" I ask with a robotic voice and then a sigh.

Yeah. Don't think I haven't noticed that I'm being a complete prick! Not much different than my football friend of yesterday who, by the way, in case you're curious, I did manage to win over. That's because I'm a professional.

"What's wrong, Marco?"

I don't look at him.

"Marco…"

"You know what's wrong."

"You chose to come here. You don't have to stay. You're free to leave at any time."

"Oh, but I'm not, am I?"

"Why do you think that?"

"You know why."

"Because your wife told you to come here?"

I look at him, pointedly.

"It's still your choice, isn't it?"

"You mean I have a choice. I just have to choose which is more important; my freedom or my marriage."

"Freedom? Do you really feel that, by coming here, you've surrendered your freedom in some way?"

"Haven't I? If a person is forced to do something against their will, at the risk of losing another person, have they not surrendered their free will?"

He shrugs and sighs. "At the risk of straying into the philosophical, I suppose that would depend on how you look at it. You could argue that free will preceded the choice. It was only once it was made that the free will, as you put it, was surrendered."

I laugh. "No wonder therapy has such a bad name."

"You don't agree?"

"Whatever, mate."

I slide out of the chair, trying to look as casual as possible, and walk over to the window.

I had to get out of that thing. Leaning back like that – it felt like I was strapped to some kind of medieval rack.

The window offers a partial view of the shared garden and the iron railing separating off the nearby street. That place where I nearly lost the breakfast I didn't have. Shit. I can still feel that cold sweat now.

I can only see part of the bench, but it looks empty. The coffee lovers have disappeared for the day. They've probably reported to an office somewhere in the city. I think about Ellie, and where she might be right now. Is she at the office? In a meeting with David? And what about Toby? What about my little boy? Is he at school? What I would give for a hug from that little fella right now.

"So, Marco, tell me, where do you prefer to live?" the doctor is asking.

I turn and frown.

"On the coast, or in the city?" he clarifies.

"So, you have spoken to my wife," I say knowingly.

"Why do you say that?"

"How do you know I have a place in the city?" I ask cockily, confident that he's just dropped himself in it.

"You put a north London address on your form," he says, casually.

I sigh, take a few seconds, and then, "The city. I prefer to live in the city," I lie.

Though, it's hard to explain, but it was only in the moment, the second I spoke the words, when I realised that they were a lie.

"With your wife and son?"

"Yes."

"How old's your son?"

"Ten."

"You must miss him."

"Again, how do you know I'm not seeing him?"

"Marco, you talked about your home in the country…"

"House," I correct.

"House in the country. You talk about being trapped here because of an ultimatum issued by your wife. Did I draw the wrong conclusion?" I hesitate, then shake my head. "It isn't much of a leap to conclude that a lot of this hostility you're displaying towards me is due, in part, to the problems you're having at home."

I gape at him. They've obviously been talking, so I rage, "You don't have the first fucking clue about what's happening in my life! You have no fucking idea about how it feels to be banished to the fucking wilderness and branded persona non-grata! My wife won't even answer my calls. That's when I can get a fucking decent signal!" I pull my phone out of my pocket. "You know what – I'm going to call her. I'm going to call her until she fucking answers her phone. I have a right to talk to her. I have the bloody right to see my son." I tap buttons and wait for the call to connect. *"Hi, this is Ellie, I can't answer the phone right now. Please leave a message."* I dial again. *"Hi, this is Ellie, I can't answer the phone right now. Please leave a message."* I dial again and again.

"Fuck!"

When I finally look up, the doctor is watching me, and you can imagine the expression on his face.

"What?" I ask angrily.

"Do you think you're in the best frame of mind to be making a call like that right now?" he asks softly, patronisingly. At least, that's how it sounds to me.

"What difference does it make? It doesn't matter what fucking mood I'm in, she doesn't pick up anyway. You know I haven't seen my son in…" I stop here, scrabbling around in my brain.

"Since…" he prompts.

But I can't remember. I bloody well cannot remember how long it's been since I've seen my own son. It's like I've been sunk to the bottom of the ocean and lost all track of time. That place! "I can't fucking remember!" I explode. "That's how long it's been!"

My breath's coming in short shallow bouts and now I've got bloody palpitations in my chest. I can feel his eyes on me, but he doesn't speak, not for a few seconds. Then, he asks, "Marco, are you okay?" His voice is soft. Sympathetic.

"No… I'm not fucking okay. My… life is… falling apart!" I say between breaths, which is quite handy, because I think I've managed to successfully mask the quiver in my voice.

Fuck, I think I'm having a panic attack.

Relax, you fool. Relax. Don't lose your shit in front of this guy.

"Marco. Why you don't you take a few seconds, just to allow yourself to recover?"

I wave him away. I'm okay. I'm a man, not a fucking kid.

A minute or so passes before he leans forward in his chair and says, all seriousness, "Marco. I'm concerned. You're obviously very anxious right now."

"You think?"

"You must be under enormous pressure, and I would like to help you through this. Let me help you through it." His voice is soothing. Reasonable.

Seconds rumble by, along with an aeroplane overhead, as I force myself to recover, but I feel tired all of a sudden. Exhausted. And, I'm not ashamed to say it, a bit emotional. It feels like I've been walking around with scaffolding propping me up and now, suddenly, somebody's come along and torn part of it down. And, I'm not too pig-headedly blind to see the symbology in that. I was resisting this guy. Why?

Eventually, I declare, "I don't want to go into therapy," before falling back into my seat like a sulky child.

"Why?"

"I just don't want to start stirring up all that shit. Begin all that self-analysis. I'm not at the right stage of my life for it."

"Why do you say that?"

"There's just too much happening."

"Well, wouldn't that make this the perfect time? To take a look at those things that are mentally disabling you from dealing with what's troubling you?"

"I've coped just fine until now."

"Have you?" he asks seriously. I look up at him, but he keeps at me. "Marco, you know better than me that you were moments away from having an all-out panic attack; that's not coping. That's your body's way of telling you that you are *not* coping well at all."

"I'm fine now."

"Until next time. Only, then you may not be in the safety of my office, but you could be driving the car, walking down the street, maybe even out with your son."

I squint at him. "Don't do that. Don't bring my son into this."

"Why not? He is a big part of this. In fact, from what I can tell, he may well be one of the triggers."

"He isn't."

"How do you know?"

"He just isn't. He has nothing to do with this."

"How can you be so sure?"

"I just know!" I yell.

He watches me for a few seconds, allowing the sound of my own voice to ring in my ears, before saying, simply, "Is that your professional opinion?"

Checkmate. Point made – and quite well, actually. You little shit.

I sigh, then look out the window, as if I can escape through it, escape from all of this, but I can't. I know that.

Even I've got the presence of mind to know that this is all in my head and, as much as it galls me to admit it, this bloke's right. I've lost all objectivity.

There's another long interlude, before the whippersnapper speaks, "Marco. You're a therapist. You know the benefits of looking at things from multiple perspectives, and especially when they're not your own."

"Seriously?"

"Just because it's a cliché, it doesn't make it bad." He smiles with another of what is fast becoming a trademark shrug.

"Look. Why don't we agree to just talk? Not examine. Not evaluate. We can then take it from there. Let's just," he looks for the word, "chat."

I laugh. "Chat? Look at this place. There's no doubt in my mind that nothing that is said in this room is just a chat."

"Maybe. But, at least you know that it's confidential, that you're safe here. That you can speak freely. Why not give it a try?"

I hesitate, and then it's my turn to shrug. I feel like a child that's just been cajoled into eating his greens.

So, I nod.

"Okay." He puts his pad down and shifts in his seat. "I'm curious.

You've alluded multiple times to the fact that your wife and I have somehow colluded in compelling you to come and see me. Why do you think that is?"

"Because she's the one who gave me your details." I swallow as I recall the meeting, and then add, "Along with divorce papers."

"Why does your wife want to divorce you?"

"If I said irreconcilable differences, would you believe me?"

"Not now," he says with a knowing smile.

I take a few seconds as the heat of shame rises to my face. "She thinks I'm an addict."

"Alcohol?"

I shake my head.

"Drugs?"

"Sex," I mumble.

I expect him to react. Obviously, not with a shock horror reaction, but a flicker of something in his eyes, but there's nothing. Like he hears this kind of stuff every day. Well, coming to think of it, he probably does. And that's when it occurs to me. Then, in that very moment. My resistance to him was equal to that of most men who must visit the doctor about something intimate. Penis, prostate exams, unusual rashes in awkward places. No man wants another bloke examining his junk. This is no different. I don't want some bloke, some stranger, poking his nose around in my business. I know what it's like to put lives under a microscope. It can be painful, stressful, not to mention harrowing because, to heal, you have to carve out the dead flesh from that wound, clean it and give it time – lots of time.

And if I allow myself to consider this fact... If I allow myself to accept that this bloke deals with this kind of shit every day, then maybe, just maybe, he might be able to help me. After all, it's not as if I have loads of people to talk to right now. I've alienated all of those. Hell, the only close friend I would talk to about anything like this is David, and I left him here when I parachuted myself into bloody Telly tubby land.

"Marco?"

I look at the young man before me. I scrutinize him as if I'm evaluating him in an interview. In reality, he isn't that much younger than me; it just feels that way. Yet still, could this boy really have what it takes to unravel the puzzle that is me?

Yep, now that's definitely bordering on the narcissistic.

"Where were you just then?" he asks.

"I was thinking about my wife," I lie.

"What exactly were you thinking? Tell me your thoughts."

"I've cheated on her." There, I've said it.

"How many times?"

"Does it matter? Isn't one time too many for a married man?"

He's nodding again.

"I know. Cliché. Gorgeous wife at home, but I still can't help following my dick. But then, you're gay, you should know a thing or two about that."

He observes me. If he was insulted, he doesn't show it.

"So, you believe that just because I'm a gay man, I'm promiscuous?"

"Well, isn't that what you guys are all about? David's always on that Grindr app. No string hook-ups are like take-out for him."

"Can't the same be said of Tinder or other dating apps?" he bats back. "That said, I don't have Grindr on my phone. Do you?"

I laugh. "Touché."

"Could it be that you're attacking my monogamous commitment to perhaps explain your own…" he looks for the word, "dalliances?"

"Dalliances? Really? These weren't dalliances, Doctor, they were fuck-fests. I drank booze, took pills, snorted shit, and fucked other women besides my wife. We're not talking mild *peccadillos*."

"Why do you think you did that?"

"You mean you haven't figured it out yet? Shit, Doc, I've been here for, what, the best part of an hour, and you haven't figured it out yet?"

He ploughs through my sarcasm. "I'm interested – why do *you* think you cheat on your wife?"

"Um, I don't know. Because I'm bored."

"Of your wife?"

"Of life." I take a few seconds and then say, cheerfully, "You know, I have a patient. Ava's her name. In her own words, she has everything she could possibly wish for; wonderful home, pair of kids, a devoted, attentive husband, and yet she's bored. She told me she's so damn bored, she could throw herself from Smuggler's Pier – that's a place in the village I live in. A bit like the French Lieutenant's wife. Have you seen that film? Anyway, only in this case, she wants to drown herself just so she doesn't have to spend another day feeling the way she does. How about that?"

"She threatened to kill herself?"

"Chill, Doc. It was a figure of speech."

"You don't think she's capable of harming herself? You know that you have a duty of care…"

"…I told you. It was just a figure of speech. She doesn't really want to kill herself, Ethan, relax. Jesus. Talk about by–the-book."

"It's not about practicing by the book, Marco. It's about making sure you provide the best standard of care. You're obviously going through a difficult time right now…"

"…So you think I'm unfit to treat my clients?"

"I didn't say that. You know I didn't."

"No, you didn't say it, but you're alluding to it."

"I just want to make sure that you aren't leaving yourself exposed in any way. That's all."

"Well, you just worry about your own patients, and I'll worry about mine."

He holds up his hands. Seconds tick by.

"So, Ava. Are you saying that you can relate to her?"

"Well, there's a rather uncanny similarity, don't you think? She has the perfect husband. I have the perfect wife. She has wonderful children. I have a fantastic son. You would have thought we'd both be as happy as pigs in shit, yet we're both so bored that I fuck around and she… well, I don't think she wants to throw herself off that pier any more than I want to throw myself from a cliff."

"What do you think?"

"I think she's just bored with her marriage. Is looking to spice things up."

"What do you think is missing from her marriage?"

I think about this. "Um, it's early days, but so far I'd say that it's pretty much like many marriages around the world; complacency. Actually, strike that. From what I understand, *he* isn't complacent."

"Okay. What do you think is missing from yours?"

"That's just it. I don't *feel* like there's anything missing. I have everything I need right there. I mean, even the sex, when we have it, it's good. You know, adventurous. Yet, I can't help following my dick elsewhere... but then, I suppose it's never really been any different."

He looks at me curiously. I can almost see his ears prick up.

"What do you mean?"

I knew that question was coming the moment the words left my lips. I rub the back of my head and sigh. "Well, I hadn't really thought about it until the other day. I was having a conversation with David. He thinks I look like this guy from *Fifty Shades*, Jamie something…" I trail off here, looking for recognition on his face and finding it. "You obviously agree."

He smiles a curious smile. If I didn't know better, I'd say it was appreciation. A bit like I smile when I see a good-looking girl, and it's odd because I feel a twinge of embarrassment, but then, he's a gay guy, after all. I suppose, like a female, he was built to view me in that way. "Anyway," I say, slowly, cocking my head to one side, "*he* thinks that because I've got the looks of this bloke and so that makes me popular with females."

"And you don't agree?"

"That I look like him?"

"That you're an attractive man."

"Um, no, I can't say I do."

"But you must be aware of your looks."

I shake my head. "Not really. Do you think I'm good-looking? I mean, you're able to give me an objective opinion, right?"

"Do you think that, in order for another man to give you that kind of feedback, he has to be gay?"

I think about this. "Well, I guess so. I don't normally make a habit of telling other blokes they're good-looking."

"Do you think that, by doing so, this would somehow diminish your masculinity?"

I laugh. "No. It's just not how I roll."

"Has it always been like this for you?"

"Like what?"

"Have you always seen girls as sex objects?"

"Don't most blokes?"

"I'm asking how you see them, Marco."

I rock my head as I think about it. "In hindsight. I suppose it is a bit like that, but then, on the other hand, I also feel some of them have used me."

"How so?"

"Well, at the risk of sounding conceited, I've never really had to try hard with girls. Many of which appeared to be into me for the sex."

"And you obliged?"

"Of course – what hot-blooded heterosexual teenager wouldn't? It's kind of how it's always been. Just fun. An itch that gets scratched. A release. For me and them."

He nods. "Okay. So, looking at your relationships with other women..."

"...I wouldn't exactly call all of them *relationships*, per se."

"Your interactions," he corrects himself, "with other women. When you see an attractive female for the first time, what goes through your mind?"

"You mean apart from fucking her?"

"I mean, what goes through your mind? Men and women, generally, looking at a potential partner, perform some kind of evaluation." He thinks into the air for examples, "Do they have a ring on their finger, do they appear interested in me, are they out of my league? What kind of checks do you perform?"

I think about the question. "None."

"None?"

I shake my head. "No. None. I just see someone I like, and I just go for it."

"You... just go for it?"

"Yes."

"And what are you thinking about at the time? For example, are you having thoughts like... she's attractive. I like her smile. I want to have a relationship with her. I want to marry her. What goes through your mind?"

I think about this again, and realise, "Nothing. I just think about having sex with her. About making her orgasm. About seeing that look on her face right in that moment and thinking, 'I did that,' and knowing that makes me cum even harder."

"So, if that's the case... What happened with your wife? I mean, if you've only ever gone through life having sex with women, but never actually engaging with them on an emotional level, then, what happened with your wife? There must have been something special about her. You married her. You have a son together."

"I love her."

"But, you didn't love any of these other girls?"

"I don't know. I don't think I didn't love any of these other girls. I think they just didn't work out."

"So, you did see some of them more than once?"

"Yes. I even moved in with a couple."

"What happened?"

"What do you mean, what happened? They just didn't work out."

"None of them?"

"None of them." I think about this. "Actually, that's a lie. There was one. I was besotted with her."

"Your wife?"

"No, somebody else."

"What was her name?"

"That's it. I'm trying to remember, but I can't. I can see her in my mind's eye, but I can't remember her name." I laugh, but it's because I'm frustrated. "I can't even remember exactly what she looked like! I just know that she had a profound effect on me."

"How old were you at the time?"

"Oh, I don't know. In my late teens."

"Is there anything at all that you can remember about her? About how she looked?"

I shift in my seat and chuckle. "As corny as this is going to sound...

her smile. Well, kind of. I can see a smile through a curtain of brown hair. No, not brown – it's red. No, not red, but it's glowing red in the sun. She's looking at me in profile, over her shoulder, in one of those dreamy shots you normally get in films. Do you know what I mean? She's looking at me with a pair of the biggest brown eyes, and I can see it, no, I can feel it. I can feel the memory, and it feels like love."

My middle-distance gaze refocuses on his face, as if I've just re-emerged from some kind of trance, and then I add, casually. "Of course, it could just be a dream. One so lucid that I'm now unable to distinguish it from a memory."

"Do you think that's the case?"

"Well, if you met some girl, some guy," I correct myself, "and he looked at you like that, don't you think you'd at least be able to remember his name?"

"And this person in this dream definitely isn't your wife?"

"No."

"How can you be so sure?"

"Well, my wife has short blonde hair, blue eyes. This girl has long dark hair and brown eyes."

"Interesting."

"What is?"

"That the two of them have completely opposite physical characteristics."

I squint at him.

"Bear with me. So, what's your preference? Blonde or brunette?"

"Haven't we already established that I'm not that discerning?" I ask sarcastically.

"Just go with it. You must have a preference. Right?"

I shrug. "Brunette, I guess."

"Anything else? Body? Eyes? Rear?"

I think about this some more. "Fit body, of course, and brown eyes. I'm a bit of a sucker for brown eyes and accents," I say, appreciatively.

He looks at me. I lift my hands as if to say, *What?*

"Well, don't you see? Your wife. The woman you decided to marry, out of all of these girls who have featured in your life, just happens to be the complete opposite to your type."

"And?"

"And it's curious, don't you think?"

"Not particularly. They say opposites…" I stop in midsentence.

He leans forward. "What?"

"Well, it's interesting that you should mention this, because I remember having a similar moment last week."

"Tell me."

"Well, I'd only just arrived at the house. I was still exploring the place, and there's this girl, this policewoman. She came to the house Tuesday morning."

"Why's that?"

"Um, well, she actually came over because there was, or at least I think there was, a break-in at the house."

"Somebody broke into your house? What happened?"

"Oh, nothing major. I came back from the pub one night to find the place trashed. I think they just broke in for food. Made a mess. In the end, I reckon it was animals," I lie, playing down the rooftop encounter and how I felt. Or, more precisely, how I feel about the incident now, in the cold light of day. I also don't want him to go off on a tangent when we seem to be onto something. "Anyway, I called the police and she came over, and wow. She's a knockout. Beautiful. Even, *especially*," I correct myself, "in her uniform."

"Describe her to me."

"Well, as I said, she's…" I stop here, as realisation dawns. "Well, you know, now that I think about it." I chuckle as I recall the image of her standing in my kitchen. "She actually reminds me of the girl from my memory. Yeah. Only she has blue eyes and auburn hair, but, I guess in that light, it could have been…" I trail off here. Trying to work out which was which.

"Okay. So, just to be clear, are you saying that this policewoman looks like the girl from your memory, or that she *is* the girl in your memory?"

I shake my head. My mind racing, scrabbling for an explanation. "I don't know," I say, thoughtfully. "I'm not sure. I told you that I had the memory while I was here, but that's after I met her."

He squints. "Are you wondering if you fabricated the memory, perhaps even a fantasy, and placed her in the middle of it?"

I nod, absentmindedly. "I'm not sure." And I'm not.

For the first time in a long time, I'm worried. Are things that dull back in the countryside that my subconscious manufactured the fantasy about the cop and then tried to pass it off as a memory when I was unable to find one to give to the doc? That's ridiculous.

"Marco?"

I look at him.

"Where were you just now?"

"I was just thinking."

"About this policewoman?"

"Yes."

"Do you know her name?"

"Yes. It's Emily. Apparently, we used to play together as children. I used to call her Emmy."

"You remembered that?"

"Kind of. She reminded me. Apparently, she remembers all of it."

"Right. So, could the memory be of her?"

"No. We were children. My memory is of a woman."

He looks at me for a while, and then asks, "Earlier, you said that Emily came around on Tuesday morning."

"Right."

"But that you discovered the break-in after you came back from the pub."

"Yeah."

"Why the delay?"

"You don't miss much, do you?"

He smiles. "It's our job. You know that. Every detail's important in therapy."

"I thought we weren't in therapy?" I tease. Then, "She didn't come out until the morning because, apparently, in the place where hardly anything happens, a child has now gone missing. They were busy trying to find him."

"Missing? As in abducted, or run away from home?"

"She didn't know at the time. Either way, it must be killing his parents."

"You say that because you can empathise with them?"

I glare at him, so he clarifies, "Only in that you know what it feels like to be separated from your son."

"Of course I do."

He must sense that my son was a sore topic, so he changes his line of questioning.

"So, you called and the police responded. Emily responded."

"Yes."

"Was she on her own?"

"Yes. Is this relevant?"

"I'm just wondering."

"Yes, she was on her own. She said she recognised the name and wanted to check if I was okay."

"Did you want to have sex with her?"

"No," I say sharply.

"Why not?"

"What do you mean, why not?"

"Why didn't you want to have sex with her?"

"Um, I just didn't."

He looks at me. "You hesitated. Why?"

I react, "Yes, I bloody hesitated. Fuck! I feel like I'm being questioned by the bloody Gestapo. Are you going to attach electrodes to my chest next?" I stall, trying to gather my thoughts. I can feel his scrutinizing eyes on me, like some kind of futuristic scanner, reading my body language, my thoughts.

Give him his due, he doesn't miss much. I pause here because I don't want to go into the whole thing about the weird stuff; Emily, being hung over and all that. I need to gather my thoughts.

"Marco?"

"Do you think I'm incapable of appreciating a good-looking bird without wanting to fuck her?" I snap.

"No, but you do."

"What?" I ask sharply, screwing up my face with disdain.

"Earlier, you described yourself, and I'm paraphrasing here, as some kind of sexual predator…"

"Hang on…"

"…You said that you didn't engage with women on an emotional level, that many of your *interactions* with other females were more a matter of *fun* than anything else. That they came easy to you. That sex with some of them was more about the power you had to make them climax. You even went as far as correcting me, emphasising that, when it comes to sex, you're not discerning. Yet, now you seem to be upset that I might be viewing you out of context. So, which is it, Marco?"

I gawp at him. He's obviously attacking me, trying to get a reaction, yet at the same time, he has a point. I don't have an answer to his question, as that's simply how I've always seen myself. Just like I don't know the answer to the question I know is coming next.

"So, once again, what do you think is different about the policewoman?"

"Emily," I interject. "Her name is Emily."

"What do you think is different about her, when you compare her to the others?"

"What do you mean?"

"Why, to use your words, didn't you want to fuck her?"

"I don't know."

"What was different about her?"

"I told you, I don't know."

"There must be something, Marco. Think about it. This is very important."

"I told you, I don't bloody know! And I don't want to talk about it anymore."

"No. I'd like to stay with this. I would…"

"NO!" I yell. Sitting forward, the best as I can in this shitty bloody chair. "Fuck! Don't you get it? I don't want to talk about her, it, anymore. Jesus Christ, you're a persistent fucker!"

He watches me for a few seconds. Obviously, letting me catch my thoughts, and then he adds, "Why are you suddenly so angry?"

I widen my eyes. "You mean you need to ask that?"

"Why does the subject of Emily make you so angry?"

"No, it's not that the subject makes me angry. It's you banging on about it that's pissing me off. Fuck." I run my hands through my hair.

Shit. You're reassuring yourself. Why does he have you rattled?

"Would you rather talk about something else?"

I don't respond.

"Marco? Remember I'm here to help…"

"…Oh please, don't start with that shit."

"You don't believe me?"

"Oh, I believe you."

"You don't think I'm qualified or you don't think you need me?"

"Need?"

"Need to sit here, talking to me."

"I resent being here talking to you."

"Because of your wife?"

"Because of your condescending tone."

There's silence for what feels like a good part of a minute as a car horn sounds outside and another jet rumbles overhead.

Then, "Why don't you tell me about your new home? You've just moved to the country. Right?"

"Well, I wouldn't say 'moved' exactly. I'm there to renovate the place so I can sell it, although, as it turns out…" I trail off. I'm not in the mood to talk about my shitty step family.

"What, Marco? Finish the thought."

"Nothing, it doesn't matter."

"I'd really like to hear what you were thinking."

"I said it doesn't matter." I follow that up with another glare, and then add, "Maybe next time."

Reluctantly, the doctor changes his line of questioning again. Yes, like he's a bloody lawyer in court. "So, how's it going? The renovation?"

"Good. Apparently, there's huge demand with all of the city folk *escaping* to the country. My agent's showing two potential buyers around as we speak."

"And that's good, isn't it?"

I shrug.

"Did you inherit the house?" he asks suddenly.

I squint. How the fuck did he know that? Am I that transparent? I play to it. "Yep. Turns out that the old man actually did give a shit about me, after all. The place was his own private haven, so leaving it to me was quite generous of him. If you leave out the part where he gave everything else to my bloodsucking step siblings."

"Did you not enjoy a good relationship with your father?"

I look at him and scoff. "Really?"

He feigns surprise.

"That's such an amateur move. And premature, don't you think? Besides, we've already been down this road, remember? But, just for the sake of clarity, I'll summarise for you. Did I hate my father? No, I just disliked him intensely. Was he there for me as a child, growing up? No, the fuck, he wasn't. He was busy shagging every piece of skirt that worked for him. Is that place a metaphorical treasure trove of childhood memories for me? Fuck, no."

"Does it hold *any* memories for you?"

I think about this. He notices but, interestingly, doesn't pursue it.

"Again, you keep telling me about your father, but nothing about your mother. Why is that?"

I shrug again. "I told you. Not much to say. She died before I reached my teens."

"Must have been difficult for you. Being so young."

I roll my eyes. "And you're supposed to be one of the best?" I scoff. "This is fucking amateur hour. I'm out of here." I stand up.

He pulls a face. "What? What just happened?"

"You know what."

"Because I mentioned your mother?"

I respond with a sneer. The guy's really starting to piss me off, and he isn't finished.

"Why is it that, every time I raise the subject of your mother, you either brush over it or, now, threaten to leave?" he asks calmly.

"Because this is a fucking waste of my time, and money."

"What makes you say that?"

I stop on my way to the door and turn to him, "Man, just listen to yourself. You sit there in your fucking standard issue therapist garb with your spectacles and your gay brogues and you think that makes you a good therapist."

"I didn't realise I was being evaluated, Marco; otherwise, I would have put on jogging bottoms and a T-shirt."

I shake my head. "You're constantly being evaluated, you moron. Any new client that walks into your office is going to evaluate you – that's because they need to establish whether they can trust you with their most intimate thoughts, secrets, fears, insecurities. They need to be able to establish a bond."

"And you think I failed you?"

"Hell-fucking-yes, you failed; you started this whole session by dredging up all of this crap about school."

"Would you have preferred it if I had lied? Would that have been a better way to have earned your trust? I mean, you tell me. You seem to have all of the answers. You talk about trust, and creating a bond, yet you would much rather I have started our session by withholding facts. Is that it? Is that your great advice? If that's it, fine. I can do that. I can ignore all of the reasons that compelled you to walk into this office in the first place, including the fact that there's something about school that you feel particularly uncomfortable with, or why else would you have reacted the way you did? Or that you miss your wife and son so much that, despite the fact that you abhor self-analysis, despite it being the very reason that made you become a therapist in the first place, you still presented yourself here today. We could even side-step the obvious daddy issues, as you've repeatedly intimated, and even allow you to continue to repress each and every memory you have of your mother, all of which have undoubtedly contributed to you standing there in your safe, casual jacket and jeans, looking down on me today."

I gape at the little shit, and am seconds away from leaping over to him and putting my fist through his dainty spectacles, when he adds, "Come on, Marco. How much more of a cliché do you want to be? Punching me in the face isn't going to solve anything, is it?" he asks, as if he's just read my mind.

"Fuck you!"

"No thanks. I'm already happily married, remember?"

He's smiling at me now. Warmly. Disarmingly. As if he hasn't just spoken on of all that shit. As if he hasn't just blown any chance of retaining me as a client.

"You think I'm worried about that," he continues. "You think I care about whether or not you dignify me with your presence? You've already alluded to my wealth, which I've obviously accumulated by doing a terrible job at helping others, and through a brilliant job at ripping off people like you."

I want to say so much, but am incapable of saying anything; the rage that's humming through me like an electric current has paralysed my tongue.

He's smiling again. "No, I can't read your mind; nor can I offer a quick fix to all of your insecurities, as well as your repressed anger and, most importantly, your second guessing my every question, but I am willing to give it a try if you are."

His voice is soft. Conciliatory. Which makes me want to smash his teeth in even more. Instead, I say nothing. I just stalk out of the room, slamming the door shut behind me.

LONDON

Friday. 11:03.

I explode out of the doctor's building and into the street to a murky grey sky, but the chilled air feels so fucking good on my sizzling red face. I was going to deck that bloke. I was going to put my fist through his pearly whites. I was seconds away from it. The only thing that stopped me was the memory of Ryan-bloody-James. A kid.

I thought about how he reacted when we started talking about his father, and how I felt. Yet, he – two decades younger than me – managed to handle his emotions. He managed to keep himself in check. So, I did, too.

But, I can tell you; it wasn't fucking easy.

I am trying to help Ryan, but this jumped-up prick of a doctor was trying to rile me. All of that shit about my parents. He was provoking me, testing me. Prodding sores with those bony fingers of inquisition, and I didn't like it. I didn't like it one fucking bit.

Just like I hate this whole situation I've unwillingly thrown myself into. I'm sick of this shit. I'm sick of Ellie's shitty ultimatum, and of being banished to the country, and of generally being told what to fucking do. But I'm going to change it. I'm going to change it right bloody now.

I pull my phone from my pocket, switch it on, and wait for it to load. My hands are shaking, my heart is still pounding, and I'm breathing heavily again, but I have to do it – I have to tell me my wife that this situation is ridiculous. I have *rights*. I am Toby's father and, no matter what the situation is between us, nothing is ever going to change that. Fuck! We even agreed that nothing would ever change that, and yet here I am, out in the freezing cold. Literally. But not anymore.

I dial my wife's number.

So, now you're probably thinking the same as that tosser or anybody else who isn't living through this shit, who hasn't been separated from their child for what feels like a fucking eternity; that I'm in no fit state to try and reason with Ellie, but hey, guess what? I'm the only one here, so I can do whatever the fuck I please, and right now…

…There's ringing on the line and then, surprise of surprises, *"Hi, this is Ellie…"*

I wait for the tone and then speak. "Hey, Ellie, I've just been to see your fucking prick of a doctor. Just as you demanded. Now, I've just left the fucking prick of a doctor's office, and I'm ready to see my son. Ellie, he's my boy, too. I have rights, and you know that, so here's my ultimatum for you. If you don't call me back as soon as you get this message, then I'm going to have to seek advice from my lawyer. Yeah, I have one of those, as well, you know. One of the best, and I'm actually on my way to see him now. So, I suggest you call me back as soon as you get this, because two can play at this game, you know. But it doesn't have to be like this. It doesn't. Call me."

I hang up, my breaths coming to me thick and fast. I'm bloody shaking. Fuck!

There's that familiar tickling in my scalp, the constricting of my lungs, hammering in my chest. I think I'm going to have a panic attack. I tug at my shirt collar; the button's already undone.

Just breathe. Breathe.

The cold air isn't cold enough, so I press my forehead against those familiar iron railings as blood burns through my veins like lava through rocks, pumping heat around my body. I can't tell – is my vision blurring? Is that park bench fading in and out of focus? My legs are buckling as the rush of adrenaline dissolves and I think I'm going to puke.

Calm down. Calm yourself bloody down.

I'm bent over, holding onto the bars again, like my bloody life depends on it. The cold of the metal reminding me I'm still here, that I'm still alive.

Calm down. You've given yourself an attack. Calm yourself.

It's at least a couple of minutes before, slowly, the sound of gasping subsides, and all I can here is the urgent, rhythmic pulsing behind my ears and the thumping of my heart pierced by the occasional siren and the rumbling of motor vehicles. Then, there's the drone of the city, distant voices, footsteps and the shrill of a text alert.

Ellie.

It isn't.

It's my voicemail, telling me that I have a message. So now I'm confused. I didn't hear my phone ring. Did I miss her call? How's that possible?

I take a deep breath. Again. Then again, before straightening myself upright while keeping a steadying hand on the railing.

After a few seconds, it becomes obvious. I switched my phone off during the session. Therapy is already hard enough without the constant interruption of ringtones.

I dial my voicemail.

You have one new message.

"Hey, Marco. I'm calling from the car. As you know, there's no signal at the house, so I may lose you. Anyway, just checkin' in with ya to let you know that the first viewing went well. In fact, it went extremely well. Older couple, lots of money, looking to retire out here. I'm just waiting on my next showing, but wanted to have a quick chat with you and make sure everything's okay. By that, I mean, I know you're in the country an' all, and that y'all are all neighbourly and whatnot, but leaving the front door wide open is probably not the best idea. You're invitin' all sorts inside. Also, what's the deal with the plants? What happened? You can imagine that it was a bit of a surprise walking in there today with potential buyers to find them looking like that. You should really either replace or remove them altogether. Okay. Hope all is well with you, and I'll catch up later… call me when you get this…. oh, and while I have ya. What happened upstairs? I mean, what have you been doing? That place is looking a bit different to how I left it last week, and if we want to get it sold, I'm really gonna need ya to keep it how it was. Anyhow, call me when you get this. Just makin' sure we're still good with the sale and everything. Okay. Bye."

You have no more messages.

I stand in the middle of the street for some time, trying to work out what the hell Lucinda was talking about. Door. Plants. Place. I have no idea what she means. So, I dial her number.

Voicemail.

Of course.

"Fuck."

I close my eyes and let the wave of anger wash over me. I can't even begin to tell you just how sick I am getting of bad reception, voicemail messages, and cold shoulders.

But then I have a thought. One that puts a smile on my face almost instantly. I'm back in the city where I can find the perfect remedy.

THE NIGHTMARE

Friday. 18:35.

Okay, so, drinking in the middle of the day is a new low, even for me. Alright, perhaps not *that* new, but going to a bar for it is.

And now, for some inexplicable reason, I'm feeling guilty. Dirty. Like some seedy old man who's lost all control over his life and is only able to find it at the bottom of a bottle. In my case, shots, to grease the so-called wheels, to borrow an expression from Ryan, and then a few beers and maybe a few more.

On the plus side, you'll be pleased to know that I haven't ended up at some hotel with a stranger. Although, I would like the record to show that it's not for a lack of opportunity. I had that.

The blonde behind the bar worked hard to initiate a conversation with me, and I suppose that, in any other circumstance, I would have been up for it – especially when you consider just how *pent up* I'm feeling right now.

I guess it's this particular accolade that hasn't helped me over the years; women gravitating to me without much encouragement.

If you're turning your nose up at me, don't. I'm not the one who thinks that – it's what the data tells me. It's how it is. From my perspective, and as much as this isn't going to ring true, I fucking hate it, like many addicts do their addiction... until next time.

Anyway, on this occasion, despite my so-called *affliction*, I chose not to. That's got to be worth something. Right?

So, are you proud of me?

Don't be. I'm a shitty liar. I was accosted by some bird, and she did talk to me like she was ready to fuck in the toilets and I, as always, was game, but I did decide not to, if not out of some loyalty to my wife or to progress, but more out of some shitty loyalty to booze. It seems that good ole' doctor dickhead managed to piss me off so much that he actually turned me off of sex and onto drink.

Maybe he wasn't such a waste of time and money after all. He put me in such a foul mood that all I wanted to do was get blotted. Fast. And that meant not pausing to stick my dick in some stranger.

Yes, I'm vulgar, and you probably think I'm horrible. That's okay. I am. I'm also a hypocrite, a cheat, and a fucking embarrassment of an imposter. I pretend to have the ability to help people but, looking at me, riding this train, feeling like I am going to yack at any moment, I can't even help myself.

So, just in case you're judging, don't bother. And just in case you're hating, don't bother with that either. You can't hate me anymore than I already hate myself right now.

Shit.

There's a tickle on my cheek. I think it's a bug, so I swipe at it, but realise it isn't an insect; it's a tear.

Wow, what's that all about? I haven't seen this in quite some time. In fact, I don't think I've shed tears for years. I think the last time these strange things slid down my face was when Toby was born.

What's up with that?

I glance around the train to make sure nobody has seen or is watching, but it's empty. Just me and the mobile device addict a few seats down. I doubt he's talking to anybody; we know all too well that there's no signal here. No, he's using it to listen to music. I can hear the song. It sounds like that Erasure Eighties song again, "Respect." But I doubt it is; I just think I've got the bloody track in my head because that's what I'm longing for right now.

Please, give a little respect to me.

Even if I don't deserve it.

I can't identify the track, since the clatter of the train is much louder than the tinny overspill of the guy's humungous headphones that are sticking up from his head like he's tuning in to a radio mast miles away. What's the bloody point of that anyway? It's like society is regressing; instead of things getting smaller, they're getting bigger. Soon, he'll be walking around with ghetto blasters on his head.

Remember those?

The image of that makes me smile, and that's a refreshing change, don't you think?

I'm not going to look at my phone. There's no point. There's only one person I want to hear from, and she hasn't bothered to return any of my calls. Yes, plural, because you won't be surprised to hear that I didn't leave Ellie one message, but several. The more she didn't return my calls, the more I drank and the more I drank and…well, suffice it to say that she knows how I feel.

Eventually, I stumbled my way to Kings Cross and onto the Coastline Express out of the city.

That's my little nickname for the magical mystery train journey that's presently chugging its way around the harbour.

The sun is setting, but I can still just about see the outline of Dolce Vita perched on the opposite peninsula like an island prison.

It's odd, but somehow the place doesn't look anywhere near as mystical as it did that first day. Now, nearly a week later, it seems to have lost some of its lustre. I mean, everything's there – that crimson sun, the glistening surf, and the train's romanticism, but… none of it is invoking the same magical awe that it did.

Of course, I don't think for a second that this is a reflection of the building, but more of me. My perception is changing. I'm most likely becoming disillusioned with all of this. The so called novelty is wearing off.

Oh, and in other news. In case you're wondering. My new lawyer, Emmerson James, a weedy middle-aged thing with bug eyes and grey hair, of James & Parker, thinks that I have a good case against my step siblings. Given the fact that they already have the lion's share of the old man's estate, he thinks they're going to need to put up a pretty good argument as to why they feel that they should contest his wishes and seek a claim on what is effectively a fraction of my beloved dad's estate. I'm paraphrasing here. You'll appreciate that my head is a bit fuzzy and that the judder of the train is doing a pretty good job at mixing the burgers and fries I chowed down on before boarding. Right now, it feels like I'm in one of those lab centrifuge spinny things, and if I don't get off this train soon, I'll be redecorating the olde worlde décor with new art of my own.

And it's as I'm considering this, as we approach the ridge of the horseshoe, that I notice the lights in the distance.

At first, they look like fairy lights strung between the trees and, for a second, I wonder if someone has started decorating the place for next week's party, but then I notice that the lights are actually moving, bobbing in and around the woods that surround the place.

I squint through the window because, to be honest, I think my pickled brain is playing tricks on me. But it isn't, and I'm immediately reminded of the phantom guests in the kitchen and at my window.

I can't peel my eyes off of the lights for the whole time it takes for the train to draw slowly and painfully closer until, finally, it becomes clear. They aren't fairy lights or bugs of any kind, but flashlights, about fifteen or twenty of them, crawling like glow-worms all over my bloody property!

We're nearing the bridge now and I can see them as clear as day. They're not just outside, but inside the house, too.

"What the fuck?" I gasp as the train passes Dolce Vita and the clearing where I catch sight of her. She is standing in between a couple of patrol cars, with a group of other cops, and she's looking right at me.

Emily.

Our eyes lock for several seconds as the train shudders by, each of us seemingly wanting to communicate with the other but unable to do so.

Then, she's gone, disappearing into the gloom of the trees.

What the fuck was that all about? What's happened at the house? Another break-in? Lucinda? Something else?

The rest of the journey lasts minutes, but it feels like hours. I want, no, I need off of this train. I need to get home.

Home?

Well, it is my bloody home. At least for now. And I need to get there; I need to know what the hell has happened.

Eventually, we pull up at the station and I'm suddenly presented with the conundrum of how the fuck I'm to get back home at all. I don't have a ride.

Then, as the train quakes to a stop next to the platform, I see the officers and I know it doesn't matter. Somehow, I know that they are here for me.

My heart is thumping again. Shit. This whole bloody day has been one giant helter-skelter of anxiety. I'm sweating, my head hurts, and I'm already having palpitations as I go through a sickening transition of alcohol buzz to hangover fuzz.

Rustling draws my attention to the one other passenger, who's busy gathering shopping bags from the floor in front of him and prepping to disembark from the train. I mirror the action, but take my time because

I want him to leave before me so that I can take a few more seconds to collect my thoughts. However, when I turn to look at him, I snap my head backwards so fast I lose my balance, slamming the back of my head against the window and sliding back into my seat once more.

The passenger, whom I thought was a young man, is not. I don't really know what he, or it, is because I can't identify it. It's dressed like a human, and moves like a human, but his face... oh God, his face isn't human. It's disfigured. No, it isn't disfigured – it's worse; it's melted like fleshy candle wax! One ear has oozed down by a stubbly chin from which an eye has just blinked at me like a grotesque cyclops.

Then, slowly, it lifts a bony finger at me and starts to squeal, like a disgruntled cat, from the gash in its welted face where its mouth once was.

I open my mouth to scream but my lips are glued together. Then, my head swims, my stomach churns as the carriage starts to turn, like a movie set on a gimbal. Shopping bags plummet all around me, like meteors, before the lights flash and die and the world turns black.

THE MISSING

Friday. 19:05.

"Marc. Marco. Marc? Marco, can you hear me?"

It's a familiar voice, and I can feel my consciousness floating towards it until my eyes slowly peel open and hers come into focus. Big, blue, almond eyes. Full of concern. She's still in uniform. Her hair tied into a bun at the back of her head.

"Emmy?" I murmur.

I watch her lips crease upward, and then she nods.

I gradually become aware of the fact that I'm still slumped in the train seat, which reminds me of the last thing I saw.

I bolt upright, eyes darting everywhere. Searching the rest of the carriage, but it's empty. Upright. And Emily and I are the only ones in here.

"That man! That thing!" I yell. "That thing!"

"What thing?" she asks while placing a gentle, restraining hand on my chest.

"That thing!" I keep saying, looking around us until my eyes catch sight of the empty platform, but for an officer talking to a young couple. The man is carrying plastic shopping bags.

"Him! Him!" I yell, pointing out of the window.

Emily leans over me so she can see. So close, I can smell her perfume.

Now, I can't explain this to you, but all I can say is that there's something about her fragrance that calms me. It's like some kind of rescue remedy. It isn't exactly a sedative, but it's enough to knock the edge off.

"What about him?" she asks, following my gaze and squinting out of the glass.

"He.... He…" I trail off here as the man's face comes into view each time he pauses his conversation to look in our direction.

Obviously, just in case I didn't already feel like I was starting to lose a grip on reality, the man's face is normal now, apart from the fact that his nose looks like it's walked into a brick wall. He's in his thirties – designer stubble, wavy black hair. I assume that the blonde next to him, wearing a beanie hat and puffer jacket, is his wife or girlfriend. She has her arm linked in his and is also glancing across at us from time to time.

"Marco. What's wrong? What happened?" Emily prompts.

But I'm unable to respond. I don't know exactly how to process what I saw, or what I think I saw. I certainly don't know how to explain it.

"Marco, are you alright?" Emily continues.

I nod absentmindedly.

"Just, you're looking really pale. Like you've seen a ghost or something."

A ghost. Interesting choice of words. But the bloke isn't a ghost. He's standing right there.

I breathe deeply, running my hands through my hair as a dehydrated headache starts to press on my skull as my body remembers that its hungover.

Shit.

I'm Tired. Exhausted, to be more precise. It's a been a long, emotional day and, if I'm being completely honest, I don't think the booze has helped one bit.

Oh well... it felt like a good idea at the time.

"Marco?"

"I'm okay," I say, but I don't mean it. I'm far from okay. I'm confused, and not necessarily about what I think I witnessed in this carriage. I've already explained that away as some waking nightmare. A kind of a sleep paralysis brought on by a particularly emotionally stressful day.

How did I reach this conclusion so quickly?

Easy.

Ask yourself. What would you believe? That the man really had a melted face that miraculously put itself back together again, or that the drunkard – and that would be me – imagined, or more specifically, dreamt it?

Exactly.

"What are you doing here?" I croak with a dry mouth as I continue to creep out the couple by staring at them until they eventually walk off.

The officer who was with them takes over the staring contest by looking in our direction.

"Um, we came for you," Emily says.

"Why? You cops that bored, you're providing a taxi service now?"

"Come on," she says, standing up and taking my hand. "I'll explain on the way."

It feels nice. I know that sounds cheesy, and especially when you consider my relationship with women, but there's something about the warm, dry touch of her fingers around mine that, not unlike her perfume, is soothing, reassuring, safe.

I know that sounds completely bonkers, but after this week of an affection drought, her one action is amazingly powerful, and I couldn't tell you if that's due to the simple fact that a female is holding my hand, or because it's *this* female who's doing it.

Something else I notice is the way she promptly lets go at the moment we reach the train doors. Instead of holding my hand, she places a guiding one on the small of my back as her partner eyes me, suspiciously.

"Everything okay?" Sasquatch asks. I've automatically dubbed him that because of his height and build. The guy is huge. Heavyset. Not somebody you'd – alright, I – would want to mess with.

"Everything's fine," Emily responds with a reassuring smile. I'm assuming that was for me. If it wasn't, I'm taking it anyway.

But everything isn't fine. Far from it. And everything feels much worse when, each and every time during the drive back to Dolce Vita, my questions about why the police have invaded my home and what I may have done to deserve a police escort go unanswered.

Inevitably, my anxiety levels are climbing once more, and now, Emily and her magic hands are in the front with her colleague, along with her mystical, magical fragrance, which is too far forward to cast its spell on me. In fact, and don't laugh when I say this, I'm actually finding myself leaning forward towards the front passenger seat and breathing in in the hopes of copping another sniff.

No, Marco that doesn't sound pervy at all.

Before long, the patrol car is scrunching over the gravelled drive and home.

Note how I'm calling it home again, now that my lawyer has given me hope.

The patrol car stops just outside the gate. The house is ablaze with light. Officers stream in and out of the front door like termites from a mound, and back and forth to the woods like ants on a mission.

I hear Emily speak into her radio as I watch these strangers stomp around my property and I feel a flare of anger. "Okay. So, I'm not exactly an expert, but I'm pretty sure that you need a warrant to come onto my property and trample all over my home, so now I think would be a good time for you to tell me what the fuck is going on!"

The last part of my sentence has come out as an angry snarl, prompting Sasquatch to mumble, "Nah, we'll have less of that."

Emily's more civil. "Everything will be explained to you, Marco. I promise. We're just waiting for the D.C.I. to join us."

I can just about make out the look in her eyes. They're friendly, yet her pupils keep flicking back and forth, which makes me think that she's anxious about something – and, I can tell you, that shit is contagious.

This means that, by the time the Columbo wannabe – a short arse in a long coat – sits in the backseat next me, tugging the door shut behind him, I'm a nervous wreck.

"Mr. Battista?" Short-arse asks as he turns to me in his seat.

I nod.

"I'm Detective Chief Inspector Grant. I'm in charge of this investigation. You probably have a few questions…"

"..Yah think?" I interrupt.

He pauses and then adds "…But I'd like you save these until I've finished asking you my own questions…"

"… What the fuck is going on? Why are you here?"

"Mr. Battista…"

"…No. Why are you here? Why are you at my house? I'm not answering any questions until you tell me what the fuck is going on."

"Mr. Battista…"

"…Marc."

TONY MARTURANO

I hear Emily's voice and look at her dimly lit and yet encouraging face. She doesn't need to say anything else.

"We could always do this down at the station, if you prefer," Grant is saying.

"Just get on with it," I snap sulkily.

"What can you tell me about the little boy that went missing last Monday night?"

It takes me a few seconds to register what the hell he's talking about, and then I remember what Emily told me that morning by the front door. The paper headlines in London. Shit, it all seems so long ago.

I shrug. "Only what I heard."

"What did you hear?"

"I heard that he'd gone missing and that you were looking for him."

"Is that all?"

"Yes."

"When did you hear this?"

"Um..." I think about this. Although recent developments have gone some way to sobering me up, the alcohol is still making my head fuzzy, as well as bloody achy, and I could really use a drink. Water, that is. "Um, I think it was Tuesday. Tuesday morning."

"How did you hear about it?"

I glance at Emily. I don't know why, but for some reason I feel that telling him I heard it from her could somehow be dropping her in it.

"I heard it on the radio," I lie.

"Tuesday morning."

"Um, yeah, I think so."

Grant exchanges glances with Emily and I instantly regret the lie. Oh well.

"Have you ever met Timothy Cooper?" Grant asks.

"Um, yeah, once."

"When was that?"

"I met him down at the pub. I was down there the night of his birthday party."

"Did you speak to him?"

"Yes."

"What did you say to him?"

"I wished him happy birthday; what do you think I said?"

"And that's all?"

"Um, no, actually we started talking about politics and he told me how the government really needs to curb public spending... Yes, that's all."

If my sarcasm has annoyed Columbo, he doesn't show it.

"And have you seen and or met Timothy at any other time?"

"I've already answered that question. Now, look, what is this about?"

"Have you ever given Timothy any gifts of any kind?"

"Yes."

"When?"

My head is feeling really tight. My temple is throbbing. I want out of this car, but even I know that losing it in front of this bloke isn't going to do me any favours.

Sighing, I say, "I gave him a remote-controlled model of a Schooner, at his birthday party at the pub. But then, I imagine you already know that because pretty much the whole village saw me hand the thing to him."

"And that was the last time you saw him?"

"Yes."

"Are you sure?"

"Am I sure? What, you think I would forget something like that?"

As I spoke the words, I watched him grimace slightly, and then I understand and nod. "Right, so I've had a few drinks and now I'm a drunk who can't remember anything. Is drinking against the law now, too?" I ask seriously, but nobody responds, so I fill in the gap. "I've spoken to Tim once in my life and that was on Monday night. I gave him a birthday gift. His parents saw me do that. That is the last time I spoke to him. Is that a suitable, comprehensive, and definitive enough answer, DIC?"

The duo in the front seat glance at me and then at each other.

"Well, that's what you are, isn't it? A DIC?"

Emily suppresses a snigger. "Actually, Marco. The Detective is a DCI, Detective Chief Inspector, not a DIC," she explains.

Well, that's a matter of opinion.

"Oh, I'm sorry," I say with a grin.

"Do you think this is funny, Mr. Battista?"

"Well, no – I just transposed the letters, that's all."

"I'm talking about the life of a ten-year-old boy; do you think that's a laughing matter?"

"No, of course not."

"Then I'm going to give you one more chance to answer my questions without trying to be a smartass."

Shit. He's looking deadly serious now.

"Detective. I've already told you. I didn't know the boy. I saw him down at the pub and then never saw him again. There really isn't much more I can tell you about it, and, again, I'm no expert, but I can't see how that gives you the right to traipse all over my property."

"You say that you never saw Timothy again after you met him at the pub, is that correct?"

I sigh. "Yes, that's correct."

"Never?"

"Oh my God, I've already told you…"

"…Then, why is it that we have two witnesses who claim that you not only saw, but talked to Timothy after the party on Monday night, between the hours of eleven-thirty and midnight?"

Those words may as well have been a blade slicing down my chest and into my scrotum.

What the fuck?

"What?"

He's observing me, and I know what he's doing; he's checking my reaction and, while I can't see through his eyes, I know what he's seeing. A scared man with the blood drained from his face.

"That's impossible," I utter, shaking my head. "Who are these witnesses?"

"That's unimportant right now. All that matters is that both their separate statements tell us that you were the last person to see Timothy before he went missing. How do you explain that?"

"What do you mean it's unimportant? Of course it's fucking important because, whoever it is, they're lying! They're fucking lying! I didn't see Timmy outside that pub."

"Timmy?"

"That's his name, isn't it?"

"It's a bit familiar, given that you've only met him once."

"Are you fucking kidding me? His dad calls him that. What the fuck is this all about? Why are you all here? You can't all be here just because someone claims I spoke to a little boy."

I look at Emily. She blinks back at me, but says nothing.

Grant observes me for the longest fucking time before he says, "Timothy Cooper's body was found this evening on a beach near here."

"What? No."

"He was slumped over the ship model you gave him. It's being checked now for prints and DNA, and something tells me that this is going to lead us back to you."

The pressure in my head is suddenly immense. It feels as if somebody has been slowly inflating a balloon inside my skull and, if I don't get out of this car right now, it's going to explode.

I nearly lose that burger and fries over *DIC* but, lucky for him, I manage to yank the car door open and fall out of it before crashing forward and spewing all over the gravel.

It takes me several minutes to recover and, during the time, it feels as if I've left my body and am remotely watching some other poor bastard laying prone on that gravelled drive. Vomit dripping from his mouth, face in the dirt and stone, as a pretty copper fusses around him, handing him wipes and bottled water.

It takes a while before I realise that that poor bastard is me, and it's with true reluctance that I return to pilot the inebriated, stunned, and confused mind.

Every question that comes after that doesn't even register. Especially since most appear to be simple and subtle variations of the those I've already heard and answered.

Eventually, when I've had enough of going round in circles, my temper boils over and I tell DIC to fuck off and take his band of unmerry men with him. He, once again, offers to continue the conversation down at the station.

Prick!

I know my outburst probably didn't help things but, oh my God. It was just relentless, repetitive, and absolutely insulting. The mere suggestion that I would have anything to do with that little boy's death is just horrendous. Unfathomable. I wouldn't, nor could, ever do anything like that, and the fact that my gift was found at the scene – with, most likely, my fingerprints and DNA all over it – is purely circumstantial, and we both know that.

But these so-called witnesses. That's what worries me. Not that they claim I spoke to and saw Timmy, but why? Is it simply because I'm the newcomer here? Is someone trying to frame me? What?

Shit.

I was pretty smashed that night, and then there was that whole thing in that alley-way. Now I'm getting paranoid. Oh God. I can't think straight. I need to sleep.

I'm starting to feel much better by around ten o'clock because that's that when the platoon of officers finally pack up their shit and leave in a convoy of lights, growling engines, and dust.

DIC tells me that I'm now a person of interest, otherwise known as a suspect, and that, as such, I need to remain in regular contact with the police and that I'm not to leave the country while the investigation is ongoing, the post mortem conducted, and the cause of death established.

That was country by the way. Not county. As if. I don't even know where my bloody passport is!

Emily doesn't stay behind. She just gives me a long lingering look, like she wants to say something but can't, before she climbs into the passenger seat of the patrol car that, eventually, is just a glimmer of red lights that rapidly dissolve into darkness.

Shit.

I don't even know how to start processing all of this. Did that just happen? Did that really just happen? Did a whole bloody legion of cops just stomp their size nines all around my home?

Home.

I stare at the house; lights blazing, front door wide open. It looks angry. Not like home. Not right now. Now it just feels like the shell of something that's been raped and probably pillaged by a bunch of strangers.

Misery slowly devours me like a sticky, toxic cesspit as I rack my brains. Did I see anybody on the way home? Could I have seen and spoken to Timmy, but forgotten? No. I didn't talk to anybody! But then, why are those people saying that I did?

Now it's loneliness' turn to smother me like a wet hair blanket. I have no idea what to do next. What is clear is that my dehydrated brain is still very unhappy with me.

Should I try to contact a lawyer? I say it like I have a choice. Grant suggested that I contact my lawyer, before *cautioning* me.

What I would give for a hug from Toby right now. But he isn't here. I am alone.

Ten minutes later, after I've tried desperately to extract some comfort from the sobering chill of the frosty night and the now seemingly uncomforting sound of the grumbling surf, I push on the gate. It protests reliably, but the sound is no longer quaint or cute – just annoying.

I walk into the house and greeted with a sight that punches me in the stomach with the memory of Lucinda's voicemail.

What happened to the plants?

Well, apparently, what happened is that that they're all dead. Every single one of them. The dwarf trees have become desiccated twigs. They've been stripped naked of their leaves, which are now brown, partially crumpled, and scattered over the floor. The plants that were once verdant and vibrant are now black with brown patches, as if scorched by the sun.

"What the…." I walk up to the feature, but snap my head back when a foul, sewer-like stench envelopes me. The water is no longer cascading over the marble, but has instead pooled into a stagnant pond.

How the fuck is that even possible? In one day?

Now my mind starts to turn like a rusty weather vane. I think about

Harvey, but push the thought aside. I feel like a dick for even thinking this way, and yet I still allow myself to consider it. To consider the possibility that maybe, just maybe, he did this. But why?

I know it's ridiculous. But he was unhappy with me, that was obvious. And, being the shit that I am, I haven't managed to make it over there to make things good, but this? Really?

The lights flicker on and off and I freeze before my attention is drawn to the sound of a creaking door and then a thump. It's coming from across the room.

"No. Oh no." I put my hands out as if I'm steadying invisible wires. The last thing I need is a bloody power outage. Yet, no sooner does the thought enter my mind than the lights die, plunging the room into darkness.

"Oh shit!"

This day just keeps getting better. What's this all about? The weather couldn't be any calmer. What's going on?

I remain still for seconds, frozen like the air that's drifting through the open front door.

Then, I duck, instinctively, as a light beam slices through the glass in the terrace doors and sweeps around the room.

Creak. Thump!

I wait for my eyes to become accustomed to the gloom and then squint into it.

Scratch.

What is that? Is it one of the policeman? Has someone been left behind?

You know it isn't.

The sound is coming from across the room and is like fingernails on wood. Something is in the house, and the realisation sends a claw of fear scraping down my spine. This is instantly exacerbated by my mind's recall of the kitchen intruders, as well as the rooftop scuttling that took place afterwards.

Shit.

I think of calling the police, but there's no fucking signal here to do it.

My frantic heart wants out of my chest, but my feet are rooted to the spot. Rooted with fear as more scratching and creaking burrows into my ears and scampers across my brain.

Another shard of light sweeps around the room, illuminating the space temporarily, and that's when, through my fuzzy, fear-numbed brain, I'm able to conclude that the light is coming from the lighthouse. The beam is faint, but distinctive.

Scratch. Creak. Thump!

Now, I'm convinced that some hideous creature, like the thing I saw on the train, is dragging itself through the shadows, across the floor to me, and I can feel a scream creeping up my throat, but it catches there when the creak is suddenly replaced by a whimpering sound.

"Hello?" I call into the darkness as another beam arcs around the den.

The only reply is the creak and thump that I've now established is coming from the photography room. The door has been left open. Now, someone or *something* is in there.

More whimpering. It sounds like a pained puppy. In my mind's eye, I can see it dragging itself and a wounded limb across the floor to the door where it's now scratching, begging to be let out of there.

"Hello?" I call again. I don't even know why.

Nothing. Just the usual background rumble of the surf. The house is, in fact, painfully, eerily – and yes, I'm man enough to say it – terrifyingly quiet, which is only making the desperate clawing more chilling, because it's echoing around the room and ringing in my ears.

There's more pitiful, painful whimpering, and I've had about as much as I can bear.

Fuck it!

I wait for the next shard of light, check that there really is nothing on the floor in front of me, and march over to the photography room. I am just about to push on the door, but jolt backward as something launches itself at it from the other side, forcing the door to creak and almost shut in protestation. Then, the scratching resumes. Desperate. Frantic. Loud. The sound of nails *or claws* scraping on wood rakes across my eardrums and warns me not to go in there.

"It's okay. It's okay," I coo, instinctively.

Creak... thump!

"Who's there?" I call through the door as I'm gripped by a vice of dread that's squeezing my guts, pushing them into my throat, making me want to spew again.

Don't go in there, Marco.

"Hello?"

Light slithers around the den and then the lobby.

Creak. Thump!

Sweat glistens on my forehead. I can feel it. It's prickling my skin, and I want to wipe it, but I can't. I'm afraid of making any sudden movements. My chest is tightening, squeezing my breath in to short and shallow rasps.

I reach for the door handle, but shy away as the scratching resumes, rocking it back and forth.

"It's… okay, boy… It's okay," I utter through a tight throat. "It's okay. But I realise that I'm not talking to whatever is in there, but to myself. I don't want to open that door. I don't want to find out what's behind it.

Then, don't!

Clawing. Scratching. Creak. Thump.

Tears prick my eyes as my head trembles with tension.

Creak. Thump.

I can hear it now. The rattle. The squelch. The spittle.

Creak. Thump.

It's getting much faster now. Desperate. It wants to be set free!

Creak. Thump. Creak. Thump. Creak. Thump.

My fingers are inches away from the handle. My heart is in my mouth. My head is going to explode.

Then…. the lights come on, and an incredulous voice that I immediately recognise asks, "What the 'ell is going on 'ere, then?"

FRIENDSHIP

Later Friday Night.

When I first see David standing in the doorway, I actually think I'm dreaming. No, not in a romanticised kind of way, but more in a practical, *if I'm going to have to deal with this weird shit, then he's most likely the person I'd want to find gawking at my sweat-drenched, blood-drained face while I'm holding a shaky hand over a perfectly innocent looking door handle* kind of way.

A door that, incidentally, has revealed absolutely nothing. The room is empty. At least it is according to David.

Well, you didn't think I was going to venture in there, did you?

Of course, I didn't explain anything about that to him. At least, not while he was busy throwing his arms around a stupefied me.

It's weird and wonderful, as if all that crap in London didn't happen. At least, judging by his demeanour, and I'm so bloody grateful for it. After the day I've had, it feels good to have a slice of my old life back.

Which means that, when David starts to going on about being hungry, I'm more than happy to cook us a plate of his favourite and my signature dish, no matter the hour.

Pasta Arabbiata, but made properly and not in that weird Frankensteinian way of chucking God knows what into the sauce and hoping for the best. My version is much more traditional, with fresh chilies, olives, and basil, some of which I pluck from the courtyard beyond the backdoor. Oh, and original Parmigiano-Reggiano cheese.

Yes, if there's one thing my little adopted village has going for it, it's the abundance of genuine artisan products.

I did bargain with David, though. I told him that, if I cooked for him, he would need to sort out the photography room for me. You know, tidy up in there and make sure that the windows and door are closed firmly behind him.

He agreed without asking questions since I made my request seem casual, as I stirred pasta. He did throw a glance my way, as if to say, *Why, what kind of practical prank have you got set up in there?* But I pretended I didn't notice and only turned when I saw him leave the kitchen through the corner of my eye. I then followed to the kitchen door threshold to make sure he was okay.

I know. Spineless.

But, you and I both know what I heard, or what I think I heard, even though it all miraculously stopped when he arrived.

I didn't know what to tell him, though. Not because I didn't trust him with that shit – he's my best mate – but I just didn't know how exactly to explain it. I didn't understand any of it myself and, to be perfectly honest, I was scared. Fuck, I *am* scared. I'm terrified of what the hell is going on. First there was that stuff on the train and now this crap with the photography room. How the hell do you go about explaining that?

No, I mean really. Take a second and have a think about that. Imagine if this was happening to you... which friend would you tell, and what do you think their reaction would be?

Exactly.

That didn't mean I wasn't going to try, though. I had already unloaded everything about my trip to London on him, as well what happened to

Timmy and the police invasion.

Of course, his reaction to all of this was to make a joke; I'd only been here one week and I was already causing trouble. The thing is, I haven't been. It's as if trouble keeps finding me.

When he comes back into the kitchen, I've busied myself with the sauce once more, but look up and scrutinize his face, as casually as I can, for signs of shock and horror – but there's nothing.

I only realise I'm staring at him when he asks, "What?"

"Nothing. Just glad you're here."

He smiles. "Bloody 'ell, mate, you'll be telling me you love me next."

"I already tell you that."

"Yeah, but rarely. You only say it either when you want something or when you're drunk."

"That's a lie," I protest, as I stir sauce into the pasta. When I realise it's gone quiet, I look up; he's sitting at the island, watching me. "Really?" I ask. He nods. "Right, well, you know that whole stereotype thing about gay men being like women?"

He rolls his eyes. I grin and fork spaghetti into a bowl.

The thing is, I do love this bloke. He's like a brother to me. And I'm so bloody happy to have him here because it's only now that I have some company that I realise just how much I've really missed it.

This also puts a thought in my head. I wonder if all of this weird stuff is a bi-product of me spending way too much time on my own. As we established earlier, I'm not good at being alone. This could all be my subconscious, fuelled by my irrational fear of the past. It's spawned this shit to scare the crap out of me. And, in my professional opinion, that makes perfect sense, although it doesn't go so far as explaining what happened to Tim, the intruders, or all of the other physical stuff that's clearly not a figment of my imagination.

Half an hour later, most of which has been spent devouring spaghetti, we're both sitting in the kitchen with empty bowls in front of us. David is sipping wine that he brought with him, and I am – wait for it! – drinking water. Not because I'm a paragon of goodness, but more because I'm still emerging from my haze, and so I have no intention of going back there. At least, not right now.

"I'm really happy you're here, you know," I say.

David observes me for a few seconds. "I know."

"And," I pause, "I am really fucking sorry about what happened in London. I didn't mean to…"

"…You don't have to apologise; you can't help being a dick," he says with mock seriousness, as if there's no hope for me.

"I can. I let my emotions get the better of me," I say, and then as I'm watching him squirm on his barstool, I add, "again, you're my best mate, and I know I don't say it often enough, but I do love ya."

"Bloody hell. What have the locals been doing to you? Where's my uptight Italian stallion, and what have they done with him?"

"Oh he's still here. Just more in touch with his priorities."

"Yeah?"

"Yeah."

"And what about your other priorities, in the city?"

"What about them?"

"Do you think calling and threatening your wife with a lawsuit is going to help you get 'em back?"

I feel the walls of shame, especially now that I've sobered up, closing in on me. "Fuck."

"Yeah, fuck. Ellie's none pleased, mate."

"Well, what does she expect, Dave? She won't talk to me and, worse, she won't let me see Toby."

"Marco, you're never going to be able to talk to her if you don't deal with this in the proper way instead of in *your* way."

"You know, it's really fucking shitty the way you sound like her!" I snap. "I am dealing with it. Why do you think I'm here? Why do you think I sat in that place with that condescending shit for the best part of an hour today?"

"And then, in your own words, you told him to go fuck himself and left."

"What was I supposed to do? The guy's a prick!" My friend raises his eyes, as if to ask, *see what I mean?* I sigh. "He is," I reiterate. "Snivelling little shit, too. I told you what he said to me. He's lucky I didn't deck him."

Now it's his turn to sigh. "You know, if I pulled something like that, you'd be the first person to tell me I was scared of confronting shit."

"But you don't confront anything," I say with a grin, taking a sip from my glass.

"I said, *if* I pulled something like that. I was offering one of those things that you lot love to talk in – hypotheticals."

"Great. Well, I guess we're both one worse than the other when it comes to dealing with *shit*."

"Yeah, well, I'm 'ere now, ain't I? I'm confronting this." He makes a finger gesture between the two of us.

"True."

"Maybe you should start asking yourself why you can't."

I stare at him for a few seconds. "Fuck me, you've been dating an American for two seconds and you're already starting to talk like one."

He laughs, and I see his cheeks flush, and I know I'm onto something. "Bloody hell. You really like this one, don't you?"

A smile spreads across his face, and then he nods while avoiding eye contact with me, of course.

I feel an unexpected warm swell of something. I'm not sure what exactly. I think it's joy, or no, not joy, but pride. I'm really proud, and yes, joyful for my friend who has spent most of his life looking for something more than just a night-time thrill. Not that he'd ever admit to it, but I can tell by the way he's talked about Ellie and me that, secretly, he'd like to settle down, and I've lost count of the amount of times I've wished that for him but, like many, he's been hurt multiple times in the past and so he'd thrown the proverbial walls up, until now.

I instinctively reach over and pull him into a hug. "He's the reason I'm here," he says, once the hug ends. He has a rare supercilious smile on his face. The boy is in love, and I think I've just had a taste of what that happy-clappy excited girly thing is like. "He's been on at me ever since that night at the restaurant. Reminding me that good friends are hard to find. I said I know, but he said that joke was getting old and to get my butt over here."

I smile. "Yeah, he's a keeper, that one. It'll be wedding bells next."

He doesn't respond and, again, he avoids my gaze, but his blazing, now red big ears, give everything away.

"Fuck, mate, seriously?" I ask.

He nods.

"Congratulations!" I say, slapping him on the back.

"Nothing's been decided yet, but he asked me just before he left for the States and," the words catch in his throat. "And, guess who's the first person I wanted to tell?"

His eyes are moist. Shit.

We hug again and neither of us speaks for a few seconds. And yeah, don't think I haven't noticed this softer side to me.

Shit, in all of the time I've known David, we've never really talked. I mean we have, of course we have, but not like this. He's the closest person to me, beyond Ellie, but this time... I don't know, this time it's a different kind of bond. And I suppose that's primarily because of me. After spending this time alone, I've craved this kind of interpersonal connection and presumably allowed my own barriers to drop slightly, and so I've become receptive. That, and the fact that David has never talked about getting married before, and seeing him like this really warms my heart.

When we finally emerge from the embrace, my friend looks me in the eyes and asks, earnestly, "So, now that we've got all of that over and done with, are you gonna tell me why the fuck you sent me into that room for ya?"

My smile disappears, instantly.

NIGHT TERRORS

Saturday. 03:07.

I don't know what it was – if it was the explanation I gave David about the noises in the photography room, the break-in, the voices outside the study door, or even the weird melting face man – but it feels like I've barely gone to bed when I awaken to the sound of his screams.

Shit. Now, I can truly appreciate the term blood-curdling. I don't think I've ever heard anything as terrifying in my life.

I fall out of bed, stumble to the door, across the landing and into the spare room, flicking lights on as I go.

I gawk at the empty bed. My semi-roused mind is just processing whether or not the screams actually came from in here when I'm drawn to a whimpering in the corner of the room.

I look behind the door – David, in nothing but his briefs, is backed up, into the corner, fingers covering his face.

"David? Mate." I drop to the floor in front of him. "Mate, what happened? Dave, what happened?" I ask anxiously, instinctively trying to pry his fingers apart.

He's breathing heavily, fast, like he's hyperventilating, and this gets worse when I finally manage to pull one of his hands away from his face and he catches sight of the bed.

"David. What happened? What's wrong?"

But the only response I get is a series of gulps, gasps, and splutters as his bulging eyes stare past me at the room, as if he's expecting someone or something to jump out of the shadows.

"David…"

"… I…I… need to go. I…I need to get out of here. I need to go. Now!"

"David. What the fuck happened?" I demand through my frustration, teeth clenched. "What happened?"

"I… n… need to go. I n … e… eed to go home," he whines through shudders.

I keep following his gaze, scanning the room behind me, but It's empty. There's nothing there.

I turn back to my best friend, and I don't really need him to tell me that he dreamt about something that's terrified him so much that his face is white, and I mean white, like those bats in the loft have visited him during the night and sucked out all of his blood.

Is that it? Did he see the bats? No. He's made of stronger stuff than that.

I automatically switch modes. "It's alright, mate. It's alright," I reassure him, figuring that I'll get answers later, once I've managed to calm him down.

I jump up and over to the bed, grab the quilt, and wrap it around him. "Come on, mate, come on, let's get you out of here," I say softly.

Reluctantly, he allows me to haul him to his feet while, all the time, his eyeballs flick back and forth, side to side, searching for something in the room.

With my arms around my shivering, quivering friend, I lead him across the landing and to the stairs, where I pause momentarily to look at something that turns my stomach. Something that brings Lucinda's words back to me; *What happened upstairs? The place is looking different...*

No shit.

There's a giant ugly crack, like the ragged teeth of an angry mouth, running from the attic into the stairs, and, for all I know, probably down into the dining room below.

BLUE EYES

Saturday. 11:03.

The clang of the doorbell awakens me from a restless sleep to a bad head and an equally bad mood. This is made worse the moment memories of last night also rouse from their slumber and start pulling at me, like demanding children.

I'm exhausted. What I would give to wake up just once in my own time in this bloody house rather than being yanked involuntarily out of sleep by a parade of uninvited guests.

And shit. Great. Now, I bet you can't guess what I'm thinking about.

I don't think describing yesterday as weird, uncanny, creepy, or with any other adjective adequately encapsulates what an absolute head-fuck it was.

Jesus. From the trip to London to the ride back home, to David's midnight freakshow, to the discovery that the house which, just a week ago, seemed to be something out of Lifestyles of the Rich and Famous, is actually falling down around my ears.

The doorbell clangs again and I've reached a decision; I hate that thing almost as much as I hate the Gestapo-knock that others seem to use as an alternative.

I tell you, for a place where I'm often feeling miserable because it's lonely, it seems I'm rarely fucking ever alone.

Begrudgingly, eyes still partially closed, squinting against the sun-drenched room, I rise to a sitting position in a move worthy of a Dracula coffin-rise.

Fuck. I'm knackered. I mean *really* knackered.

David decided that, when he said he wanted to go home, he meant literally half an hour later: not this morning, or tomorrow, or whenever the hell it bloody could be, but as soon as he could pack up his shit and leave.

There was absolutely nothing I could say or do to change his mind. Asked what exactly he had seen up there, he told me he'd had a nightmare, but I knew it was more than that. Much more. He just wouldn't or couldn't tell me.

It was only when he was dressed, his overnight bag in one hand and his car keys in the other, and by the front door, that he turned to me and told me not to worry, that he would get in touch when he got back home, but that he needed to leave straight away. Then, to add drama to all the creepiness, he glanced into the house, pursed his lips, and said, "The sooner you sell this fucking place and come back to London, the better."

Then, he hurried down the pathway, flung the gate open, got into his rather sexy Porsche Carrera, and was gone.

And what was that all about? I have never seen him that way. Never.

I stood at that door for ages, waiting for the growl of that Porsche's engine to fade before I turned and closed out the night behind me.

Then, I remembered. So, I crossed the entrance hall to the dining room, bare feet slapping loudly as I went, flung open the doors and snapped on the light.

Shit.

The crack, like a bolt of lightning, travelled from ceiling to floor, but I was just so tired at the time, I didn't even want to contemplate what that meant. Although, the thought of having to call in some overweight builder so he could scratch his belly and suck the air in over his teeth and tell me, "Aw, this doesn't look good, does it, guv'?," did push itself into my head, along with the fact that fixing or pointing or whatever the hell he would need to do to put the shitty thing right was going to cost money I don't have.

And do you know which bit of that scenario I hated the most? Having to walk to the top of the fucking lane to make the call!

So, I kicked a chair, stubbed my toe, swore some more, then leant on the dining table to wait for the ball-churning pain to subside. And that's when I noticed that my hand was full of it; thick dust that I then realised had covered the whole room. And I'm not talking dust like a week of neglected housekeeping, I'm talking about something you can plant stuff in. It's almost as if the builders had already moved in!

So, I stomped, or more like hobbled up the stairs, deliberately avoiding eye contact with the wall's mocking, gaping grin, before stalking into my bedroom and slamming the door behind me.

In bed, I wished for sleep to claim me quickly, to put me out of my misery by switching off the thoughts buzzing in my head, the pain in my foot, and the smouldering anger I was feeling about pretty much everything.

But no such luck.

Even the lighthouse seemed to be working overtime and, for reasons I cannot explain, appeared to have moved bloody closer. It was like having a fucking disco ball in the bedroom.

The sound of the doorbell brings me back to the present. Morning. Birds singing. Surf rumbling. Normality.

Then again, do I even know what that is around here anymore?

I run my hands through my hair, will myself awake, and slide my legs over the side of the bed.

My mood hasn't changed any. I could quite cheerfully punch someone in the face. So, whoever it is down there, they better have a bloody good reason for ringing that bell first thing in morning.

Again, I'm in my boxers, because I don't give a shit. I wrench the door open and my bad mood dissolves like the morning mist in sunshine.

"Hey," Emily says brightly. She's out of her uniform, in jeans, a white shirt, and a blue sweater. She's a fantastic sight for my literally sore eyes.

"Oh, hey." I smile. Anger smothered.

"I was starting to think you weren't in."

"No, I was, um, I was in bed."

"Ooh, late night last night?"

"You could say that."

We stand at the door, awkwardly, for a few seconds. Awkward only because part of my mind is telling me to make conversation, invite her in. You know. The other part – the sexually deprived heterosexual – is admiring how absolutely gorgeous she looks in those clothes. Petite. Trim. As if everything she's wearing has been tailored to fit her slim body and pert breasts.

And, as technical as this is going to sound, I also snatch a few seconds to consider my reaction to seeing her. Yeah, you can thank Doctor Holmes for that. I want to understand if my reaction to the sight of her is purely sexual or if it's something else.

Bet you can't guess what the result is…

"Is the underwear thing some kind of fetish, or do you just enjoy walking around half-naked?" She interrupts my thoughts with a grin as she looks me up and down. I feel that familiar heat rise to my cheeks again.

I laugh. "I'm sorry. I just…"

"…woke up. Yeah, you said."

"So, look, I thought I would come around and that maybe we could have lunch together?" She holds up a brown paper bag. "Pasties, homemade and fresh from the bakery."

"Sweet," I say, stepping aside. Then, I glance at myself and, as much as I hate to say it... *Do you mind if I jump in the shower?*"

She looks me up and down again, and, if I didn't know better, I'd say that she's just picturing me without my boxers on.

"Oh, no problem," she says quickly. And follows that up with a wink. There's definitely a mischievous twinkle in her eyes. Not a come-on. I know what they look like, and this is something else. Something that I realise has already improved my mood, considerably.

I take the stairs two at a time and am naked before I even hit the shower which, of course, of all of the time I've been here, has chosen this morning of all mornings to spit at me like a disgruntled reptile. Hot. Cold. Hot. Cold. In the five or so minutes I'm in that thing, I alternate from yelping at being scalded to losing my breath in the freeze.

Fuck!

I'm not even going to think about it now. Emily's downstairs. I'm in a good mood for a change and I'm not going to let anything spoil it.

I pull on jeans and my blue knitted jumper that Ellie says always brings out the green in my eyes. I also, childishly, like the idea of us dressing similarly.

Emily is surveying the dead plants when I reach the foot of the stairs, but she looks up when I join her and, again, she unashamedly looks me over, as if approving my outfit.

"Nice jumper," she says with a smile.

"Thanks," I say, and I'm about to explain that I thought it would be fun to match outfits, but I can already feel that warmth rising to my cheeks again, so I chicken out.

"What happened here?" she asks sadly, nodding at the graveyard of plants.

I shake my head and grimace. "I really don't know. If I hadn't received a call from my estate agent telling me that they were dead early yesterday morning, I'd be blaming you lot for trampling all over the place and leaving it looking like a tip."

She averts her gaze. Seemingly embarrassed. "I'm sorry about that," she says seriously, as if she'd personally authorised the search.

"It's okay. I know you were just doing your job. Speaking of which," I wave my hand between us both, "isn't there some kind of conflict with you being here?"

"You don't want me here?"

"No, of course not. I mean, no, of course I do," I say, quickly. *Shit, get it together, Battista.* "I mean, with me being number one suspect and all," I lift my eyebrows dramatically. "Sorry, no, what was the term your boss used, *person of interest.*"

"Well, first, he isn't my boss. ... Well, he kind of is, but indirectly. And secondly, well, we don't know what happened yet, hence why the investigation is still ongoing and hence why it's something we shouldn't be discussing."

Our eyes meet for the longest of moments, and I wish she would stop doing that, because it keeps making me nervous.

What is happening? It feels like I'm not even involved in this whole discourse. It's like I'm watching it from somewhere else, like through a cinema screen. These two protagonists, flip-flopping between awkward flirtation and professionalism.

We're both bloody married!

And yes, given my reputation, it's perfectly logical for that statement to bring a cynical smile to your face. But, again, after my session yesterday, I'm looking at this from a different perspective. And it feels like, for the first time in a long time – or in as long as I can remember – I'm actually thinking with my mind and not with what's inside my shorts.

That's because the conclusion to my little self-examination at the front door is that I think Emily is beautiful. Yeah, that we already know. What I didn't know, until I took a few seconds to consider it, is that my initial reaction to her is not to have sex, but... I don't know, to just enjoy being around her. I mean, I wouldn't mind sex but... oh, why am I even explaining it to you? You probably don't believe me anyway.

"Hey, listen," I croak, as of course, my throat is suddenly dry, "what do you say to us going for a walk, down on the beach, and taking your scrumptious gifts with us? A bit like a walking picnic?"

"I thought you'd never ask," she replies, waving me to the door in an invite to lead the way.

I do.

I lead us out through the terrace doors and into the fresh air, which feels and tastes good. I can't even describe it to you. It's like being released from jail. Not that I would know, of course. You'll be pleased to know that my rap sheet of misdemeanours doesn't extend to any time spent at *Her Majesty's Pleasure.* But hey, give me time.

It's odd, because it's almost as if I've forgotten exactly where I am. I've temporarily lost sight of the fact that I'm living in a house next to the ocean, with an abundance of autumnally fresh sea air, cloudy but with sunny skies and a bloody killer view. And, yet. It feels like I've spent my days cooped up in that building.

I lead Emily by the tree, where I go through the ritual of touching the bark, as if the act might restore some energy to my disillusioned cynical self and enable me to deal with the beauty by my side.

No, I'm not talking about the view anymore, but this woman who has spontaneously thrown her arms around the tree trunk as if it's a long lost relative.

I smile at her spontaneity and revel in the fact that she adores the tree as much as I do. There's no need for introductions – these two are like old friends.

"I love trees," she says, placing her cheek against the bark as if listening for a heartbeat.

Eventually, she relinquishes her new squeeze and, paper bag in hand, skips the rest of the way down to the garden gate.

"Have you been here before?" I ask, squinting into the sun that's temporarily made an appearance from behind a big fluffy cloud that looks like a giant marshmallow. It's hanging so low, I feel like I can reach up and touch it.

"No, why do you ask?" she returns casually as she reaches for the handle and pulls the gate open.

I watch the act and the way that her shoulder-length auburn hair is fanned by the ocean breeze and set alight by the sun.

"No, no reason," I say, stepping through the open gate.

"Oh, by the way, would you like a drink?" she asks, reaching into her bag and plucking out a bottle of water.

"Thanks," I say, wishing there was some alcohol in there.

"So, is your wife planning on joining you? I forgot her name…"

She's looking at me expectantly now.

"Ellie," I say.

"You told Grant that your wife was in the city, but that she was planning on joining you soon… but you've been here a week."

She's skilfully descending the rocky coastal path ahead of me, so I can't see her face, but I'm sure she's making a point, and I'm momentarily unable to find the words. Her candidness takes some getting used to. Yes, even for someone like me.

"You checking up on me?"

"Oh no, I was just wondering. Well… Okay, I was being nosey." She stops abruptly and turns to face me, hair flying across her face, sapphire eyes wide and mischievous.

I can smell her shampoo. Something you and I know doesn't normally bode well for my self-control. But I'm, um, surprised to report that, while I could quite cheerfully kiss those beautifully plumped lips, my thoughts don't stray anywhere beyond that.

Now, I'm really confused.

I smile. "Truth be told, we've been having some problems lately."

"Oh no, I'm sorry to hear that. How's Toby taking it?"

And just like that, she punches me in the stomach, knocking the foolish schoolboy fantasy out of me.

I take a moment.

"Oh, I'm really sorry. Me and my big mouth. People are always telling me that I have no filter. I promise, I'll shut up now," she says, turning and resuming the descent with purpose.

I laugh, since there's no other possible way to react to her candidness and, the thing is, I like it.

My whole life's work is about getting people to face up, to talk about the things that they would much rather keep buried, things that affect their everyday lives. I can't help but wonder what life would be like and what would happen to my profession if people were more like the gazelle in front of me.

We've reached the beach now. The surf is loud. The water is a blend of grey and emerald green as the sun flashes in and out of those giant cotton-wool clouds floating overhead.

Emily pauses as the wind styles her hair, and I feel a bizarre compulsion to touch it. To just simply allow my fingers to be tickled by those deliciously soft strands.

She turns to look at me over her shoulder. "I love the ocean, don't you?" she asks, dreamily.

I nod, since that's all I can do because here, in this very moment, she's reminding me of that memory. The face looking at me on the beach through a curtain of hair. Was it her?

"You okay?" she asks, her thin eyebrows arching.

"I'm good."

"Not all the time, I bet," she says with another of her cheeky smiles. She delivers the line as she searches in her bag of delights and produces a pasty that's semi-wrapped in a paper pocket.

"Thanks," I say, taking the traditional savoury pastry.

"These will be the best pasties you've ever eaten," she declares, as if she personally baked them.

I'm still looking at her. "What?" she asks.

"You just say what comes into your mind, don't you?" I laugh. It's refreshing.

"Doesn't everyone?"

I give her a squinted sideways glance.

"Okay, well, most people do, and if they don't then they should. If you think or are feeling something, what's the point in keeping it all bottled up?"

"You make it sound so simple," I say, taking a bite from my pasty.

"That's because it is."

I shrug and rock my head.

"See? You don't agree, but rather than say it, you just shrug. What's so terrible about speaking your mind?"

"You know, if I didn't know better, I'd suspect you were trying to get me to confess to something."

She laughs. Then, "Are you talking about Timmy?" Seriousness making a rare appearance on that face.

"Well, I wasn't, because you said we're not allowed."

"We both know you didn't do anything to that little boy."

"How do you know?"

"I just do," she says, bringing back one of her smiles and walking forward.

I follow her. The waves reach for us and yet dissolve just feet away.

"Shame you didn't share your conviction with your boss last night," I say, taking her up on her encouragement to speak my mind.

She looks at me, and arches her brow like she knows I'm making a point. "It's a process, Marco. Something awful has happened to somebody's son. Witnesses claim you were the last person to speak with him. We're obliged to look into that."

"I didn't talk to that boy," I say emphatically.

"You didn't or you don't remember talking to him?" she asks, casually, before taking a bite from her pasty.

"What's that supposed to mean?"

"Well, we both know you had quite a bit to drink that night. Maybe you don't remember talking to him."

I stop walking and turn to her. "What is this?"

She stops and turns to me. "Oh, I'm sorry, I really am. This isn't why I'm here, I promise. Just, you raised the subject, so..."

I sigh. "No, I'm the one who's sorry. I know you've got a job to do, and if it were my son, I'd..." I trail off here because the thought of something happening to Toby takes my breath away, and I'm reminded, once again, that it's been weeks since I've seen him and it's bloody killing me. I can't even imagine what it must feel like to know that your son is actually gone, forever.

"Come on," she says, linking my arm as if she's read something on my face. "Let's walk, and I'll let you grill me with questions for a change."

"Sounds good to me," I say, accepting her arm.

After a few seconds, I ask, "So, where's your husband today?"

"The two men in my life are out today. Some Laser Quest thing."

"Oh, Toby loves those places. Why didn't you go with them?"

"Not my kind of thing, really. Plus, I like them having their own quality time together. I read somewhere that it helps strengthen paternal bonds."

"Huh. So, as a cop, you don't enjoy rolling over barrels, skulking in corners, and stalking prey? I would have thought it would be right up your street."

"This is England, not the States," she says, rolling her eyes.

She's downwind from me, which means that every now and then I get a waft of her fragrance and I surreptitiously breath it in.

Oh God.

So, I hesitate a few seconds, but then, taking a page out of her book, I ask, "So, how are things with your husband? Everything good at home?"

Shit! What's wrong with me. I'm supposed to be a therapist, but here, talking to this woman, I'm a bloody bull in a china shop.

If she's surprised by my directness, she doesn't show it. "Oh, you know. It's okay. He's a good man, and he's great with my baby boy, but… you know, like most, we have our ups and downs."

Easily interpreted as, *there's more to this story*, but she's thought better of it and has decided not to tell me by playing down the seriousness of any potential problems at home. This only goads me, though, and I consider asking her outright, 'Why are you here? What do you want from me, you gorgeous and unusual thing?'

But again, I chicken out. Instead… "In answer to your question, Ellie isn't joining me," I say suddenly.

She glances across at me, presumably because she's expecting some melodramatic announcement about my marriage to follow, so now it's my turn to play it down. "We're kind of on a break."

"Oh, one of those, eh?"

"Yeah. Well, you know, every marriage has its ups and downs," I say, winking at her.

She laughs. I like that laugh. I like it a lot, but I was just talking about my marriage. To someone else. *Get it together, Battista.* But I'm on a roll. "You see, Emmy, I haven't been totally honest about…"

She stops walking abruptly and, because our arms have been linked, I stop with her. Then, she turns to me and says, cheerfully, "You know, there's a film, I can't remember which one, but the heroine turns to the man and says, *let's not tell our sad stories.*"

I grin. "That's *Jerry McGuire.*"

"You've seen it?"

"Who hasn't?"

We look at each other for the longest time, and it's one of those moments. You know… the pulse quickens, stomach flutters, and, well, I'm ready to kiss her.

NO!

This is insane, even for me. We're in the middle of talking about our marriages *to other people* and all I can think about is kissing those lips of hers.

"So, there's something I do want to ask you," she says, finally breaking the spell. "And, well, you know it's completely up to you…"

"…Seriously? You mean there's actually a subject that you're struggling to bring up without preamble?" I ask with mild amusement.

"Yeah, well, occasionally, I do remind myself to engage my brain before speaking."

"What is it?"

"It's this housewarming you've got planned for Saturday."

"What about it?"

"Do you think it's still a good idea, given what's happened?"

"Code I'm interpreting as, you *don't* think it's a good idea."

"Oh no, it's just…"

"…Come on, Emily. You're all about the naked truth, remember?" She looks at me and she doesn't need to say anything. "How much do you think they'll despise me if I go ahead with it?" I ask, and then watch her rock her head as she ponders the question. "Oh, bloody hell. That bad, eh?"

"It's just that it's a small village," she begins, as if she's going to say more, but she doesn't, and she doesn't need to.

"So, are you counselling me against the party because it's in bad taste or because it's me, number one suspect, who'll be hosting it?" Again, she doesn't respond, but simply glances at me with a sympathetic expression. "Blimey, Emily. I think I prefer it when you speak your mind."

"I'm sorry. I don't know. It's just that I've been thinking about it, and I know Shawn, Spencer, and the guys are excited, but…" she lets the sentence

TONY MARTURANO

hang in the air until it's snatched and carried off by the breeze.

"Wait, you've spoken to them about this?"

"Well, actually, they spoke to me – told me how much they're looking forward to it and, well, that got me thinking. But, it's just a thought, that's all. I mean, actually, no... forget it, forget I said anything."

"Oh no, no, no. You can't drop something like this and then try and run away from it."

"It's stupid. Really, just forget I said anything."

"No, you obviously mentioned it because you're worried and, to be honest, the thought hadn't even crossed my mind until you mentioned it. There's been so much going on around here, I didn't even think, but after last night... Maybe you're right. I'll talk to Spencer, make sure he hasn't started buying in loads of stuff."

We resume our walk for a few minutes, each lost in thought, until she stops again and looks at me, her face brimming with resolve.

"Uh oh."

"Do you know what?"

"What?"

"Fuck them!"

I burst out laughing. That word just sounded so wrong coming from those lips. "I can't believe you just said that."

"Well, it's true. Bad things happen to people all the time, and I mean this with absolutely no disrespect to Pete and Deedee, but whether we come round yours for a few drinks or we stay at home, weeping, it won't change anything. Will it?"

She searches my eyes for validation. "Don't look at me, you're on a roll," I say.

"Really. Please ignore what I said."

"Well, maybe...."

"...Promise me you'll ignore what I said," she insists.

I couldn't say no even if I wanted to. "I promise. Blimey, it wasn't even my idea in the first place; it was..."

"...I know," she interrupts.

"You know?"

"Yeah."

"Don't tell me. Shawn told you."

She shrugs, and I roll my eyes. "It's a small village," she repeats. "Besides, he said that he had to suggest it because it looked like you never would."

"And she's back to speaking her mind again," I say. "So, anyway, thanks. I feel so much better about this party now. If I wasn't looking forward to it before, I'm thrilled now."

"Good," she says, patting me on the arm. "Glad I could help. Just don't expect a huge turn-out," she adds with a mumble.

"Wait, what?"

She laughs. "Just kidding." But she probably isn't. "So, when exactly are you going to give me the guided tour?"

"Oh, well." I remember the crack in the wall, the plants. "Ugh," I groan.

"What?"

"Want to hear something strange?"

"Strange, how?" she asks with mock suspicion.

"Strange, as in, by the time I've finished talking, you'll probably think I've lost my bloody mind."

"Tell me *everything*," she says. "Leave nothing out." Then, we're walking once more.

I don't know how long we spend down by the ocean, but it must be a couple of hours, at least, although it feels like minutes.

I tell Emily everything that's happened since I arrived at Dolce Vita – and I mean everything.

Why? I haven't got the foggiest. There's just something about the woman that demands a confession.

There's no doubt in my mind that, had she not quoted *Jerry McGuire* to me, I'd probably be adding in everything else about London, too.

By everything, though, I do mean everything. Not just all the rubbish I've shared with you, but everything that came before it, and it would have been easy. Very easy. Because this woman has a way of making every single word I say seem so important. And this isn't a feeling I'm unfamiliar with. It's something I often experience with clients. Some of them are so desperate, they'll hang onto anything I say in the quest to understand the puzzle that is us.

With Emily, it is slightly different, though. In that it feels like she really wants to know. Like she is isn't just interested in what I'm saying, but actually interested in me, in who I am as a person, in what makes me tick. Flaws and all.

This is how I know I could have confessed everything to her, but, luckily, I don't, because there's no doubt that would change everything.

Instead, I steer the conversation to her, to what it's like being a cop in a small town, to her son and her marriage. I even ask her to tell me more about those memories of us, to fill in the precious moments that I have somehow managed to lose. Now, even more regretfully, since I can only imagine the mischief she must have got me into.

And she does – plenty of it. Including our stealing apples from next door's orchard, taking possession of somebody else's sandcastle and passing it off as our own, and playing hide and kiss in some of the caves, despite her parents' express instruction not to. Apparently, she was always daring me to do stuff, and I did. I followed her like a puppy dog, even then.

We laugh a lot. Occasionally, I feel sad. How the hell could I forget this stuff? These were some of my best memories, and to hear Emily recount them like they belonged to somebody else is as compelling as it is fantastic, because it means I get to rediscover them all over again, and I love them – as much as, I realise, I've already come to love her.

There's only one problem; we're both already married.

THE FUNERAL

Sunday. 14:03.

I spent most of today clearing out the dead plants, and holding a funeral for them at the end of the back garden. Okay, I dumped them there, along with the remains of the dwarf trees.

But I did a mini speech in my head, telling them that they would never be forgotten and that the beautiful legacy of the marble stone steps that they've left behind will always be sure to forever keep them in my heart.

And that marble really is bloody beautiful. I wouldn't be surprised if the old man had it specially imported. It's black, featuring a series of white veins, like cream stroked through coffee, and a 3D galaxy of tiny glittering stars.

I've convinced myself that the feature looks much better now that the pots and plants have been removed, fully exposing the marble. I can only imagine what it would look like with water cascading over it.

By *imagine*, I mean just that by the way. After I cleared away the fetid, stagnant gunk that I presume started out as clear water, and switched the pump on, the thing spluttered, made some weird and disgustingly rude noises, and then died.

That was the end of that.

"What the fuck is going on?" I yell at nobody in particular. God, I'm sick of this shit. Everything is falling apart. It's like I take one step forward and fall five feet back.

Oh well, mustn't grumble. At least I have my health. And no, of course I'm not being sarcastic.

I take a seat on one of the steps and imagine the pump springing to life automatically, giving my backside a douche.

It doesn't.

What does happen, of course, in my new spooky house of horrors, is that suddenly and spontaneously, without any open windows or doors that I am aware of, the door to the photography room clicks and creaks eerily open.

"Are you fucking kidding me?" I growl, launching myself from my perch, stomping over there and tugging it shut with a loud slam.

I am in no mood for this crap right now. I'm not going in there! I'm not. So, leave me alone or, I swear, I'll bloody hammer the door shut!

Of course, I don't know who I'm saying or, more specifically, thinking all this to. Perhaps some invisible cosmic force that's here and trying to give me the creeps, and bloody well succeeding.

Unsurprisingly, all I have to do is think, 'Creepy, spooky,' and who do you think pops into my head? That's right, David, and what happened in that room on Friday night-slash-morning.

There's only one way to find out, although that does involve climbing to the top of the hill or hanging out of the window.

Shit.

I make tea and climb the stairs to my bedroom, where I unplug my mobile phone and check the screen. I don't even know why I do it anymore. There are never any messages there, probably because there's no bloody signal!

Then, I walk out onto the landing and towards the window where I catch sight of the attic door. It's a tiny, creepy thing set in an alcove, and it looks more like a cupboard or some secret passage for imps than the doorway to Spooksville.

Have you noticed how everything is creepy now? I can't move in this house, for stuff that now insists on giving me the wrong vibe. This place doesn't feel anything like it did when I first arrived.

Of course, I know this is stupid because I'm supposed to be a rational person who believes in tangible things, such as proof and evidence. But then, if that's the case, why do I spend most of my life listening to people's fantasies?

Because you seek to rationalise them, you fool. That's the whole point.

I suppose.

Bloody hell. Since when did I become such a miserable git? I guess this perpetual state of exhaustion isn't helping. My mind feels like it's on a constant hamster wheel. Round and round. If it isn't one troubling thought, it's another.

I think about this and, in a scene worthy of any melodrama, I allow my weary body to slide down the wall until my backside hits the creaky wooden floor.

Coming here was probably the worst thing I could have done. It really feels like I've locked myself in a prison haunted by the ghosts of my past, present, and future.

And they won't leave me alone.

Ghosts?

See? It's just a constant chain of something, and now I'm feeling miserable again.

The thing is, I recognise the signs. They're regular and constant. I am spiralling into a depression here. If I don't get my act together, it'll soon become clinical depression, too, although I think I'm probably already there. And marooning myself here, alone with no distractions, none of the things that I really want, isn't helping.

Ellie.

Emily.

Toby.

Ellie.

Emily.

Oh, shut up!

Well, she is the only good thing about this place right now. *Are you going to try to deny that?*

I consider it. I suppose I can't deny it. We had such a great time yesterday, and it's my favourite kind of pastime. Not doing much of much, and still enjoying every single second of it. I loved being around her and I loved hearing about the past of this strange little boy who was trouble, but cute with it.

Her words.

Maybe I should invite her over for dinner.

She's married.

It's just dinner. There's nothing wrong with that, right?

You're married.

God. I'm feeling depressed again.

No you're not; you're using this reality as an excuse to be depressed, feel sorry for yourself, and maybe drink yourself into a stupor.

Snap out of it, Battista, and call your friend. Who knows? He might even make you laugh. He normally does.

Sulkily, I drag myself up from the floor, open the window, hold the phone near it, and wait for the bars to appear. Sorry, I said bars, plural. I meant I was waiting for one little bar, singular.

As I'm doing this, I spot the door to the attic again.

No, no way. I'm not going up there. I don't even want to go into the photography room.

Yeah, but that place has memories.

And an attic, the place where most people dump their unwanted crap, doesn't? Get real.

If you're getting a bar down here, you're bound to get a better signal at the top of the house, where there aren't more walls blocking the reception, right? It's logical.

Maybe, and stumbling around in some dingy attic may well make for a good story, but it sure isn't a good thing to actually experience first-hand.

Are you scared?

What do you think? I am scared, but probably not in the conventional sense. I just don't want to be reminded of stuff. I'm just about keeping all of this together now, and I don't want to add any additional complication to that.

I glance at the phone's display. One bar.

Make the most of it.

I tap David's contact picture, which is a snap of him sticking two fingers up at the camera. I smile as I remember the day I took the shot. Then I wait for the phone to ring. It takes a few seconds, but eventually it does, for quite a long time, and I'm half expecting it to go to voicemail.

Then, "Hello."

"Hey, you. What did I do, get you out of bed, you dirty slut?"

"Hello?"

"David, can you hear me?"

"Marco?"

I bend my head so that it and the phone attached to my ear are hanging out of the window, "Yeah, it's me, buddy," I say casually, despite the fact that I must look like a complete weirdo to anyone who might be watching from the outside. "I'm just checking in after the other night. How are you doing? Are you okay?"

"Marco. Mate, I can't … 'ear you properly… ate. I think yo… asking how I'm do… "

I try to arch my head out of the window some more, as if I'm attempting to garrotte myself. "Is that any better, Dave?"

"Marco… you… out… house…"

"What was that?"

"Out… need… out…"

"What? David? Dave? David?"

But the only response is that now familiar disconnection beep.

"FUCK!" I yell, and slip back into the house that I now realise is only a tad warmer than the outside.

Then, I allow myself to slide back down the wall until my butt hits the floor again.

I close my eyes and listen to the sound of the surf, which is louder through the open window. I clench my jaw then listen, in the hope that the earthquake that is rumbling in all of my extremities will subside, but it doesn't. The bubble of rage, like a leviathan deep from the ocean floor, rises up my legs, through my crotch, into my gut, and over my chest until it explodes with me slinging the mobile phone across the landing.

The useless thing skitters across the wood floor and slams into the attic door.

SHAWN AND JESSICA

Monday. 17:58.

No, contrary to what you may have thought or in fact be expecting, I didn't and don't plan on going into the attic. There really are enough skeletons down here. I don't need to go climbing into some dusty old memory mausoleum to unearth more.

No.

Instead, I spent most of the day repairing, where I could, some of the fissures that have spontaneously appeared in walls around the house.

You know, if I didn't already own the bloody place, I would go so far as saying that I've been duped. I get here and everything's fine, and then there's dead plants and cracks in the dining room and on the stairs.

Today, it's been pretty much more of the same. So, now that I've finished labouring, am showered, and in my jogging bottoms, I am ready for some peace and quiet... but, guess what? That's right, the doorbell rings.

Front door open.

"Evenin'," says Shawn. He's out of his overalls, in jeans and a black Woolley jumper. "Yep. I'm on time this week, but it looks like Jessie ain't."

I step aside so he can come in.

He glances at my casual attire and asks, "You given up on us?"

"Um, well, given how things ended last week, I wasn't sure you'd be back."

"Well, don't get too excited, Doc. It may not happen," he says, slapping me on the shoulder. "I don't know if Jessie's going to show."

I consider this, and it's weird, but I'm actually glad for the company.

"I should go and get changed anyway," I say, looking at myself.

"What? For me? Nah, don't worry about it," he says, feigning flattery.

"No, not for you, but…"

"…for Jess? I wouldn't worry about her either. She's seen me in my joggers plenty. And complains every time. In fact, if she sees you, she might go easier on me next time," he says with a wink.

"Not sure that's helping," I say. There's a pause and then, "Listen, Shawn," I start, "I just wanted to… um." He leans in and pulls a curious face. He knows I'm trying to say something awkward, but he isn't helping, and I get the impression he'll probably end up annoying me by making a joke instead. God, now I know how Ellie feels. "I just wanted to say thanks."

"What for?"

"I don't know. Just. Well, it's a bit unorthodox, you being a client and all, but, you know, thanks for making me feel welcome. You know, down at the pub. Can't say I'm thrilled that you volunteered me for a house warming, but still. I don't know anybody here and, well, I appreciate it."

He laughs. "No worries, mate. It's cool. Oh, and don't sweat it about the house warming; Spence and I have got you covered. Besides, we're under strict instructions."

"What do you mean?"

"Well, I quite like ya. Not in *that* way, of course – you're not my type." He laughs. "Nah, Uncle Harvey told me you'd take care of me, but that in return, I need to make sure I take care of you."

"Harvey told you that?"

"Yeah, before you even got here."

Good ole' Harvey.

"Oh, right."

"So, we cool?" he asks.

"Oh yeah, of course."

He looks at me for a while and I can't help but wonder what's going through his mind. "What?"

He leans in again. "Doc, can I ask you a personal question?" Now *he* looks awkward.

"Um, only if you call me Marc. What's up?"

"Are you, you know, happily married?"

Well, I wasn't expecting that. The paranoia bell sounds loudly in my head. "Why do you ask?"

"Oh, no reason. Just wondering."

He's watching me with eager eyes and I know he wants an answer, yet I don't know how to respond. I mean, I really don't. From what I know, Ellie and I are... were?... could be happy, if I wasn't such an idiot. Sure, we have disagreements, like most couples, but generally we have been happy, if not for me ruining everything.

"Well, you know. Like most marriages, we have our disagreements." I give him my stock answer and hope it's enough. Hope that he doesn't see through it to the truth, which is that, no, we're not happy. Or, correction. My wife isn't happy because I'm a dick. Even more specifically, I think with it.

He's nodding. "So, you've never, you know, cheated on her?"

"Shawn, what's this all about?"

"Oh, it's just... Jessie."

"What about her?"

"Last week, she said something, and now I can't get it out of my mind."

"What did she say?"

"What if..?"

I wait for him to finish the sentence, yet when he doesn't add anymore to it, so I lift my shoulders. "You've lost me," I say as he gazes into space, obviously recalling something.

"Last week, after we left the session, we got into a fight…"

"…you and Jessie?"

"…Yeah. She accused me of having doubts about the wedding, and I was like, 'What? You were the one who was having doubts during the session.' Anyway, she accused me of not being committed, and then she said, '*What if.* What if you wake up one day and realise that this is all some terrible mistake?'"

"Shawn, I'm still not sure I follow. You're having doubts about getting married?"

He looks me straight in the eyes and asks, "What if? What if Jessie isn't the one? Now that she's planted those two words in my head, I can't seem to get them out."

I'm about to speak, but my sentence is cut short by the sound of the doorbell.

Shawn widens his eyes as if to say, 'Brace yourself.'

Front door open.

Jessica, in customary suit, is standing in the doorway, but she isn't looking at me – she's looking at the garden.

"What did you do to these?" she asks, dismayed.

I step out and follow her gaze to the wall flowers.

Every one of them, not unlike the house plants before, has shrivelled up to a black crisp, as if they've been burned.

I shake my head. "I didn't do anything," I utter, stupefied. "They started to wilt last week and…"

"…Oh well," she shrugs, walking by me into the house.

I survey the rest of the garden, like I'm expecting to see the culprits scuttle off back into the trees, but there's nothing out here, but for a deep chill. So, I turn and go back inside, closing the door behind me.

In the study, we assume the same seats as last week. Shawn and Jessie on the couch and me in my armchair.

"How are you this week, Jessie?" I ask, shuffling into my seat.

"I'm fine," she responds enthusiastically. "How are you?"

"I'm good, thank you," I nod.

"Shawn?"

"Brilliant," he says with a cock of the head, but I know he's being sarcastic. I know, because it's probably what I would have said in this situation, especially after how things ended last week.

In therapy, sometimes, the very seat you've parked your backside on can be a trigger to making you feel a certain way. Specially, if you've been looking at particularly painful things. Which means that the next time you sit on that chair, you automatically associate it with what came previously.

So, I try to address that head-on. "I'd like to start by saying how happy I am that you both chose to come back this week. I know things got a bit tense last time."

"You don't need to thank us, Marco. We know you're happy we're back. I think we both fully understand the benefits of repeat business," Jessie says with sickly smile.

Wow, we're just minutes into the session and she's already staring me out. I notice Shawn look at her, and I hope he doesn't try to stick up for me. It's one thing being friendly and another to compromise your own therapy for it. This is exactly why fraternisation between therapist and patient is frowned upon.

He moves to speak, but I head it off, "You think I'm only interested in you for your money, Jessie?" I ask with a smile.

"Aren't you?"

"Well, I wouldn't say that…"

"…But you should make the most of it because this will be our first and last official session."

Shawn looks at her, as if he's just hearing this for the first time.

"Well, I'm sorry to hear that, Jessie. Can I ask why?"

She purses her lips, then says, "I just can't see how sitting in here, spilling our guts to you, is going to help us solve our problems. Surely, the only way we're going to do that is by taking action."

I rock my head. "Well, don't you think the two can be related, Jessie? Generally, it's only through analysis that you can determine the action."

"I already know we've got problems, Marco. I don't need to pay you for the privilege of telling us the same."

"Okay. Let's talk about that."

"What's the point?"

"Well, you're here now. As you say, this is your last session, so why not make the most of it?" I bridge my hands. Something I normally avoid doing, as it's a somewhat stereotypical gesture, but I think I'm making a point here.

She turns to look at the garden.

"Shawn?" I direct my question at him. "You booked these sessions. You must have felt there was something wrong. Something that maybe you wanted to understand or perhaps even tell Jessie," I ask, perhaps too pointedly, which is obviously a side effect of the discussion we've just had. This is exactly why things should not be discussed out of session.

He looks at me, as if I've put him on the spot, and I'm expecting him to bail, to make up some excuse, but what he actually does is turn to her and say, "You're obviously stressed out about the wedding, but I don't know why. It's always been your thing. So, I want to know if the problem really is your mum taking over or if it's something else."

We both watch the side of her head for a few seconds as birds tweet outside.

"Don't you just hate days like today?" she asks, suddenly, without turning to us. "This is what I call a grey day. Just a flat sheet of grey sky with no actual cloud definition, no rain. Nothing. Just flat greyness."

"Are you still talking about the weather, Jessie?" I ask softly.

Her laugh is hollow. "Is that your therapy? Everything has meaning?"

"Doesn't it?" I ask. And I would know. "More than often, it isn't necessarily the things that surround us, but more the importance we attach to them. Um, say, for example, a person sitting in an office. He or she has no control over the weather, but they do have control over how it makes them feel. Sunny skies generally make people happy, and rain often makes them sad. Then, there are others – those who enjoy nothing more than a downpour, a blanket, and a good book."

"I'm sorry. Is there a point here, somewhere?" She asks apathetically.

"It's not always the things around us that influence how we feel, but it's more than often our reaction to them. Perhaps it isn't necessarily the wedding preparations, but more your reaction to the same. How they make you feel, Jessie."

She doesn't respond, but looks back out of the window. I can see Shawn's gaze flit from her to me through the corner of my eye, but I don't engage with him; instead, I continue. "This is only the second time I've met you, Jessie, and it's quite obvious that you're not particularly thrilled about being here. But, at the same time, you want to be. It's almost as if you want or need to say something, but can't. Similarly, it's like you want to be married, as you seem to be going through the motions, even to the point of enduring your overbearing mother, while at the same time you seem disinterested, dissatisfied with a process that generally fills most brides with genuine excitement."

Now she gives me her gaze, although it's more of a glare. "You expect me to skip around like some love-stricken schoolgirl?"

"Why not?" I ask.

She sneers.

"Why not, Jessie? It's your wedding – you can do whatever you like."

More silence. More sounds of nature beyond the glass.

"Could it be, perhaps, that you like the idea of getting married, but that you don't necessarily trust it?" I ask.

She's staring at me now, tapping her foot, and I know I've struck a nerve. She doesn't say anything, though. It's like she's challenging me to read her mind or something.

And okay. I'm up for that.

I shift in my seat. A symbolic movement in therapy as we move onto another subject or line of questions. "Last time we spoke, you told me that, when you met, you were both already in relationships – is that right?"

Shawn looks at Jessie, at me, and then nods.

"And, if I remember correctly, Jessie, you were already engaged. Is that correct?"

She nods.

"Shawn, was your relationship serious? I mean, I can't remember exactly what you said." I make a show of trying to remember. "I think, if I'm not mistaken, you actually used the word *stolen*. You said, Jessie stole you from your, what was she... girlfriend, fiancé?"

He looks at Jessie and then back at me again, hesitates, and then says, "Wife."

"Oh." Okay. I wasn't expecting that. How did I not see it? "So, you were married?" I ask. He doesn't respond, nor is he making eye contact. "You *are* married?"

He nods, shamefully. I say shamefully because, guess what, I recognise the look. The hanging of the head. The dropped eyes. The reluctant nod.

"Right," I say, considering exactly what I've just learned. This changes everything. "Um, why didn't you tell me this last week?"

He rocks his head, uncomfortably.

"So, you're separated from your wife?"

"Yeah. We live in different houses."

"How long?"

"It's been a few months now."

"Not long then."

"Well, obviously long enough to plan a wedding," Jessie contributes.

"Well, that's the bit I'm wondering about, Jessie. If Shawn's still married then, how is it that you're planning a wedding?"

"My wife's already filed for divorce."

"Because of your relationship with Jessie?"

He nods, and I can't help but wonder if there's more to this, but I don't push it. I can already sense Jessie's hostility, and I don't want to make things worse – yet.

I nod. "So, how does all of this make you feel, Jessie?" I watch her jig her crossed legs up and down for a few seconds before she holds her chest and says, "Oh, sorry, are you talking to me now? You're actually interested in hearing what I have to say?" The sarcasm in her tone is as thick as the angry burn in her eyes.

"What exactly has made you angry, Jessie?"

"Angry? I'm not angry. Why would you think that?"

"The jigging of your leg. The flash of your eyes. It's quite obvious that you're upset about something. Did I upset you?"

"You mean, did your fascination with his marriage annoy me? Of course not. Why would it?"

"You see. There it is. You're being sarcastic rather than telling me exactly what's on your mind."

She stops jigging, leans forward, and jerks a finger in my direction. "You don't want to know what's on my mind, mister," she hisses.

"Isn't that why we're here," I say, holding out my hands.

She sinks back into the sofa, crosses her arms, and starts jigging again. "You know, it staggers me why you think I'd want to sit here and listen to you drone on about his marriage to another woman. Are you really that dim?" she asks.

"Because it's important. It speaks a lot to what may well be on Shawn's mind – or yours, for that matter. This must have a profound effect on how you feel about your relationship. Doesn't it?"

"Of course, it fucking does!"

"Then, that's why it's important that we discuss it, because there's no doubt in my mind that it's this very thing... this, this sense of insecurity that brought you both here in the first place."

"Wait, what? You think *I'm* insecure?" she asks, slapping her chest again.

"Aren't you?" I ask abruptly.

She glares at me.

"Jessie, it's obvious. It's been obvious from day one that you don't trust what is happening between you. It's the very reason why you want this wedding. You want it to happen. You *expect* it to happen. You want Shawn to make the commitment – despite your feelings, despite your mother, despite the other *minor* detail that he's still married and has commitments with his wife."

My words are forceful, and if I'm being completely honest, it's probably because I've allowed myself to become irritated. What the hell is going on here? It's as if they've both boarded this ridiculous marriage train and didn't even stop to consider whether it even has a track to run on.

She's staring out of the window again now, completely disinterested in making eye contact with me, or with Shawn, for that matter.

Then, I hear him clear his throat. "Um, do I get to say something here?"

"Oh, he speaks!" she says, without turning.

"Please, Shawn," I say, inviting him to talk by holding out a hand.

He turns sideways on the couch to his fiancé. "Jessie, last time, you said that you *used* to find me sexy" – she doesn't look at him, but rolls her eyes – "to me this kind of means that you're not actually, you know, *into* me anymore. Is that what this is about?"

Both of us wait for a reply.

Nothing.

"Jessie?" I call.

"Every time we talk about you getting a divorce, you always change the subject."

"But, I am."

"Not because you want to, but because your wife filed for it."

"Does that make a difference?"

"Of course, it makes a fucking difference!" she hisses, finally turning to face him. "What kind of a message do you think it sends me when you visit me, fuck me, but go home to her?" The words choke in her throat.

"But, I don't go home to her anymore."

"Not now, but you used to."

"So, let me get this right. You're pissed off that I used to go home to my wife? That's bloody stupid."

"No, what's fucking stupid is that I believed you were ever going to leave her."

"She's my wife. I've known her since we were kids. Of course, it's fucking difficult! We're divorcing because of me, because of what I did; it's not because we hate each other, and that makes it bloody hard."

"Then maybe you should fucking go back to her!" she shrieks. Eyes blazing.

"You know, when you behave like this, that's exactly what I want to do," he says angrily.

"Oh really? Then what are you waiting for?" she retorts with a growl as angry tears well in her eyes, and then, louder, "Go on, then, go on! GO!" she yells, lifting her feet onto the couch and kicking him away from her, "GO ON! You fucking bastard! GO! Get out! GET OUT! GET OUT!"

"JESSIE!" I yell, lifting myself out of my seat and holding out my hands as if I can telepathically stop her.

Shawn doesn't react to her attack, except to hold out his hands in defence and gawk at her incredulously.

There's a long silence, but for the rumble of the surf and Jessie's panting. She's retreated to the far corner of the couch now. Her hot and tearstained face looking every which way but at us.

I can't believe it. Since I can remember, I don't think anything like this has ever happened in a session, and I don't really know what to say. I just know that it's unacceptable.

Eventually, after a minute or so. "Jessie, you know, there are many things that I'll put up with in a session, but one thing I won't put up with is that kind of behaviour."

She looks at me, smudged black eyeliner complimenting her tempestuous demeanour, and sneers, "Fuck you!"

Then, she pulls on a shoe that fell during her attack on her fiancé, grabs her bag and coat, then clicks out of the place without so much as a glance back.

Moments later, *Front door open*, before it's slammed shut, sending the sound reverberating around the building.

Shawn and I are both shell-shocked. And it's another minute or so before I ask, "Are you okay, Shawn?"

He takes a few seconds, then looks at me and nods, before getting up from his seat.

"What if, eh, Doc?," he says with a faint smile. "See you Saturday," he adds softly before turning and leaving the room, closing the door behind him.

AVA

Wednesday. 17:58.

Thank God for yesterday. It's about the only day, since I've arrived here, where someone didn't just show up at my door, demanding attention.

And I took full advantage. I spent most of the time snoozing, since, as you know, there isn't much else to do around here. And, when I wasn't doing that, I was down by the beach – running, exploring, and loving it. In fact, I've decided that I'm going to go running every day while I'm here. It's the perfect location for it, and it makes sense.

I've kicked the booze, and I'm sorting out my mind because, well, there's nothing else to do but sift through all the trash that makes me the weird and wonderful thing I am today, and so, keeping my body in shape is logical.

Who knows? If I get really fit, I might be able to win my wife back. What do you think?

Don't answer that.

Today, I did more of the same, and I feel much better for it. I'm feeling energised, and relatively happy compared to the miserable git I've generally been since arriving here. The only thing that I'm not particularly thrilled with is the fact that the hot water appears to have taken on my temperament, and this morning I found several roof shingles shattered on the front doorstep.

Needless to say, this only reinforces some of the creepy goings-on around here, but I soon dismissed them. I realise now that much of what happens is a matter of my own imagination.

Okay, so, let me rephrase that. The shingles that were blown off the roof are not my imagination, and nor is the temperamental immersion heater, but I'm just going to get someone to sort these issues out. When I mention matters of my imagination, I'm talking about creatures in the attic and people behind windows and scratching on doors. This stuff is only as bad as my imagination allows. I understand that now. Just like I also understand that, given free reign, and in the absence of any other stimulants, the mind will seek its own recreation, like imagining more than actually meets the eye. But that all stops, now.

Unlike yesterday, though, today I did received an unexpected visitor – Shawn. And, to be perfectly honest, I was happy to be infected by his cheerful disposition.

It was a flying visit, to let me know that plans for Saturday are coming along and that I don't need to worry about a thing. He said that *they* have taken care of everything – including food, booze, and even the disco – so there really isn't anything for me to worry about. When I asked him about paying for this stuff, he told me we'll settle later.

When I touched on Monday's session, he didn't seem particularly fussed to talk about it, other than to deliver an uncharacteristic '*Everything happens for a reason*' line. When I asked him if that meant reconciliation with his wife, he just gave me a wry smile, tapped his nose, and drove off with a promise to see me early Saturday evening.

Blimey. Did I do some good after all?

I've vowed to find out at the party, after I've managed to get a few drinks into him. Yeah, I know, sounds a bit dodgy but, right now, I think it's important for me to establish if I am actually helping around here. I would like to believe that I am, but I don't really know and, while it's certainly a bit cheeky, I could really use the psychological boost. You know, to make sure I'm moving in the right direction and all that. Besides, as far as I can tell, Shawn's no longer a client, which means…

The doorbell interrupts my thoughts. Shocker!

Front door open.

And it's a sight to behold; the top of a wide-rimmed black hat.

"Hello?" I ask, trying to peer under the rim. The wearer is looking down.

"Oh, hello, Marco. Sorry. Just brushing lint off my dress."

"Ava?"

At least, I think it is. This beauty looks nothing like her. Or, more specially, nothing like the woman who gave me a lift that day in her nineteen-forties spy garb, or even the plainly dressed housewife who graced my couch last week. This woman is wearing a stunning black lace dress with matching sleeved gloves, and is wrapped in a long red coat. Her lips are black cherry red, complimented by thick, dark eye shadow.

"Sorry, were you expecting someone else?" she asks, allowing a wide smile to emerge from those immaculately painted lips.

"Um, kind of... wow. You look great," I utter.

"Thank you. May I come in?"

"Oh, of course." I step aside and watch her enter the house with the confidence of a catwalk model. After I've allowed the breath I was holding to escape, I follow her inside.

Before I've even joined her in the study, Ava has removed her coat and is sitting on the couch, one long leg folded over the other.

I take a seat opposite her, still in awe of the transformation.

"Thanks for seeing me a bit later today,. You got my note?" she asks in a silky, confident articulation, as if she's a very busy person and could only fit me into this slot.

"Yes. Thank you. I did. And, it's no problem. Are you going somewhere?"

"No, I dress like this every Wednesday to clear out the oven."

I cock my head and look at her sideways.

She smiles. "Sorry. I'm feeling naughty today."

"I can see," I say appreciatively. "So, where are you off to?"

"Oh, I'm meeting someone," she says with deliberate mysteriousness.

I play along. "Okay. Do you want to tell me about them?"

She mulls the question and then says, teasingly, "Maybe later. Don't you want to ask me about my week first?"

I gesture to her. "Yes, absolutely. The floor is yours," I say with a smile.

"It's been quite a week. I've had a sick child, a boiler breakdown, an absent husband and, ugh, a family gathering at the weekend. Well, it wasn't exactly a family gathering. Just a get-together with my sister. She lives in London. They came down to visit us. You know, spend some time in the country."

"What was that like?"

"Noisy. Not her son. He's adorable, of course, but more the twins. They can get really boisterous when they've got company."

"Twins?"

She smiles.

"Why do you enjoy that?"

"What, keeping you on your toes?"

"Yes."

"I don't know. Why does it matter how many children I have? Is it really relevant to what we're doing here?"

"Well, the environment, the people that surround you on a daily basis, is very important to therapy, yes, as those people will undoubtedly affect you in one way or another."

"I don't really like to talk about the twins. I'm with them most of the time and, well… they drive me crazy." She puts up a hand. "Don't read into that. I love my children, I do, but I don't necessarily love every waking hour, nor am I thrilled with what they did to my body. Do you know I used to be today's equivalent of a size zero?"

"Your body still looks very good from where I'm sitting." The words just fell out of my mouth.

She eyes me for a few seconds. "Ah, well that's very sweet of you to say, but I'm definitely not the body I used to be." She smooths out her dress and tucks herself in subconsciously.

"Is how you look important to you?"

"Isn't it to most women? Actually, don't answer that. Yes, it can be important to me. Depends what mood I'm in."

There's a pause as a pair of crows squabble in the tree outside. Then, "You mentioned that you have a sister. Is she older or younger than you?" I ask.

"Younger, of course. High achiever. Great body, despite her son. Gorgeous husband, even if he is naughty." The last bit is emphasised.

I look at her and smile. "What do you mean?"

She nips her lip ever so slightly. "Don't read into that. He's just easy on the eye, and there's something about him. Like he's trouble. He's someone who takes what he wants and sod the consequences."

"You seem to be quite taken with him."

"Didn't I say, don't read into that? Although, I am – quite taken with him. I do like a man who knows what he wants and goes for it, no matter the consequence."

"Is your husband like that?"

She laughs. "Mick? Um, no. Complete opposite. Everything is planned and there's a strategy for everything." She sighs and brushes more invisible lint from her dress. "No, my husband is all about the Ps."

I lift inquisitive eyebrows.

She puts on a gruff voice, "Proper planning and preparation prevents piss-poor performance." Then she adds, "Yes, he's ex-army."

"But he's a salesman now, right?" She nods. "Aren't they all about passion, aggressiveness, tenacity, and all that?"

"Oh, he is, with work – oh, and football."

"But not with you?"

She laughs, bitterly. "No. Mick's idea of sex is us finding the right position so we can both snooze while doing it because he needs to be in Newcastle by eight in the morning." She straightens on the couch, rearranges a cushion. "Don't get me wrong, he's a good man. A great father, provider, and I do love him, but…" She trails off and looks out of the window, wistfully.

"But? Ava, please finish the thought."

"But…" She holds her chest, almost as if she needs to burp the words out of herself, "Not a great, um, partner. And by that, I'm not just talking sex, of course. I'm talking life. Kids, bills, broken boilers. Me. He tends to leave all that to me."

"Have you talked to him about it?"

She snorts. "Talk to Mick? My husband is commonly known as a *man's man*. He doesn't do touchy-feely, talking." She starts to laugh.

"What's funny?"

"Well, I'm just imagining him sitting here now. Oh God, what I would give to see that!" she says with another chuckle.

A few seconds drift by. Leaves float to the ground outside.

"You don't strike me as a woman who enjoys touchy-feely, Ava."

She weighs the statement with a cock of the head. "I enjoy everything in moderation, Marco. And some things to excess," she says with a wry smile as she swings her leg.

I nod, take a few seconds, and then ask, "So, where's Mick now?"

"He's travelling, for work."

"Does he travel often?"

She nods.

"How do you feel about that?"

"Well, he's got to earn a living, hasn't he?"

I nod. Thinking about my own situation, I project, "Must get lonely, though?"

She thinks about the question, shakes her head, and then replies confidently, "No, not really. I'm fifty-two years old. I'm way beyond being an attention-hungry teen; I've learned to enjoy my own company, my own space. You know, settling down with a nice book and enjoying the solitude."

I think about the statement. "Huh. That's interesting."

"Really? I thought it sounded rather dull."

"No, the way you reemphasised the same meaning in that sentence. You say you've learned to enjoy your own company, to enjoy solitude. Does that mean that you used to feel lonely?"

She clucks her tongue, as if I've just caught her out on something. "Um, doesn't everybody? I mean, physically, theoretically. Don't we all get used to being alone after a while? I mean, sometimes you can feel alone even when you're with company. Right? For example, you must have gotten used to being out here on your own, no?"

"Um, well…"

"…Unless your wife and son have joined you." She makes a show of looking around the room, as if my family is going to jump out from behind the desk. She knows they aren't here and she's making a point.

I smile. "So, getting used to your own company and enjoying your own solitude are things that you've had to do, rather than choosing to come to terms with them?"

She shrugs. "Again, there are few women, or men," she adds that last bit with a nod towards me, "who have the luxury of being with their partner twenty-four-seven. You just make do with it. You learn to adapt."

"And yet, it's left you feeling bored."

"Sorry?"

"Last week, you told me that you were bored. Your demeanour reflected that, and yet, this week… There seems to be a change. Has something changed, Ava?"

A mischievous smile cracks those luscious lips.

I settle in my chair. "Want to tell me about it?"

She glances out of the window as she considers my question, waits a while, and then, "Have you ever let yourself go, Marco?" she asks, without looking at me.

"It depends what you mean by that."

"I mean, really let yourself go. Forgotten duty to house, spouse, and offspring, and done something that's for you? Have you done something that's selfish, indulgent – something that's exclusively for your own gratification and not the collective?"

I swallow. I'm not sure if she's asking a question or making a point about me. Either way, I make my answer cool, casual. "It depends."

She turns to me. "How so?"

"Well, if what I was about to do would hurt my family, then, no."

Liar!

"Not even if you believed you wouldn't get caught?"

I force a smile and sit forward in my chair. "Is there something you want to tell me, Ava?"

She holds my gaze while occasionally batting a set of those lashes, that are so long I'm almost expecting to feel a breeze. A breeze doused in that fragrance that wafted through my front door with this embodiment of seduction.

"Um, right now, I'm asking a question. That's allowed, isn't it?"

"Of course, but…"

"…So?"

"So?" I linger on the word, as I'm not sure what she's getting at exactly.

And she must have read my mind, because she sits forward in her seat and asks, "If you had a chance to do something naughty, and knew you'd never get caught. Say, for example, have an affair. Would you?"

My heart skips a beat and I pause because I'm not sure how to answer, given my history, and, for some reason, I don't want to lie either.

"Ooh," she says with a wry smile. "You're hesitating."

"I'm considering the question…"

"…come on, Marco. Handsome man like you. Are you telling me you've never been tempted? Propositioned? I mean, for Christ sakes, you look like a movie star. In fact, now that I think about it. Has anybody told you that you look like…"

"…Ava, are you flirting with me?"

She considers the question. "Maybe. Is that so wrong?"

I rock my head. "I'm your therapist."

"So?" She sits back once more, crossing her legs, causing the friction to make a subtle swishing sound. "What difference would it make? Nobody would know but you and me."

She's making direct eye contact with me, and I know it's going to be a matter of seconds before I feel a burn on my cheeks. Our gaze lock lasts seconds that feel like minutes – until she starts laughing, loudly. Then she points at me. "Ha, I had you there for a second, didn't I?"

I eventually allow myself to smile with her.

"Relax, Marco. You're incredibly handsome, but I'm already kind of extramaritally committed."

I cock my head.

There's that knowing smile again, and then, "I have a secret to tell you," she declares.

I sit back in my chair. "Okay. I'm listening."

"I've met somebody."

"By *met*, you mean…"

"…I'm fucking someone who isn't my husband." Her words are almost a whisper, as if the walls can hear, yet they're spoken with childlike excitement. "Well, technically, so far, he's fucked me, and it's sublime." There's an unmistakable glint in her eyes.

"Would you like to tell me about it?"

"You want details?" she asks, seductively.

"When did you meet?"

"A few weeks ago."

"So, you knew the last time you were here."

"Yes, but, well… it had only been once, and I didn't know if it was going to come to anything."

"Come to anything?"

She laughs. "Oh God, no, nothing like that. We're both married."

I nod. "So, how did you meet?"

"We kind of already knew each other," she explains, awkwardly.

"Okay."

"He's younger than me. Almost ten years," she declares, proudly.

"Is that important to you?" I ask.

Another hollow laugh. "Really? Are you expecting me to say that it isn't?"

"I'm not expecting anything. I was just asking."

"Yes, age is important, and those who say it isn't are lying. In this case, I think it's particularly important."

"Why? Because you're older than him?"

"Absolutely. And it isn't for that whole psychological mid-life crisis rubbish, but it's just, just…" She pauses here as if to catch her breath. "It's just so fucking exciting, you know, to be desired like that by someone younger than me. A cliché, I know. But it bloody well is." She rearranges the cushion again, avoiding my gaze, as if she's suddenly heard herself. "A cliché which, by the way, men reinforce all the time," she throws in.

"Be desired like what, Ava?"

She looks up, eyes wide. Breathless. She thinks about the question and then responds, "I don't know… Hungrily. Greedily. Lustily. Like he's ravenous for me and can't get enough. It's bloody intoxicating."

"The power?"

"Yes. I don't think I've ever had that kind of effect on anybody, in my life. I mean, not even when Mick and I first started seeing each other. It was never this way. Never like this."

There's a quiver in her voice, and she has her hand on her chest as if to still her beating heart.

I smile.

"What's funny?"

"Well, I just think it's interesting that you think you have this power over this man when, in reality, you're the one who's breathless." I nod at her hand, "And presumably in some way overwhelmed just by the thought, the memory of him."

She drops her hand and laughs. "If you had been fucked the way I was, you'd be breathless, too."

I smile, disarmingly. "And you say you already knew this man?"

"Yes, and it's precisely that that makes it so hot! Knowing that we share an exclusive secret. It doesn't matter where we are or who's there. It only takes a certain glance, look, or a discreet brush of the hand, and it bloody electrifies me." She's breathless again. "For example, just the other day. I was talking to someone and the twins were running around, driving me crazy, and then he walks in with Mick. They'd been to the store or something, and everything changed. Instantly. I mean, he just said hello, looked at me, and that was it. Suddenly, everything was tolerable, because I knew I had him – sexually, that is – and we were the only two people in that room, the world, who knew, and it's that secrecy that makes it so bloody sexy. Do you know what I mean?"

She's looking intently at me. The tide of saliva has gone out in my mouth. I know exactly what she means, even if my instinct is to say I don't have a clue... but you and I both know that would be a lie. So, instead, I just nod at her.

Eventually, she releases me from the intensity of her gaze by turning to look through glass wall. Then she sighs with deep satisfaction as she presumably recalls the memory of being with him.

Seconds later, she's looking at me again. "You know, it's something else, when you're in a room full of people, including your husband, children, and other family members, and you can still smell this man on you because you've both just come back from doing it fast, furtively, in one of the outbuildings."

"The secrecy?"

"Yes."

"So, is that why you're all dressed up tonight? Are you going to see him?"

"Yes. I'm going to his work, of all places."

"Really?"

"After hours and all that. What do you think?"

"What do I think of what?"

"Should I go?"

I shake my head, slowly. "I can't answer that, Ava."

"Why not?"

"Because I can't tell you what to do. You need to decide for yourself."

"Oh, come on. You must have an opinion. Just tell me."

"Do you want me to stop you?"

"What?"

"Is that why you came here all dressed up? You knew I would notice, knew I would ask about the occasion, and perhaps you would even get a reaction from me?"

She doesn't say anything. Instead, she proceeds to unnecessarily plump the cushion once more.

"Are you feeling remorse, Ava? Is that what this," I gesture at her, "show is all about? You want me to stop you from doing something over which you have no control?"

Yes, I can hear my words, too. Yes, of course wish the same. I wish there had been someone to stop me. And, it's as I consider this that I realise, I *do* want to stop her. I, in probably one of the most hypocritical acts of my entire life, do want to tell her that what she is doing is wrong. But, that isn't my place. I'm not here to give advice. I'm here to help her understand herself so that she can make her own decisions. I cannot project my own feelings onto her and, to be honest, right now, I'm struggling with that. And yes, I'm painfully aware of the fact that I wasn't feeling this righteous a few weeks back.

"Ava, I can't tell you what do," I repeat.

"Good. I'm glad," she says. "I didn't really want you to. I like this," she states emphatically. "It's something that is mine. It's something that's for me for once, and I'm taking it. And I'm going to make the most of it, right there, at his work."

"Is that the masterplan?"

"Yes."

"Because of the element of danger?"

"Yes. He works with other men, and I just love the idea of us doing it and having one of them walk in on us."

"So, this was *your* idea?"

"Of course. As much as he likes it, he is a bit of a stickler about getting caught. He worries about his wife finding out, getting upset."

"What about you?"

"Me? Care about her finding out? No. I have my own confliction to deal with."

"I wasn't talking about that. I was talking about your husband, Mick."

She looks at me for a few seconds, then shakes her head and tuts. "Ooh, very good, but very naughty."

"I don't understand."

"Yes, you do. You humanized him. You said his name and the word *husband*. Like I haven't already considered that a hundred times over. And so, I'll spare you the trouble. I do love my husband, and I love our children, even if they do drive me mad, but, right now, I love this, too, and I'm not giving up on it." The words are spoken like a seasoned politician who doesn't particularly want to alienate her audience while at the same keen to convey her resolve.

I can only nod.

"Anyway," she sighs, "I suppose that's enough for one day. Perhaps we should go back to talking about the mundane," she says, distractedly, plucking an imaginary strand of something from her dress.

I want to stay with the subject, but I can sense a shift in focus and I know better. So, instead, I force a smile and ask, "What would you like to talk about?"

She looks up and shrugs, "I don't know…things that go bump in the night, maybe." She's pulls a spooky face.

My ears prick up. "What do you mean?"

"Exactly what I said. Go back to talking about home and…"

"… no, you said things that go bump in the night? Why did you use that expression? Specifically, why did you say that?"

"Oh, you know, Mick and his weird rubbish."

"Tell me."

"It isn't that important."

"Please. I'd like to know."

She frowns at my insistence, but eventually gives another apathetic sigh and says, "Well, remember how last week he said that he'd seen faces looking into our bedroom window?"

I nod, eagerly.

"Well, this week it's gotten worse, so much worse."

RYAN

Thursday. 10:43.

"Ryan, would you mind putting that away?" I ask the teenager sitting on the couch opposite me.

He looks up. "Ooh, someone's got up on the wrong side of the bed today," he says, pushing the phone back into the front pocket of his jeans. "Fine, there's never any signal here anyway."

"Exactly. So, what's the point, eh?" I ask.

He squints curiously at me. "What's going on with you?"

"What do you mean?"

"I don't know. You seem different."

"No. I'm fine. I just don't think it's productive for you to be looking at your phone while we're in session."

He holds up his hands and makes another face, like, 'Okay, chill out.'

"You were late this morning. What happened?" I ask casually.

"Ah, right, so that's your problem. Me being late."

"Well, it didn't make me happy, put it that way, but only because I think, especially in therapy, that it's important for the two of us to respect each other's time. It inspires trust."

He grins, then leans back into the couch, stretching his arms out over the rest. "Me being on time inspires trust?"

I nod.

He laughs. "I tell you what, Doc. I'll pay you for the extra hour – how about that?"

"No, you're missing the point, Ryan."

"Am I? Then what is your point, mate?" he asks seriously.

I hold up my hands. "You know what, let's forget it. Never mind. How's the leg?" I ask, changing the subject.

"It's better, but still hurts like fuck."

"Have you been having physiotherapy?"

"Every day. Part of my contract. I'm no good to the club if I'm not playing."

"What's that been like?"

"Hurts like fuck. Did I mention that?"

He pulls out his phone again. "Bloody hell, mate, how do you stand it 'ere, disconnected from the outside world?" he asks, frustrated.

"It has its positive sides."

"Yeah? What are they?"

I don't indulge him with an answer. "Why's it so important to you?"

"What?"

"To be permanently connected to that thing. To tweet. You seemed particularly distressed when you weren't able to do it last week."

He shrugs. "I don't know. People just like to know about my shit. They like to know what I'm up to."

"How does that make you feel? I mean, does it make you feel wanted?"

"Fuck, Doc. Straight in there with the shrinkage this week, huh?"

"Can you answer the question for me, Ryan?"

He shrugs again. "I don't know. It's what I do. It's what most celebs do. They tweet about their life because there are thousands, millions of people out there, who want to hear about it. I've got five and a half million now."

"There it is again."

"What?"

"You're telling me about your followers again. You did the same last week. Do you think it changes how I see you? If I know how many people are interested in what happens to you. In what you're doing. In what you have to say."

He's looking at me like I'm some kind of super-intuitive god. And, well, I am intuitive, but to be perfectly honest, in this case, it's more because I recognise this. I may not be a football star like this bloke, but one thing I do remember about being a teenager is how important it was for me to be liked by others, to be popular. I'd realise many years later that this was a direct reaction to the attention deficit that I suffered as a child.

Ryan doesn't respond. Instead, he's looks down at brand new trainers. These look different than the ones he was wearing last week.

"Ryan? Where are you?"

He looks up at me, pulls a face. "What do you mean?"

"What are you thinking about right now?"

He holds my gaze for the longest time, as if he's about to say something. It's the same look he gave me last week, right after I questioned him about his night out.

"I'm not thinking about anything."

I nod. "Okay." I shift in my chair. "Last week, you told me a story about going out with your friends after the game. Do you remember?"

"Yeah, of course I remember. You're the old man here."

"Did you finish telling me that story? I forget."

He considers the question, then says, "Yeah. I finished it."

"Really? Because I can't remember how it ended."

"Yeah, you can. Even your memory can't be that bad."

I rock my head. "Well, you'd be surprised. I think you got to the bit where you were telling me you'd met someone."

"No, I didn't tell you about that," he answers quickly. "I left that bit…" he leaves the sentence unfinished as he realises. "You bastard."

"What?" I feign innocence.

"You tricked me."

"How did I trick you?"

"You said I'd told you about that bloke, but I… fuck!" He gets up from the chair and limps over to the window. "That's got to be uneffical, mate. It ain't cool," he grumbles. His dialect strong. Something I noticed last week – it tends to happen every time he's annoyed or angry.

"Why don't you want to tell me about this, Ryan?" I ask, ignoring the complaint.

"Because it's fucking embarrassing!"

"It can't be any worse than some of the things I've done."

He turns to me, instantly, with the curiosity of a hound. Clearly eager to steer the conversation away from him. "Yeah, like what?" And there's an expectation in there. I shouldn't have said that. This is a slippery slope. I know it. Yet, it's obvious that he responds much more positively to this kind of approach. I just need to be careful. "Let's just put it this way. I've had my fair share of embarrassing moments. Believe me."

"Like what?" he asks. Eyes locked on mine.

"Oh I don't know. I haven't been the best husband to my wife, for example. And I've made a fool of myself in front of mine and her friends."

"Tell me about it," he says, eagerly.

Shit. If I'm being perfectly honest, there's something about confessing to this boy that feels good, but… "Oh no. I've given you something. Now it's your turn," I say, gesturing to the couch.

He follows my hand with his gaze and, after a few seconds of hesitation, he limps his body there and reseats himself. Then, after a few more seconds, "Well, you know I told about those cocktails we had?"

I nod.

"Well, I drank loads of other shit too. I can't even remember what exactly. All I know is they kept putting 'em in front of me and I kept knocking 'em back. Thing is, mixing doesn't really agree with me. Normally, I get a buzz from booze, but this time…well, it was about ten fifteen minutes later when I start to get this heavy feeling in the pit of my gut. You know, like I've swallowed a bloody bowling ball or something. So, I figure that some fresh air might do me good. Obviously, I don't wanna leave through the front door because, you know, paparazzi, fans and all that shit. So, I decide to go out through the fire door at the back. It opens to an alleyway, and when I step out there I'm like, holy shit! As soon as that fresh air hits me in the face, it's like bam! I start to feel worse. Then, it's only pissing down with rain. Bloody freezin'! So, it's a bit of a shock to the system. Anyway, I barely reach the other side of the alleyway and this gutter flooded with water before I upchuck everything." He pauses, bites his lip, and looks at his feet. Then, adds, timidly, "Only, you know, as I'm going through the motions, you know, retching and all that shit. I slip, lose my balance. Next thing I know, whack! Face-fucking-first in a gutter full of water."

I suppress an instinctive laugh. And I don't know if it's because the scene is comical in some way or if it's because the little prick got his comeuppance. Either way, I stay professional and make the right sympathetic noises. Then, I ask, "So, what happened next?"

"Some dude comes along. He was having a cheeky smoke out there. Saw everything. Helps me up, recognises me and's like, 'Oh, you're that footballer' and everything. Anyway, long story short. He checks to make sure there's no one else around and literally gives me the clothes off his back. Tells me to take off my shirt, gives me his jacket. Luckily, my jeans were still fairly dry, and after a quick trip to the men's for a wash, it was like nothing had 'appened. In fact, none of the people I was with even noticed that I'd got changed and was wearing a fucking jacket with nothing on underneath."

He shakes his head and turns to look out of the window.

I wait a while. Then, "So, is that it?"

"Yeah, that's it."

"What happened to the good Samaritan? Did he just disappear?"

He nods, without giving me his eyes. "Yeah. Kind of. We went back into the club and I didn't really see him again." His voice is distant, like he's busy recalling what happened.

"You never spoke to him again?"

"No."

"Are you sure?"

He turns to look at me now. "What do you mean am I sure? Of course, I'm fucking sure."

"Ryan. Come on," I say, softly and knowingly. I can see that his cheeks are changing colour. Yeah, I know that feeling, mate. There's more to this story.

He rounds his shoulders, cricks his neck, then moves his leg and grimaces.

"Nah, it's your turn now," he says decisively.

I take a few seconds. Instantly regretting my previous share. On the other hand, we've made progress. "What do you want to know?" I ask, knowing that open-ended question can go two ways; innocuous subject or something I just know is going to come back and bite me on the arse later.

"You cheated on your missus?" he asks.

It's the latter.

I hesitate. "Yeah. Yes, I have."

"And how do you feel about that?" He asks, mimicking my voice.

"Not good. Like shit, actually. All the time," I say.

"Is that why you're hiding out here?"

"Kind of."

"How many times?" he asks.

"I think it's your turn now…"

"…How many times did you cheat?" he pushes, and I know I'm going to have to answer.

Fuck.

I think about the question. Not because I have to think about it. I have quite a good idea of how many times I've been a cheating piece of shit. No, it's more because saying it out loud is far worse than thinking it. I should know. That's one of the main points of therapy. Being able to declare and accept our failings. Fuck, I can't, though. The words just stick in my gullet until I'm eventually able to garble, "Too many."

"Shit, man." He seems genuinely shocked. I'm assuming because I have not only shared something so intimate, but because I've broken a cardinal rule. Not that I expect him to appreciate that. "So, was it different women?"

"Oh no. You've heard enough. Now it's your turn," I say, relieved that I can bat this hot potato quid pro quo back at him.

He leans forward on the couch and hold his hands. "Okay, well…

As I say, I didn't really see the guy again after we walked back into the club. Didn't take his details or anything." He lets out a big sigh. "And, I'd forgotten all about him until a few days later when I went to my wardrobe to pull out some clothes, and spotted the jacket with a note from the maid – saying that the bill had been washed with the jacket, but that it was still intact and in the inside pocket. This bloke had an overdue bill; I think it was telephone or something. Anyway. It had his address on it."

"You contacted him?"

"No. I sent someone 'round there at first. Gave him my number. Said to get in touch. Next thing I know, we're meeting up and I'm returning his jacket."

He looks at me.

"And?" I prompt.

He scratches his short hair. The rasping sound is loud in the still of the room. "And, we start to hang out. Drinks and shit." He lets out an involuntary laugh as he recalls, "He even got me to go knockdown terror with him."

I pull a face.

"Don't worry, Doc. This one isn't because you're old. I didn't know about it ether. Knockdown terror, it's a bit like knockdown ginger, you know? You knock on someone's door and then run away? Anyway, this is when you sneak into the ghost train at a fair. Do you know the ones I mean? Those ones you sit in?"

I nod.

"Yeah, so, with this, you sneak onto the tracks and you hide at the bit where it's really dark, so those on the ride can't see ya. Then, after the curtain, skeleton, or whatever it is has jumped out in front of them, you lean over and slap them on the back of the head or trail fingernails through their hair." He laughs again. "It's fucking hilarious! I mean, we must have spent at least an hour doing that before someone clocked and reported us to the operator, because then they start chasing us with fucking flashlights!"

He's still laughing at the memory, and I can see that his whole face is alight. It's probably the happiest I've seen him since he limped into this room. It's an instant transformation.

"So, you two became good friends, you and this…" I trail off here and wait for him to fill in the blank.

But he's busy gazing into middle distance still. Eventually, after what looks like some kind of internal struggle, he speaks his name. "Andy, his name was Andy."

"Was?"

He looks at me, then at the chunky watch on his wrist. "We must be shit out of time now, right?" he asks.

I glance at my own watch. "We've still got a few more minutes. Plenty of time. Besides, I want to stay with this."

"Why?" he asks, the petulant teenager back once more.

"Because I get the impression that there's more to this, Ryan. More that you aren't saying, that you don't want to tell me. Why?"

"I just don't want to talk about it."

"Why?"

"How many women did you cheat on your wife with?"

"Ryan, I really don't want us to get distracted by this."

"Why?"

"It just isn't the best use of our time."

"Says who? You? I think it's brilliant."

I knew telling him was a mistake.

"Go on. Just answer this one question and I promise I'll tell you everything," he says.

"I really don't know."

"Oh, that's a bullshit cop-out and you know it."

"It isn't."

"Yeah, it is. It's a load of crap. You must know. You're a fucking hypocrite..."

"It isn't…"

"You sit there, lecturing me, wanting to know all about my shit, but when it comes to you, you suddenly can't remember, start making excuses…"

"…It ISN'T a fucking excuse. I can't fucking remember how many!"

Shit! My voice is so loud, I can still hear it ringing in my ears seconds later. I don't even know where that came from.

Ryan's gawping at me. I'm not surprised. I lost it in the middle of a fucking session!

"Holy shit. Keep your hair on, Doc. I didn't realise it was that bad. But then, maybe now you know how I feel."

I'm breathing heavily. I can hear myself and I can feel my heart tapping against my chest. I swallow, but my throat is dry, so I take a sip of water. I can feel his eyes on me. I clear my throat. "Okay. So, um, I'm sorry about that. But, um, well, as you can see, just like you're having a hard time sharing... um, I am too… this isn't something I'm proud of, and the fact that I can't remember how many, well, yeah, it only makes it worse."

Shit. It feels like someone has just run me over, but I've got to keep it together.

The boy is still staring at me. I go on the offensive. "So, now that I've, um, shared," I wave at the both of us, "with you, maybe you can finally tell me why you keep trying to hurt yourself."

I see his eyes widen like a rabbit in the proverbial headlights; not only is the subject back on him, but I'm obviously right. Add this to that the fact that he's just made me confess to something I've been actively avoiding, and I charge like a wild bull. "Oh, come on, Ryan. It's hardly a secret. These so-called accidents you've been having obviously weren't accidents. They're a rather unimaginative cry for help. It's textbook. Something's obviously troubling you. Something bad. Something you feel so shitty and so guilty about that, like me, you feel locked in a perpetual state of shame, which in turn makes you feel unfit, unworthy, undeserving to even be thinking and breathing – so what do you do? You keep pretending to kill yourself, but never quite succeed."

I pause to take a breath and notice that his face is already red and creased into a grimace that gradually worsens; his eyes well with angry tears, his lips curl back, and he snarls, "You don't know the first fucking thing about me."

"Nor do you about me, yet it doesn't stop you asking. The only difference is, I'm not in therapy, Ryan, you are. You're the one who's trying to hurt himself; you're the one who needs the adulation of others to function. Now, I don't know what happened, but what I do know is that you're not going to find absolution from a bunch of faceless social media followers. As you say, I, they, don't know you. They don't know your life. Your struggles. They don't understand what it's like to go to bed some nights wishing not to wake up in the morning. They have no clue about the immense pressure you're under to be out there on the pitch, on the screen, in the media and having to perform, project this image of a young, up-and-coming and more than capable testosterone-fuelled heterosexual bloke in a clearly homophobic industry."

He gapes at me. His body trembling. A tear streaking down his face as he utters, "How, how do you…"

"…Oh, come on, Ryan. It's hardly rocket science." I plough on, belligerently. "Me thinks thou doth protest too much, and all that," I throw in, arrogantly, before sitting back in my seat.

There's a few seconds of silence as I consider what the hell just happened. Then, suddenly, I hear him garble something through tears.

"What was that?" I ask, dumfounded. I don't know what the hell came over me.

"He…He's d-dead," he stammers. "He's dead, because of me."

FIGHT OR FLIGHT

Friday. London, 10:30.

"Marco?" Doctor Ethan Holmes is calling to me.

Yeah – surprise! I am back in his office again.

Well, I couldn't exactly bail, could I? Wait, you didn't expect me to, did you? No, I'm not quitting that easily. Not on my marriage. Especially after everything I've learned this week. I know now more than ever what I want. My wife. My son. My family. And if that means eating humble pie with this guy, then so be it.

"Are you with me?" the doctor is asking.

"Yes. Unfortunately. Where else would I be?" I respond. "I was just thinking."

"What about?"

"Do you remember me mentioning one of my clients to you? Ryan?"

"The footballer?"

"Yes."

"What about him?"

"I had a major breakthrough with him this week."

"What kind of breakthrough?"

"Well, you know I told you about the fact that he'd been in a few accidents and that his management was concerned."

"Right, and you suspected self-harm?"

"Yeah. Well, turns out, he might be gay."

"Okay," the doctor says, as if I've just told him that it's sunny outside, which it is by the way.

"I take it you don't follow sports then? Football?"

"Not really."

"Well, you may have noticed that there aren't many openly gay footballers out there."

He muses on this. "Huh, is that so? Why is that?"

"Well, football's a man's game… And before you come back at that, what I mean is, it's predominately played by blokes. Or, you could argue, kids thinking they're blokes. The bottom line is, these players want their teammates to focus on *the* ball, not on their balls."

He laughs. "Right. That's interesting," he says thoughtfully.

"Oh, you're not all offended now, are you? Because, obviously, for once, that wasn't my intention to…"

"…Actually, no. It isn't that. I just find it curious that at our first meeting you didn't seem particularly interested in sports, certainly not football, and yet now…." He doesn't finish his sentence, but lets it hang in the air for a while like dissipating vapour.

"I said that?" I ask.

"No, you didn't say it per se. You just kind of implied it."

I nod. "Right. Well, I don't know why, but I can tell you, that the idea of a pint down at the local with the game on the big screen sounds like a wet dream right now."

A distant siren fills a short silence between us, which is then broken by the doctor, shifting in his seat and switching gears. "So, what happened, to Ryan? You said you had a breakthrough."

"Yeah. Well, he befriended some bloke, or more like the bloke befriended him."

"They had a relationship?"

"Um, no, I don't think it got that far. I'm not sure. I'm hoping to go through it during the next session. From what I've heard, I get the impression that this guy, this fan, developed a bit of an obsession with Ryan, but that he spurned him. This guy didn't take it well and, you know, took his own life."

"Oh. That must be weighing on him."

"Yeah. Exactly. And I think he's been carrying the guilt ever since."

He's looking at me now, or more like staring, and I'm just about to say something when, "You seem to have developed a bit of an affinity with him, Ryan."

"You think?"

"Yes. Is it because he reminds you of yourself?"

I think about the question. "I suppose. You could say that there are elements of him that remind me of me, yes. All apart from the conflict he may have with his sexuality, of course," I say with a lift of my eyebrows.

"You think he's conflicted?"

I stop to consider the question. "I don't really know. I just know that, for some reason, he feels responsible for this fan's death and is having a hard time dealing with it."

The doctor nods, takes a few seconds, and then shifts in his seat. "Marco, don't bite my head off when I say this, but do you think you're equipped to deal with something like this right now?"

I shake my head, knowingly. "I knew it. I bloody knew it!"

"What…"

"I just knew that the moment I told you about this, the second that I mentioned that there'd been a death, you'd start to question my ability to deal with it. I have years of experience, you condescending prick."

"That isn't what I'm saying, Marco."

"No?"

"No. I just think that you're emotionally fragile right now, and I don't know if taking on a case as potentially complex as this one is the best thing for you."

"Noted."

"Marco…"

"… No, it's fine, Doc. What shall we talk about instead, then? Perhaps you'd rather dwell on me and sex, maybe throw in the fact that I don't enjoy talking about my mother and then shake it up a little, see if you can find some incestual genesis in there somewhere? Would that be safer? Oh, or, while we're on the subject, I could tell you about how Ava came onto me during a fucking session…"

"…Marco…"

"…about how she's undergone some weird sexual awakening that has led her to shag some stranger while kindling a fucking crush on her brother-in-law…"

"Marco…"

"…Actually, coming to think of it, maybe it's actually her brother–in-law that she's shagging…"

"…Marco!"

"What?" I glare at him.

"Do you want to talk about why you're so angry at me all of a sudden?"

"No, it's not all of a sudden, Ethan. It's the moment you started to question my abilities as a therapist."

"I wasn't questioning your abilities. You know that."

"Um, are you sure? Maybe we should play back the session. Ah, that's right, you don't record your sessions; you're the mighty Doctor Sinclair.

You, who are barely out of nappies, think you know it all."

He waits for me to finish my rant, but says nothing; he just observes me. Then, "Do you really think I was impugning your ability as a therapist?

But I'm not hearing him. I've just heard my rant in my head, and realise that I must sound like a bloody spoilt brat.

"I'm just thinking about you. About your well-being. That's why you're here, Marco. And, I am your therapist, not your supervisor. I'm here to hear about you, not your clients."

"If you're so worried about my well-being then you'll be happy that I'm seeing clients again, that I'm busy dealing with other people's crap, so that I stop obsessing with my own."

"Yes, but you and I both know that therein lies the problem. I'm concerned that you're so busy dealing with other people's," he makes quotations with his fingers, "crap, that you aren't looking at your own."

"Oh, and what's so fucking wrong with that?" I ask wearily. "It's been weeks, although it feels like months – hell, it feels like a bloody lifetime that I've been dealing with nothing but my own fucking demons, so it feels good to be taking a break from them."

"And, you believe that's a good thing?"

"Hell fucking yeah, it is! Of course it bloody well is. I've done nothing but pine over family, life, circumstance, a crumbling new bloody home... and I'm sick of it! I want a break. I need a break from feeling so FUCKING SHITTY ALL THE TIME!"

My voice rings around the room and yet the doctor doesn't stir. Instead, we sit for several seconds, listening to the hum of the city outside.

"What's happening to your home?" he asks, casually, breaking the interlude.

"What?" I ask distractedly. I'm still recovering from my outburst.

"Your home, you said it was crumbling."

"Um, yeah. For reasons I'm sure are purely coincidental, ever since I started seeing you, the place has started falling apart."

"Do you think I've been sticking pins in a model of your house?" he asks with a smile.

"I don't know. Have you?" I ask with mock seriousness. We smile, but then I add. "Yeah, some weird stuff has been happening at that place."

"Go on."

"I can't really explain it. It's a collection of small things, really. Plants dying, cracks appearing in walls. But then, there's the other stuff."

"What other stuff?"

I shift in my seat and notice that my heartbeat's suddenly elevated.

"Marco?"

"Um, yeah. The other stuff. The visit from the police, them trying to link me to the disappearance of this boy, Timmy, and then the shared dream."

I pause here. I can feel the tell-tale beads of sweat tickling my scalp again. My chest feels tight.

"Marco? Please, tell me about it. Can you remember?"

I hesitate, then, "um," I swallow. My throat's suddenly dry. Something's wrong with me.

"Marco? Are you okay?" The doctor's staring at me.

"What? Yeah. Um, well, the first thing I noticed was…"

Stormy weather. Dark clouds overhead. Pain in my head. Pain in my hair. Crashing surf. Pebbles clicking. Crying. Screaming. Seagulls flying overhead. Grazed skin. Pain. Crying. Loud water, sloshing and crashing and fizzing. Splashing. Ice cold. Freezing cold. Water encircling, restricting. Can't breathe! I can't breathe! I'm drowning! I'm drowning! I'm dying! Help me! Help! Help! I'm dying! I'm dying!

"NOOOO!" I hear myself scream as I leap out of the chair, run to the corner of the room. "What the fuck?" I breathe. I'm doubled over. Hands on knees, sucking in air, as my surroundings slowly come back into focus.

It's sunny again. I'm in Ethan Holmes' office. We're in London. The traffic's rumbling, sirens are blaring, a jet thunders overhead.

Relief floods through me like alcohol.

"Marco. What's wrong? Marco?" The doctor is on his feet, staring at me. His face, a mask of concern. "Marco, breathe slowly. Control your breathing. Breathe slowly."

That's when I become aware of my breathing. It's too fast. Shallow. I'm hyperventilating. "What… What… the… fuck did you do… to me?" I ask, eyes bulging, searching him and the room, as I stand gulping, sucking in air.

It feels like I've just emerged from the bottom of the ocean.

"I didn't do anything to you. We were talking and you suddenly jumped out of your seat."

"What… wh… what… were we talking about?" I ask.

He frowns as he recalls, and then confidently comes back with, "We were talking about the changes you've been experiencing at the house. Things falling apart. Your clients and shared dreams."

I study him for a few seconds. Then my eyes darting around the place again, taking in everything, every detail as if I'm seeing it for the first time. And I'm shaking. Scared. Distrustful. I'm half expecting the giant yawn of a jagged mouth to appear on the walls, and for them to break away, *Inception-*

style, to reveal the pebbled beach back at the house.

Yet, nothing happens. Everything is as it should be. The desk, the computer, the armchairs.

Holmes is still staring at me like I'm a wild animal trapped in his lair.

"Fuck!" I run my hands through my hair and shake my head. Am I awake? I think I am. I pinch my arm so hard it hurts, then grimace; the pain is sharp, but it feels good. I'm alive. I'm still alive!

"What the fuck did you to me?" I repeat anxiously. "Did you hypnotise me without my consent?" I glare at the man and realise that my hands have turned into clenched fists as I enter fight or flight mode.

"Marco. I have no idea what just happened. Please, come and sit back down. Tell me about it." He moves forward to touch my arm, but I shrug him off and observe him, suspiciously. He looks honest enough, but he's a therapist like me. We've mastered the art of the impassive look, no matter what we hear. It's what we do.

"No," I eventually say. "I think I want to go home now." I'm eager to get out of here. Eager to see the rest of the world, even London, to make sure it's still there, as I want it to be.

"Marco, please. Take a seat. I'm really interested in what you think just happened to you. Please?" He's gesturing to *the* chair.

And I consider it. I want to, but I'm too fucking scared. No, I'm terrified. And Parched. I walk over to the seat, grab the glass of water, which I notice is still full, and down it in one continuous gulp.

Then, I gingerly walk over to the window, all the time glancing at the doctor, who has retaken his seat. Only now he's sitting forward, watching me, seemingly with concern.

Beyond the window, everything is as it should be, although the sun has already packed up for the day and is napping behind a sheet of grey. The park is there, but empty. Everything looks normal; the bench, the trees, the railing, the street. It's all there.

"Marco?"

I turn to my therapist.

"Marco, please, tell me what just happened."

I shake my head as my tongue tries to wrap itself around the words. "I don't know. I, it, I... phew," I breathe deeply. "I don't know what happened. I just, for a few seconds... It felt as if I was somewhere else." I hold my hands out in front of me; they're shaking. My heart is throbbing and that familiar tickle is now happening behind the shirt on my back. "I think..." I swallow. My throat's dry once more. "I think I had some kind of a waking nightmare."

"Tell me about it," the doctor says eagerly.

"I can't."

"Marco…"

"…I can't. I've got to go."

"Marco, please. Let me help you with this," his voice lifts as I make for the door, but I don't turn back – not even when his head appears over the handrail of the stairwell. "Marco!"

But I don't stop.

THE TRUTH

I explode out of Doctor Holmes' office building and into the cool air. I would have called it fresh, but it isn't. It's nothing like the ocean breeze, but it's better than the air in that room, which was stuffy, stifling.

I stop to fill my lungs.

I want to go home. Not to Porthcove, but to our home in North London. I want to see Ellie. I need to see Toby, and this time, nothing's going to stop me.

I pull the mobile phone from my pocket and dial Ellie's number, lingering a few seconds to watch the picture I've assigned to her contact as it fills the screen.

The picture of her smiling up at me, sunshine glistening off her skin, blonde hair partially covering her face, was taken first thing in the morning. We'd just made love. Her face is flushed. Her eyes sparkle as they always do after sex. It's why I took the picture. I love that look on her. She, of course, hated me snapping the candid shot because she said her makeup was smudged, but I don't care. She looked then, and does now, perfect to me.

There's ringing on the line.

"Pick up. Pick up," I chant.

"Hi, this is Ellie. I can't take your call right now, but if you leave a message, I may get back to you."

I hang up. Dial again.

"*Hi, this is Ellie. I can't take your call right now…*" Again, and again.

"Fuck!"

A woman in a supermarket uniform glances at me and then quickly away as she passes me. A black cab trundles by.

I look up at the doctor's window, wondering if he's still there or if he's already moved on to his next patient, and forgotten all about me and my episode.

Maybe I should go back and speak with him. Share what I saw. I know from experience that this alone should make me feel better. He might be able to help me work out what happened since I'm not normally prone to losing my shit in the middle of the day – or, not like that anyway. And, as much as I dislike the condescending prick, I trust him. Or, more specifically, I trust that he's intuitive, perceptive, and professional enough to help me with this.

That said, I'm a therapist. I should be able to work this out for myself. But, I know that's a stupid idea. It doesn't work that way. It would be a subjective and not an objective view, which is what I need right now.

Oh shit. I'm feeling breathless again.

Just breathe normally. Short shallow breaths are going to make you feel dizzy. Now, come on.

I don't want to throw up here. Not now.

You're not going to. Relax. Breathe normally.

I focus on a couple of cars as they growl past me, their diesel engines belching plumes of carbon monoxide. Ironically, my breathing is improving, which means I'm able to suck in a whole cloud of that shit.

Okay. Focus. Focus.

I turn my thoughts on myself as I lean on the black railing for support once more, just in case my body decides to eject whatever I have in my stomach, which can't be much because I'm bloody starving.

Focus.

Think about this logically. What do I think happened?

Seriously? You're going to try self-diagnosis?

A van revs by. Two men in suits laugh on the opposite side of the street.

I look up at the doctor's window. Part of me wants to go back up there. The other… well, the other thinks that it's too soon, too real right now. Maybe next week.

Another cab goes by, and I think about flagging it down. I'm not going back to the country without at least talking to Ellie. I have to see her.

So, I as near as throw myself in front of the next black cab, invoking a blare of its horn as the driver swerves to avoid me.

"You fucking off your rocker or what? I nearly hit ya!" the cabbie yells out of the passenger window.

"I need to get to Camden."

He looks me up and down. "Fuck off!" he yells angrily, as he drives away.

It's several minutes before the next free cab makes its way towards me. This time, I avoid acting like a crazy person. Instead, I take a deep breath and casually flag the man down.

It works. He indicates and pulls over.

"Camden Lock," I say calmly, but my stomach's in knots.

The driver nods and I climb in the back seat. Relieved to be out of the cold. It's drizzling rain so fine that the city is shrouded in mist. And, it's only now, as I sit in the back of the cab, that I realise just how bloody freezing it is out there.

I'm a ragdoll as we bump back and forth over the cobbled street to get out onto the main road. Meanwhile, that griping in my stomach is getting worse. I can't decipher if it's hunger or something else and, like an oil well that's about to blow, I can feel that I'm pent up, primed, and in no state to be doing this, but what choice do I have?

None.

Ellie isn't picking up her phone and, after David's communication breakdown, I feel it's high time I confront the both of them, face to face.

There's no point in going home. Ellie will be at work. Toby at school. I'd be going home to an empty house. At least, if I go to David's, I'll be able to speak to them both. I can talk to her and find out what exactly freaked him out the other night.

Easy. Right?

Well, it is in my head.

Okay. So, let's get this clear. I am fully aware of the fact that this is probably a giant mistake, but I've spent my time in purgatory. I've given my wife space. I've respected her boundaries – kind of, at least – but I'm done waiting. I need to deal with this, now.

You understand that, right? I'm in crisis here.

I could do with a smoke, though. And no, I'm not talking about conventional cigarettes, but something else – just a little something, you know, to knock the edge off. Maybe even a drink or two, or three. It'll probably be difficult to get my hands on the former at such short notice, but the latter...

I ask the driver to pull over.

When I return with a bottle of Jack Daniels camouflaged as a plastic bag, the driver looks up in his rear window. "You can't open that in 'ere, mate," he says, pointing to a NO FOOD OR DRINK sign mounted on the back of his seat.

"Nah, mate, course not," I say, but as soon as he takes a call that must be from his wife, given the animated tone of his voice, I shimmy over to the seat directly behind him, out of the line of sight of the rear-view mirror, where I quietly break the seal and take a couple of furtive glugs.

Oh fuck, just feeling that mouthful of warm nectar burn down my throat is making me feel so much better already.

I'm sorry. I know you're probably thinking that this isn't going to help any, that I'm probably going to make a pig's ear of things, but don't worry. I'll be fine. It's just a couple of drinks, you know; just to take the edge off.

I need it.

I'm so wound up right now, the veins are literally throbbing in my temple. I need to release the pressure and, as you know, I normally do that by hooking up with some stranger, but I'm trying to stay on the straight and narrow. You *know* that. So, you don't begrudge me this, do you? Besides, I've hardly touched a drop since being exiled to the country. I deserve this.

I reward myself with another generous swig, screwing my face up as little as possible to avoid being busted by the alcohol policeman who's driving like he needs to attend a crime scene. Shit! I'm bouncing all over the place here.

After weeks of being given the cold shoulder by Ellie, the weird stuff at the house, David's visit, Timmy going missing and the police suspecting me for it, I'm not ashamed to say that I'm scared. Really scared.

I have no idea of the reception I'm going to receive when I finally see Ellie, nor of how I'm going to react to that, but I need it. I really need some normality right now.

You'll have noticed that, if there's anything that's consistent about me, besides my addiction to sex – shit, did I just say that? – well, in any case, it's my temper. I'm way too hot-headed, I know that. I don't often think before I act, but it's going to be different this time. I'll have had a few drinks, just to calm me enough so I can walk in there, have a private chat with Ellie, and see how I go about fixing all this. At least to the point where I can see Toby.

Toby.

Tears spring to my eyes and I glance up. The alcohol inspector is still too busy talking to his wife about the weekend to see me swipe a tear off my face.

Then, I blink more away before taking another swig, because I'm loving the suspension that good ole' Jack is adding to my ride. Phew. My empty stomach means he's already unscrewing the tension and smoothing it out with each twist, weave, and turn we make in and out of parked cars. Wow. It's almost like my driver knows I'm on a mission, and it isn't long before he's pulling up near the Lock.

As always, the place is heaving with locals and tourists.

My driver puts his missus on hold and barks out the fare, which I think is extortionate. And now, bottle safely hidden back in its plastic bag, I frisk myself for my wallet. I should say, I'm surprised that a swarm of moths doesn't come flying out of the bloody thing. It's empty. I'm boracic.

Luckily, I clocked the VISA sign when I boarded, so I hand the man my credit card and stop short of doing a victory dance when the charge is approved.

Then, I step out and the chill slaps me across the face.

"Hello," I say, as I wait a few seconds to reacclimatise to being on my feet, as it feels like I've just stepped off a fairground ride.

David's place is about a five-minute walk on the other side of the canal. I pull my coat around me and break into a brisk walk in that direction, dodging people who are shuffling along like zombies, oblivious to the drizzle hanging from their hair and hats.

It's late morning, so assuming they're not out with clients, David and Ellie should both be in the office. I'll speak to her first and, assuming I don't manage to get myself thrown out again, him after that.

I slow down as I approach the building and listen to the market callers in the distance, to voices chatting about the inane, and banter about the vacuousness that has an overwhelming sense of the familiar. It's home. Which is weird because, the last time I was in London, I was missing the ocean.

I resolve that I'm probably feeling like this because I'm in crisis and looking for reassurance from what I know. David, London, and, of course, my wife and son.

The feeling grows stronger as the bustle of people fades and I reach the refurbished red brick warehouse, where part of me tells me to turn around. The other says, 'Just get on with it.' This confrontation has been a long time coming. And I agree. It has.

So, I search around the entrance and home in on what I need; a relatively empty trash can.

I carefully place the bag inside, but not before taking another good swig. With a bit of luck, I should be able to easily recollect it on my way out. I just hope some homeless drunk doesn't come along and nick it while I'm in there.

I straighten myself up and turn to face the building.

There's no lock on the entrance lobby, or at least there isn't during working hours. I know this because I've mentioned it to my best friend several times. "Mate, anybody can walk in off the street."

"And?"

"And… murder us in our beds! Didn't you watch The Strangers?"

"The only strange thing around here is you. And when you're strange…" he then proceeded to sing verses from the song by The Doors.

Anyway, the unlocked door is the reason why I'm now able to walk through the entrance lobby and back into that famous open-plan office where I first snooped through Ellie's diary so that I could cause a scene at that restaurant and get myself banished to the back of beyond.

"Oh, hey, Marco," says a petite twenty-something blonde, casually, as if we've only just seen each other.

Her name's Lucy. Lucy has a great rack. Yeah, I'm sorry, I don't mean to reduce everything about the female of the species to a part of her anatomy, but hey, it's been a while, and Jack Daniels on an empty stomach is like the devil on my shoulder.

Oh, interesting fact, too. According to David, Blondie has, had, a crush on me. And right now, I'd love to crush those giant things beneath my fingers. But David's already warned me off of her. Told me to avoid all contact if I don't want my testicles removed. That, and this new thing that…

…Hang on, I've just realised. While I like the idea of a fun time with Lucy, I'm not entirely sure I would act on it. Hold on here – let me think about that… no, not right now. Maybe never! I can't even explain it to you. I just, well, I like the idea of sex with her, but I'm not in a hurry to *have* sex with her. Does that make any sense at all?

Anyway, I dial down my smile and ask, "Hey, Lucy, is Ellie here?" I'm asking the question because I've already looked across the office and spotted her empty desk.

The girl's smile disappears, and I don't know if that's because I've mentioned my wife or because my wife has already instructed her on what to do and say, should I ever decide to show up here, asking for her.

The girl's looking a bit flustered now, but I don't have time for it. "Never mind. Is David here?" I ask, but my eyes have already homed in on the giant fishbowl conference room at the far end of the building.

"He is, Marco, but he's in an important meeting," she adds quickly when she sees me move in that direction. "You can't go in there, Marco, he's with investors," she says, jumping up from her seat and trailing me down the aisle of desks and office workers, like an anxious puppy.

The place looks busier than I remember, and you'll be pleased to know that this gives me pause for thought, since I have no intention of giving a repeat performance of what happened at the restaurant.

That said, it doesn't stop me from barging into the meeting room where everybody stops talking and looks up.

Lucy's loud supplication turns into a whisper behind me, "Marco… You can't be in here."

But it's too late.

"Can we talk?" I ask David, and then I swallow hard because he's wearing a bloody tie! He never wears a tie. It means this meeting is really important, after all.

The three suits around the table watch me in bemusement, but I avoid eye contact with them, so that the extent of my intrusion is limited.

"Marco, I'm in a meeting," David says with a clearly forced smile. I'll catch up with you in a bit, mate."

In case you didn't notice, that wasn't a question, but a statement. His way of telling me to fuck off, he'll talk to me later.

Then, he turns back to the chart that is being projected onto the glass wall. It's kind of like a Google Glass, but on a much larger scale. And, I have to say, pretty bloody cool.

For me, it obviously isn't cool enough. "Actually, Dave, it's pretty urgent. I kind of need to have a quick word with you now," I say, with my own forced smile.

"Marco…" Lucy's girly tone pipes up.

"It's okay, Luce," David says. Then, turning to the three suits around the table, he says, "I'm sorry about this. Please help yourself to more food, drinks." He gestures at the bounty of pastries and beverages on the table. "I'll be right back… Lucy?"

David gets up from his chair and leaves the room as Lucy enters and starts chatting in her unique girly way by asking the men how the meeting has been so far.

David guides me out of the room and waits for the door to close before speaking through clenched teeth and a fake smile, "What the fuck are you doing here?"

"I know. I'm sorry, but I need to speak to Ellie."

"What?"

"I need to speak to Ellie, David. Where is she? Is she in the office today? I just need to see her. I just need to have a quick word."

He looks around the building, as if to check that nobody is listening to our conversation. Then, he walks me further away from the meeting room door, turns his back to the meeting, loses his smile, and says, "She ain't here, Marco. You know that."

"What do you mean?"

"What do you think I mean?" he asks

"That's exactly it. I don't fucking know!" My voice is loud, and part of the office staff stop what they're doing to look up.

David glances at the meeting room, smiles, and then turns to me, "Marco, we're not doing this shit. Not now," he warns.

"What do you mean, *this?*"

He wipes his hand over his mouth and I can tell he's pissed off because his big ears have turned crimson. They always go like that when he's either embarrassed or angry.

He chuckles, but I know it's not amusement. "Okay. So, I know you've had a shitty time of late, but I swear to God, mate, you carry on and ruin this for me, and you'll be out so fucking fast that your feet won't even touch the floor, you hear me?"

I nod like a castigated child, and that's probably because I feel like one right now. I can't make head nor tail of what the guy is talking about, and these riddles aren't helping. So, I roll my shoulders in an attempt to shake off the anxiety that's gripping me like a straightjacket.

"Just tell me," I say to him. "Just tell me where Ellie is," I supplicate, keeping my voice as low as I possibly can, given the frustration that's squeezing on my lungs. "Why isn't she here, and why isn't she picking up her phone?"

I can tell I have his attention because he's obviously responding to something he's seeing on my face, and his stance relaxes. "What the fuck's wrong with you?" And, despite the phrasing, there's concern in there.

I close my eyes in frustration. "Just tell me," I say slowly.

He sighs. "Marco, you already know this. She resigned after what happened. She said she knew we were best mates and didn't want to put me in awkward position. I was pissed off, remember?"

"What do you mean she resigned? After what happened at the restaurant?"

He frowns. "What restaurant?"

I choke down a flash of anger. "You know, the poncey one you took her to introduce her to your boyfriend. Sorry, fiancé."

He stares at me. "You know about that? How do you know about that?"

I grit my teeth. "Oh, what the fuck is going on?" I groan.

"You tell me, psycho. How the fuck do you know about Aaron? Did

Ellie tell you about him?"

"He told me."

"You spoke to him? When?"

"A couple of weeks ago."

He forces a laugh. "Aaron wasn't here a couple of weeks ago. What the hell have you been taking?" Then he leans into me. "Thought so. Fuck. You're already on the booze? After what you promised?"

I can see disappointment in his eyes, shortly followed by anger, and I'm instantly ashamed, so I react and cut him off before I'm affected. "Tell me what happened last Saturday."

"What?"

I squeeze his arm, "Tell me what you saw last Saturday, when you came out to Dolce Vita. I need to know."

"What are you talking about? I didn't see you last Saturday. I wasn't even in the country, Marc."

I pause to take in what he's just said. "Why are you saying this?" I ask, stupefied. "Why are you lying?"

He seems affronted, asking next, "What? Why would I be lying? What the hell's wrong with you?"

"You came to see me at Porthcove last week!"

"Marco, I don't know what the fuck you're talking about." He said slowly, calmly. "Where the fuck's Porthcove?"

"You know. My dad's place."

"Are you 'aving a laugh? You hate your dad. That place. You've always banged on about how you'd rather live on the street than go there! That's why you still live here, with me, but it won't be for much longer if you carry on like this."

That is when I feel the room capsize, and I don't know if it's because of what I've just heard or the booze, which I must say is starting to play havoc with my brain. I shake my head and then speak, although I think it's more of a slur. "You visited me at my dad's house, on the coast," I tell him.

He shakes his head and pulls a face. "No, mate. I didn't."

"You were there. I cooked pasta. You told me you were gettin' married."

He laughs, but it's a mixture of mild amusement and concern. I can see it in his eyes. He hasn't got the foggiest what I'm talking about, and the enormity of what that means hits me like an avalanche.

If David's telling the truth, there's something very wrong with me. And by 'wrong' I'm not talking about your average screw-up; I'm talking about fruit loops.

Oh God.

"David?" Lucy is back.

"Yeah, I'll be there in a sec," he mumbles.

"They're waiting for you," she presses.

"Yeah, I said I'll be there in a second." He pulls a reproachful face at her. Then, he angles his head to look me in the eyes. "Marc. What the fuck is going on with you, mate? You're really starting to freak me out."

I slowly shake my head, and I realise that I'm trembling. "I don't know," I whisper.

"Mate, you don't look too clever. You need to see a doctor or something."

I stare at him. So many things I want to ask, but I don't know how to formulate the words in my mouth. I don't know how to structure the question to get the answers that I need, yet somehow I manage to garble, "You said that Ellie resigned after what happened. But if it wasn't what happened at the restaurant, then what are you talking about?"

His eyes flick away from me, then back again, and even with my pickled brain, the action gets my attention. "Dave. What, what is it?" I ask again.

He shifts the weight on his feet, glances around the office, at the meeting room and then back at me.

"David? Just fucking tell me," I hiss.

He bites his lip. "Alright… alright… After you lost your job…"

"Right, my job. At the clinic. At the Wellbeing Institute," I jump in, to make sure I'm following him correctly.

"What?" he asks. "You don't…"

"…David." It's Lucy again.

"I've got to get back in there, mate. We'll talk about this later," he says, moving away from me.

"No," I say, forcefully grabbing his arm. "Dave, I'm your best mate. Just tell me, please!" My voice is imploringly loud.

He looks around us and then back at me. "Are you having me on? Can you really not remember any of this shit?"

"No, that's what I've been trying to fucking tell you. Something's happening to me. I don't know what, but something…"

I must look worried or like I'm going to be ill or something, because he quickly says, "You were sacked, Marco. You were sacked from your job…"

"Yeah. I know. At the clinic."

"What? No. Why do you keep talking about a poxy fucking clinic?" His voice is a mixture of frustration and, I don't know – I think it's panic.

"That's where I used to work, isn't it?" The last bit of that sentence was spoken slowly, as if I don't really want to hear the answer. Nonetheless, I search his face for a reaction, but there isn't one. Just confusion. "Isn't it?"

I repeat.

He shakes his head, slowly. Probably still wondering if this all some hideous joke. "No, Marco. You don't work for any clinic."

My stomach turns over. I can feel my shirt sticking to me again. "Where, where did I work then?" The words come out, but I know I don't really want to hear the answer. This is insane. Is David lying to me? Why would he?

"Mate, you worked in a garage. Harvey's Garage. In Islington."

I laugh. At first, it's one of those short laugh-out-loud kind of things, and then I'm laughing like my best friend has just told me a joke while he stares at me, nonplussed. Yet, despite that, despite the fact that the expression on his face is telling me that he didn't just share a joke, I can't stop laughing, and I think that's because I keep getting flashes of me in overalls and, well, the thought's just too funny, and I tell him so.

"Oh, thanks, mate. I haven't laughed like that in a while. Shit, I've no idea why, but that was bloody funny. I've got this image of me in blue overalls, shimmying in and out from under cars…"

But he still isn't sharing my amusement, and I gradually lose my smile. "Come on, David. I know you're having me on now." I speak the words, but I don't know… there's something about the look on his face that worries me.

"I'm not joking, Marco. You used to work there before you got the sack."

"Yeah, and why did I get the sack?" is my automatic response.

"David?" Lucy, who is still hovering nearby, whines.

He glances at her and then looks at me, his face a mask of unfamiliar seriousness. "I've got to go," he says, moving from me.

I catch his arm again. "No, tell me, why did I get fired?"

He looks at me, squints, and then spits, "You fucked one of the customers, remember?"

"What?"

"Yeah. In the storage room. Your boss found you."

He moves to leave again, but again, I intercept him. "No, wait! What? What you're saying doesn't make sense on so many levels, but even if what you're saying is true and I was sacked, why the fuck would Ellie resign over it? You're not making any sense, mate."

"It wasn't just that." He glances over his shoulder at the meeting room, and I know it's to avoid my gaze.

"What then?" I shake his arm to make him look back at me. "What then, David?" I demand, and when he finally gives me his eyes, I repeat, "What?"

He scrutinizes me, as if I'm the one pulling a prank here, pretending like

I don't remember any of this, and then he says, "It'd become a habit with you and the customers. You'd been warned about it before. Only this time, you hooked up with the worst bloody person," he says through his teeth, as if disgusted by the very notion. "You got caught with Ava."

"Ava?" I ask, thoroughly confused. "My patient, Ava?"

He scowls. "I don't know what you even mean by that. No, I'm not talking about a patient, Marco, I'm talking about Ellie's fucking sister!"

It's his turn to make the office staff look up from their computer screens, only to look straight down again when he shoots them all a glare.

I stagger back from our conversational intimacy, and I don't think it's the alcohol.

Meanwhile, my friend continues, his voice now subdued and yet full of repressed emotion, "And, after what happened, Ellie just couldn't take it anymore. Marco. Mate, I'm telling ya, you're out of control. If you want any chance of seeing your family again, you need help."

"David!" Lucy squeals.

"Look. I've got to go. I'll check in on ya later. Okay?"

He doesn't wait for a reply, and starts to walk toward the door and an impatient Lucy.

"Wait," I mumble, gawking into space. My brain processing a zillion thoughts, yet comprehending none. "Wait. David. What do you mean after what happened? David? What do you mean?" I repeat.

But he doesn't respond. He's already back in the goldfish bowl, back to his meeting.

APARTMENT 3

Friday. 13:03.

I think I stood outside of that meeting room for at least five minutes as my brain scrambled to understand what I'd just been told, and yet, I was still unable to make any sense of it. My thoughts were like a runaway train, and no matter how hard I ran to try and catch up with them, I couldn't.

Eventually, and most likely in some kind of a catatonic state, I left the building with several pairs of curious eyes gaping after me.

What's odd is that I remember bracing myself for impact. I knew that the moment I stepped out into that fresh air again, my intoxication was going to hit me like a brick wall, but it didn't. I assume that's because my mind was already overworked on other critical issues, and it thought, *Fuck it, your inebriation is secondary to the fact that all of the shit you've been taking over the past decade is now coming back to haunt you.*

And that's gotten me thinking; maybe the mental confusion I've been experiencing has nothing to do with my recent alcohol consumption, and everything to do with a bad trip. Did I take something? Maybe It was so bad I don't remember taking it. Unlikely, though. I've had bad trips before and they were nothing like this. More rabid Furbys and rainbows than a twisted edition of *Twilight Zone.*

Both of them equally terrifying.

Okay. So, pushing aside all the other crap for just one second... Who can help me? The doctor can. Surely. He knows about me and he must have an inkling of what I'm going through.

And Ellie.

Oh my God. Ellie. Ava? What kind of mind trip is that? Ava is Ellie's sister? It can't be. It can't. I've never had sex with Ava. Have I? It could explain why she's so angry with me. Why I don't remember her seeing much of her sister lately…But then, I don't remember much of anything!

NO! This isn't possible. I did not have sex with the crazed housewife who visits my study on Wednesdays. I know that for a fact. Don't I?

Oh God, my head hurts. This is a bad dream. This is all a bad dream and I'm going to wake up from it, but first I need a fucking drink. I really need a drink.

I look down to where I left it, but the plastic bag is no longer there, and I'm no longer at Camden Lock, but travelling in another cab.

I must have boarded it in my stupor about twenty minutes ago, and asked the driver to take me to Putney in North London, because some of these buildings look familiar.

Home.

I don't have a key, but I know where to find a spare one. I'll lay low and wait for Ellie and Toby to come home. With a bit of luck, she might already be there. Where else would she be if she gave up her job?

A smile spreads across my face as, despite everything, the thought of seeing the little man sends a warm glow through me. It feels like forever since I've seen him. Shit, I can't even remember the last time I saw my boy – I can only feel it, like an aching phantom limb.

Putney is a far cry from Dolce Vita. It's pretty much a red brick and grey concrete jungle overcrowded by herds of people and smoke-belching vehicles that have seen better days. We actually live in what's a fairly nicer part of it, though; a block of flats near a tiny green park. Toby's favourite haunt. We've been taking him to there ever since he could walk and it's his, our, favourite place to be. A little bit of heaven in what I used to dub hell.

Which is odd, because right now, forget the seaside, I'm happy being consigned to hell as long as my wife and son are there with me. As wrong as that sounds.

The cab drops me on a corner of the park at my request; since the traffic is so shitty, I've decided to walk the rest of the way, but not before going through the hold-my-breath ritual in waiting to see that the cabbie's charge to my card goes through successfully.

It does.

So, I let my breath go and step out into the drizzle that has now turned into a light rain. It's freezing! And I hurry to get inside, but not before pausing to take in the area.

The park is deserted. The swings are dripping rainwater, the slide is glistening cold. So, I picture, in my mind's eye, summer and my son's squeals of delight as he plummets down that thing and into my arms. I can feel the warmth of his body. The smell of soap on his skin.

"Who do you love more than anybody else in the world?"

"You and Mummy."

"Me and Mummy? You mean you don't love Daddy just a teeny tiny bit more?"

He looks at me with a grown-up exasperated smile and complains, "Dad."

"Just kidding, little man."

The memory makes me grin, and then instantly sadden, because that's how twisted the fucking mind is. Gives me a mental image exploding with colour and beauty, and then fades it back to a cold winter's day in North London.

I hurry down the pavement, dodging people who don't have much else to do with their day than to parade about with ridiculously large umbrellas sporting promotional messages. Doesn't anybody bother buying anything anymore? Or are we all happy to become walking billboards for a fucking freebie?

We live in a Victorian red brick block of flats, creatively named Acorn Mansions. Needless to say, our flat doesn't look anything like one. And I would know. We're reminded every time Ellie's parents invite us to their mansion by the river. I've always been in awe of that place, but Ellie, who grew up there, has often said that it never felt like home to her. Home is anywhere Toby and I are, including this place.

Home.

The word alone hugs me like a warm blanket.

I hurry out of the rain and climb steps to the third floor because, not surprisingly, the dilapidated lift is out of service.

I pass Tracy Lee's door, behind which, I can hear Lady Gaga squealing that she's born this way. No, wait, I think that's Tracy warbling *to* Lady Gaga.

It doesn't smell very nice in the stairwell. It's smells of yesterday's fast food, and as disgusting as it is right now, given my sensitive disposition, it makes me feel hungry and queasy in equal measure.

I stop outside the brown door with a faded gold number 3 and listen. I don't know why, but I guess part of me is hoping to hear noises from beyond the door – even if, given my luck so far, I'm not expecting much.

That said, I'm sure I can hear the faint, enthusiastic voice of a television presenter. Daytime TV? Ellie hates daytime TV. But then, she has just given up her job.

My heart soars and my stomach twists. Shit! Ellie's home and I'm suddenly excited as I reach down to the giant plant pot housing a dwarf lemon tree. We've never harvested any fruit from it, but it seemed like a good idea at the time.

There's a hollow at the base of the pot – small, but big enough to house a single key. I tip the plant over and am both happy and disappointed to find that the space is empty.

I've been nagging Ellie to remove the key from here for months. She's actually very organised when it comes to her work, but not so much when it comes to her life, which means that she often forgets her keys and loves the idea of having a spare one here for emergencies. I, on the other hand… well, this is London.

Anyway, of all times to listen to my advice, she's decided to do so on this, just now.

So, I stare at the door for a few more seconds before summoning up the courage to knock on it.

Seconds tick by. Neighbours argue in one of the flats down below. Then, I hear the faint scuff of slippers and my heart is in my throat.

Ellie. Toby.

I hear a key turning in the lock and then the door opens.

"Yeah?" says a legging-clad, overweight twenty-something woman with scraggly brown hair and large looped earrings hanging over her shoulder. She's holding a grizzly baby with a snotty nose in her arms.

I am struck dumb.

Well, what do you expect? There's a chav in my home. So, I hear myself squeak, "Um, is Ellie home?"

"Who?"

"Ellie, Ellie Battista."

"I think you've got the wrong house, mate," she says with a smoker's gravelly voice. Her working-class dialect is as thick as her apathy as she bounces the drooling baby up and down.

Then, she moves to push the door closed.

"Wait!" I say, putting a hand on the door. She glances at my hand and then back at me while all the while jiggling that baby, causing its drool to spill over her arm. "Look…" I don't even know how to put it. "Um, I, well, I live here. My wife and son live here."

Now her eyes look interested. She sizes me up again and then suddenly bellows, "Martin!" Her loud voice startles the baby and it starts crying. "Oh, bloody 'ell," she moans, and then, "Martin!" she squeals, louder this time.

"What?" comes a grumpy male's voice from inside the flat.

"Get your arse over here!"

"What do you want?"

"Just get here!"

I suppress my impatience as a grumpy skinhead in a T-shirt and shorts appears behind the earringed girl. He's as tall as me, yet carrying much more weight. "What?" he asks unhappily, glancing at me and then pulling a face at the now screaming child.

"This bloke thinks he lives 'ere," she says casually.

The skinhead glances at me and then back at her, "What?"

"He thinks he lives 'ere," she repeats, nodding at me while jiggling the child, this action no different than what she was doing when she first showed up at the door. The result is that the baby is really unhappy now, and its screams are drilling though my last nerve, but I force myself to remain calm.

"What are you on?" the bloke whom I now know is an avid Arsenal supporter, given the oversized canon tattoo on his right arm, says. "You can't live 'ere, mate," he begins sarcastically, "because, ya see, we live 'ere." His voice is deep and gruff. My urge to punch him in the face, equally so.

But I reason that that's not going to get me anywhere and I'm certainly not going to start something with a baby nearby. Still, I somehow need to snap these two dopeheads out of it and get them to at least pretend to show an interest in my fucking plight because, right now, I want to elbow this girl to one side and kick this guy in the balls.

He's in my fucking house!

Calm down.

"Look. I know this probably sounds weird," I begin, forcing a begrudging smile, "but I've lived here with my wife and son for years now. I was here just the other week, I…"

"…Mate…"

Stop calling me 'mate.' I'm not your mate.

"…I don't know where you fucking live, but what I can tell ya is that it ain't 'ere, alright?" he says in a patronising tone, but then adds much more severely and with a bulge of football hooligan eyes, "Now run along. You've already pissed off the little'n; you don't want to piss me off, too."

"Get 'im inside, will ya? He's driving me nuts!" he barks at Earring Girl who, after giving both of us dirty looks, turns on her heels and disappears inside, relieving my ears.

"Ya still 'ere?" Football Guy asks me, leaning out of the door.

"Just, just one more question," I ask. He blinks at me. "How long have you lived here?"

"No idea, mate – a few months now."

"Three months maybe?" I ask.

"Yeah, probably about that. Now, best be on ya way," he says, glancing at the stairs.

Prick!

The urge to say something forms at the back of my mind, because at the front is me asking myself, what the hell is going on? And I want to scream. No, I'm actually spoiling for a fight. I'm confused and not knowing, not understanding, what is going on – well, it's making me volatile. I know it. I can feel it. It's like a beast inside, clawing to get out.

Yet, I've barely turned around when I hear my front door slam shut behind me.

Then I stand in the stairwell while Lady Gaga's squeals echo up to me as I try to make sense of all of this, but I can't. I mean, I really can't. I'm trying, but my brain is not only fuzzy, but aching.

Yet, my instinct is to turn around and hammer on that door again, kick the skinhead where the sun doesn't shine, and barge my way into the apartment so that I can check for myself that those people do live there and that Ellie isn't slumming it with her friendship circle. Although, I know my wife well enough to know that those two aren't the type of company she'd normally keep. As bad as that may sound.

My wife may have rejected her parents' wealth when she met me, but she's still a snob at heart. She always has been. I know this because it's something we either laugh or argue about. But it isn't just that. Something in the back of my fucking worn-down brain knows that those people in there are, despite the fact that I can't wrap my head around it, telling the truth.

And, speaking of truths. I'm done. I have no fucking idea where to go from here, nor what is happening to me, and nor do I want to entertain that bastard shitty thought that has been trying to assert itself in my brain since the moment all this began.

I won't let it. I won't. I'm nothing like that.

Instead, I've started to vacantly descend the stairs when the music stops abruptly and the door to Tracy's apartment flies open.

She halts the moment she spots me.

"Marco," she breathes, heat rising to her cheeks instantly. "What are you doing here?" she asks.

At first, it doesn't even register, but then, after a few seconds... fucking hell, yeah!

"Tracy, you recognise me?"

She laughs, sheepishly. "Of course I recognise ya," she says, touching the fringe on her bobbed blonde hair.

Relief floods through me like a warm spring. I step forward. "Tracy, I'm looking for Ellie. Do you know where I can find her?"

I wait, eagerly, for a response, but she just stares at me blankly, and asks, "Ellie?"

Now it's my turn to let out a laugh, "Yeah, you know, Ellie, my wife."

Her eyes widen. "You and Ellie are married?" she asks with a gasp.

I frown. "You know we are. We have a son, Toby."

"You've got a baby together? When did that happen?"

And instantly, that collar of frustration tightens around my throat and is choking me once more, "Tracy, we've lived next door to you for years."

"I'm... I'm sorry, Marco." The flush from her face has diluted and I can see an awkwardness darkening her eyes. "I don't know what you're saying to me."

"What do you mean, you don't fucking know?" I spit, angrily.

And I know I've lost her because she flinches at my outburst and then says, quickly, "I'm sorry. I've got to go. I'm going to be late for work."

I realise my mistake and quickly move to recover. "I'm sorry, Trace. I'm really sorry," I say in a softer voice, reaching out to touch her arm. "It's just, I've had a really rough couple of days and I've," I think on my feet, "I've, I've, been in an accident," I lie.

Her eyes widen again behind thick glasses, which by the way, I don't think I have ever seen her in before.

"What happened?" she asks, concern instantly returning to her voice.

"Oh no, I'm okay. It's nothing to worry about. Just, well, I banged my head and now, you won't believe this, but I'm struggling to remember stuff. Doctor thinks everything will come back to me eventually, but, you know, until then... I need all the help I can get." I force a patient smile, but it isn't at all how I'm feeling. *I just want answers, Tracy!*

 She looks at me sceptically. "What... what do you need to know?"

I take a deep breath, because here we go again. It just feels like I keep boarding these fucking rollercoasters to the unknown each and every bloody time I ask a question, and I hate that I don't want – but need to know the answers. "When I told you about Ellie, my wife. You seemed surprised; why?"

She hesitates and looks at her arm, which I realise I'm still squeezing, probably too tight. I instantly let go. "I'm sorry," I mumble.

"Well, um…" She pauses.

"What?" I prompt.

She squirms on her feet and glances around the stairwell.

"It's okay, you can tell me. I'm a big boy." I offer another encouraging smile.

"Well, as far as I know, you and Ellie aren't married. Not as far as I know," she quickly emphasises the last bit as if she can sense I'm going to flip out.

"What?" I squint at her, and then I hear that familiar hollow laugh. "Of course we are. We're married, we've lived here for years. Look, I have a wedding ring." I show her the wedding band on my finger. "We have a son together, Toby. You know him."

Fuck. She's shaking her head, *No*.

"No?"

"No. I've never seen the him here, but I heard that you have a little boy… with your wife."

Claws of ice scratch through my nerves and I'm suddenly feeling queasy again, like I'm standing on the bow of a ship, facing into a storm.

"You're talking about Ellie, right?"

She looks at me, curiously, as if she's trying to work out if I'm toying with her. As if all of this is a hideous practical joke, a sick edition of *This is Your Life, Marco Battista*.

My whole body is quivering now, and I don't know if that's because of what I've just heard or what I believe I'm about to hear, or just because it's so fucking cold and stinky in the stairwell.

Every fibre of my being is telling me not to ask the question, and yet those very words escape through my lips once more. "Tracy, you are talking about my wife, Ellie. Right? Right?" I repeat.

But she shakes her head. "No, Marco. Ellie isn't your wife. She's your… your…"

She doesn't finish the sentence. She lets it trail off and hang dramatically in the air between us. And the terrifying bit is, she doesn't need to. You, like me, will probably already have guessed what she means, but you, like me, will be thinking that it can't be, right? Right?

Then, I have an idea. A fantastic idea that's going to clear this up once and for all. I reach into my pocket and pull out my phone. I swipe and tap on it until an image fills the screen, and then I turn the device to face the woman before me.

"This is Ellie, right?"

Tracy looks at the contact image, nods her head, and says, "Yeah."

I release the breath I've been holding, then add, "And she's my wife." I nod for her, but Tracy doesn't follow suit.

Instead, she shakes her head again, then looks up at me. "That's Ellie, Marco, but she isn't your wife. You two were, um, having an affair. Your wife's name isn't Ellie. It's… it's…" she struggles to remember.

"No," I say, swallowing hard. "No."

"You two have been seeing each other for some time," she continued.

"No. It can't be."

The enormity of her revelation is obviously reflected in my eyes, because she quickly says, "I'm sorry. That's all I know. I'm really sorry."

"Where is she now?" I ask solemnly, waving the device at her.

"She's gone," she squeaks.

"Gone. Gone where?"

"I don't know. You two broke up a few months back and she left a bit after that."

"A few months?" I echo. She thinks about it, then nods. "Was it about three months?" I ask. She nods again.

I suddenly lose my balance. That ship I was sailing on is now capsizing under a freak wave.

Tracy's arms shoot out to steady me. "Oh ma God! Are you alright?" She panics.

"Yeah. I'm… I'm fine." But I'm not. I am either going to puke what I haven't eaten or pass out; I'm not sure which will come first. I don't think I really care, either.

"Are you sure? You look really bad," Tracy is asking. Eyes wide. "Do you want me to call someone, an ambulance?"

"I'm fine," I say, shrugging her off. "When Ellie left, did she say anything? Leave word, a message?"

My ex next door neighbour shakes her head, slowly. "No. She was just really upset. Came home one night, crying. I could hear her through the walls. When I asked her what happened, she just told me that you two had had a fight, that it was over and that she was leaving."

"Did she say where she was going?"

She shakes her head again. I can see that she's clearly rattled by the conversation we're having. But not as much as I fucking am.

"Think, Tracy," I say. "Did she mention anything? Anyone? Did she mention her parents?"

"No, no one," she squeals, "but I doubt she's gone to her parents. She hasn't spoken to them in years."

I consider this. Why would Ellie lie about seeing her parents? She visited them regularly. She hated visiting them, but felt it was her duty as a daughter, and she was keen for Toby to see his grandparents.

Then it occurs to me. "Has Ellie ever mentioned Bray to you?" I ask.

I watch her shake her head yet again. "Bray? No. Who's that?"

"It's not a person," I say. "It's a village just outside of London."

And it's a far cry given what I've just learned, but it's the only place I can think of. The last place where I'll have any chance of understanding what the hell is happening to me.

BRAY

Friday. 16:00.

Bray, also known as Bray on Thames, is a village in the county of Berkshire. It's about a thirty-minute drive from London, assuming the roads are empty, but given that they rarely are, and today being no exception, it takes the best part of an hour before concrete gives way to countryside and high rises are replaced by age-old trees.

And I must have spent most of that time glancing at the cab's fare meter and watching the digits rise along with my anxiety.

I know there are only a couple of hundred left on my card, if that, before it's maxed out, and the way I've been spending today on cab fare alone, I also know that it's not a matter of if, but when, my card is going to be declined.

As the cab sloshes through puddles and gets pelted by rain, I look out of the misty glass of my window and see one big question appear in it: how the fuck can I be a mechanic? I mean, really, it's just laughable. I don't even know how to change a flat tyre, do I? But I do know about psychology. I know about stuff like cognitive behavioural therapy. I mean, how would I know anything about that if I wasn't a therapist? I know about repression. Anxiety. Erotic transference. How would I know this stuff if I wasn't who I thought I was... think I am... think I was?

Fuck.

No, I know exactly how to explain all of this. It was the first thought to pop into my head when things started getting weird, and it's the only logical one still screaming in there now; I am in a dream. I'm trapped inside some kind of parasomnia. If you don't know what that is, it's a type of abnormal sleep behaviour. Those suffering from parasomnia exhibit abnormal movement, emotions, and can even dream while falling asleep rather than when in deep REM. That's Rapid Eye Movement to the uninitiated, and it's one of the five stages of sleep.

See?

How would I know this stuff if I was just a bloody mechanic? That's not a slur on all of the grease monkeys out there, by the way. I mean, Shawn's one of those and he smacks me as very intelligent. But, there's knowing about cars and knowing about human behaviour, and I bloody know about the latter.

Shit. What the hell has happened to me? A few months ago, my life was perfect. Okay, I'm guessing it probably wasn't since I'm now stuck in a dream and trying to work through what happened back then, but close enough. And, I need to wake up from this; I need to wake up now... and perhaps I should stop eating cheese.

Yes, I know that sounds weird, but it's true. Apparently, cheese does make you dream, although the jury is still out on whether or not it gives you nightmares.

Well, hello! I can report that it does!

Yeah, so, I may be losing it just a little, but that little factoid could go some way to explaining what is happening to me and, right now, given the intensity of this mind trip, I'm ready to latch onto anything.

Shit. Things must be bad. Cheese? Really?

Okay. But again, I'm obviously looking to make light of this predicament because I don't know how to handle it, let alone the thought that I am about to visit the two people who probably hate me the most on this earth. Ellie's parents. Who, rightly or wrongly, believe that I stole their daughter from them, as well as from bigger and better things, to make her my wife. The fact that she was slowly withering and dying under their roof and couldn't wait to be out from under their clutches is something that they've always conveniently brushed aside. It's much easier to blame me than accept that it was their controlling ways, and the enormous pressure that they continuously put on their daughter, that drove her from them.

And, do you know what? I'm happy to play that role. I'm happy to be the cliché of the undeserving son-in-law with nothing who marries the frustrated, misunderstood daughter with everything.

At least that's who we are in their eyes, and probably in yours, too, and if that's the case, well, you're entitled to your opinion, but you should know that I disagree. I know we're more than that. We may not have money, but we're filthy rich in other ways. We have our son and each other, and for us, that's all the currency we'll ever need – discounting for a second the necessity to eat and pay bills, of course.

On a serious note, I may not know what is happening to me, but what I do know is that I love my wife. I love our son, and I'll do anything to get my family back.

Yes, I know that, maybe... well, okay my behaviour *doesn't* always reflect that... but I try. I really do. Although I understand now more than ever, thanks to this hideous dream, that there's something fundamentally wrong with me. I am fundamentally flawed.

There, I said it.

Don't get me wrong. I don't think anybody is perfect. Are you? But there are basic comportments and behaviours that most of us automatically subscribe to when exposed to different types of relationships.

For example, generally, if we're dealing with clients, our behaviour towards them tends to be respectful, professional. In intimate relationships, our natural impulses lean towards trust, empathy, sympathy, monogamy.

Me, I obviously have a problem with that last one, and there's got to be a reason for that. Before, I wasn't able to see it. Or, I did see it, but was paralysed to act.

Yet, most of us know – even you, by now, no doubt through me – that the first step to healing is understanding that there's a problem.

I know that now, truly.

Admittedly, I don't think I needed this pseudo-psycho-mind-fuck dream to come to this conclusion, but, hey, the mind is a mysterious and sometimes terrifying thing.

Now, does all that sound plausible to you?

Fuck. Who the hell am I trying to convince? Me or you? You can't help me. I can't even help myself, so you certainly can't help. You, who are just sitting there, witnessing my world implode!

On the other hand, just in case you can... please, please, just help me understand. Please help me wake up from this. Please let this be the hideous dream I think it is, because the alternative... the alternative is just too unbearable for me to even contemplate.

I reach for the button and crack the window. This cab smells of the driver's I-don't-know-what – food? genitals? – whatever it is, it's making me gag. Making my head spin.

Yes, that's good... that fresh air feels and smells nice.

I lean my forehead against the cool glass and inhale the sweet, fresh scent of rain. It's really chucking it down out there and I'm finding that strangely comforting. It's like being undercover, hiding in the precipitation, somewhere where no further ugly revelations can find me.

Shit. It's late afternoon, yet it feels like early evening. Darkness is opening its big yawning mouth and slowly devouring the land.

I think about Ethan. Yeah, I'm on first name basis now. I'm no longer compartmentalising the good doctor and that's because I need him. I need all the friends I can get right now, and he is the only friend I can think of who I believe can help me through this. That's why I called him, the moment I boarded the cab. I gave him a synopsis-size version of everything that's happened today, including the journey I'm making and what I'm hoping to do when I get there, and asked him to please call me as soon as he gets my message.

That was nearly an hour ago, and he hasn't called back. I know this because I keep checking my phone for messages, just as often as I check the damn fare that seems to be counting up even faster now that we're getting close to our destination. I've already seen the obligatory sign welcoming us to Bray and asking us to drive slowly, along with a whole parade of super-rich, fuck-off mansions. Some visible from the main road and others set back amidst trees.

Some seriously wealthy people live in Bray. Popstars, actors, stock brokers, lawyers, and successful business owners have made their homes in this little village, and my cab has just pulled up outside of one of them.

THE STEVENSONS

Friday. 17:25.

This time, I don't wait for my card to clear before I get out of the cab, and I don't know why. Well, actually, I do. It's because I don't want to be stuck in that stuffy, confined space while the man puts through a two-hundred-and-something charge on my card.

The downside is that it's pouring down with rain out here and my jacket is little defence against the driving freeze.

Didn't think that one through, did I?

Then, the words I've been dreading all day: "Sorry, mate, it ain't going through," my overweight and generally already disgruntled driver says through the slit in his window.

"Could you try it again?" I ask, pointlessly, as I squint into the precipitation.

Then I turn and look up at the giant pillars supporting a seven-foot-something iron gate as if it's a fort I'm about to breach.

How are you going to do that?

I have no idea – beyond ringing the buzzer, of course.

I look up the gravelled drive. I can just about make out the silhouette of the mansion in the distance. Lights burning orange like small campfires behind arched windows.

Of course, I'm probably thinking about that analogy right now because it's bloody freezing. I mean, I know people say that when they're cold, but I am truly freezing. The sensation in my fingers is actually diminishing, and I already have pins and needles in my toes, which are soaked from the rainwater scurrying down my legs.

Yeah, getting out the cab probably wasn't the best idea. Or was it?

"Oi, mate! It ain't going through. I've tried it two more times now and it keeps getting declined. I'm gonna need another card or cash."

But I don't answer. I've already moved over to the intercom mounted on the stone column and am pressing the button.

It was an impulsive reaction. A bit like leaving a car when it's raining cats and bloody dogs, both of which I'm already regretting.

There's ringing, and then, "Yes?" It's a man's voice. It's James Stevenson. Ellie's father.

I swallow. "James, it's Marco!" I shout over the din of the driving rain, giving a wave to the recessed camera.

There's a pause. Then, "What can I do for you, Marco?"

"Well, I was wondering if I could borrow a cup of sugar…" I begin sarcastically, and then follow with, "I'd like to speak to my wife, please."

Another pause.

"Oi, mate!"

I'm shivering now, hunched next to the speaker, stupidly pulling my sodded coat around me.

"She isn't here."

"Come on, James. We both know she is. Just put her on, will ya?"

"I told you. She isn't here. Besides, she doesn't want to speak with you."

I smile. "Well, which one is it, James? She isn't there or she doesn't want to speak with me?"

"Just clear off or I'll have to call the police," he says in a particularly snooty and oddly high-pitched tone.

"James, you don't need to do that; just let me speak to my wife, please."

"Oi! You! Don't make me get out of this fucking cab!"

"I told you, she isn't here."

"Do you want me to scale this gate? Because that's exactly what I'll do if you don't put her on right now."

"Try it and I'll have you arrested for trespassing."

"Mate, after the day I've had… just let me in, will ya? Oh, and while you're at it, do you think you could lend me a couple of hundred quid?"

I've added this last bit because I've just heard the slam of the cab's door along with a series of disgruntled expletives.

My friend the cab driver has left the warmth of his vehicle and, by the sounds of it, he's thinking it's pretty cold out here, too. Oh, and he isn't happy.

Before I know it, he's grabbing me by the scruff of the neck and slamming me up against the intercom. He's a heavy-set fella, which means there's some momentum behind the action, and my already fuzzy head is suddenly seeing stars.

"What's going on?" asks James' tinny, girly voice.

"He's got your money," I say to the stubbly man with a balding head as he bears down on me.

Ew, is that rain or spittle on my face?

"I'm waiting for my fucking fare!" the bear yells at the intercom behind me.

"I've already called the police. Leave, now!" is James' response.

"Not until I get my money!"

I can feel the rain on my face. And by *feel*, I mean I can sense the impact of the droplets on my skin, though I can't actually feel much else because I think my nerve endings have frozen over. A bit like the rest of my brain, really. That fuzziness that's been dogging me for most of the day has transformed into dizziness, and I can feel my body being swung from side to side, like a ragdoll, in the clenched fists of the grizzly that's manhandling me.

He's screaming now. Yeah, that's definitely spittle mixed with rainwater spattering my face, but I don't feel it. In fact, I don't feel a thing. Instead, I shrink into myself; I shrivel up, crawl into my mouth, and slide down my throat and into my chest. It's dark in here. Nothing like what I expected. Dark, cavernous, and when I call to Ellie, the only thing that replies is my echo over and over again, like waves of sorrow washing over me. And I realise – I am inside the hollow of where my heart used to be. It, like my family, has gone, and there's no other reason to be here. None, so I may as well go and never come back.

Now, like Alice after taking the pill, I'm shrinking smaller and smaller, but not before I see blue fireworks explode in front of me to a chorus of angry voices, none of whom I recognise, but for one, and then I'm smiling, right before the world turns black.

AWAKE

Saturday Evening.

Oh ye of little faith. I told you it was all a shitty dream!

How do I know? Because I've woken with a start to find that I'm lying on my lovely, gorgeous, delicious, fantastically orgasmic sofa in the den at Dolce Vita.

And thank God for that. Thank you!

Oh, and guess what woke me? No, not the sound of the drumming rain on the skylight, and not the sound of the surf because, well, the rain's just too loud, but the urgent clanging of the doorbell.

Yay!

No, I mean it. Literally, yay! I'm so bloody pleased to be hearing that sound today. I can't say I'm super-excited by the fact that whoever it is appears to have fallen asleep against the button, but I don't care. I just don't care. I'm so happy, so grateful to be back here.

Fuck, that was one shitty, hideous dream, but I'm awake now. I'm awake.

I take a second or two to calm my breathing and to reacclimatise to my surroundings. Then, I glance at my watch. It's just gone six-thirty, and it's already dark outside, thanks to some seriously angry black clouds.

"I'm coming!" I call, relatively cheerily, because the whole euphoric I'm-not-stuck-in-a-hideous-nightmare thing is already starting to wear off, thanks to that repetitive clanging sound.

"Alright, alright!" I say as I make my way over to the door, snapping on lights.

Front door open.

"Seriously, dude? It's chucking it down out here!"

It's Shawn and his band of merry men, otherwise known as the guys from the shop.

Shawn's hair is plastered to his face and the five groupies behind him aren't fairing much better as they each struggle to carry and-or roll large, black, chrome-studded trunks into the house.

"What's this?" I ask with a grin, automatically stepping aside.

Note that I am actually grinning. I am so bloody happy to see these boys, I can't even tell you.

Once inside, and after shaking the rainwater from his hair like a dog, Shawn says, "It's Saturday. Party time!" He injects typical Shawn enthusiasm into the last bit of that sentence, and his pals echo this by cheering.

"Oh, yeah. I'm so sorry, mate. I fell asleep and completely lost track of time."

"Well, you better wake up because we've only got an hour or so to get this stuff set up before the whole village gets here."

"So, you still think they'll show?" I ask seriously.

"Why wouldn't they?" he shrugs. "It's free food and booze."

His upbeat demeanour, despite the fact that he's got rainwater dribbling down his nose, makes me chuckle, and I imagine that now that he's no longer a client, we'll probably become good friends.

"What's all this stuff?" I ask as I watch the guys roll trunks, mud, and water around the house.

"You'll see," Shawn says with a wink. "But, for now, let's get this party started!" He yells again, punching the air and eliciting yet another cheer from his crew.

I laugh, running my hands through my tousled hair before moving to close the front door when a voice calls out from the gloom beyond the gate, "Wait for me!"

It's Emily. I watch her scurry up the garden path, carrying a large cardboard box while squinting and hunching against the downpour.

"Hey," she says, pausing only to give me a smile before making her way inside.

"Hey." I grin back.

Okay, so strike what I said earlier. I'm psyched, to use an American expression, to see the lads, but seeing Emily... oh God.

I close the door and turn to a room that is already bustling with activity as, one by one, the *clunks* and *clicks* of locks prompt the cases to fall open.

I can see what they contain now. Speakers, decks, lights; it's the DJ gear that Shawn mentioned at the pub.

"Are you okay, or do you need a towel or something?" I ask Emily. Her hair is wet and hanging, beautifully, in loose curls over her shoulders. What can I say? I like the wet look. Her hair is chestnut brown under the house light and smells shower-fresh gorgeous.

"No, thanks, I'm okay," she says, peeling off a large chequered shirt that I imagine is her husband's, to reveal a tight-fitting black T-shirt. And, I guess you know what I mean by tight-fitting, right?

Yeah, I'm trying not to think about that, but you'll be pleased to know that I'm okay. I'm telling myself that this is just me appreciating an absolute stunner of a woman, but I know where my priorities are, I do.

Emily proceeds to dab her face and hair with the shirt, and as she does this I get damp wafts of her perfume. It's delicious.

Anyway, "What are you doing here?" I ask, suddenly, because I need to get my mind off every movement she is making.

"I'm here to inject some sparkle into your palace."

I cock my head.

"You'll see," she says with a cheeky smile. I can't take my eyes off of her. "Anyway, I best get started," she adds, pointing towards the stairs as if checking for my permission, and then walking in that direction.

Behind her, in the den – "Hey, Marco! I'm setting the bar up here, is that okay?" It's Shawn asking the question.

He and his brigade have already moved the sofas to the side of the room, opening up the floor space in front of the terrace doors where the men are now unfolding and assembling what looks like a giant black lectern.

"What the…" but my words are interrupted by another clang of the doorbell. I'm still watching the assemblage when I pull it open.

Front door open.

"Coming through!" It's Spencer. He's carrying a crate of beer. "Evening, Marco," he nods. "Bloody chucking it down out there." He stops suddenly. "Blimey, this is amazing..." he says, taking in the room.

"Thanks, Spencer. Do you need a hand with anything?"

"No thanks, mate. It's all in hand. Some of the regulars helped me load and unload. He nods at the door. As if by magic, a precession of people, a couple of whom I recognise, follow him inside, each carrying their own box or crate.

"Over here, Spence!" Shawn yells from the far end of the room.

And that is how, half an hour later, the den is transformed into a mini-club with a half of a glossy black bar and a resident DJ.

And I'm smiling. For the first time since arriving here, music is playing, loudly, at Dolce Vita. And it's accompanied by some very serious looking disco lamps, mounted on T-frames, directed at the newly unveiled dancefloor.

It's impressive. These guys obviously take their partying seriously. I like that.

Emily has transformed the rest of the place into a Christmas-worthy light extravaganza by draping strings of fairy lights from the balcony and hanging light curtains from the patio doors. She's even scattered a series of micro pulsating LED dots on the marble of the former water feature, bringing the constellation of gems to life in a dazzling array of colours.

Now, she and Spencer are busy unpacking food in the kitchen.

So, do you remember that famous film with Kevin Costner, *Field of Dreams*? And that now famous line, *Build it and he will come*?

Well, they don't.

By the looks of it, it's pretty much what Emily predicted. The turnout at somewhere around eight-thirty is nothing like what it was at the pub that night.

I guess you can't blame them. It's a small village, and anybody who knows about psychology and the societal practice of people confined in small spaces will know that, generally, these people band together like one big family. So, the loss of one affects many. Add to that the fact that I'm still allegedly the number one suspect, and nobody is going hurry over to a house warming they probably think is in bad taste anyway.

But, I didn't do anything. I didn't see Timmy that night at all. At least, not that I can remember.

"You okay?" It's Spencer. He's carrying a box of plastic glasses. Yeah, he thought of everything.

I nod and smile. "Of course. Look, Spence, I really don't know how to thank you. This, it's incredible," I say sincerely. I feel humbled that these people have done all of this with hardly any intervention from me.

"Well, it was a team effort," he says.

"Yes, and wow, what a team."

"We take care of our own around here, Marco."

I nod in response, and he must have read something in that, "Don't worry about the others. They're grief-stricken right now. It's not a slur on you."

"Really? Because it kind of feels like it."

"No. What happened to Timmy is a shitty, crappy, tragic accident. Nothing more."

"How can you know for sure?"

"She knows, and I would trust her any day of the week."

He's referring to Emily of course. Most likely because I've been watching her and his wife hand out plates of food to the twenty or so people who did turn up tonight. Although, I think most of them were part of the crew who helped set it all up.

I snatch my eyes off of Emily and busy myself by plucking drinking glasses out of a box, and setting them out on the bar.

"Who are we talking about?" I ask, feigning ignorance.

"Emily," he says, playing along with me, but without taking his eyes off of her.

"Yeah, she's been really helpful," I say casually, and almost instantly hear him snigger.

"What?"

"Helpful?"

"Well, she has," I say, trying to keep up my pretence despite the fact that that bloody heat has already returned to my cheeks. I can only hope the image gets lost in the subdued lighting.

"Yeah, right. And you'd be the only bloke who hasn't really noticed her. You're not gay, are ya?"

"No, I'm not!" The protest is much stronger than I intend, which only prompts the barman to shoot me a knowing wink.

"You wouldn't be the first to fall in love with her. Most of the married men around here have. You know that rubbish people say on Facebook and whatnot, about people being, ya know, beautiful on the outside and on the inside? Well, I think Emmy's the only person I know who really is. She's a lovely girl. Really cares about people, about the community."

We're both looking across at her now. To an onlooker, we both probably look like Dippy and Dopey, two love-stricken teenagers with doe eyes, and this makes me smile until I find myself asking, "Emmy?"

"Huh?"

"You called her Emmy."

"Right. And?"

I turn to him, "Oh, it's just interesting, because she told me that was my nickname for her. When we were kids."

"Course it was," he says with a chuckle. "She likes people to call her that."

"Right," I say, thoughtfully.

"Hey, when you two have finished gawping at the talent, some of us would like a drink."

It's Shawn.

"Don't know what you're talking about, lad. We're born ready," Spencer says, flipping a glass and pumping lager or whatever that nectar stuff is into it. The process takes only seconds, and he presents it to Shawn with a flourish.

"Anything else I can get ya?"

I laugh, and as I'm doing so, something catches my eye. It's something about these people in my house who are dancing, milling about, eating and laughing. Something that I can't quite put my finger on.

"Hey, Mr. Host, you have a customer." Spencer elbows me, and I look up.

"Lucinda, you made it."

"Of course, I heard there was a free bar!" the American says.

She looks completely different, out of her suit and in a generously fitting red dress. Her makeup is immaculate, her hair pinned up with a gem encrusted comb.

"You look great," I say earnestly.

"Why, thank you. I try," she says, grinning and patting her hair. "Say, can I have a word with you?"

"Yeah, sure."

"It doesn't have to be right now, honey, just when you get a chance tonight. I'm a pleasure before business kind of gal," she says, eyeing Spencer.

"Just my kind of girl. What'll it be?" he asks, as if reading her mind.

"Martini, please," she says, flashing her brilliant white smile. "Not shaken, but stirred, baby," she adds the last words with an enthusiastic wiggle of her ample body.

Spencer grins. "Stirred, it is," he says.

If I didn't know better... Actually, strike that, I do know better – they are flirting with each other.

Lucinda's arrival reminds me of those who aren't here. Namely, Ellie, Toby, and David. As well as Harvey. But then, he didn't come to Timmy's birthday party either. Never mind, though – I'll be visiting him first thing tomorrow. It's time I apologised for being such an ungrateful shit.

And it's as I'm considering this, while absentmindedly watching Shawn walk up to a couple of friends and snap a selfie, that I realise what it is about the guests that caught my attention earlier.

Most of them are holding their mobile devices and are either tapping out messages, snapping photos, or reading from them.

So, I leave Lucinda and Spencer to their chatty banter and make my way around the people shuffling on the dancefloor, towards one of the groupies, a man named Stuart.

He looks up from his phone when I approach.

"Great party, Marco."

"Thanks to you," I say with a grin, and I'm just about to ask him about phone signal when something wet, cold, and sticky is thrown at me.

"What the…"

I snap my head up and am about to yell when…

"Sorry. I'm sorry, I'm so sorry!"

It's a girl I've never met before. She looks across at a group of people who are doing some weird Cossack dance to some disco hit on the dancefloor. They're obviously not spatially aware, and have bumped into the girl who in turn has emptied her glass down my shirt.

Shit.

I smile at her. "It's no problem. Don't worry."

"I'm so sorry," she continues.

"It's no problem, really," I repeat, holding my hands out helplessly as the wet patch dribbles down and grows on my shirt. "I'm just going to go and change," I say with a forced smile, making my way away from her, around people, and up the stairs.

I'm already unbuttoning my shirt and pulling it out of my trousers before I've even entered the bedroom.

The sickly-sweet smell of coconut is nice, but the sticky sensation dribbling into my shorts, not as much. So now I'm thinking I'm going to need to change everything.

And, I'm loosening my belt, unbuttoning and unzipping my trousers, when the sound of running water reaches me from beyond the bathroom door.

Shit.

Someone or something is in there.

Something?

I'm already attempting to rebutton myself when I hear footsteps, and then the door is flung open.

Me and my visitor are both startled by the sight of each other.

"Emily!"

"Marco! Oh, I'm really sorry," she says, putting her hand to her chest as if to stop her heart from jumping out of it. "I'm so sorry. I just needed the loo and the others are busy, have been busy most of the evening, and…"

She's babbling. Nervous. As am I for some inexplicable reason. I suppose it could be something to do with the fact that we're in my bedroom and that I'm looking sideways onto her, Hollywood movie style, and that I'm naked from the waist up – and oh, my belt and trousers are half undone.

Interestingly, my beautiful intruder doesn't avert her gaze... not that I'm surprised by that. In fact, her eyes are all over me, but something is different

TONY MARTURANO

this time. It's not like it was at the front door. That was light-hearted, and this... well, this instantly feels like something else.

"I-I was just getting changed," I croak.

Yeah, my mouth's dry again. Shocker.

"I can see that," she says with a wry smile.

Shit.

My traitor of a bloody body is already reacting to her like an anxious hound. My heart is thudding. Thick. Fast. And I have to repress the churlish action of putting my arms across my naked chest because I fear that she may be able to see my heart throbbing behind my skin. And, oh yes, there goes that familiar tickle in my hair. Already? Down my back, like the gentle stroke of fingertips. Shit, I'm already sweating. She's making me sweat.

"You know, we really should stop meeting like this. People are going to talk," she says teasingly.

Panic is my initial reaction to that statement, but then I notice her smile and realise that she's referring to the fact that I'm semi-naked in front her, once more.

I look at myself and laugh. "Somebody decided to throw a drink down my front," I explain.

She just nods, and seconds seem like hours when your brain – you know, that amazing thing that works three hundred and sixty-five days a year, twenty-four hours a day – suddenly decides to take a break just because you're faced by a beautiful woman.

"So, um," I swallow, clear my throat, and then blurt, "your husband wasn't able to make it tonight, then?"

"No, he decided to stay home and babysit."

"Oh, that's a shame," I say, but it isn't. I know it isn't. I know that I'm glad her husband isn't here. On the other hand, I haven't got the foggiest what to say to her. It's like the aphasia she keeps giving me has kidnapped my tongue.

"So, anyway, I wanted to tell you just how grateful I am, for you, for all your help, that you've, the support you've given me."

Oh God. Now I'm babbling and it's ridiculous.

"Oh no, it's no problem. It was my pleasure. It's a good opportunity for people to meet and get to know you."

"Does that include you?"

"Of course. Although, I had a private audience on my last visit, and I prefer that," she says softly as she takes a step closer.

I don't want to ask, but my traitor tongue has other plans. "And, what did you see? In me," I ask.

She mulls my question over with a knowing smile. Then, "I see a man who isn't in a particularly good place right now, but is keeping it together. Someone who has a good heart, but has been hurt, so is terrified to show it. Someone who's so busy helping everybody else break down their walls that he's incapable of letting down his own." Another step closer. "You've been hurt, we all have, and now you're scared, but you don't need to be."

Her voice is silky smooth. It's like a lullaby to my ears and a pickaxe to my defences.

I swallow. "Wow, I wasn't expecting that. You sure you're in the right job?" I ask, in an attempt to distract her from the colour in my cheeks.

It's times like these when I'm grateful that I don't have David's ears. Random, I know, but those things are like two giant flares when he's embarrassed. I'm hoping that the bedside lamplight isn't enough to illuminate my own self-consciousness.

It's interesting and typical, how I preoccupy myself more with my reaction to her words than the meaning of them. But then, I never have enjoyed talking about myself. I suppose this is the very reason I decided to become a therapist; if I'm busy talking to others about their problems, I'm not looking at my own. Those who can't, teach.

"Am I right?" she presses.

"I..." I actually don't know how to respond, because you and I both know how I feel about this. I would have felt uncomfortable if a bloke had said all that, but I certainly can't allow myself to get into it with this wondrous creature whose blue eyes are devilishly black in this light.

I'm paralysed, but I manage to croak, "Hey, if you're really into this, we can bin all these people and go to my study; you can take my chair and…"

I break off there. She's smiling at my deflection and stepping closer.

Oh shit.

"Are you okay?" she asks.

"I-I'm fine," I stutter, like the virgin schoolkid this woman keeps reducing me to.

"Are you sure?" she asks, moving closer.

It takes all my willpower not to step back. And that's when I realise… I'm afraid of her. Of me. I know what I'm like and how this usually ends up.

Although, I have to say that, unlike most of my usual encounters, this particular one is completely different. For a start, I don't feel like I'm in control. Normally, it's me either initiating or allowing the charge, but that's normally because I know what's coming, and what I want, and it's normally at my speed… but this. This is something else. She is in the driver's seat and I know I have no control whatsoever over anything when I'm around her.

It's as if she's already bound me to the bed. I'm scared, yet excited. Terrified, yet turned on.

Get a grip, you limp-dicked idiot!

But that's the problem. I'm not limp. Far from it. I can feel a gradual stirring in my shorts and all I can think about is what that is going to look like. Can you believe that? Me? Marco Battista? With my history? This is what I do. I never shy away from it, because I've been like a bloody druggy who needs to score. I need it because I'm addicted to it.

Yet, something is different this time. Something I don't understand. The compulsion, it's is different. So different, it's making me want to bang my head against the bloody. I just can't figure it out. All I know is that this tension, this electricity, that has charged the air between us, is more about intimacy than release.

"Marco?"

She's standing really close now. Less than an arm's length away. I can feel the radiation of heat from her body, like a solar storm against the shield of my resolve as her scent intoxicates and hypnotises.

"Are you sure you're okay?" she asks. Her voice breathless, seductive as she places a red-hot hand on my naked chest. It is a cattle prod to the senses that jolts and jangles all of my extremities. I wrestle with the instinct to jump away from her.

But I know I've been made. Her cool slender fingers are spread open like a heart monitor on my chest and I know she's discovered the frantic thump, thump, thump of my heart.

"Wow. Your heart's beating really fast," she says in what I can only translate as mock alarm. She knows what's happening to me. I can tell from the twinkle in those big eyes, and she's enjoying it.

The rain is drumming on the window like the pulse in my veins as she brings her body closer, ordering the small hairs on my arms to attention, deploying the flow of blood to my loins.

"Emily, I…."

"It's okay," she whispers, reassuringly, "It's okay."

She leans in closer. As she does, her hand slowly and teasingly tickles its way down my chest to my midriff, where her fingers linger on the band of my shorts.

"Emmy?"

She looks up at me. Her almond eyes are giant aquamarine pools smothered in a mist of desire, and I just want to let go, to fall be drowned in them.

Oh God… her lips call to me and I respond by lowering my head to kiss her, but hesitate when I hear someone whisper, "Emmy, I'm married."

What? It's me! It's bloody me!

"I know," she responds, and she's about to pull my lips down to hers when a loud, jarring phone alert pierces the moment and pops it like a giant balloon.

She wrinkles her face apologetically. "Sorry."

I smile at her as the steam from the pressure cooker of our encounter is invisibly released into the air and I pull back.

"It'll be my boy wishing me goodnight," she explains, pulling the phone out of the back pocket of her perfectly moulded jeans.

I suppress the mental image of what the naked version of this looks like and instead go through a flip-book of reactions in my head. The first is mild irritation, that she should interrupt the moment just to take a bloody message. The second is relief because that was way too close for comfort, and the third... the third is, how the hell is she receiving text messages in this dead zone of a house anyway?

I look at her. She's reading the text and smiling. I unconsciously smile with her as I imagine what it would feel like to get a goodnight text from Toby.

Then, she looks up, her face brimming with pride.

"Your boy?"

"Yeah. He's so sweet." She turns the phone to me and I slowly read the text: *Goodnight Mummy. I love you.* It makes me smile. Then, just as I'm about to look away, I catch sight of the tiny thumbnail image next to the speech bubble, and catch my breath.

"That's your son?" I ask as my eyed widen, because I think I'm seeing something that isn't possible.

"Oh, yeah, you said you wanted to see piccies of him." She takes the phone from me, swipes, and taps a few times before showing me the device's screen once more. The effect it has on me is akin to handing a crucifix to a vampire. If vampires were to exist, of course.

I'm paralysed, unable to do anything but watch as she proceeds to swipe through a whole series of photos while proudly introducing them. "These are from the other day, flying his new drone, and this is him all dressed up for Laser Quest. Oh, and this is him playing football…"

I tune out from the rest of her words as I involuntarily stagger back, away from her, away from the slideshow of confusion until my back is up against the wall.

Her smile disappears almost instantly. "What's wrong?" she asks.

I can't speak. I just stare at her. Eyes bulging, beseeching. "Wh… wh…

why are you doing this?" I stammer.

"What are you talking about?" She asks with a curious smile.

"Why would you show me those?" I gasp as my skin crawls with invisible insects.

"I don't know what you're talking about. What's wrong?"

"Why would you do this?" I demand again, my voice louder now.

She steps forward. I squirm against the wall.

"Marco, I don't understand. What's wrong?"

But, once again, I can't talk. I'm moving my tongue, but it's thick and heavy. The words won't form, they won't emit, because I don't know what to say, I don't know how to explain it. I don't know what to do.

"Marco!"

I refocus on her face. She's walking slowly towards me. "What's wrong with you?" she demands. Her face now creased into a frown.

"Stop where you are. Don't come any closer!" I say, putting out a restraining hand.

"What is wrong with you?" She demands.

"Why the fuck do you have photos of my son on your phone?" The words spew out of my mouth with a snarl.

It's true. I'm not imagining it. I thought I was at first, when I first saw the thumbnail and then when she showed me a larger image, and then another and another. There's no mistaking it, though. No fucking denying it. The sandy coloured hair, the big brown eyes, that broad little nose, the one that looks just like mine.

"What the fuck is happening?"

"Marco," she begins, her face a mask of seriousness.

"Answer me!" I yell.

"I don't know what you're talking about."

"You know exactly what I'm talking about! Why the fuck do you have pictures of my son on your phone? Why are you doing this?" I ask. Angry. Stupefied.

"Marco, I don't know what you think you've seen, but these are not pictures of your son. They're my pictures. Of *my* son."

"Why are you lying?"

"I'm not lying," she throws back.

"You are!"

She swallows hard and moves in, arms outstretched in front of her like she's approaching someone who's about to leap from a cliff.

"Tell me why you're doing this."

She doesn't respond, yet continues her approach.

"TELL ME!"

She blinks rapidly, flinching against my raised tone. Yet continues to move in closer…closer.

"Get the fuck away from me!"

"Marco, I think you're suffering from some kind of a psychotic break."

I let out a short, hollow laugh. "I'm suffering a break?"

"Yes, you are."

"Get the fuck away from me!"

"Marco…"

"I said, get the fuck away!" I growl, fists clenched, face burning. "Get away from me or I swear…"

But, she doesn't stop.

"I want you out of here. I want you all out of my house! Get out! GET THE FUCK OUT!"

I turn from her and stumble out of the door, fully prepared to grab people by the scruffs of the necks and throw them out if I have to, but that's when I realise it. There's no hubbub. No chatter. No laughing, and the music has stopped.

I look over the bannister. The space below is silent, but for the whirring of the disco lights and the relentless precipitation dinging off of the skylight.

Everybody is frozen. Each and every one looking up at me. Eyes unblinking. Glaring.

"Get out of here! GET THE FUCK OUT OF MY HOUSE! GET OUT! NOW!"

But they don't move. They just watch.

A creak startles me and I snap my head around. Emily is at the door now. She followed me out of the bedroom and is moving towards me again.

"Get back! Get away! Get fuck away from me!"

"Marco. I need to talk to you. I need you to listen to me," she tries to reason.

"I don't want to talk to you. Get away from me!" I scream, backing away from the balustrade and moving towards the stairs.

"Marco, I need you to listen to me. I need you to hear what I have to say," she continues in a measured, authoritative tone.

"I don't want to listen to anything you have to say. Just get out! Get out! Get out!" I shrill. I'm hyperventilating again. Bordering on the hysterical.

But she's not going anywhere. The more I back away from her, the more she advances on me. It's like we're tethered to each other. She's inching closer and closer.

"Emily, I swear. Come any closer and I'm…"

But she doesn't care. She won't stop! Whatever I say or scream seems to have no effect on her. So, I turn to run, but miscalculate distance between step and landing.

"No." I flail, reaching for the bannister, but my fingers narrowly miss the purchase. "NOOOOO!" I scream as I fall sideways, cartwheeling helplessly down the stairs as the world, the lights spin round and round until I slam to a stop in a crumpled heap. Then, everything turns black.

IM NOT DEAD

Saturday Evening.

I'm dreaming. No, I'm not dreaming – I'm sleeping. No, I suppose I'm not doing that either because the world is still black, as if I simply have my eyes closed, as if I can open them at any moment…

I'm fully aware.

I know I'm lying in bed and I can hear what's happening around me. That stink of disinfectant is back again. I must be in my bedroom. And it's raining still. I can hear it tapping on the window. There are voices. Actually, they're more like hushed tones, because I can't hear exactly what's being said, but I can sense that there are people in the room, standing nearby.

There's no birdsong, though, or surf. No matter how hard I try to focus on that low rumble, I just can't hear it above the sound of the rain.

Yet, I know I'm in my bedroom because the lighthouse beam keeps falling across my eyelids, searing the floaty alien world behind them into an orange blur. Although, it's much brighter today. Stronger.

Somebody, close the curtains!

Oh, I thought I spoke those words aloud, but I didn't. I couldn't have. My tongue feels like lead, as if it's been anesthetised, but I don't think it has. I just seem to be unable to move it, to articulate.

Hello!

Yep, still in my head.

Meanwhile, the hushed sibilance continues unabated. Now, I'm annoyed. I am so bloody sick of people just walking into this house, and now into my bedroom, like they own the place.

Get out of here! Get out!

Shit. Again, I'm saying the words, but they're not actually leaving my mouth.

What the hell is wrong with me? It's like I'm too tired to open my eyes, yet I'm wide awake.

Oh, what's that? Hey! There's someone leaning over my bed now. I can hear them breathing. Smell coffee on their breath. It's not a woman. They're breathing way too deeply – not a woman unless she's had a sex change.

Oi! What's with the intimacy? Step back!

Again, nothing.

Then, the bloody light burning my eyelids again. I grimace. Fuck! Stop that shit, will you? Stop! Close the fucking curtains!

"Marco? Marco, can you hear me?" It's a male voice. One I vaguely remember.

"Marco?" He's speaking loudly, as if talking to an old man. I am right here, you know, you don't have to yell.

Fuck! There's the light again. Ow! Close the curtains… close them!

Oh God… I've just been stung by a memory. Oh shit! That's not a real memory, is it? It can't be. Please tell me it was a dream.

I'm falling down the stairs. The world's spinning. Everybody's watching me.

Oh God. Am I okay? Am I hurt?

I move fingers, but I can't tell if they're actually moving. I try wiggling my toes because, well, that's what doctors always ask you to do in these situations.

Oh God. Is that it? Have I been injured? Did I break my neck in the fall? Am I paralysed? Oh fuck! No! Fuck! Please tell me I'm not paralysed.

An electric current of fear zaps through me, down my spine and up through my legs. That's good, right? That must mean I'm not paralysed. I'm not a cripple because I felt that. Didn't I? Didn't I?

Oh no, please, God. Please, no.

I will my fingers to move.

Nothing.

I will my legs to move.

Nothing.

I try to peel my eyelids open.

Nothing.

Oh no, please, no! NO! I'm dead! I'm dead! This is what it's like to be dead! I'm dead! But, I'm not dead!

You're dead!

I'm not dead! I'M NOT DEAD!

Tears build at the backs of my eyelids until one breaks the seal and trickles down my cheek. I can feel it! I can feel it!

So why can't I open my eyes? Why?

Something is wrong. Something is fucking wrong! Why do I have all of these sensations, but can't open my eyes?

I'm paralysed, physically and metaphorically, and the thought of that pushes me into a bottomless well and I'm drowning. I'm drowning in icy, arctic water. I can't breathe! I can't breathe! It's squeezing the air from my lungs like a vice. Like a bloody vice! I can't breathe! I'm dying! I'm dying!

"Marco?"

Help me!

"Marco. Can you hear me?"

"Help me!"

"Marco."

"HELP ME!"

I jolt up into a sitting position, spluttering and sucking in air like I've just been unearthed from a premature grave.

I sit there for what must be minutes – coughing, gagging, and wheezing – and I suck in the stagnant air from the room. "Oh shit! Fuck!" I touch myself. I'm here. I'm alive, but where the hell am I?

I'm sitting up on a bed in a room that I don't recognise. When I say that I'm sitting on the bed, that's exactly what I am doing. I'm fully clothed, and have just bolted upright like a fucking vampire.

The box of a room is generous in size, but sparsely furnished, with a bedside dresser, a lamp, and an armchair in the corner by a black window. Night is pressing on the glass and, from that tapping sound, yes, it is still raining out there.

The rest of the room is blue pastel drab and resembles a hospital room, only not as grim or as clinical. This place is more like a sanitised hotel room.

There's a man standing at the foot of my bed. His fingers are fiddling with something silver. It's a pen. No, not a pen, but a penlight. Which would explain that glare burning my eyes.

He's looking at me. FUCK! I recognise him and I'm filled with relief. Blissful relief. Thank God. Thank God for Doctor Ethan Holmes.

He's frowning at me. He seems worried, but I'm smiling. As much as

I could never have imagined myself admitting to this, I'm really fucking happy to see him.

But where's everybody else? Who was he talking to? And, most importantly, "Where the fuck am I?" The words are a croak. There's that dry mouth again. Only this time, it's worse. Much worse. My throat is sore. Like I haven't used it in months.

Shit.

"You're in a private hospital, Marco. Tell me how you're feeling right now."

Oh God. I fell down the stairs. I look at myself. I'm wearing grey jogging bottoms and a black fleece. I touch my arms and legs systematically – checking for breakages, bandages, but finding that there are none. I wiggle my hands and toes, and everything seems to be in perfect working order. I even give you-know-who a twitch to make sure he's still there and in working order. I'm sure that you'll be pleased to know that he seems to be okay.

"I think I'm okay," I utter. "Did you bring me here as a precaution?"

Holmes frowns, so I show and tell. I move my hands and wiggle my feet for him. "I don't think I've broken anything in the fall. I think I'm okay."

He observes me from behind those neat glasses of his, but says nothing for a few seconds, during which I can see that water droplets are still clinging to his jacket, and his hair is wet. He's been outside. Did he just get here?

"You fell?" he asks.

"Yeah. Down the stairs," I say slowly, as I observe him for clues. He seems a bit off tonight. Not his usual plucky self.

He hands me a plastic cup of water and asks, "Can you tell me what happened?".

I down the water in one go. It's cold. Refreshing.

"You don't know?" I ask, through breaths.

"No, I just got here."

"Huh." That explains it. "Well, I was…" it takes a few seconds for the memory to come back to me. It's like it's been sitting behind some firewall or something. "Um, I was having a party at the house, and I was talking to Em." I pause as the memory, like a developing photograph, comes into focus while simultaneously knifing me in the gut.

Fuck.

"… Emily had pictures of Toby on her phone." I speak the words more for my own benefit than because I'm in the mood to share. I can't believe what I'm remembering. I can't believe that what I'm recalling is true. Why would she do that? Why would anyone do that?

Holmes must see the horrified look on my face because he quickly asks, "What happened, Marco? Tell me what happened."

But I'm too stunned by what I'm thinking, to the point where I can't get the words out, and sitting on this fucking bed isn't helping!

I swing my legs over the side.

Holmes moves in to help me, but I wave him away.

I stand up and nearly fall over. I've got cramps in my legs. Holmes moves, but again, I swipe him off. I don't need his help; I just need to walk around a bit.

So I will my legs to step forward, to move around the room so that I can restore some circulation and steal a few seconds to think, since I'm still wrestling with that whole nightmare of believing I was paralysed.

Holmes backs away towards the door to give me space, and I'm grateful.

Eventually, I go on. "She, she... Emily had pictures of my son on her phone," I utter in disbelief as snapshots of what happened in my bedroom are replayed to me. "She had photos of Toby and she told me that..." the words catch in my throat, "she told me that he was *her* son."

I screw my face up, both with incredulity and because my fucking legs are hurting!

"What else?" he asks calmly.

"What else?" I echo. "That isn't headline enough for you?" I ask in amazement. "The woman has pictures of my son on her phone and you're holding out for something more sensational?"

He doesn't respond. He just watches me with that fucking poker face of his. And, shocker, he's annoying me again, already. He's supposed to be my bloody therapist, and I could use a little support right now because I'm fucking losing my mind with this shit. "Why would she do that?" I press him.

He observes me for the longest time, then says, suddenly, "Marco, can you tell me a bit about Emily? Can you tell me what you know about her?"

"Um, I can tell you that she's a fucking psychopath." I shake my head, slowly, as I gawp at him. "So, let me get this right. I tell you some bird has my son's pictures on her phone and is passing him off as her own, and all you care about is knowing more about her?"

"I'm just trying to understand all the facts. Would you mind explaining them to me so that I can better understand?"

He seems earnest and very calm which, I have to say, is contagious. Because if he's like this, I don't feel like I have to rally against him. It's Therapy 101, but he and I both know that it can go two ways. In this case, he's lucky – it calms me but, again, I think that's more because I'm actually grateful he's here to work through this with me.

I sigh and lean against the wall next to the window, because I like the idea of breaking the glass in case of emergency. In this case, filling the room with fresh air because the atmosphere in here is stifling. The air is thick, stuffy and stale. It's like a bloody windowless attic. Except for that sickly disinfectant stench that occasionally slices through it, making me feel bloody nauseous. And my legs; they're fucking killing me. It's like they've atrophied. So, I start rubbing them.

"Marco?" Holmes prompts.

"She's a copper. Told me we knew each other as kids."

"From London?"

"No, she's local."

"Local to where?"

"Come on, Doc. You know where. Bloody Porthcove."

He nods.

"Anyway, she introduced herself as a friend. Told me we were old playmates. She visited the house a few times. Not including the night she showed up with a posse of her police pals and a fucking search warrant to tell me that I was the number one suspect in the death of that boy. You know, Tim, the one who went missing."

I watch him for a reaction but, as usual, there's nothing behind those bloody glasses, that are currently reflecting the lamplight, to the point where I want to jump across the room and rip them off of his bloody face, just to see if there's any life beyond them.

Obviously, I don't. Instead, I continue. "Anyway, you know most of this. She came to see me the next day, acting like she was sorry for the home invasion and reassuring me that she doesn't suspect me." I hesitate here. I want to add that I liked and trusted her, but all of that's changed now. Now she feels like my fucking nemesis. So, I don't mention it, and instead continue, "Then she encourages me to throw the housewarming party where it all goes tits up."

"What happened exactly?"

"I told you. She turns up with the rest of them. Shows me pictures of my son which, by the way, I have no idea how she managed to get. I mean, the woman's fucking twisted!" I pause here, allowing the cloud of confused rage to blow through me like a fiery backdraft. I swallow. My throat's tight. Dry. "The next thing I know, I'm falling down the fucking stairs," I say, bitterly. "Can I have some more water?"

Holme's doesn't speak. He reaches over to a tray on the bedside table, picks up a bottle of water, breaks the seal and hands it to me.

I snatch the bottle from him and gulp half of it, before pausing for air.

I notice him take a few steps back. Again, as if respecting my space. Then, "I'm sorry. Are you saying she pushed you down the stairs?" He asks.

I think about this. "No, I fell, trying to get away from her."

There's silence. Thunder rumbles overhead as I watch Holmes, willing him to say something, to make some sense of this crap. But, yet again, he has no reaction to that story, which, you can imagine, is getting on my nerves now. I mean, I know why he's moderating his behaviour. Obviously, if he starts reacting, I am going to pick up on that and there's nothing constructive nor progressive about two blokes losing their shit at the same time. But still…

"Where am I?" I find myself asking.

"You're in hospital."

"Yeah, I got that, but where?"

"You're in a clinic on the outskirts of London."

"London? Why did they bring me all the way back here?"

I wait for an answer, but instead Holmes takes a deep breath and gestures at the armchair in the corner of the room. "Marco, why don't you take a seat"

"I'm fine standing," I say, leaving the ache in my legs and folding my arms across my chest, defensively. The doc's long brooding silences are already doing my nut in, and him asking me to take a seat, as if he's about to tell me something really upsetting, isn't helping.

I look at him, pointedly, and wait.

"Marco…."

The buzz of his mobile phone seems particularly loud in the stillness of the room. We both stare at it, as if it's a hornet caught in his jacket.

And fucking hell, I realise now just how tense I've become. My shoulders have been hunched and I've been alternating between holding and intaking shallow breaths the whole time since popping up in this place, to the point where I'm feeling light-headed.

I breathe deeply. I desperately want to open the window, but I've already clocked that it's locked. Suicides and hotel rooms. Only, I know this isn't a hotel. It's a hospital. A private hospital. Who the hell's paying for this?

"Yes?" Holmes says into his mobile phone while averting his gaze for some reason, as if I'm able to read his expression. "Already? Um…" He looks at me and then away once more and, in a hushed tone, says, "Okay, give us a couple of minutes and then come in. Thanks."

He slips his phone back into his pocket, looks up at me, and shit, I swear my blood freezes, because there's something about that look. In fact, there's something about his whole demeanour tonight. I mean, I don't know if they got this guy out of bed to come here or what, but he looks like he's aged ten years. He doesn't look anywhere near as fresh, young, or as poncey as he normally does. Tonight, he looks like he's carrying the weight of the world on his shoulders and, now, he's staring at me, grim-faced, like a policeman with bad news.

"You may not have noticed, Doc, but your poker face has slipped and you look like your cat's just died. What's going on?" I ask through a grin, but it's a nervous grin. I can't see anything about this particular situation that is in any way, shape, or form funny to me. Far from it. I'm suddenly feeling weighed down with overwhelming dread. It's restricting the movement in my achy limbs like I've just been locked into a metal suit of misery.

"Marco. You mentioned that you were at a party with Emily. Was this back at, um, Porthcove?"

"Yes."

"And there were lots of people at this party?"

"A few. Not as many as I'd hoped."

"And Emily was there with you?"

"I've already told you she was."

He looks at me for way too long before saying, "Marco, you weren't in Porthcove." His voice is solemn, his eyes locked on mine.

"What do you mean?"

"You weren't in Porthcove this evening," he repeats, firmly.

My face falls into an equivocal squint. "I, um, why are you saying that?"

"You've been in London all evening."

A snicker leaves my mouth. "Yeah, I teleported here. Doc, stop talking shit. I couldn't have been in London, because getting to London is a whole fucking saga. Takes hours to get here. You know that because you've asked each time I've visited you. You know, stock questions. How was your week? How was your journey? All of that crap."

He goes silent again, and I'm getting worked up now.

He obviously spots the look on my face because he says, rapidly, "Marco, something has happened…"

"…No shit! I told you that. But I also told you that I'm fine."

"No, I mean something else has happened, but you weren't necessarily physically involved."

"What the fuck are you talking about?" Then realisation dawns. "Oh shit, is this something to do with Toby, Ellie?" I ask anxiously. He just stares at me. "Oh no, it is, Isn't it? Isn't it?"

There's a rap on the door and it startles the both of us.

"Not yet. We're not ready yet!" Holmes shouts to nobody in particular.

My eyes dart to the closed door, at the doctor, and then back to the door again. "Not ready for what?" I ask warily, my stomach churning.

"Marco, I need you to listen to me…"

"…Ready for what? What are we not ready for, Doc?" I repeat.

Holmes steps back towards the door while all the time keeping his eyes on me, almost as if he doesn't want to startle the scared little boy in the corner.

That would be me, by the way, because I'm suddenly feeling scared. No, not scared… terrified. I asked him about Ellie and Toby, and now he's gone all quiet.

"What's behind the door?" I ask.

Thunder cracks, then rolls away. Rain spits loudly at the window.

"Marco, I need you to focus on my voice; I need you to listen…."

"What the fuck's behind the door, Doc? Tell me!" Someone whines, and I realise it's me. Tears prod at my eyes. Fear restricts my breath like a tight collar around my neck.

"Marco, it's okay. I promise it will be okay," Holmes reassures me as he continues his regression towards the closed door.

"Tell me who's behind the door!" I shout. My skin itching. Eyes bulging, heart thumping. I swipe my forehead with the back of my sleeve, and then, "Tell me what's behind the door," I wail, as if I know the man's about to set a rabid dog on me.

"It's just a friendly face, Marco. A friendly face. I promise, but I need you to trust me. Okay? I need you to trust me. Do you trust me?"

Those words only make me feel worse because I know there's something horrible behind that door. Something hideous is waiting for me on the other side. I can sense it. I can feel it. I know it.

Holmes rests his hand on the door handle. I unconsciously back away to the corner of the room until the armchair pushes against my legs.

The doctor turns the handle.

I bring my fists up to my face.

Lightning flashes. Thunder moans.

Holmes opens the door, slowly, painfully, inch by inch by inch. It squeals eerily, as if it, too, is afraid of what might be revealed.

And that is when my heart stops. The hammering ceases and the blood freezes in my veins like cooled molten lava.

"What the fuck are *you* doing here?" I ask, coldly. The words leave my mouth without any thought from me.

The visitor does not respond, but instead steps into the room, donning a nervous smile.

"You can't be here!" I say, emphatically shaking my head. "You can't be here. You have to leave. You need to leave. NOW!"

"I don't want to leave," the visitor says, standing timidly in the middle of the room, dripping rainwater.

"You have to. I don't want you here! My wife will be here soon, and you have to be gone before she gets here! Get out! Get the fuck out!"

I'm trembling now. Nerves taught – so tight they're tugging the occasional nervous twitch from my face.

Tears bubble and spill from the visitor's eyes. Her lips quiver, and then she utters, "M… Marco… I *am* your wife." The words are choked out through a lump in her throat.

Rain pelts the window, demanding to be closer to the melodrama unfolding before me.

I shake my head because what she said isn't true. It can't be true, obviously. "What the fuck are you talking about? No, you're not. Why would you say such shit?" I ask, my voice and incredulous whisper. She doesn't respond. Instead, she does a terrible job at holding back a sob.

I turn to Holmes. "Why is she saying this? Why does she keep doing this?"

"Because it's true, Marco," Holmes says gently.

"It's not true," I snap. "It can't be fucking true! My wife's name is Ellie, short for Elizabeth."

The woman in front of me blubbers loudly, and through those convulsions garbles, "That… the… that's me, Marc. I am your wife, I am Elisabeth."

"No, you're not!" I yell angrily. "You're not Elizabeth! You're Emily, Emmy, or whatever the fuck you like to be called! You're a fucking policewoman! My wife works for David."

"She's your wife, Marco," Holmes continues softly. Then, with a faint smile on his lips, he adds, "You created Emily, or Emmy the police officer, to protect you from the intruders. The intruders being the truths that your mind struggles to handle. So, you assigned someone close to you. Someone you can trust to protect you from them."

I stare at him, and I'm assuming my face looks like a mask of fucking incredulous horror because that is exactly how I feel – confused. Horrified. Like I'm stuck in some film noir and people are trying to make me think I'm going loopy, but I'm not. I'm not fucking crazy! "Why are you doing this to me?" I ask through clenched teeth.

"Marco, I know this is hard for you, but I need you to stay with me,"

Holmes continues in that measured tone of his, and I just want to kick his teeth to the back of his throat. "I need you to stay with me, Marco. Stay with me. *This* is your life. *This* is your reality. Right here in this room..."

"...No. No. It isn't!"

"Can't you see? You compartmentalised this whole thing. You created a home – not a house, a home. Think about it. Think about how you described it. You described it as a fortress with a drawbridge. And then you locked everything that happened inside. You created rooms and filled them with memories. Memories of your mother in one room and those with your father In another. Think, Marco. The study. The ships. Your childhood. You compartmentalised everything inside of an idyllic place so that you could then systematically deal with every aspect of it."

"You're fucking insane!"

"Marco. Please think about it. I need you to see. I need you to accept. You know what I'm saying makes sense. You conceived, idealised a location, and built a world. Then you, you brought in characters, real characters and alter egos from your present and past, to help you deal with what happened."

"No. No!" I shake my head. "It's a lie. It isn't true. No. It isn't true! Why are you are saying this stuff? Why are you doing this to me?" I yell, trying to smash through the white noise of his words.

"Marco, I'm not doing anything to you. You are doing it to yourself. I promise you, I am trying to help you. Think about it. Deep inside, you know I am telling the truth. You know, because you've been working all this time to heal yourself. Heal yourself from both the traumatic events that happened to you as a child and the traumatic event you've been ignoring. The one that eventually brought you back to my office."

I don't want to hear what the fucker is saying. In fact, I try actively to ignore it, because I know he's trying to screw with my head. But I can't – it's in there now. His words have burned and burrowed deep into my skull, making me slap my head, instinctively. Slap myself so hard I'm seeing stars.

The woman who is pretending to be my wife throws her hands to her mouth in horror as tears stream down her face while I smack my head and chant, "It can't. It can't be."

"It is," Holmes repeats.

"It can't!"

"It is, Marco," Holmes responds. His voice forceful now. Like he's my dad. Like he's my fucking father telling me what to do. What fucking right does this arsehole have in telling me what to fucking do?

"What did you do for me? What have you done for me, huh? What gives you the right?" I growl.

"Your father tried the best he could, Marco. And I, I have no rights. I just want to help." He's back to his soothing self and I feel like my head is going to explode. I just want out of here, out of this room, and I glance at the open door. "Marco. Please stay here. Stay with us," Holmes says. As if he's read my mind.

I look at him, at the snivelling wreck of the woman whom, despite her ordeal, is still bloody beautiful. Now even more so with her damp hair and tear-stained eyes.

I can tell you, in some other place, some other universe, I'd be lunging across the room right now and taking that sad, wretched thing in my arms, but not here, not now, because I'm onto her. I'm onto them. I don't know what their fucking game is, but I'm not falling for it again. I'm not!

"Okay, alright. Okay," I say with a shaky voice, as I attempt to straighten myself up and get a grip on the wild horses of emotions kicking and bucking inside of me. "If she's Ellie, then where's Emily?"

"I told you. You created Emily."

"No, I mean the other woman. My actual wife. If she's my wife," I say, nodding at the woman standing before me, "then where's the woman with the short blonde hair, and where's my son, where's Toby?"

The doctor and Emily, as I know her, exchange a fleeting glance. Fleeting perhaps, but long enough for me to notice, and my eyes flick back and forth between them.

"Marco," Holmes begins.

"What?" I snap.

"Marco…"

"Why did you two just look at each other like that?" I ask suspiciously.

"Marco," the doctor perseveres. "The woman whom you believe is your wife isn't. She, she was actually your lover."

I let out a laugh and snatch a look at the woman in front me, and I catch something. I don't know what it is, but it's something. Like a dark shadow across her face as she registers what Holmes just told me. Was that a flicker of jealousy? Resentment. I keep my eyes on her for several seconds as I try to read her face, but she just sniffs back tears and then drops her eyes to her feet.

I turn to Holmes and shake my head. "Ellie is actually my lover. That's what your telling me?" I ask, mildly amused. If only. How hot would that be? Yes, I am thinking that. Give me a fucking break. You try taking in all of this shit about your life and then come back to me with how well you coped.

"Look at how you cast her, Marco." Holmes is talking again. "The villainous wife who won't let you see your son. Who doesn't return your messages. This is your subconscious telling you that she is wrong, so you painted her as a villain. You cast her as the estranged wife who won't talk to you."

"You said *she* was my wife," I toy with him, nodding at the woman before me.

"She is."

"Then, what are you talking about?"

The doctor takes a step closer to me and speaks, seriously, "You know what I'm talking about, Marco. You heard me perfectly. The woman, Ellie, whom you believe is your wife, is actually a woman you had an affair with, but it's over now. It's over. You broke it off with her." He says the words slowly, like I'm hearing impaired or from a foreign country, and I don't know why, but it makes me titter, and then chuckle and then laugh.

Now, when I say 'laugh' I mean I give out a real belly laugh that must go on for at least a minute or so. And I know what it is. I recognise it. It's hysteria. My world has just imploded, or at least it has according to these two, and the only way my mind can cope with that is to laugh. Until what started out as a natural reaction turns into something that's being artificially oxygenated by me because the alternative is to go back to truly accepting what I am being told.

Eventually, once I finish flogging the proverbial corpse, I say somewhat dryly, "You know, I bet there are thousands or maybe even millions of husbands who would love to wake up to the realisation that their wife is actually their bit on the side. I mean because, come on, let's face it, that's fucking hot, but…" I trail off here because big Almond Blue Eyes over there is watching me again with a pained expression on her face, as if all of this is excruciatingly raw for her. And I search those eyes once more, looking for the truth in there. *Who the fuck are you?*

But I can feel Holmes' gaze on me also. He no doubt clocked that I stopped short of dismissing the whole wife/mistress mind-fuck and was instead seeking acknowledgement from the stranger in front of me.

"Marco," she speaks, imploringly. But I don't know what she wants from me. Does she really expect me to take their word at face value and assume that everything I remember is just a figment of my own imagination? Is she high?

"Marco, I know this is difficult for you to accept."

Ya think?

"But…" the words, along with a whole anguish of tears catches in her throat, "I love you. I really do. I love you. Please come back to me, baby. Please come back to me."

She starts blubbering some more. Deep convulsive shudders. She seems genuinely distressed, but I don't believe it. I can't believe it. Would you?

"So, where is this woman now? My so-called mistress," I ask relatively brightly, considering the *Twilight Zone* I've just woken up into.

Woken up?

Yeah, that's what this is. I'm bloody dreaming again! This is exactly what happened last time.

"She's gone." Holmes says quickly. "You know this."

"Gone where?"

"You ended it. Over two months ago."

I shake my head. "No, no, no. You see, this is where this dream falls apart. I met her the other week. I met her for lunch. I remember it like it was yesterday. I even decked a bloke while we were there."

"You didn't meet her for lunch, Marco. You created that scenario to help you deal with what your wife told you. Then you placed her in that situation, because you wanted her to play the part of the villain, to act out the part of your wife because, to you, she's the one who caused all of this."

"That's bollocks! Why would I do that? Why would I invent that whole ultimatum shit?"

"You didn't invent that, Marco. That bit is true. Your wife, Ellie, did give you an ultimatum. You did come to see me."

"And why did my..." I wrestle with the words. I can't say it, it just doesn't feel right. "Why did *she* give me an ultimatum?" I say, nodding at the tear-stained woman in front me.

"I wanted you to get better, Marco. You needed help and I wanted to give us one last chance," she contributes.

"For what?"

"You know what," Holmes says in that trademark authoritative voice of his.

"No, I fucking don't!" I explode. "I have no fucking idea, because you two," I wag a finger at them both, "you are trying to make me think I'm off my rocker, that I'm insane, but I'm onto you. I know this is all crap, that it's all another shitty dream, but what I don't know is…" I falter here, because I'm scared, I'm fucking petrified, that all of this just might be true – and I want to wake up, I need to wake up, right now, right fucking now!

I see Holmes actually bite his lip. Like he's getting desperate, like he's thinking I might just take a run at that window and smash my way out of this. There's an idea.

I glance at it.

He notices and swallows hard. "Marco, I need you to listen to me…"

"No! I'm done listening to you."

"Marco, please. Just let me explain…"

"…Why? So you can spin more crap!"

"Marco, these aren't lies; you've suffered what's known as a psychotic break."

I hear myself emit another hollow laugh. "I know what a fucking psychotic break is, Doctor. I'm a fucking therapist."

They exchange looks, again.

"There's that fucking look again! If you have something to say to me, just fucking say it. You haven't held back on anything else!" I explode.

Although, I don't know if I can handle much more.

"Okay, Marco. Alright," Holmes says in a soft, conciliatory tone while maintaining constant eye contact with me. I know what he's doing, keeping me in the moment, keeping me with him. Then he speaks, "Marco. You're not a therapist." He delivers the words like he's just told me that I don't take sugar in my coffee.

And my already beleaguered mind reacts in the only way it knows, with amusement. "Oh really? What am I then?"

More dramatic hesitation. He seems to have become proficient with this, and I imagine a camera zooming into his mouth. "You're a mechanic," he says.

Now someone else is laughing. Only it isn't me, and it certainly isn't the husk of the policewoman in front of me, or the doctor. They both have stony faces.

Oh, fuck, it *is* me.

Holmes continues. "You created Shawn and Jessie to help you deal with the struggle between you and your lover. To help you come to terms with the fact that your marriage was falling apart and that you were seeking solace in the wrong place." He takes a step forward. "You know it's true, Marco. You can see it. Just think about it. The social divide between Shawn and Jessie represents your marriage to Ellie and her parents' wealth. This has always been a source of acrimony between you. In your marriage.

"As has Ellie's relationship with her parents. You felt abandoned by yours, especially your father, so you fabricated a world featuring a friendly father figure, an uncle, someone close, but not too close.

"Captain Birdseye. The man from the packet of your favourite childhood food. The affable older guy who owned his own garage, one that you could take over. Only you don't have an uncle, Marco. Harvey doesn't exist."

I just gawk at the man in bewilderment. I think I've heard what he said, but I'm not sure because, well, it's just... I don't know what it is. I look at the woman who goes by the name of Emily, the woman who is pretending to be my wife, for validation, but she says nothing; she just watches me with those giant, tear-soaked eyes of hers. She hasn't moved once from her position. Not a step, not a weight shift. She's completely immobile, as if the floor is made of glass.

"Why are you doing this?" My words sound like a defeated whimper. The tension that was keeping my body upright now dissipated like a sandcastle at high tide. Now, I just want to crumple to the floor and sleep. It feels like I've been drugged. Something in the water, maybe? I don't know. I do know that these two are colluding to make me feel like I'm losing my mind. I just don't know why. "Why are you lying to me?" comes another whimper.

"Were not lying to you, Marco. I promise you that. You're not well. Let me, us, help you," Holmes says.

"I can't. I don't. This isn't real; it's just a dream."

"It isn't, Marco. This is not a dream," my doctor barks quickly and assertively.

I glance at the window again. "I want to wake up now."

"Marco, no!" Holmes snaps.

But I'm already sliding down the front of the armchair to the floor. My mind shutting down like an office at the end of the day, an exhausting day in an exhausting, ridiculous nightmare, but now it's time to sleep so I can wake up from this. Sleep so I can wake up.

Suddenly, I can't breathe. It's as if a trapdoor has closed in my throat, blocking my airway. I'm dying! I'm not waking up, I'm dying!

I can hear Holmes talking still. "I know this is a lot to take in…"

I claw at my throat.

"…But I need you to trust me. Right now, you're so confused that nothing makes sense. Your mind will be a blank and it will feel like everything has been erased. It hasn't. You're just processing a lot all at once. That's why I need you to calm down for me. Take some deep breaths and calm down. Marco. Your brain is overworked. A bit like a computer hard drive running too many routines at once. I need you to calm down and breathe, Marco. Calm down and breathe for me so your brain can start catching up. Marco? Marco?"

But I can't answer; I'm scrabbling, gripping the armchair, furiously sucking in air, but it's having no effect. I'm choking! I'm dying! Help me! Help! I'm dying! The tension's building in my head again, dimming the lights. I'm dying!

That woman steps forward, but through my blurred vision I can see Holmes holding his arm out to block her.

What the fuck? Help me. I'm dying. My face is hot, contorted, the room fading to black. I've lost control. I've lost control of my body and I can't get it back. I can't get it back because I'm dying. I'm dying!

Emily's anguished sobs echo and fade into the distance.

"Marco?" Holmes is calling out to me through the gasps. "Marco, you're not choking. You're trying to escape from the reality of this again. Marco, listen to my voice. Listen." His voice is strong. "Marco, you're lapsing into another anxiety attack, but I need you to regain control. I need you to calm down. Marco! Marco! I need you to slow your breathing, regain control of your breathing."

He's towering over me now and I reach up to him, imploringly. "H… e… lp… Me. Pl… ease… he… lp."

Then, I'm clawing at my throat once more, choking and spluttering, supplicating the doctor to save me, because I know I'm fading away. I'm dying.

Now she's on the floor next to me. "Marco. Please, baby. Please breathe for me! Please!"

She sounds hysterical, but I'm tired; I'm too tired.

I collapse into her arms and the world turns black.

THE INTRUDERS

Saturday. 23:50.

I wake with a start, bolt upright in my favourite awaking Dracula pose.

The sheets are soaking wet and I can't tell if this is because of the leak that's magically appeared in the ceiling, and which is now dripping water onto the bed, or the cold sweat that's drenched my hair and making the sheets sticky.

Shit. It's like I've woken up in the eye of a bloody hurricane; the Atlantic gale is screaming around the house, throwing furniture around outside and launching hailstones, like bullets, at the window.

"Jesus!"

It's freezing, too, and when I say freezing, I mean it's fucking freezing, like this place hasn't been heated in days. And to make things worse, I'm wearing my favourite outfit again. At least, according to Emily.

Emily. This all started the moment she showed up. These dreams I keep having. These episodes that keep taking me to a ridiculous alternate life... but I'm back now. Thank God, I'm back at Dolce Vita and I'm not returning to London anymore. Never again. I'm done with that. Even if it means no more sleep.

I'm okay, though. I'm okay.

Just breathe. Breathe.

I do this for a minute or so until my breath is less fast and my heart not so furious. Then, I swing my bare feet off the bed and yelp when they step on something gritty and hard.

"What the…?" I look down, but the only light offered is from the occasional flash of lightning.

I flick the switch on the lamp, but nothing happens. I try it again, a few times, and still nothing. So, I try the overhead light. Nothing.

"Great. A bloody power cut."

I reach for my phone. It's plugged in, but the light is out, which means it isn't charging. I tap the screen; 30%.

"Great."

But then, why do I care? It's not as if I can take calls here. *They did, though. She did.* I check the signal. One bar.

Was that a dream, too?

I hold the home button down, the phone beeps, "'Turn on flashlight." The powerful LED light springs to life and I train it at my bare feet.

What is that? I lean down, closer to analyse what it is, and I can't believe what I'm seeing. It's plaster. It's bloody plaster! I turn the light up at the ceiling and then pan across. There's a bloody giant spider's web of cracks spreading from one side of the room to the other.

My mouth falls open. Unbelievable. It's almost as if the house is literally falling apart around me, but I can't deal with something like this right now. I can't.

I get up from the bed, side stepping the debris on the floor, and hurry over to the bathroom.

Jesus. When I came here, I was worried that it would be this place that would turn into a mind-fuck, but it's the opposite. Or is it? I mean I've been having these nightmares about London ever since I arrived here...

I smack my head like people smack television sets or radios that aren't working. I know it's pointless, but it makes me feel better.

Wake up! Wake the fuck up, Marco. You need to make sense of this. You need to understand why you've started having these dreams.

You know why. It's obvious. You came back here and started raking up all of that historic crap and now you feel like you're going insane.

Is that it? Am I going insane? Am I insane already?

Stop it. Stop. Stop doubting yourself. Right now, you're the only friend you have.

I grab a towel and dab all over my body, as if I've just stepped out of the bloody shower.

I suppose I'm not completely alone, am I? I still have you. You're still following this mind-trip, aren't you? Psychologically hitchhiking with my suffering. Watching my world literally crumble around me. How's that working out for ya? Am I doing it for ya?

If you could talk, I bet you'd have an opinion, wouldn't you? I bet you think you've figured all of this out – but you can't share it with me, though, can you? More's the fucking pity.

Probably just as well, for the use you'd be. You see, just for the record, I'm onto you. I know what you're doing right now; you're trying to second guess my every move, trying to work out why shit has happened the way it has rather than focusing on helping me. Help me!

I guess there's only one conclusion, and as much as this is going to sound paranoid, I realise that right now there really isn't anybody I can trust, but me.

I step back into the bedroom, pull on jogging bottoms, socks, trainers, and a jumper from the wardrobe. Yes, probably not the best look, but hey, you'll appreciate that I'm not trying to make a fashion statement here.

I feel instantly better, but I can still see my breath fog out in front of me in the occasional beam of the light. I need to get the heating on in here, but with no power, I don't even know how I go about doing that. I mean, does this place have a back-up generator or something? Did Harvey mention it? Because I don't remember him saying anything about it. I suppose there's only one way to find out.

I cross the room as more plaster crunches underfoot, and I feel a jolt of anger just as lightning lights up the room. Yeah, you and me both, mate.

I pull the door open with a loud scrape and step into the hallway, where I'm instantly assaulted by a tempestuous cacophony; the skylight's squeaking and then groaning as if the gale is performing some kind of medieval torture on it, coercing it to let it inside. Doors creak in invisible drafts. Tree branches, like talons, keep leaning in and scraping on windows that are rattling in fear in their frames. Then, there's the building, creaking a moaning like a disgruntled giant prematurely roused from its slumber.

"Shit!"

That familiar rat of fear scuttles down my spine and into my shorts. I thought my bedroom was the eye of the storm; I was wrong. The whole building is shaking.

Get a fucking grip, will you?

I move across the landing and there's more crunching underfoot. The house is being torn apart, and I can't get out of here because I don't have a car.

I'm stranded.

I could go and see Harvey. He'd probably tell me to fuck off, but it's worth a try.

Why? Where exactly are you planning on going? And what exactly are you running away from? A storm?

I don't know.

A gust of wind tugs at the skylight so hard that one of the screws comes loose and falls into the den with a loud ding.

"Jesus Christ!"

I'm still gawking at the stricken screw when a door slam makes me jump.

Slam! Creak! Slam! Creak! Slam! Creak!

It's the photo room again. A window must be broken in there because that door is shaking back and forth so violently I think it's going to come off its hinges. And if it isn't a gust of wind, then it must be someone or *something* else.

Something? Like what? A ghost?

Ghost?

Why do I always jump to those bloody thoughts in these situations? And why is it that, each and every time, I insist on drawing on my vast mental repertoire of horror films to heighten the experience?

Shit.

Get a grip, Battista! Are you a man or a mouse?

Do you really want me to answer that? Fuck off!

I'm angry again, which I know is a direct reaction to the fear. It's textbook psychology. I'm disliking how the fear is making me feel. Therefore, my instinct is to remove the cause. However, since I'm unable to manipulate meteorological phenomena, I'm angry at my inability to be able to change this situation.

Or some such shit.

Of course, there is one other way of dealing with this. A man's way, or a woman's, for that matter, I'm not sexist. To just fucking face it.

Face it, Marco! You know invisible hands are not moving that door, nor is there a malevolent entity lurking in the shadows. It's all in your head!

How can I know for sure?

In my head? That screw jumping to its death is not in my head. The house groaning like an ancient demon isn't in my head and nor are the creaking window frames that are threatening to implode any second now. This is real stuff. It's really happening.

True. But your fear of that room is not real. It's mental. Irrational.

Fear of spiders and baked bloody beans is irrational, but it doesn't make it any less fucking scary for those who fear them, does it?

There are only pictures in that room. Just pictures, Marco. Memories.

That kill!

They don't kill. Pull yourself together.

I can barely make anything out down there. Just shadows. I have to keep waiting for the intermittent beam of the lighthouse or the flash of lightning to see. This, of course, makes everything ten times worse because I've seen enough horror flicks to know that on the next illumination there's a good chance I might be presented with an altogether more terrifying apparition. Maybe a dead body wrapped in a plastic sheet, or perhaps a dark shape, or maybe even the bloody intruders from the other night.

Oh Shit. I've got the world's most sadistic imagination.

I'm conscious of the limited battery on my phone. I need to light candles, but they're downstairs.

I pick my way across the landing and snap my head back to the other side. I'm sure I saw someone or something standing over there on the door's threshold. Something that darted back into the room, the very second I glanced over.

It's just your imagination.

No, I saw something.

Go see, then.

What?

Go and see. There's nothing in there. You're imagining this. Your mind is taking inspiration from the elements and then fabricating the rest. You know this.

I hesitate, then, taking a deep breath, I march across the landing as bony fingers tap on the window. I whirl around to see the tree branches and rain drops taking centre stage in the spotlight from the lighthouse.

Oh crap. My heart is thumping, and it doesn't matter how much I talk to myself – I'm scared. Thing is, I don't think it's all about the storm or even about being alone in this house. There's something else. Something on the fringe of my mind. It's there, but I can't quite reach it. Like an itch you can't scratch.

I step cautiously forward, using the phone's light to scare away the shadows and anything else that may be lurking in them, and I catch sight of the door to the spare room. The same room David slept in.

What did he see in there? What did he try to say on the phone? Get… house? Get *out of the* house, maybe?

Oh God.

Ignoring the doubts and more clips to horror movies I had to cajole Ellie into watching with me, I stride across the landing and fling the door open.

There's nothing in here. Just an empty bed, a bedside table, but nothing else. Just inky darkness. Unusually so. But, it's okay, I can justify that. This room is normally dimly lit by the overspill of light from the village but, looking out of the window, it's easy to see that it, too, has suffered a power cut... and that's why I'm currently longing for daylight and… why do I keep talking to myself like a crazy person?

Can we please get on with the task in hand?

Maybe I should sleep in here tonight. Seems dry enough. You know, try and get some sleep, weather this so-called storm and sort everything out in the morning.

Sounds like a great idea.

But the creak and thump from the room below doesn't agree. Something is moving that door back and forth, and if I don't go and investigate, don't stop it, there's a good chance I'm going to wake up to a bloody river running through the den in the morning. This place is already falling apart. If I want to sell it, I've got to try and preserve it in the best possible condition.

So, it's with purpose that I stomp across the landing to the stairs and pause there as lightning brings a flashback. I fell here. I'm sure I did.

By the light of my phone and the occasional strobe from the lighthouse, I slowly make my way down the stairs, being sure to use the handrail as an anchor, and I tell you, it feels bloody good when I reach the bottom without mishap.

You're fine. You're safe.

The bluster, creaking, rattles, and groans are much louder down here, though. The pressure of the storm pushing against the terrace doors is palpable. I can sense them bulging and buckling, straining against the onslaught, and I secretly pray that they won't give because, if they do, I'm fucked. And the furniture is fucked, because there's absolutely nothing I'll be able to do to patch up that gaping hole.

Thunder cracks overhead and I instinctively duck. "Shit!" That sounded like it's coming from inside the house. Inside the attic.

I glance at my phone; 20% battery life remaining. Then, I lift it, resurrecting shadows as I make my way into the kitchen where the glass windows are still shaking in their frames.

I know how they feel.

I search drawers while the wind whistles outside and moans through gaps under the door inside. Eventually, I manage to find candles and matches that I'd set aside specifically for this eventuality. I know there are flashlights here somewhere too, but I can't remember where exactly they are so these will do for now.

I light a couple of candles just as a familiar sound cuts through the meteorological turbulence. It's the gate outside. I just heard the latch and the squeak it makes when it's opened.

It might be Harvey or somebody coming to see if I'm okay, or it might just be the wind.

I cross over to the window, the candle's flame flickering wildly as I go, and I stand there, leaning over the kitchen sink. I can barely make out the white gate in the dark, and, I don't know if I'm seeing correctly, but it looks as if it's still closed. I hold the candle up, but the action's futile, as it only illuminates my reflection in the glass. I move it away and, as I do so, what I can see of the gate suddenly disappears and then reappears from view, as if something has just walked in front of it.

The candle's shaking and sputtering now as if it's going to go out at any time, and I'm wondering what the hell is happening when I realise that it's me, I'm breathing on it – rapidly, shallowly.

I wait. But there's no knock at the front door, and nor will there be any kind of alarm. It just occured to me. No electricity means no alarm, doesn't it? Anybody can walk in here, and I won't even know it. I rack my brains, but I can't remember. Does the door announcer run on batteries?

I whip around, almost snuffing out the candle in the process, as the handle in the backdoor starts to rattle, like somebody's testing it to see if it's locked.

My heart is in my throat as I back away from it, squinting through the gloom in an effort to see through the glass and beyond, but I can't see anything, even though I know something's there. Someone or something is out there. I can sense it. And whatever it is, it's staring right at me.

Get a grip. There's nobody there, it's just the wind.

I jump when I feel something cold touch my back; it's the wall. I've backed so far out of the kitchen that I'm now in the doorway.

So, I turn and leave as fast as the flickering flame will allow.

Back in the den, another screw jumps to its death and the skylight shudders and screams as the wind violates the space and attempts to rip it from its casing.

Creak! Slam! Creak! Slam! Creak! Slam!

I tune back into the photo room door that's contributing to the din down here. Just like the other day; it seems as if there's someone or something in there trying to get out.

There's nothing in there, Marco. It's a stormy night. The door is moving in the draft. Come on. Pull it together because you can't ignore it. You need to go and check.

Reluctantly, I move across the floor, the candle's flame invoking a legion of giant, ghoulish shadows and ordering them to encircle me.

Shadows. They're just shadows. Stop adding creepy words into every thought.

You're doing this to yourself. It's psychosomatic.

You think?

I know.

I'm at the door now and, like a naughty child, it appears to have calmed in my presence. Funny that – when I was upstairs, it was like a mudslide was going to burst through at any moment... and yet, now?

Scratching draws my attention and, at first, I think it's the photo room door, but it isn't. The sound is coming from the study, but it's fine. It's okay. I know exactly what it is; it's the tree branches. They're scraping against the glass wall in there, that's all.

Are you sure?

I'm sure.

Oh, fuck it. I shake my head and laugh. Can you believe this? I'm behaving like a scared little boy. That's because I am scared, but that's okay.

Just accept this is how you feel and deal with it. Come on. This is what you do.

I can't.

This is what you do.

I don't want to.

This is what you do.

I don't want to go in there.

Get on with it.

No.

Get on with it. NOW!

Against all of my instincts, I move forward.

I push on the door and it opens effortlessly, with a nerve-jangling creek. I hold the candle out in front of me and an army of different smiles appear and disappear like candle smoke. My stomach lurches. My hands are shaking. I can tell by the effect this is having on the candle, its flame dancing back and forth like it too is afraid, is terrified, of what we'll find in here, and it wants to run, break free from its waxy shackles and leave this place, never to return.

Like me.

But, I keep the flame aloft in front of me, deliberately avoiding eye contact with the subjects inside the myriad of rectangular frames adorning the walls in here. Even though I can still see them through my peripheral vision... calling, urging me to look at them.

Look.

No. I don't want to. It's only going to make me feel worse.

Worse? How much worse can you feel?

Something's being blown across the front lawn. I don't know what it is, but it flaps in front of the window like a fucking ghost, scaring the shit out me before it disappears on its journey to God knows where.

And that's when I realise. That is when I remember.

I swing around in a three-sixty, the candle flame shivering in protestation. Nothing.

Then I swing again. Still nothing.

Except for the rapid, jerky, scared shitless movements of my own body, nothing is moving; there are no open windows in here. No open doors. No drafts. Yes, there's all hell breaking loose outside. Yes, the window frame's joints creak like it's in agony. But there's no serious draft in here. No open window.

A shudder ripples through me just as the door slams shut.

"Fuck me!"

Oh God.

There's something in here with me. No, not something singular, but some *things*, plural. They're all around me, watching me.

And I close my eyes, because I don't want to see. I don't want to see, and it works, but I can still hear. I can hear the rattle of the window, the mournful howl under the door, the creak and jangle of the handle as well as something else... something that plants a dagger of terror in my back.

A dog. A puppy. It's whimpering, just like it was the other day, but that isn't possible; it isn't possible. There's nobody here but me.

My whole body is quaking now and that familiar tickle of sweat is back, beading on my forehead, despite the fact that it's cold... it's so bloody cold in here. So cold.

There's scratching behind me, and as much as conscious thought doesn't want me to, my subconscious has me whirling to see what it is, to make sure that there's nothing there. But there is, and it's flickering in and out of focus, in the candlelight.

It's a ten-by-eight-inch, black and white photograph that looks sepia in the gloom. It features an eight or ten-year-old boy with a mop of black curly hair who's running, laughing on the shingled shore. I recognise the beach. It's one I've walked on many times since arriving here. The one where Emily and I ate our pasties.

Behind the boy is a woman with long black hair. She's wearing a summer hat and is laughing. Next to the little boy is a puppy. A black Labrador.

My Labrador. Blacky. *What happened to you?*

I almost drop the candle, but I recover it and move in closer.

"Mum?"

Tears prick my eyes. I don't even know why. I think it's because I thought I'd forgotten how she looked, but I haven't. I remember her. She looks exactly how I remember her. Beautiful. So beautiful.

There's nobody else in the photo, but someone snapped the picture, and I know it can't be my father because he was never around. He was always leaving. He always left.

I lift the candle up and across, to the next image. It's the same size, also black and white, and it drops stones into my gut. It's an over-the-shoulder shot of the same woman. She's looking straight at the camera through a curtain of hair, and she's smiling, enigmatically, seductively, at the person behind the lens.

I move the light across the wall as the storm outside intensifies.

Another photograph. This time in colour. It's a family portrait, seemingly taken on the same day. My mother, large brown eyes as wide as her smile, is holding a pair of small legs. A distinguished looking man, with grey hair, dark eyebrows, and a salt and pepper beard, my father, is holding the other half of the little boy, whose face is contorted into a fit of laughter.

It's me.

But, I don't remember this photo. I don't remember that day. I didn't remember having a puppy. My mother was allergic to dogs. To pets. She *hated* them. I'm sure she hated them. Didn't she?

I don't recognise this.

I allow the light to roam over other images; the walls are covered with them. They are in all shapes and sizes, and I feel a pang of anger because most of them feature my father and me; at the beach, fishing, trekking through woods, riding bikes and sailing. There are even photos of us in front of this house... only it looks completely different. Nothing like it does now. The building looks smaller, humbler.

I'm moving fast now, flickering from frame to frame, photo to photo, high and low on the walls, in an effort to understand, but they're all pretty much the same. The same duo. Where's my mother? What happened to her? Why isn't she in these photos with us? These photos that I don't remember. And Blacky? What happened to Blacky?

On the other side of the room, next to the window, I come across another black and white image. This one is more of an artistic shot of the beach, empty now, with dark, solemn clouds on a tempestuous shore. The shingled beach is in focus and the cliff face backdrop is blurred. There's nothing in the image, yet I can't take my eyes off of it. I can't wrench my eyes off the pebbles, and I find myself leaning in, closer and closer...

.... *Dragging. Pebbles grazing skin. Screaming. Drowning.*

"What the fuck?" I snap my head away from the image. "What was that?"

I'm breathing heavily again. Shaking, shivering once more, or maybe I never stopped.

The candle flame is flickering violently now, as if I'm still blowing on it, but I'm not, I'm not breathing on it... but I can see the plumes of my breath. It's so cold in here. So cold.

I pull back from the wall, but in doing so, I knock something off the wall unit and it plummets to the wood floor with a loud smash.

I look down to identify the fallen object, but freeze when something else catches my attention – something through the corner of my eye, something that when I glance back up has me leaping backward, tripping on my own feet and crashing to the floor.

Hot and cold shivers drown me as I sit on my backside gawping at the window where, behind the glass, I see a group of torchlit faces watching me. Only, they're not faces, but hideous, melted blurs. Horrifying. Disfigured. Unrecognisable, and yet I know they're glowering at me. I know that they're here, for me.

A high-pitched squealing sound slices through the air and I realise that it's me. I am the one screaming like that. The one incapacitated with terror, until I will myself to move, to get out of here.

Move!

Without ripping my eyes from the dysmorphic faces, I crawl backwards, like a spider, until my back slams against the opposite wall. I press against the hard, cold surface and want to be absorbed by it so that I can hide, but I know that's not going to happen... so instead I wish, I wish that this could be a dream after all and that I'll wake from it.

Please, I don't care! Just get me out of here! Get me out of here!

I squeeze my eyes shut and reopen them seconds later, but I'm still here. I haven't woken up anywhere. I'm still here. This is real! This is real!

The wind is shrieking around the house now, threatening to carry it away. The rain is pelting the glass, demanding to be let inside, but I don't look. I refuse to look. I cannot look!

"Marco…" a scratchy whisper calls to me from the corner of the room. "Marco…"

I yelp as the window explodes into a shower of glass and imaginary hands reach for me out of the gloom. "Marco…" They're calling. "Marco…!"

"Leave me alone!"

The room is a cacophony of turbulence as the wind squeals around it, ripping frames from walls and hurling them in all directions, smashing them to the floor in a dissonance of tinkling glass. I throw my hands up in a defensive gesture as projectiles and debris land on my head and arms.

I barely have time to register the pain before my attention is drawn to other sounds at the window – crunching and dragging sounds. Something is crawling through! Something is crawling towards me!

I squint into the dark rain that is now whizzing around me like a mini tornado, but I can see nothing. So, I reach to my pocket, pull out my phone, and yell, "TURN ON FLASHLIGHT!" There's a beep as it responds, "Turning on flashlight."

I lift the device, shining the light at the window, and instantly wish I hadn't.

There, like creatures from the deepest pits of hell, anthropoids are slithering through the window and onto the rain-drenched debris, moving towards me like a knot of snakes. I can only watch in stunned horror as scabbed scars, where there were once mouths, move, but make no sound except for an incomprehensible, muffled, phlegm-infused wail.

I jump to my feet but slip on the crunchy debris and fall to the floor once more, my phone clattering forwards and slamming into the door.

Staggering and slipping, I reach for it and the door, which I yank open and jump through as fast I can, slamming and locking the turbulence behind me as I slide down the other side.

I'm panting loudly as my body struggles to recover. I don't know what the fuck I just saw in there, but I want out of here, and now! I train the light on the front door and tell my body to go there.

I do. In several giant strides, I am over there and almost ripping the thing off of its hinges.

Front door open.

The voice cuts through my shredded nerves, but it's nothing compared to how I feel about the sight that greets me.

My garden, the driveway, and pretty much every space as far as my eyes can see is full of people. Silhouettes of all sexes and sizes glow in the light cast from a sea of flickering lanterns. They are all standing perfectly still under the driving rain. They are unblinking, unflinching against the downpour. They are watching the house. Watching me.

A lynch mob.

Oh my God. Is that it? Is that what this is about? Do they think I did something to Timmy? Is that why they've all come for me?

"NO!" I shriek at nobody in particular. "NO!" I rail angrily against the injustice. "I didn't do anything to him! I did nothing wrong. Leave me alone! Please, leave me alone!" I blink into the rainfall that's drenching me and washing into the house.

They don't respond. They just continue to observe me with accusatory eyes I cannot see. "What do you want from me? What do you want?" I scream.

Thunder groans in their stead. Lightning snapshots the immovable mob under sheets of rain.

Still, there's no reaction. Not a cough, not a snuffle, not a shudder. But I know it's coming. I can sense it. I know that, any second now, they're going to charge at the house and there'll be nothing, not a thing, I can do to stop them.

Suddenly, the ground starts to shake. I can feel it underfoot. It's like a giant bulldozer is making its way towards me. I wipe my eyes and squint into the deluge, looking for it among the throng. Are they going to demolish the house? With me in it?

"NO!" I shriek. "N…."

But my words are cut short as the screech of bending metal fills the air, followed closely by the sound of smashing glass. Then there's a series of *thud, thud, thuds.* The sound is like giant, heavy footsteps, on the roof! I look up, into the blur of water.

Thud!

Closer.

Thud!

Closer.

Thud!

Silence, then…

…CRASH! The whole window module of the skylight smashes onto the path in front of me like something out of a fucking disaster movie.

I yelp, leap back and, for the second time, slip on the wet floor, slamming onto my backside.

The action knocks the air out of me and dispatches a shockwave of pain up my spine and into my brain. I lie still for a few seconds, giving shock a chance to dissipate, but movement grabs my attention.

The congregation is shifting. One by one, they begin to shuffle forward, towards the house, like a herd of zombies.

"NO! NOOOOOO!"

But my voice is lost in the meteorological onslaught. Worse, now that they're closer, now that lightning is strobing the scene in a series of flashes, tears of terror spring to my eyes. These things aren't the villagers; they aren't even human. They're demonic creatures with melted, liquefied features that flicker in and out of the focus of the lantern lights.

"NO! NO! YOU'RE NOT REAL!" I scream. "YOU'RE NOT REAL!"

But they are.

As crazy as it sounds, I know and feel that they are.

I crawl then jump to my feet, slam the door shut, throw all the bolts, and step back while straining to listen, but with the skylight gone and the turbulence howling across the gaping wound in the roof, I can't hear them.

But I do feel something else.

It too starts as a rumble, vibrating through the floor and then my body, causing me to spin on the spot, to search for its origin, but I can't see anything. Yet, the sound is moving closer. Growing louder.

Closer….

…Louder….

Closer…

…Louder…

…Whoomph!

I'm knocked off my feet as a gargantuan jolt hits the building, shaking it like a doll's house. It feels like the place has been hit by an articulated truck.

I scramble to my knees as an eerie groan is promptly followed by an almighty smash of breaking glass and a percussion of exploding bricks, mortar and dust as the giant tendrils of the oak tree burst out of the study door, flips the couches onto their sides, and skid to a halt in the middle of the den.

My incredulity makes momentary way for a slash of grief, for it feels as if I'm watching the lifeless body of a relative.

"Oh, Jesus…" is all I can mutter before a slow and methodical pounding on the front door spurs me back into action, because I know that those things aren't knocking – no, they're trying to pickaxe their way in. I can see the blunt tooth of something poke its way through a hole in the door. It's followed closely by the blade of an axe that gleams under the white light of my phone which is now beeping, warning me that it too is dying, a mere 10% battery remaining.

More smashing sounds. This time from the kitchen.

Back door open. Back window open.

I jump to my feet and I'm running forward, towards the stairs, just as the terrace doors shudder, whine and then implode, launching glass, water, and a hail of debris in my direction.

I lift my hands to fend off the projectiles and slam into the wall to maintain my balance.

Terrace doors open.

Without looking back, I race up the stairs, my phone light bobbing in front of me as I climb to the balcony and look over to see those creatures, those things, juddering and slithering over the remains of the furniture and tree.

Climb as high as you can. Call for help! Go now!
Front door open.

I race across the landing to the tiny door of the attic, yank it open, and pull it tightly shut behind me. Then I stomp up wooden steps.

The rain is much louder up here. Deafening as it beats and dings off the shingles.

"Fuck," I gasp as my phone light brings to life a series of boxes, old suitcases, trunks, and Christmas decorations. I've backed myself into a corner. Into a dank, dark fucking corner.

They're at the door now. I can hear them shuffling at it, so I grab the first thing I see, which is a wooden trunk, and hurl it down the steps, along with a bunch of suitcases.

My phone beeps; 5% battery remaining. But there are two signal bars. I dial 999.

"Police Emergency. How can I help?"

"There are people in my house," I whisper.

"Caller, you've reached the police, how can I help?"

"They're in the house!" I repeat.

"Who, who is in the house?"

"They're going to kill me," I say, but the words choke in my mouth.

"I'm sorry, I can't hear you. Can you speak up for me? What's your name? Can you tell me your name?"

The door pushes open. They're climbing over the suitcases, making their way towards me. I can hear them in the inky blackness; rasping, croaky breaths, mournful groans, and the cricking and clicking of limbs as they move their jerky, spasmodic bodies closer and closer.

"They're inside now! Oh God. Please send someone. Please help me!"

"Can you tell me where you are? Can you tell me exactly where you are in the house?"

"They're…." I turn the glow of the screen in front of me and I can just about make out the contorted humanoid shapes. They're advancing on me!

"Hello? Caller. Are you still there?"

I can feel and smell their hot, fetid breath against my face. "They're killing me! They're killing me!" I scream, as first the phone and then I go black.

MOTHERS LOVE

Sunday. 10:16.

Grazed skin. Grazed legs. Pain in my hair. The sound of the ocean. Screaming. Pebbles clicking and shifting. Crying. Shouting. Waves crashing. Pebbles rolling. Screaming. Crying. Arms flailing. Arms reaching. The water, freezing, engulfing. Spluttering. Wheezing. I can't breathe. I'm drowning. Help me! Mummy. Help me! I'm drowning. I'm dying. I'm dying!

"Marco? Marco? Stay with me. Marco?"

It's Doctor Holmes. I hear his voice calling to me and I wake up with a start. Spluttering and choking, hands clawing at something invisible in front of me.

But there's no water. No ocean. No pebbled beach.

"It's okay, Marco. You're safe. You're safe."

I'm breathing heavily. Hyperventilating again.

"Just breathe for me. Just breathe." Holmes' voice is reassuring.

"Stop saying that! Stop… fucking…saying… that!" I choke through gulps of air as I climb out of my chair and make the usual beeline for the window.

Oh God. It was a dream. Thank you, thank you. Or, not?

It's daytime. Sunny with blue skies. And, I don't know, but despite the soundtrack of the city, I think I can hear birds in those nearby trees.

There are people sitting on the bench, clutching Starbucks, and I want to run down there, snatch it from them and replace their dainty sips with my own generous glugs.

"Marco?"

He's calling to me again, but I don't want to talk to him. I don't want to talk to anyone. I certainly don't want to hear anymore weird crap. I don't think I can take it. I can't. I can't. I don't want to process it. I don't even want to think about what I saw in that house. I certainly don't want to try and rationalise it – because I can't.

I can't!

Can't or don't want to?

I have to wonder, because something is bugging me. It's that same thing that's been bugging me for a while now. That same itch that can't be scratched. There's something at the back of my mind that I just can't get at and it's driving me mad!

"Marco?"

"What?" I snap.

"Would you please come and sit back down?"

"Why?"

"So we can finish our conversation."

"You mean so you can finish your interrogation?"

"Where did you go, Marco, just now?"

I turn to look at him. My laugh is empty. "I was at Dolce Vita and there was some really strange shit happening on a rainy night, but now it's the middle of a sunny day and I'm in your office. How the fuck do you explain that?"

"You don't remember?"

I shake my head. Hold up a hand. "And don't give me the psycho interrogation crap. Stop trying to make me recall. I don't want to fucking recall! Just tell me what's going on or I swear to God I'm jumping out of this window right fucking now!" I explode. "Right fucking now, and then maybe all of this will stop."

"Okay. I will, I promise. But please, come and sit down so we can talk properly."

"I don't want to fucking sit down!"

He gives me a few seconds, and then says, "Marco. Please."

I don't want to sit down. I just want to stay here and keep looking out of this window at this blue sky, at those people outside, in the open air, on the park bench.

"Marco?"

Oh God. If he says my name one more time I'll…I don't know. I'm confused. Maybe a little scared. Okay, maybe a lot, and something tells me that this man that keeps saying my name, to the point where I want to smack him in the mouth, is the only person who can help.

Reluctantly, begrudgingly I turn, but a thought enters my head, and I don't want to look because, if I look and discover what my mind is starting to suspect then, fuck, I just don't know how I'm going to deal with that.

So, of course, the masochistic side of me forces me to look at myself. I'm wearing jeans, jumper, shoes. I touch my hair. It's short. My beard feels trimmed.

I breathe a sigh of relief. Thank God. Thank God. The tension in my shoulders dissolves like the tiny white cloud that was hovering above the trees just a minute ago.

I turn to Doctor Ethan Holmes and, as always, he's watching me through those square spectacles. He's looking fresh again. Like he's had a good night's sleep. It's alright for some. He's wearing that familiar blue pullover again with a white T-shirt underneath.

I glance at *that* shitty chair, walk over, and allow myself to fall into it like the petulant teen I seem to be reduced to every time I'm here.

Holmes looks at me for the longest time and I'm just about to grunt 'what?' when he speaks. "Marco, can you tell me why you just did that?"

"Did what?"

"Looked at yourself that way."

"I don't know what you're talking about."

He cocks his head and gives me a knowing look. Of course, I might have known he'd spotted it. This guy doesn't miss anything. It's why I love and loathe being in this office. I get a sense of security, in that he seems to understand me, while at the same time I feel like I'm under constant observation. I hate that part. It's like sitting in a fucking goldfish bowl. I'm surprised he doesn't invite his colleagues over for a good gawp. Maybe they're already here, watching the spectacle through hidden cameras.

"I was checking myself," I say sulkily, as I notice that I've developed a twitch in my leg, and now it's bouncing up and down like I'm bored. Am I bored? I don't think I am, not yet.

"And why were you doing that?" he asks.

Again, I'm still feeling sulky, but I tell him. "I, um, I was checking that I wasn't wearing a hospital gown or a, um, straight jacket."

"Why do you think you might be wearing either of those things?" Now it's my turn to slump my shoulders, like he's the one avoiding the bloody elephant in the room. "Please tell me," he continues. "I would really like to know."

"Doc, this is the second time I've woken up in your office after some seriously messed up shit. Even I have to admit, something's a bit off."

"What exactly do you think is off? Are you able to put it into words for me?"

"Isn't that why you're here?"

He nods and smiles. "Marco, can you tell me who you are?"

I shake my head, hopelessly. "Seriously?"

"Please, would you just indulge me?"

I roll my eyes. "Oh, for fuck's sake. My name is Michael Jackson," I begin in a very soft voice, "or is it Caine?" I continue in a working-class Cockney accent.

Holmes laughs. "That's pretty good."

"Yeah? You think so?"

"Yes, very good."

"I'm Marco Battista. I'm forty-something and I live in Putney with my beautiful wife, Ellie, and my gorgeous boy, Toby," I declare.

Holmes nods. "And your wife. Can you describe her to me?"

"Doc, have I lost my fucking mind?" I ask anxiously.

"Do you feel as if you have?"

"FUCK'S SAKE! Do you ever just answer a bloody question?" I explode, jumping out of my chair and walking back over to the window.

The Starbucks brigade has gone now and that makes me feel sad. They felt like my only anchor to the real world. Proof that there are other human beings out there, and not just me and this shrink, in this office.

Yes, that's right. I'm sanguine enough to know that, if I keep waking up in different places, there must be something very wrong going on upstairs. And, like most, I've railed against the concept, but look where that's gotten me. So, I've decided to try, although I know it's going to be tough, to keep an open mind. At least to hear what the man has to say, and then I can make up my own mind. Assuming I still have one.

"I'm sorry, Marco, but it isn't that simple," he states.

"I know it isn't fucking simple! If it was simple, I'd be able to work it out for myself. Isn't that why I've been coming here for the past two weeks?"

He gestures to the chair once more. I hesitate, because I hate sitting in that fucking chair. "Do you know how fucking uncomfortable that chair is? I've been meaning to tell you that from day one," I say angrily. "It's a shitty chair! It's a fucking shitty chair and I hate it!"

"Okay," is his calm response. "Would you like me to fetch you another chair?"

"No." My sulky tone is back, as is my demeanour while I return and allow myself to fall back into the thing he calls furniture.

He gives me a few seconds and then he puts his notepad down to lean forward. "Marco, did you hear what you just said? You said you've been coming to see me for the past two weeks." I nod. He hesitates, and then, "It hasn't been two weeks, Marco, but two months."

And there's that sickly merry-go-round feeling. "What?"

"Yes, it's been a little over two months since you first came to my office. Do you remember any of that?"

I shake my head.

He continues, "You started seeing me once a week at first, and we made some progress. Then things, um, changed, so you started coming more often."

"Progress? How much progress? And what changed?"

"Before I answer that, can I ask you a question?"

I shrug. Like I have a choice.

"Do you trust me?"

I'm both surprised and wary of the question. So, I think about it. I think I do trust him. "Um, well, I don't hate being here. No... correction, I definitely *do not* like being here. No offence, but there's something about this room. I hate *it*. I hate being stuck in here with you; yet, at the same time, I don't know – it feels safe."

"Safe? From what? Can you tell me?"

"Safer than being there."

"By there, do you mean Porthcove?"

I nod, as if I no longer want to acknowledge that place, and I don't. Certainly not after what happened the last time I was there.

"Thank you," he says.

"For what?"

"For your trust."

"Yeah, well, just so you know, it wouldn't take much to change my mind."

He nods and holds up his hands.

"So, Marco. Given this *bond* between us. I need you to trust that I have your best interests at heart. Do you trust that?"

I nod, warily, as I don't know where he's going with this.

"I know you have questions and I know that you simply want me to answer them, but if I do without us following best practice, without us following a process, I could end up confusing you even more. Do you understand that?"

I nod, but I don't care. I just want to know what's going on.

"Okay. So, with that in mind... Would you just relax for me? Just relax into the chair you hate, and just go with me, okay?" He smiles, reassuringly.

It feels like I'm being handled, and no, not in a nice way, but I'll go along with it, for now.

"Earlier, you said that you couldn't breathe, that you felt as if you were dying. Can you tell me about that?"

"You mean you want to revel in my misery? Oh God, don't answer that, as it's bound to be another question like," I put on his measured tone, "do you think I want to revel in your misery?"

He smiles.

I take a few seconds and stare into middle distance as I try to recall exactly what I've been seeing. Then, "I keep having this dream. Actually, I don't even know if it's a dream. It feels more like a flashback, but obviously it can't be – but, it's weird, because I can *feel* it. I mean... It's like I can feel what is happening in this thing. It's a bit like – well, like giving yourself a deep-cut finger. Every time you remember it, it feels almost like it's happening again. You know, real." I lift up my arm and look at it. "I mean, I can feel the graze, the sting of the stones on my skin."

"Can you tell me about it?"

"There isn't much to tell. It's just snapshots. There's a beach. Stones. No, pebbles. And it feels like I'm being dragged over them into the water."

I look up at him, make a spooky face, and say, "Now, you're going to tell me that it's all symbology or some shit, aren't ya? Something to do with repressed adolescent rage or some crap like that, huh?" I say this with a grin. But, I'll be honest, his stony face does a pretty good job at deconstructing my smile. "Or not," I add.

He's still leaning forward. "Marco, firstly, I'm going to tell you that this isn't the first time you've told me about this dream, this flashback."

"No?"

"No. We've talked about it a few times before. Do you not remember?"

I shake my head.

"Okay, do you remember at least thinking about it before? For example, did you have this flashback while you were at Porthcove?"

I nod.

And he nods. Like something has just made sense to him.

Well, at least one of us is making progress here.

Then, he takes a very long time before asking, "Marco, excluding your step siblings. Do you know anything about any other brothers and sisters you may have, or that your parents may have wanted?"

The question pulls an inquisitive frown to my face and I laugh, "You going to tell me I have a long-lost brother or sister now, Doc?"

He smiles. "No. Could you answer the question, though, please?"

I shake my head. "No."

"Nothing? No mention of, no memory of your parents ever telling you anything about a brother or sister?"

"No."

"Think, Marco."

"I've answered the question."

"Nothing? No memory, no recollection of your mother being pregnant?"

"I said no!" I snap. "What the fuck are you driving at? Just tell me what you're trying to say."

"Marco, we agreed we'd go through this my way, remember?"

"Yeah, but that's before you started talking shit about bloody siblings and pregnant mothers."

"Do you remember your mother being pregnant?"

"I've already answered that fucking question, Ethan; what's wrong with you?"

"Okay. Okay."

"Jesus." I shrug then roll my shoulders, as they suddenly feel tense, like the man is attacking me.

"Marco…"

"Jesus Christ! Why do you have to prefix every bloody sentence with my name? It's just you and me here, remember? I know you're addressing me. I know you're talking to me. I also fucking know that by prefixing every sentence with my name, my label, you're trying to instil confidence, importance, reassurance. We all know about the psychology of the fucking label, so why don't you just dispense with the training and talk to me like I'm a fucking human being?"

I glare at him.

He closes his eyes and, when he reopens them, he apologises. "I'm sorry. It's not deliberate, just a force of habit," he says. "Are you okay now? Are we okay?"

I sigh, nod, and run a hand over my hair.

He takes a few more seconds and I end up tuning into the drone of the city beyond the window, and can't help but compare it to the rumble of the ocean. I miss its rhythmic rumble in contrast to the chaotic sound of traffic, which is irksome, disjointed.

"M…" He stops himself. "Did you see what just happened there?" he asks, suddenly. I blink at him. "I mentioned siblings, your parents, your mother, and it made you angry."

"No, you overused my name again and again, and it was that that made me angry. You've got a bloody knack of doing that, like always answering a question with a fucking question. It's bloody annoying."

"I'm sorry. Again, occupational hazard." He waits, then. "Why can't you... don't you want to talk about your mother?"

"Jesus Christ…"

"Marco… this is important. It's really important…"

"… I already told you…

"… I need you to stay with this, please…"

"… I don't see the point in going on about my…"

"... I need you to see this…

"… No…"

"… I need you to accept this…"

"… I don't want to talk about it..."

"… I need you to face this…"

"NO!" I scream at the top of my lungs. And it's like a gun has gone off in the room. Each of us is frozen, waiting for the fallout.

I reach for the coffee table between us, break the seal on a bottle of water, and drink, thirstily. It's so bloody quiet in the room, I can hear myself gulping.

When I've finished, I set the half empty bottle down again and then look at him, expectantly.

"Marco…" He begins, and then lifts his hands, apologetically. "How much do you know about Postpartum Psychosis?"

"Eh? That's random, isn't it?"

"Please, just answer the question."

I shrug. "I don't know. Not much, really. Why?"

He looks at me and I can see those bloody cogs whirring. I know he wants to say something, but is wondering how to structure it. "Oh, for God's sake, man, just bloody say it!"

"Did you know your mother suffered from it?"

I cock my head and frown. I'm surprised, yet eager to show him that I'm in control and that I don't always lose it, as he's implied, when it comes to the subject of my mother. Why do fucking therapists always go there?

"When she had me? No, I wasn't aware of it."

"No, not when she had you. When she gave birth to her second baby," he says.

I try to sit forward in that fucking chair. You already know how that is. "My mother had a second baby?"

He nods. "Yes."

I shake my head. "You're suggesting that my mother had another baby after me, but that I didn't know about it?"

"No, I think you knew. I believe that you've chosen not to remember."

I sneer. "You're on crack."

"Marco, your mother gave birth to a second child. A baby boy."

I nod. "Right, and now you're going to tell me he's waiting outside and that you're going to introduce us like a pair of sad muppets on some talk show."

He shakes his head. "No, I'm not going to say or do that."

"Then, what are you going to say?"

"He died, during birth."

His words are casual, like he's just told me how he likes to take his coffee. I simply stare at him while trying to process what I've just learned. Although, he doesn't give me much time to chew on that information nugget, before continuing in the same newscaster tone, "Not long after you were born, your parents' marriage started to flounder. Your father started to spend more time at the office and your mother, she started to suspect that he was having affairs with some of his models. They argued a lot, which resulted in your mother spending more time at Dolce Vita while your father stayed in the city. That's when you met Ellie or Emily. Do you remember?"

I shake my head. Because I don't. I mean, I remember some things, which is what I told her, but I don't remember us spending a lot of time together.

"There's a reason why you can't remember," Holmes continues. "You see, you met Ellie round-about the time this happened, so when you repressed the event, you also appear to have suppressed everything associated with it, including your relationship with her. But, you two remained close for quite some time. And I believe that it was this event that eventually led you to rediscovering each other and becoming, well, childhood sweethearts." He's delivered the last bit with a smile. Part of me wants to absorb both the beauty and enormity of what that means, but I'm still busy dealing with what he's told me about my mother and my childhood, in all its strangeness.

"What happened?" I hear myself ask.

"Would you like to take a moment to…"

"What happened?" I repeat, forcefully.

Now it's his turn to take a sip from his coffee cup that, for all I know, is full of alcohol.

Fuck, I could do with a drink right now.

He puts the cup down, and then, "Your mother, afraid she was losing your father, convinced him to have another child and, before long, she fell pregnant, and it was a good pregnancy. But," he hesitates, "Um, tragically, in the third trimester, there were complications and…" he leaves the sentence unfinished. "Naturally, your parents were devastated. Your mother particularly so because, rightly or wrongly, she believed that the baby was going to save her marriage."

"And let me guess, it didn't," I say, caustically.

He shakes his head, "No, it didn't."

"Right, so now that you've made absolutely sure that I feel like shit, are you going to tell me why you felt the need to share this stuff with me? I mean, if I repressed all of it as you say, then I must have been pretty cut up about the whole thing, right?"

"You were. Apparently, you were very excited to be having a brother or sister, and talked of nothing else, but then, after it happened, you just stopped talking about it – along with most things. You withdrew. As did your mother. Not surprisingly, the loss put an additional strain on your parents. Your father pretty much stopped going out to Dolce Vita while your mother never wanted to leave the place. She just wanted to live there alone, with you."

There's something about the way he's said the last bit of that sentence, as well as the way his eyes kept shifting from me to my bottle of water, that sends a chill through me. I don't even know why.

So, the bravado that has seen me in good stead for most of my life kicks in. "Great, and I'm still none the wiser. Are you actually going to tell me something or do you just want to keep dancing around it?"

"Your mother became sick. Depressed and, eventually, alone in that place, she started to see things…"

My heart prods at my rib cage and I ask, "What things?"

He shakes his head. Pulls a face, like he's struggling to put it into words.

So I repeat, "What things?"

"Shadows. Shapes. Humanoid creatures."

My heart leaps to my throat. It, like me, remembers the photography room. The faces at the window. And I shiver. "Well, I can relate to that," I contribute, flippantly.

"Your mother thought the house was possessed."

"Don't tell me – by demons?"

He shakes his head. "No, by you."

The words slice through me like a razorblade.

"What the fuck are you talking about?"

"Your mother believed that the house was haunted by these things she'd refer to as 'the intruders.'"

I gulp down bile.

"She'd alienated herself from most of the neighbours because she believed they were involved. They were the intruders that, according to her, would stand outside of the house at night, watching, waiting..."

My scalp feels prickly again. "For what?"

"For you."

"Fuck me... here we go again. Can you hear what you're saying?"

"Your mother was ill, Marco. She was really ill, she needed treatment, but nobody knew it at the time. She was suffering from Postpartum Psychosis. Do you know what that is?"

I shift in my chair. "I already told you, I don't know."

"It's a very severe form of mental illness. Sufferers become depressed, withdrawn. They become paranoid, delusional. If untreated, they'll go on to fabricate and live inside completely fictitious scenarios with fictitious characters…"

I laugh again here. "Wait, are you saying that, at some point in my life, I was pregnant? And that I'm now suffering from this thing, too?"

He doesn't laugh. Instead, he ploughs on, "No. But, because of her illness, your mother wrongly believed that you were evil, that you were responsible for the death of her baby. She believed you were a demon and that you sucked the life from her baby so that you could live…"

Screaming. Crying. Begging. Crunching footsteps. "Mummy, please... Mummy! Stop! Mummy! Please stop! You're hurting me!"

"Shhhh… it needs to stop screaming because it is not my baby. It is evil! Dear Father, thou art in heaven, hallowed be thy name…"

Clicking pebbles. Grazed arms. Searing pain.

"Thy kingdom come, thy will be done…"

"Mummy…!" Crying. Anguish. Pulling hair. Roots ripped. Pain. Sobbing. Pain. Tears. Begging. Tears. Water sloshing, splashing, and fizzing.

"Mummy! Please!"

I leap out of the chair again and run back to my sanctuary by the window; only, it isn't comforting anymore. In fact, it's worse – the sky, the open space.

I'm doubled over. Hyperventilating. The flashback was much more vivid this time. I can still feel the grip of cold, the burn of pain, the water in my nose. Choking.

I cough. Gag. "Oh fuck, oh no, oh fuck…" I'm trying to breathe, and I stagger then slide into the corner of the room as the wall falls away and I can see the beach. That beach at Porthcove! I can feel my mother's bony fingers in my hair. "NO! MUMMY! NO!"

"Marco? Tell me what you see. Tell me."

"No. I don't see anything. I… I can't see anything." I'm shivering. Cold. Terrified.

"You do, Marco. You do. Tell me what happened. Tell me."

"I don't see anything! I can't see anything!" I chant.

"Marco. Tell me what you see."

"I don't know!"

"Marco. Remember. It's time to remember!"

"NO!"

"Your mother tried to drown you that day, Marco. Didn't she?"

"NO!" I scream. Eyes bulging, throat constricting.

"Your mother tried to murder you, Marco. You know this. She tried to murder you because she believed that her little boy, *you,* took her baby from her."

"NO, IT'S NOT TRUE! YOU'RE LYING! YOU'RE FUCKING LYING!" I glare at him, and I want to kill him. I want to choke the life from him.

"I'm sorry, Marco. I'm not. You know I'm not. It's time to face it. *You must* face it."

"No, you're the one who needs to face it; you're a liar! You're a fucking liar! And I'm going to kill you!" I snarl, through gritted teeth, "I'm going to fucking kill you!"

With one leap, I'm sailing through the air, arms outstretched, until I connect with the bastard's windpipe, knocking him over in his chair. Then I clamp my hands around his throat and squeeze with all my strength. "I'M GOING TO KILL YOU! I'M GOING TO KILL YOU, YOU LYING COCKSUCKER! IM GOING TO FUCKING KILL YOU!" I scream, spit flying all over the place as I watch the prick's face turn red and then purple.

Then, I feel strong hands pulling at my arms until I am wrenched, then lifted, backward, but I don't let go. I won't let go, and the doctor comes with me until I feel the jab of a needle in my arm.

Seconds later, things don't seem anywhere near as bad until, eventually, my grip slackens and then the lights go out.

MARCO BATTISTA

Two weeks later.

Do you remember that nineties song by Joyce Simms? You know that one that goes... *Come into my life, I've got so much love to show you. Come into my life, boy, I adore you?*

Yes? No? Anyway, that's been going through my mind over the past few days, along with the bloody janitor's obsession with other eighties' classics. I tell you, if I hear that Erasure's bloody "Respect" song one more time, I'm likely to create a shiv from his mop handle and shove it up his backside.

As you can imagine, they don't like weapons here at the Wellbeing Institute because, well, the purpose of this place is to promote well-being.

So, yeah, if you haven't already guessed it, according to Ethan – and yes, we're on first name terms and have been for some time now – I haven't been luxuriating at some village by the ocean for the past two weeks, but instead, I've been detained at the doctor's pleasure under the mental health act since it was believed that there was a point, a couple of months back, where I posed a danger to myself and, I think, quite possibly, others.

Fancy that, eh? Yeah, I know it's hard to believe. As is the fact that I've been stuck in this place this whole time and that I haven't been flitting back and forth from London to the Southwest coast of England after all.

But then, I bet you guessed that already, right? At which point exactly did you realise? If it was anywhere before my little moment in the doctor's office, then you could have bloody well told me since I had no fucking idea until a rather spindly bloke and his overweight sidekick dragged me off the doctor and pumped me with I don't know how many CCs of get-the-fuck-to-sleep that had me out like a lightbulb. I'm telling you, that stuff is bloody good. I've decided that, when I get out of here, because that is likely, I'm going to stock up on that shit.

Now, I know you're probably thinking that, given my behaviour, they've locked me up and thrown away the key, but that isn't true. At least, not according to the doc. My so-called detention is really for my own *well-being*. See what I did there?

Apparently, a few months back, I suffered what is commonly known as a psychotic break. For the uninitiated, this is when a person perceives and or interprets the world differently from other people around them. It often involves delusions or hallucinations. Basically, all contact is lost with the real world.

Interestingly, it's not so dissimilar to the same thing my mother suffered from, only without the whole pregnancy bit.

Yeah, as I say, weird shit.

Oh, and speaking of my mum. Did you notice that? I said *speaking* of my mum. Something that, according to Ethan, I've been resisting for months now... she is no longer with us. I mean, I already knew that, but I just didn't want to discuss the fact that my mum was so convinced that I was the devil and that people were out to kill her, to the extent that, before my dad managed to get her help, she stepped out in front of an Underground train. Security cameras apparently recorded her running from some invisible being right before it happened.

So, yeah. You can imagine why I didn't fancy chatting about that, or allowing myself to dwell on the fact that there was mental illness in the family. Since studies show that it can be hereditary in blood relatives.

Yeah, I'm able to look at this objectively now. Which is good and bad at the same time, because it feels like, now that the damn has burst, all of this other stuff has come flooding through. Stuff that I knew, but had repressed this whole time, and it's all thanks to the fact that I called Ethan a cocksucker and tried to choke the life from him. There's a joke in there, but someone braver than me is going to have to tell it.

So, yeah, as I say – every cloud, eh?

It just goes to show, acting on stuff, sometimes, really pays off. I'm just kidding, of course; do not try this at home. I don't recommend it, and especially because it'll generally lead to you spending the next few days in a drug-induced haze that's followed by several more days of talking about and coming to terms with some of the shittiest things about yourself, so that you have to realise why you hid them in the first place. It's like stumbling around in a sewer while stopping off occasionally to create shit angels and not washing the stuff off for days, sometimes months. Or, in my case, years.

It seems that the trauma of what happened to my would-be brother or sister, coupled with the fact that my mother tried to drown me, led to my so-called withdrawal. I stopped engaging with people and developed an almost autistic reaction to those around me. I generally didn't enjoy being touched, and hated anybody going anywhere near my hair. I acted up by knocking down anybody who invaded my space at school and at home. Which meant that, when my father finally got over the death of my mother and started seeing my stepmother, I couldn't handle it.

Yeah, it appears that that also was a bit of a fabrication. My dad may well have had affairs, but I wasn't aware of them. It was just easier for me to paint him as the villain than to accept what my mother did. From what I understand, he loved her deeply, too; he just didn't know how to deal with what was happening to her because he wrongly believed he was the cause, that she had stopped loving him and that his mere presence made her angry. What he didn't realise was that it wasn't just his presence – it was everyone's, including her ten-year-old son's.

Of course, I didn't know this at the time and, the more I grew, so did my rage. My resentment. It started eating at me like a cancer, and was always there, always on the surface, ready to strike out before I was struck. I wasn't going to let anybody hurt me ever again. My father knew this because, the one time he tried to manhandle me to my room, I punched him in the face – which resulted in him sending me to a whole bunch of therapists, all of whom did nothing but spout jargon with little to show in return.

I had become a real problem child.

Eventually, as his relationship with my stepmother grew, his patience with me dwindled until, eventually, he packed me off to a boarding school where I was bullied, regularly – not only for being the little runt that I was, but also because I was the boy who'd driven his mum to top herself.

And, surprisingly, I took that shit because she was my one Achilles heel. I hurt, I ached for her love, and I found it really hard to come to terms with the fact that she hadn't cared about me, and that I'd made her so unhappy that she first tried to kill me, and then actually succeeded in killing herself.

I was ostracised at boarding school. The other boys would often play tricks on me; they'd leave shit in my bed, literally, and spiders and other crap. That's when they weren't pissing in it, and generally messing with all of my school stuff, which meant I'd often get into trouble.

Then, one day, shortly after my thirteenth birthday, something changed. Gregory Barker, some chubby little fucker who was always leading the others against me, made the fatal mistake of grabbing hold of my hair as he attempted to drag me, uniform and all, into one of the school ponds.

I lost it. First, I managed to spin around and sink my teeth into his wrist, and then I punched him in the balls, and then I gave him the results of all of my pent-up rage in one almighty uppercut. The blow sent him flying through the air, and when he landed, I pummelled his face to a pulp, and was just about to stomp on it when the other kids pulled me off of him.

I was suspended for behaviour not becoming of a gentleman, and I was still a minor, which meant I had to go home. Inconveniently, my step-mum was already pregnant with her first child and, well, told my dad she didn't feel safe with me in the house.

Which, shocker, ended up with me managing to get back into boarding school, just months later, because my father, now one of the kings of spin, knew someone who knew someone.

But, when I returned to school, a fully-fledged teen with raging hormones to prove it, everything was different. Everybody knew I had been suspended and why. Nobody dared to mess with me and I sought to capitalise on that. I dominated the boys in my dorm, as I did any brown-eyed girl that came into contact with me.

Yeah, my mother had brown eyes. And yes, according to Ethan, and as perverse as it sounds, it appears that my predilection for brown eyes is actually my need to *possess* that which my mother denied me for most of my childhood.

Yeah, you can imagine my reaction when the doctor tried to explain that to me.

Apparently, it was here that my dysfunctional relationship with girls began. With each and every sexual encounter turning into an opportunity to dominate the female of the species, to exert control over them for my own pleasure and gratification. At the same time, I kept them at a distance. I used them and never forged anything meaningful so that they could never hurt me.

 Fun fact. It was around this time that I met the future Doctor Ethan Holmes. Well, I didn't exactly *meet* him. We went to the same school and he had heard of me or, more specifically, of my reputation. I was someone you didn't mess with. I was crazy, like my mother, and I had nearly killed someone.

Before long, my peers became my clan. They looked up to me. I'd also grown into my looks, which meant that I became the cocky heterosexual stud as well as the fighter, the leveller. But then, something disastrous happened and everything changed, again.

What exactly triggered my psychosis remains unknown. The doc and I are hoping for a breakthrough today. But as you can imagine, and to be perfectly honest with you, I'm finding the whole process fucking exhausting, albeit perversely enlightening.

It's that whole computer hard drive analogy. I spent years of my life just opening the occasional document, sending the odd email. But now, I'm having to process terabytes of data in a complex search query designed to discover truths and to understand and accept not just what happened to me that day on the beach, but everything else that came after.

Apparently, this process is much easier now that I'm *receptive* to the therapeutic process. It's a bit like being an alcoholic, and finally having the guts to stand up and declare that you have a problem.

Speaking of which, you'll be pleased to know that I've been sober for over two months now.

Nah, you're not really impressed, are you? No, you're not, because you're not stupid. You know that I didn't really have a choice in the matter. There's no alcohol served at the Wellbeing Institute. More's the pity. It would make all of this stuff much more bearable.

That said, and don't take my word for it because we won't know this for sure until I get out of this place, but I don't think I'm that way inclined anymore. I'm not saying I'm healed by any stretch of the imagination, but what I'm saying is that I no longer feel the need to obliterate myself to stop from thinking about the things I don't want to think about.

You get that, right?

PSYCHOSIS

Monday. 10:06.

The door opens and Ethan hurries in, carrying his notebook and his mug.

"I'm sorry, Marco. I'm sorry, I got held up."

"It's okay. I was just thinking."

"Really, what about?" I watch him organise himself and then settle into his chair. "Oh, you know. Stuff. Therapy."

"That's handy, because that's exactly what I wanted to open up with today. I wanted to ask you, how do you think things are going? What do you think of the progress we've been making here?"

I stretch and yawn. Yeah, that's how relaxed things have become. "Well, if I say it's been good, that would be a lie, but it's been productive. Generally, it feels as if a weight has been lifted. Like I've been walking around with a whole vat full of crap on my back. I mean, it's all still there, in my head, but now that I'm able to see it clearly, it doesn't feel as dark or as heavy. Does that make sense?"

"It makes perfect sense. And I'm really pleased to hear you say that, by the way. It's great news. I think we've been making excellent progress. So," he adds, shifting in his seat, "today, I would like to start by talking through everything we've achieved over the past two weeks. A kind of a summary, if you will. Is that okay with you?"

"Would it make any difference if I said it wasn't?"

"Come on. You've been doing really well."

"Okay. But only after you tell me when I can see my wife and my boy."

He cocks his head.

"You promised," I add.

"I know I promised. But, as you've seen, we've made great progress over the past week…"

"…Exactly, so seeing my family is only going to improve that, no?"

"Well, I just want to make sure you're the best that you can be for that reunion, because it's undoubtedly going to be emotional for you."

"Have you changed your mind?" I ask, slumping my shoulders.

"No, I haven't changed my mind, Marco. But…"

"But what?"

"You said you trusted me. You still trust me, right? Please trust that I will let you know when I think the time is right. First, I need to make sure we've covered off this stage before we move onto another."

"Seeing my family is a stage?"

"Contact with your real life, as it is now, yes, I would say that qualifies as a stage. Wouldn't you?"

I say nothing.

"Marco?"

I shrug.

"Please, Marco?"

I gulp down the flame of frustration that wants to flare from my mouth and douse it with another sigh while I shift in my seat.

Do you know what I've been thinking about? I've been thinking about how weird it is that this bloke often talks to me from a position of authority, yet he's younger than me. Alright, not much younger, but it still fucking feels like I'm the adult and he's the child telling me what to do.

"Okay," I finally say, "but this conversation isn't over."

"I would expect nothing less," he says with a big smile. "So, we've talked about your mother, and I think we've done excellent work there. Obviously, the new reality of your memory of her is going to take some getting used to, but at least you can now start the healing process. Right?"

I nod since, quite frankly, I'm sick of talking about it. I'm still of the opinion that there's a reason why we repress crap, and I'm not entirely convinced of the usefulness of dredging all that stuff up. But hey, I'm just a passenger here, as are you.

The doctor shifts in his seat again, as if settling in for the duration, and then says, way too enthusiastically, if you ask me, "As I mentioned before, I think we're at a good point where we can pause, review, and summarise the progress we've made. In this case, I want to focus on Porthcove and that whole alternate world that you've been retreating to each time things become difficult here in the real world. Is that okay?"

I nod, but there's something about the matter of how he emphasises those facts being unreal that makes me want to punch him. To me, outside of this place, this room, that world still exists, and until I see proof with my own eyes, that's what I'm going to believe.

"You're thinking about it again, aren't you?" he asks.

I look at him. "Well, it makes sense, doesn't it? That I'm trying to process this."

"Yes, it does. But there's a lot of preparatory work that we need to complete, before you're confronted by that new reality. We've talked about this, right?"

I nod.

"And we've talked about the symbolic relevance of Porthcove and how you fabricated this fort, this safe place, inside of which you compartmentalised thoughts, feelings, people, and events from your life, and then tried to rationalise, make sense of them, by becoming the therapist. Right?"

I nod again.

"What we also know is that this all began when you received that letter about your father's inheritance and, of course, there was the affair with Ava."

Ava. I have to say, each and every time he says that, I am picturing this woman in that station wagon, the stunning, sexually dissatisfied housewife. But he isn't talking about her. He's talking about my sister-in-law, Ellie's sister.

"Are you still struggling with the reality of that?" he asks.

My cheeks are burning. "Yeah, I am," I croak.

"Remember what we discussed? It's perfectly understandable that you should feel like this, but you need to remember that your mind created your version of Ava based on what you knew about her. You knew that she was unhappy in her marriage even though she believed that her husband was a good man and father, and yet she featured as your patient because she represented a serious catalyst in the collapse of the real world for you."

I nod. This time because shame has tied my tongue. I can't even begin to imagine what this did to Ellie. And, to be honest, out of everything I've done, it's this that cuts me the most.

"Then, when your wife, Ellie, gave you the ultimatum about seeking treatment for the sex addiction, the drinking, you were already teetering on a precipice. Right?"

Another nod.

"What came next? Can you tell me what came next?"

I look at him. We've been over this what feels like a hundred times, and each and every fucking time, it feels like he wants me to say something else, but there is nothing else! "Why don't you just tell me what you want to hear?" I suggest, clearly irritated.

"Come on, Marco. You know it isn't about what I want you to say, but more about what you feel, what you remember."

"Well, according to you, everything that came after was all some crappy figment of my imagination. The only thing that wasn't is the fact that I probably destroyed Ellie's relationship with her sister. My son's relationship with his aunt."

"How does that make you feel?"

I glare at him, then growl, "How the fuck do you think it makes me feel?" I launch myself out of my seat and walk over to the window. The room is suddenly stifling. I long for some fresh air.

"I'm sorry. I know this is hard, but it's important that we don't become distracted by one specific element today," he says, seemingly disinterested in how I'm really feeling.

And I can't help but think about this, as I watch the trees bending in the breeze. For someone who seems obsessed with how I feel about things, he doesn't seem particularly interested in how I feel.

For example, right now, I can *feel* his eyes on me. "I am sorry, Marco," he repeats softly. "I know how frustrating this is for you, and you know I mean it when I say that. I'm not patronising you."

A smile tugs at my lips. He's saying that because of the last hundred or so times when I berated him for saying words he does not mean.

And I think about that, too. I think about how he's been putting up with my crap all this time, and I feel like a shitty ingrate.

Slowly, I turn around. "No. I'm sorry."

"Don't be sorry. It's fine. You don't need to be sorry. This is difficult, but you're doing really well. Come on. Come and sit back down. We'll move onto something else. Okay? You okay to move on?"

I nod and reluctantly return to my seat.

He's consulting his notebook now. "So, the house itself. Dolce Vita. We talked about the rooms, which we'll come to in a bit, but we also talked about the various links that you retained to reality. Do you remember those?

The lighthouse.

"Which was effectively me shining a pen light in your eyes, because you were catatonic for quite some time. It then became a permanent landmark that, in your own words, appeared to move closer each day. Which could have been a side effect of you emerging from your fantasy."

The eighties music.

"…Courtesy of the janitor's radio station. You were still hearing his music even in your delusion."

The disinfectant.

"Also used by the janitor to mop the floor in and around your room. And, you've got to appreciate just how fascinating this is. I mean, the way it permeated your delusion."

The voices.

"Not echoes from the past, but people at your bedside, talking to you. Me, your wife, nurses."

The dog scratching and whimpering.

"The puppy was the first thing you learned to truly love. A gift from your father. But it vanished, allegedly drowned by your mother, who wrongly believed it was a hound sent from hell."

Ships in bottles.

"Your father did actually collect these, didn't he? But there was one ship. The galleon, the schooner that was different from all of the others. Can you tell me why?"

I think about this. I've been thinking about it for days. Ever since we got onto this subject. But for the life of me, I can't work out why that thing is different from all of the others. Yes, my dad did collect ships, but they were all in bottles.

I shake my head.

"Nothing?"

"No, Ethan. How many times?"

"This is obviously a very important element, Marco. There's a reason why you brought this particular ship into your delusion."

"Well, if there is, why don't you just tell me? I mean, has it ever occurred to you that the bloody thing may have a completely different meaning? That, symbolically, it could mean fuck-all!"

"Do you really believe that?"

"Now I do."

He watches me, as if trying to read the truth on my face. Then, eventually, "Okay. So, why don't we take a look at some of the people from your version of Porthcove. Okay?"

Guess what I do? That's right. I nod.

"Now, we've already talked about Ava."

Shawn and Jessie.

"Shawn, we know now is actually you, that you are not a therapist, but actually a mechanic."

I bite my lip here, because no matter how many times I hear this, I still can't wrap my head around it, even if it does kind of make sense.

"…I know this was one of the hardest things for you to come to terms with. You believed so strongly that you were the person in control, the therapist in that situation, when, in reality, it was your introspection, your own self-analysis, your own therapy."

I've noticed that he seems to find this exact mind-crash of my life particularly interesting, and does a shitty job of hiding it. If he's even trying. Eventually, he pulls himself together.

"How do you feel about that right now?"

"How the fuck do you think I feel, Ethan? You've been trying to get me to come to terms with this shit for weeks. I'm doing my best, but you know, you wake up one day and somebody tells you that everything you thought was, isn't. It takes some fucking getting used to."

"So, you're still angry, then?" he teases, which probably isn't the most professional of interactions, but I think I've worn the guy down and now, well, now, it's just how we roll. "All you need to think about…"

"Yes, yes, I know. All I need to think about is the fact that I can't explain where I studied, when I graduated, how long I've been practicing, nor any clients beyond those who visited me at that place. But that's the bloody problem, because it's like I told you. In my head, I have the sense of there being many cases, but they're just like a dream. Blurry, and I can't focus on any one in particular."

Now it's his turn to nod and, to be fair, he does look pained. It's as if I've projected my anguish on him, so I give him what he obviously wants to hear. I lead. "Jessie, she's actually my so called," I make quotation marks in the air in front of me, "lover. Roughly translated as the woman I had sex with more than once. Which is a whole mind-trip in itself, because if it's really true that I'm the bi-product of my own history and that my sex addiction was born out of the need to be wanted while at the same time being in control and," I form quotation marks in the air again, "*taking* my so-called release, then you would think I wouldn't bother going back to feed from the same trough."

"You would, but remember…The addiction may be primarily about *control* and getting *the release* – but it's still an addiction and, as such, it needs to be fed. Jessie made it, for want of a better expression, easier for you to score."

"Interesting analogy, Doc."

"I try my best," he says with a wry smile.

"Hence why," I continue, "*Jessie* or *Emily*, as I knew her in the real world, took it badly when I told her I wanted to break it off. She'd also become addicted to the control she exerted over me, despite how much I loved my family. She knew that she only needed to click her fingers and I'd come running."

"…but she wanted more," the doctor chimes in. "She didn't take the split very well, because she wanted you to be together and, ultimately, maybe even get married, have children."

Oh fuck. And here comes that shame again. Pressing on me like a steamroller. The doctor must see it because he adds, "But you loved your wife, Marco. You wanted the affair to be over because you were able to see that you had other priorities."

"Still doesn't make it right, though, does it? I mean, Jesus, this woman, then Ellie's sister. Christ."

"It wasn't right that you suffered as a child either." He ignores my handwringing. "Shit happens to all of us, Marco. Remember? You said that."

"Gosh, Doctor, did you just say a bad word?" I tease.

He laughs. "Oh, I can say much worse than that, trust me."

"Oh? Go on, then."

"No," he laughs.

"Oh, go on." But he continues to shake his head. "You know, I read somewhere that people who swear a lot are less stressed. Do you think that's true?"

"I haven't read anything about that, but I can see the benefits of expressing yourself regularly and comprehensively."

We pause, and I take advantage of the break to drink from my plastic bottle. It's that or a plastic cup. Yeah, that all makes sense now too. This may well be a private clinic, but they still don't like patients having access to things they can break and use as potentially lethal weapons.

Oh, and in case you're wondering, this stay-cation was kindly brought to me by the lovely folks at Stevenson, Incorporated. Well, kind of, indirectly. I don't know the details, but from what the doc tells me, it's something to do with Ellie and an early inheritance she extorted as payback for her parents' manipulation in her life.

"So, that only leaves Ryan and Harvey," the Doctor announces.

"Well, we already know about Harvey, don't we?" I say, sombrely. "I actually feel bad that I'll never get to meet Captain Birdseye. If it wasn't for him jumping out of his boat and into the water to save me, I wouldn't be here today."

"Hence why you spent most of the delusion feeling conflicted about him," the doctor adds, as if to press the point. And, as before, it makes perfect sense.

Ryan.

"Now, I don't have any idea what he was all about," I say. "Apart from reminding me that I love football, but then, who doesn't?" He's looking at me. "Except you, of course. But you're an anomaly."

"Thanks. Do you really believe there's nothing more to Ryan, Marco?"

I cock my head. "You're doing it again."

"What am I doing?"

"Every time we talk about him, you question what I remember. Like there's something else. Like I'm holding back."

"Is there?"

"Ethan. Seriously, dude, you've got to quit with the bloody leading questions, because of all the stuff you say, that gets on my wick the most."

He holds up his hands. "I'm sorry. But, remember, it's important that it's you who imparts the information, or I'm in danger of planting ideas in your head that could lead us both to a false conclusion. We discussed this."

"I know we did, but it doesn't make you any less annoying."

He nods. "I'm sorry about that. But, at the end of the day, my job here is to help you. I can't do that if you keep gagging me from asking the relevant questions."

"I don't remember anything else about Ryan," I state, emphatically.

He nods, but I can tell he isn't satisfied. Well, tough, he's just going to have to deal with it.

"Marco, do you remember us talking about boarding school, post expulsion?"

"Why are we discussing this again, Ethan? It's almost like you want to torture me by re-visiting the shittiest parts of my life. We've been over this. Isn't the point of therapy to examine, accept, and move on? Why can't we just move on?"

"Because I don't think we're done with this."

"Why? What exactly do you think I'm withholding?"

"Well, if I knew that…"

"You might leave me the fuck alone!"

I launch myself out of the chair. Not because I want to flounce or anything, but more because, as you know by now, it's the easiest way to get out of the damn thing.

I walk over to the window and look out onto the park bench that feels so different now that I know is actually an enclosed garden, and the only people who occasionally enjoy Starbucks there are staff on a break. *Everything* feels so different now. It's like looking at my life with completely different eyes.

"Marco?"

I don't turn around. "I'm okay. I just need a second. It's just… we've been at this for days now. I'm exhausted. I just want to go home to my family."

"Marco…"

I hold up a hand, still not turning around. "Don't say it, alright? Yes, I know the London home isn't there anymore, that Ellie let it go pretty much the moment I ended up in here, but just, for a second, let me just enjoy the best bit, okay? Just for a second."

I can feel the tears welling in my eyes, but I blink them back. I try to picture Toby at the park that time, but I can't, and it's so fucking frustrating! But, I don't want to tell the doc, as that'll just lead him down another path, and it's only just starting to feel like we're reaching the end of all of this.

I don't know what's been happening, but lately it's becoming more and more difficult to remember that day at the park with Toby. I have no idea why and I'm finding this particularly distressing – because it's all I have. That used to be the one happy place I could retreat to, but now…. It just feels like the memory's become pixelated, and the more I try to zoom in for details, the blurrier it becomes.

Instead, I keep coming back to some other memory. One I don't even recognise. One where we're on a pier next to the ocean. I don't know where exactly, but I think it might be Brighton. I mean, there's nothing wrong with this memory; it's a happy one, although the details are still sketchy. Anyway, it isn't the memory I want. I want to go back to the park, but I can't. Now, it seems impossible to focus on one specific thing when all of these other thoughts keep intruding, and my mind starts to wander.

"Marco?"

"Yes. Alright," I snap.

"Where are you?"

I rub my face, instinctively, to make sure that no tears actually managed to escape, and turn to him.

"Where do you think I am, Doc? Where I have been for what feels like a year, stuck in this stuffy office with you."

I walk back to my chair, but avoid his gaze because there's something about this guy that makes me feel like he can read my fucking mind.

"Marco?"

"So, where were we?" I finally look at him and we have a mini stare-off. I know he wants to know what I was just thinking, but I'm not going to give in to him. Instead, I reroute the conversation. "Oh yeah, you want to dig around school days some more. Yay!"

"You know, it's interesting to me, how eager you seem to steer clear of those days."

"Are you fucking kidding me? We've talked about that time ad nauseam. It's how we discovered all that shit about my need to control situations, to dominate, about how I became a sex freak, and a quick-tempered fucking psychopath…"

"You're not a psychopath…"

"… who's unable to express, to emote. It's why I make jokes, why I have this in-built avoidance system. The very thing you're bitching at me about right now."

I can still hear my voice ringing after I've stopped talking, and it's another one of those long silences while the doctor waits for the metaphorical feathers to fall, before continuing.

"You're not a psychopath, Marco, and I would really appreciate it if you didn't sling those words around so casually. Especially since you and I both know that, while you may be frustrated right now, you're also using that outburst as a way of avoiding what we really want to talk about."

"Oh, fuck you… *You*, it's *you* who wants to talk about it."

"Marco, do you remember? This is exactly how you'd react when you didn't want to talk about your mother."

"This is fucking bullshit. I'm done for today. Can we call it quits? I've had enough. I'm tired."

"Marco, I want to stay with this. What is it about school that you don't want to discuss? What are you trying to avoid?"

"I'm not avoiding anything; I just want to go back to my room now."

"Not yet. Marco, I want to stay with this."

"Of course you do, because you're a fucking sadist who enjoys wallowing in all of my shit! Fuck you!"

I jump up from the chair and make for the door.

"Marco?"

"I told you, I'm done."

I reach the door.

"Marco, please, we need to talk about this."

I put my hand on the door handle. "Fuck off!"

"I think this has something to do with Ryan!" he yells, and it stops me in my tracks. "I think *this* is why you're unable to explain one and don't want to talk about the other," he adds, softly.

Dragging. Screaming. Laughing. But it isn't me; I'm not screaming this time. Laughter. People laughing. Dragging, through the woods, leaves rustling. Sunlight filtered through leaves. The smell of moss, decomposition. Wings fluttering. Traffic in the distance. Dragging, rustling. Screaming. Dragging,

rustling, screaming.
"NOOO!"
I wrench the door open and run through it.

LOVE

Tuesday. 11:16.

I couldn't sleep last night. I kept tossing and bloody turning. And when I wasn't doing that, I was dreaming, and I bet you can't guess what I was dreaming about, can you?

Of course you can.

I don't know what it was yesterday, but as soon as the doc asked me that question about school, something just clicked in me. It was as if some other room in my brain had been unlocked, and out came another precession of grotesque memories, none of which I could even interpret until I managed to sleep. Then, it was there, buried deep in the dark forest of my dream, that I remembered exactly why Ryan sat on my metaphorical couch... and I can tell you, the enormity of that revelation filled me with such an overwhelming sense of anguish and sorrow that I can see no other solution than to push my way out of that window. Because between you and me, these feelings... well, I want them to end, I *need* them to end, because now that I'm aware, I just don't know what to do with them, and it's bloody terrifying.

Again, in stark contrast to how I'm feeling, the sun is shining in a pale blue sky. Ethan is sitting in his chair, patiently waiting for me to continue, to dish more dirt, like you are.

"You already know about how things changed for me after I was expelled. When I went back to school, everybody saw me differently."

"The boys wanted to be you. The girls wanted to be with you," he contributes with a smile.

I shake my head. "Well, I didn't see that at the time. I think I was just doing whatever I wanted to do. As you know, going through the motions, not really giving a shit about what anybody thought of me. Ironically, it was through doing *that* that my popularity sky rocketed."

"You certainly had an impressive reputation. As I said, we never met and yet I knew all about you. Or, more specifically, of you."

"You mean you knew what a dick I was to everyone?"

"Um… not always." He smiles.

"Anyway, there was this one kid. He was new. Andrew Armiger. Remember him?"

"How could I forget? His death almost got that school closed down."

"Yeah." I swallow. My mouth's gone dry.

"He struggled to integrate. I remember, that place wasn't easy…"

"…It was my fault," I blurt.

"What?"

"It was my fault he hung himself."

"What are you talking about?" Ethan whispers, sitting forward in his chair.

I fight off the mental image. "Did you know he was gay?"

"I didn't really know him that well. It was a big school, but…"

"He was." I'm staring at my plimsolls. I can't face looking at the doc, but I can feel his eyes on me.

"Marco, it's okay. It's alright."

"Don't fucking start with that. It's not okay, and it fucking ain't alright!"

"Just talk to me. Tell me what happened," he soothes.

"He used to bunk with one of my mates, and, one night… um," I hesitate. Squirm in my chair. "Andrew must have thought my mate was asleep. Only he wasn't. And when he rolled over, he could hear a noise, and when he looked, well, you know, he saw Andrew wanking to a pile of photos."

"Right."

"Well, this bloke, my mate, whose name, funny enough, I can't remember – I don't think we were that close – he didn't do or say anything at the time. He just went back to sleep.

The next day, when Andrew went back to the dorm after P.E., he found that all of his photos had been taken from their wallet and stuck on the notice board. Some had been photocopied, enlarged, and stuck on walls as posters with captions underneath."

"What kind of captions?"

I swallow hard as I recall the images, then, "You know, usual kid shit, *Andy hearts Marco. Andy's loves Italian. Andy loves cock.* You know… the usual rubbish."

I feel queasy. I don't know if it's the memory or the reality of the memory, but recalling this stuff makes my stomach turn.

"The pictures were of you?" the doctor asks.

I nod, slowly. "Yeah, playing football. You probably already know that I was team captain for some time. Apparently, this guy had amassed quite a collection of these things, because I'm telling you, they were fucking everywhere."

"How did it make you feel?"

"Creeped out. Disgusted. Homosexuality wasn't something I'd really been exposed to up until then and, well, to be perfectly honest, it made me sick. Particularly because the photos were of me, and especially after what my mate told me Andy did with them the night before. I mean, he made me a fucking laughing stock! Not that anybody would dare tell me that to my face, but I knew it was what they were thinking."

"So, what happened?"

I roll my shoulders. Crick my neck. "We decided to teach him a lesson. My so-called mate, and a bunch of the other lads, grabbed him during a free period, I think it might have even been a weekend, and dragged him into the woods."

Moss. Earth. Rustling leaves. Screaming. Rough bark. Screaming. Traffic in the distance. Golden leaves rustling. Wings beating. Screaming. Sun, filtered through leaves. A dog barking in the distance.

"We figured that if he liked to get his dick out that much, then we would help him out. And if he loved cock, then we were going to feed it to him."

Screaming. Leaves rustling. Feet kicking. Screaming.

"We dragged him through the woods, butt naked, to the river, where we ripped out my crotch from some of the photos and made him eat them."

I haven't realised it till now, but there are tears in my eyes. I swipe at a renegade runaway on my cheek. "He never recovered from that. They found him a couple of days later, hanging from a tree branch by his belt."

I clear my throat in an attempt to dislodge the bile there, but it doesn't work, so I gulp down water instead. Then I force a bitter smile. "And, once again, you can see why talking about this shit doesn't do anybody any good. Certainly not me."

Ethan doesn't respond, but I can tell he's thinking. He's processing the data he's just received, but all I want is for him to talk. I want him to tell me what a despicable piece of shit I am. I want him to tell me that there's no fucking hope for me and that I should go ahead and put myself out of my misery. Not that I've realised it, but I'm already staring out that bloody window.

"You think all of your problems are going to go away if you jump out of there?" he asks.

"Um, you tell me, Doc."

"Well, assuming you get through the toughened glass, Marco, knowing your luck, mate, you'd probably just break your legs."

I laugh, bitterly, wiping my face. "Using my own lines against me?"

He shrugs as if to say, *Well, needs must.*

"I can't even begin to imagine how humiliating that must have been for that poor boy."

"Oh, don't start, Ethan," I comment.

"What?"

"You're going to try and explain this away like you have everything else…"

"Is that what you think we're doing here?" He says, sharply. "Justifying your behaviour?"

"Isn't it? You seem to have an answer for everything."

"No, Marco, I think you'll find that it's you who provides the answers. You provide answers to the questions that you do not want me to ask, to the places you don't want me to take you. Marco, *you* provide the answers. I just help you understand them, to see the truth, to see reality for what it really is, and not the polarised versions your guilt wants you to see." His voice is forceful again, like he's irritated.

I like it when he's like this. The bloke is always so meek and mild most the time, so I like it when he gets irked. It shows me that he's alive and that, like me, he feels. Because I'm feeling right now, and I hate it. I can't fucking stand it! It's like wearing a crown of thorns; just enough to hurt, but not enough to kill, to put me out of my bloody misery.

"What wrong?" he asks quickly, like he's read my mind.

"I'm just sick of this."

"Of what?"

"Of this!" I yell, and throw myself out of the chair, again. I need to move, I need to pace. "I can't stand *this* anymore! I've had enough of pouring over all of this shit under the guise that it's supposed to make me feel better. That's such a load of fucking rubbish! There's nothing about any of this that makes me feel better – it just goes from shitty to shittier!"

"Is that how you really feel?"

"Oh fucking hell," I say slowly, through gritted teeth. "Ethan, I swear, if you ask me that question in that tone one more time… what do you fucking think? Of course, it's how I feel; otherwise, I wouldn't be pacing up and down, telling you about it!"

The boom of my voice echoes around the room, and my doctor, as always, doesn't say anything; he just watches me. FUCK! I feel like a trapped animal at a fucking zoo! Under constant observation.

Then, "Are you done?"

"No, I'll be done when I stick your head through that window."

"Why are you so angry?"

I stop pacing and glare at him for a few seconds, and then resume my journey around the room, shaking my head and muttering words I don't even understand.

"You're angry again, Marco. Are you seeing that? And it's a pattern. One that we're both familiar with now. You've been using it your whole life. It's your armour. Your shield. It's how you deflect the things that hurt you. It's how you deflect the things that are uncomfortable for you. You're like a growling bear. Anytime somebody threatens your space, threatens to expose a vulnerable part of you, you growl, sneer, and snipe your way out of it. And it's time to stop, Marco. It's time to stop and let me do my job because that's the only way this will truly end – the only way you're going to get back home."

I'm still pacing, but I'm not looking at the fucker, although he might be making sense. I don't know anymore.

He continues, "Right now, you've dumped that story on me. You pull the pin on the grenade and then you throw up your defences, assuming you've inflicted mortal damage without even checking if that's true. You're so caught up with feeling so bloody shitty, to use your word, that you're only truly happy when you're actually feeling that way!"

I shoot him a glare.

"Oh, please. You think that look is going to dissuade me from telling you what I think? From telling you the truth, about yourself?" His words are flippant. I'm surprised he doesn't follow them up with a roll of the eyes. But then, he changes gear. His stony face is one of resolve, mixed with a whole lot of compassion. "Marco, what happened to Andrew was terrible. Humiliating. Awful. I mean, I can't even begin to find words to describe it, but it wasn't your fucking fault!"

I stop pacing and stare at him. "Yeah, I can use that language, too – especially when it seems it's the only one you seem to understand. Because I need you to understand the words that are coming out of my mouth. This was *not* your fault. It wasn't. Andrew, like the rest of us mortals, developed a crush on the object of his desire. Maybe he even fell in love with him, though we'll never truly know. And in this case, it just so happened that

that person was you." His tone is much softer now, and I swear this guy is much wiser than his years.

After several seconds, I collapse back into my chair.

"I let it happen, though, Doc. I bloody let it happen," I say through gritted teeth as fight back both the lump in my throat and more tears.

"No, you didn't."

"I did. I was fucking there!"

"No, you *were not*." I look at him like he's the one losing his mind. "You weren't there, Marco," he continues. "You were away that weekend. I saw you leave with my own eyes. Your father picked you up in his Maserati. I remember, because everybody was fawning over it. Except me, of course. I never did like noisy cars." The last words are spoken with a flourish, and it's probably the only thing this man has ever done, since I've known him, that seems remotely gay.

"But I remember the woods, how they smelt. I, I remember seeing what happened."

"No, you don't. You just remember how the woods smelt, because we'd all been in there enough times for... um, well."

I see a smile creep across his lips and then hide behind his neat teeth. He continues, "For our own different reasons. You had already imprinted that memory, and then your guilt did the rest. This guy repulsed you. He disgusted you. He made you a laughing stock. To the point that when your so-called friends talked about teaching him a lesson, you did nothing to dissuade them. Perhaps you even encouraged them. But you did not participate, Marco. You weren't even there.

So, as you moved to suppress yet another disappointing chapter with your father, you did what you've always done, you erased or revised what really happened, and you allowed your guilt to convince you that you were responsible. You fabricated a false memory. A bit like some exes do with a relationship that was quite shitty, yet they end up romanticising many years later.

You know this now. The mind is a powerful and terrifying thing. We see what we want to see. It's a state of denial."

I don't know what to say. I mean, my first thought is that the guy is lying in some weird way to make me feel better, but then, I know that's unlikely. So, I refocus on the memory and gradually, somewhere in the blur, I think I see snapshots of me leaving that place, of feeling proud that my father had picked me up in that car, from right in front of the school so that everybody could witness it.

Wind through my hair. The sun on my skin. The sound of sloshing water.

"Oh, fuck. That's right," I gasp. "He took me sailing. He loved sailing. I hated it. Hated the ocean... but when he surprised me that day and said I was going to be the first person on his new boat, I was grateful. I was so grateful that he deemed me worthy that I just sucked it up. I faced my phobia just so I could spend the day with him. Oh God, but I walked around that thing with my head lowered for most of the time so I wouldn't actually see the water, and I clung to anything that was screwed down. Even puked a couple of times."

I look up. Ethan has that knowing look on his face. "This is how strong your false guilt was; it was so strong, it overwrote what was probably one of the worst and best memories of your life. But it wasn't and isn't true, Marco. You were not responsible for what happened to Andy any more than you're responsible for what your friends did in your absence. It's why your subconscious introduced you to alter ego, Ryan, and why you've always shared a special affinity with David. It's your mind's way of processing and making amends."

Bloody hell. I can't believe this. Can you? For once, just once, a revelation that makes me feel better, not worse. But, I'm tired. I'm bloody exhausted.

I look at Ethan and grin. "You said a rude word, doctor?"

He chuckles. "I'm just glad you didn't pick up on my comment about the woods."

"Oh no, I heard that," I say, deliberately widening my eyes. "I heard that clearly, but I'm saving it. You know, stockpiling it in the back of what's left of my brain as ammunition for the next time you piss me off."

"Yes, I have no doubt. So, anyway... Really good progress today and, at the risk of sounding patronising and having you yell at me some more, I'm really proud of you. Really proud."

I rock my head. I don't feel proud of myself. I feel sad, but it's not like the doctor is going to let me linger on that – he's already on to the next thing.

"So," he continues, way too enthusiastically for my mood, "we've covered all of the main characters now, and we've been in every room of that house."

"Good, which means you might be able to see it in your good self to let me get the fuck out of here," I say, getting up as if the man is going to sign the papers here and now.

"Not quite."

"What do you mean?"

"There's one more room in your fort that you didn't venture into."

"No, there isn't. I went all over that place; all of the downstairs rooms and all of the upstairs, including the bloody attic!"

"All, but one," he says gravely.

And he's right. There's one room that I didn't even think of going into, and you would have thought it'd be the first; my old bedroom. And, I don't know what I've hidden in there, but it's obviously the worst of all.

THE ONE CONSTANT

Wednesday. 10:46.

So, you won't believe where I'm sitting right now. In fact, I still can't believe it. I can't even put it into words. Well, I can... But I'm just, well, lost for words. Here's a clue: Starbucks.

You've guessed it.

Fuck me. I'm sorry, but I don't know how to describe this delicious scent of fresh air, tinged with the subtle aroma of carbon monoxide, but, you know, compared to the stuffiness of Ethan's office, it may as well be pure oxygen. Especially today. It's a beautiful day. Not too cold, not too hot. The wind is blowing through the semi naked branches of the trees. The birds are singing. I'm all wrapped up, and, do you know what I'm clutching in my hand?

That's right.

I'm sitting on the park bench, I've got this little paradise all to myself, and I'm loving it.

I've been here for some time now. Ever since the doctor walked into his office and said that he had something to show me. The next thing I know, we're walking down the stairwell and into the dazzling sunlight. Beautiful. It did take some getting used to, but... well, it's just sublime.

Ethan said that I could use the vitamin D, and he was right. God, I don't know how to feel about that bloke. One minute I want to kill him, and the next I love him. I don't really need to prefix that for you, do I? The love is platonic – you know, in a friendship way.

Shit. I've noticed this about me, and I think it's gotten worse since we had that breakthrough about Andy and what happened at school. I want to express how I feel, but at the same time, I'm always trying to second guess how the person I'm talking to is going to perceive it.

Ethan said I should walk before I run. That won't be difficult. I've been an emotional cripple for years. Out of necessity and not by choice, apparently. It was my defence mechanism after the affection deficit left from both my parents. And then, what happened on the beach that day and the subsequent perpetual chasing of my father's affections like a little boy after an ice cream van.

My mother, as we've discovered, was sick. My father – well, he was a dick. Not as big of a dick as I previously believed, but one, nonetheless, since it's my dysfunctional relationship with him that led me on my lifelong quest to please him. This despite the fact that we'd cut off all ties. It's part of the reason why my so called alternate reality featured me as a psychologist, someone who'd studied and achieved, as opposed to someone who had not. Say, a mechanic, for example.

A fucking mechanic. Could I be any more boring? No wonder Ellie's parents were pissed when she ditched that city guy for a bloody mechanic. As you know, they have money. Lots of it. We've always shared a strained relationship because of it, too. Now I know why. Yeah, my wife and I are that cliché. Poor guy steals rich girl, gets her pregnant, and spends the rest of his life feeling he isn't worthy or deserving of her or their beautiful boy.

Toby. I love you.

Ethan and I have been working on my coming to terms with this. In so far as there's nothing wrong with being a grease monkey. I mean, it's an important job, as people need their cars, right? It's really important. Probably not as important as a brain surgeon, but almost. I mean, men of my profession are helping to keep the economy moving.

Oh shit. See? I'm doing it again. It's here where Ethan would ask who's struggling with this more; me or my memory of my father?

I would hate for Toby to go through anything like this.

The thought of my son brings a smile to my face, though. Do you know why? It's not necessarily because, well, he's my son, but because I know that, out of all of this mess, he is real.

Thank God.

Because there were a few anxious times where I thought Ethan was going to tell me that he wasn't, and I just don't know how I would have coped with that.

And what about Ellie, my wife?

I still can't get used to the fact that I am actually married to that policewoman. Well, I'm married to the woman, I mean. She actually isn't a policewoman, but a public relations executive. At least she used to be, for David's company.

Yes, he's real, too. And also, thank God. I mean, I'm not a religious person by any stretch of the imagination, but I'm ready to worship whoever may be responsible for these blessings.

I take a sip from my coffee, which is close to cold now, but still tastes bloody good, and I contemplate what's next. It's weird, because I feel as if the moment I've wished for, for weeks now, is finally here. The journey Ethan and I have embarked on what feels like many months ago is coming to an end, but I also have a hideous sense of impending doom... that something's going to happen, last minute. You know, like in the movies where the hero's just about to break free, and has just a few more steps, and then, BAM! The villain manages to grab him by the ankle and drag him back down the steps, into the basement with a thump, thump, thump!

And you know what happens in the basement, don't you? In the basement, *No one can hear you scream.*

Cue evil laugh.

"Hello."

The voice startles me and I almost drop my cup.

When I look up, it's into the sun, and I have to squint to make out the person standing over me. I mean, I'm doing this, but I don't need to see the face clearly to know who it is. All I need to do is look at the fiery auburn hair that's being fanned about those slender shoulders.

Ellie.

"Can I sit down?" she asks.

All I can do is nod, because my heart is startled, too, and it's thumping against my rib cage. At least it's decided to stick with me, unlike my tongue that appears to have left my mouth and has scampered off into the hedge somewhere.

I can smell her shampoo. Oh, Ellie.

In some weird comedy sketch kind of way, she's also carrying a cup of coffee. When she notices me looking at it, she offers, "Doctor Holmes' idea."

I smile. That guy thinks of everything.

"He's up there, watching us through the window right now, isn't he?"

She nods. "Probably."

I can't look at her. I don't know how to. There are a hundred things running through my mind and I can't identify any of them. It's like my brain is scrambling to find some purchase, but can't.

"He said I need to take it easy with you," she says.

"Really? Why? What are you planning to do to me out here, in public?"

"Well, given how handsome you're looking today, anything's possible," she says.

Oh yeah. That's Ellie.

An awkward teenage snicker slips through my lips and drags a curtain of heat up my face.

Oh shit.

Help me! Stop listening to my plight and make yourself useful; what should I say to this gorgeous woman, my wife, who's just paid me a compliment, and all I can think to say is, "You smell lovely."

Oh fuck.

She laughs.

It's like awkward teenage fumbling. On my part, of course. I think she's perfectly capable of dealing with this.

Seconds go by that feel like very long minutes.

"Ellie…"

"…Marco"

We interrupt each other.

"You go first," I say.

"Please, look at me," she says, and she may as well have belted me over the head with her shoe. "Please," she insists. But I don't know how. I don't know how to face her. I'm crippled with guilt. Racked with shame. Not only for the things I did, but for this, the here and now. For being stuck in this place, a mental case.

Which, by the way, is something that Ethan hates me saying, but, come on, you've thought it, haven't you? I bet you thought it from day bloody one. I don't blame you. I don't. Because I agree with you. I'm a fucking nut job that also happens to be a financial drain right now.

I feel delicate, cold fingers on my cheek. They linger, feeling the stubble where my beard used to be.

"You've shaved it."

My head moves, robotically, up and down against cold fingers, enjoying their touch on my skin. But I can't speak. I'm enraptured by it. I lean into the touch as a warm cloak envelopes me.

Ellie.

Slowly, gently, the fingers turn my head. At first, I resist it. I can't turn. I don't want to. I'm ashamed. I'm ashamed. I'm so ashamed. And yet, I'm now looking into those almond blue eyes that are glistening with tears, as are mine.

Ellie.

My lip starts to quiver, as does hers, and we fall into the tightest, most invigorating, most beautiful embrace I have ever experienced.

THE BEDROOM

Thursday. 10:05.

Rain is pelting the window and it's dark inside Ethan's office, to the point where the lamps on his desk and next to my chair are still blazing.

And it isn't just the weather that's a complete contrast to yesterday – my mood is, too. I don't know why. I just feel edgy. Confined. Like a bloody tiger pacing up and down its enclosure.

"Is everything okay, Marco?"

"Everything's fine, thanks, Ethan. Although, I am curious."

"Oh, what about?"

"I'd just like to know what yesterday was all about? You know, sending my wife out there with coffee in her fucking hand. Is that what you planned all along?"

He puts his notepad down and sits forward. "Wow. Okay. What's wrong?"

"I just told you what's fucking wrong! Why would you send my wife out there like that?" My eyes are wide. I'm tensed. And I have no idea why.

"I thought you'd enjoy the fresh air, a break from our sessions, and seeing your wife. Was I wrong?"

I'm about to answer, but I can't. I want to say yes, but... Of course, I was bloody happy to see Ellie. Even if we didn't do much talking, I felt that we at least re-established a connection. So, what's my problem?

"Marco?"

I wave him away, distractedly.

"What's wrong?"

I shake my head. "I'm sorry. I.." I don't know what to say.

"I thought you enjoyed seeing Ellie," he says.

The bedroom.

"I did. I… I'm…" Fuck, I can't get the words out.

Sun shining. People talking. Kites in the sky.

"Marco? Are you alright?" He's still leaning forward in his chair.

"I'm, I'm fine. "Um." My head feels fuzzy. My mouth dry. I take a sip of water. "Um, what, what were we talking about?"

He's looking at me, curiously. "You kicked off the session by telling me about your dream. Then, you just stopped."

The bedroom.

"Marco?"

I'm still staring into middle distance because I can't recall the images that keep flashing in my head. "I don't know what's happening. Um, I keep having these flashbacks to this memory," I say, distractedly.

"What is it? Tell me," he asks eagerly.

"Um, it started the other day; I was trying to picture me and Toby at the park here in London, but instead, I kept coming back to this other memory. One I don't recognise or remember. Then, yesterday, after Ellie left, it got stronger. More vivid. Then, last night I dreamt about it." I sigh. My head feels hot. It's warm in here. People talk about throwing up walls. Ever since we started doing this. Ever since I became aware, it feels like my wall has been smashed down. Now any ugly beast of a thought can wander around at will. Fuck.

"Tell me. Tell me exactly what you saw, what you dreamt."

I try hard to remember. "I'm, well, I can't work out if I'm in this dream or not. But if feels like I'm at a fairground or something. I only really know because I can hear that music – you know, an old-fashioned carrousel-type thing."

"What else?"

"I can't remember much else. It's just that music, the sun, and the sound of people talking. I don't know if I'm there, but it feels like I am. This doesn't make any fucking sense!" I laugh, then look at him, and see that he's staring at me, intently. "What?"

"I was just listening to what you were telling me."

"Okay. Well, can you be less intense about it? You're giving me the creeps."

"Sorry," he says with a smile, sitting back in his chair. Then, "What do you think it's about, your dream?"

"I've no idea, Doc. I thought that's why you're keeping me locked up here like a caged animal."

"It's that how you feel? Like a caged animal?"

"It was a figure of speech, Ethan, don't get excited. On the other hand, yeah. I guess that's how it feels. I mean, yesterday you seemed to have the whole petting zoo thing going on, too."

He pulls a pained face. "I don't know what you mean."

"Oh, come on, you know exactly what you were doing yesterday. You let Ellie out there with me and then you watched us from your ivory tower, like we were two fucking animals in heat or something. You were watching us like you wanted us to mate." I can hear my voice. It's bitter, but even I don't know why.

"Wow. So, we're back to yesterday again. Are you mad at me for yesterday?"

"You see? And that's just it. So fucking annoying," I say through clenched teeth. "When you pull that Uriah Heep shit."

He pulls another face and I want to slap it. "So, what I'm hearing is that you're feeling like a caged animal, that asking Ellie to visit was my own social–slash-animal experiment, and you hate how I speak, because I sound like an obsequious hand-wringing Dickens character."

"Yeah, that pretty much sums it up," I say.

"What are you afraid of, Marco?"

"Oh, God, Ethan," I moan, standing up and retreating to my window position. "Why does there always have to be subtext with you?"

"Because, there generally is. You should know this by now. And, don't get me wrong, I'm not demeaning how you feel in any way, I'm not. I can only imagine what it must feel like to be so confused about your life, your feelings, and I appreciate that that's part of the reason you're attacking me. But…"

"Of course, there's always a but…"

"*But*, I also think this has something to do with your memory, the dream you had last night, and your bedroom."

"My what?" Now it's my turn to screw up my face.

"We still haven't explored your old room…"

"Oh, fucking hell, not that again…"

"Marco, there's a reason why that room existed and why you never went in there, the whole time you were in that place."

"There's no fucking reason, Ethan!" I make claws with my hands and put them toward him. "None other than you wanting to poke your sticky little fingers inside to see what other shit you can rake up from my past to make me feel awful about myself." The last words have choked in my throat as a lump suddenly appeared there. What the hell's that all about?

We stare at each other for the longest time. Me, because I'm suddenly too paralysed to look away, as if by doing so I'll be alienated the only ally I have in all of this, and he, that bloke, probably to let me know that it doesn't matter how much I talk to him like he's dirt, he'll always be here. He isn't my father. He's here to help and he won't give up until his work is done.

No, I'm not insightful; that's pretty much been his mantra since I arrived here. It's probably why I'm always attacking him. According to him, it's my way of testing his word.

I finally break the stare-off and turn to look out of the window. I don't feel well. I feel queasy. Something is off today. Like I have this overwhelming need to retch, but I'm not able to. In this case, both physically and mentally.

There's something at the back of my mind. Something I can't quite get at. It's that bloody itch inside a cast again, and, as always, it's driving me fucking nuts, because I know it's there, and I can feel it getting worse, but I can't do anything about it.

"I'm sorry," I say, "I didn't mean to…"

"I'm sorry, Daddy, I didn't mean to make you cry."

"You realise that they're happy tears, right?"

"I know. It's because I'm cute and I say cute things."

I stagger back from the window like somebody has just hit me with a flamethrower.

Ethan is on his feet. "What's wrong? What happened?"

"I don't know," I gasp, blinking rapidly to clear the image from my eyes. "I just had a flashback to something. To that day."

"The day from your dreams?"

"Yeah. I was there. Toby was there." My eyes are wide, like I'm trying to see through them to the back of my head, back to the memory.

"Sit down, Marco, please," Ethan says, touching my arm and guiding me back to my seat, like I'm a bloody invalid.

I fall into it. "Cor, that was weird. It's like somebody smashed the memory over my head. It was like severed, electricity cables making contact then falling away again."

"What did you see exactly? Tell me what you saw."

"I, um, I... we were getting out of the car, walking across the car park, and um, well, I got out and had tears in my eyes. Toby said something and I was feeling emotional."

"Do you remember what he said? What made you feel that way?"

I'm staring into space, hoping the memory will come back. "No, I, um, he just said that... he must have said something cute. I don't know what. Ethan, look, I have to see him! You need to let me see him," I say desperately. "Please. Do you want me to beg, Ethan? Because I will!"

"It's not that simple, Marco."

"Why isn't it? You let Ellie visit. Why not my son? Come on, Ethan, he's my son, I need to see him."

"Do you really think you're able to deal with that right now?"

"Well, you set Ellie loose on me. And I know she's an adult and everything, but I need to see my boy." It occurs to me. "Jesus, I didn't see it before, but it's obvious now! That whole delusion, all of it. Everything at Porthcove was about my son. The pining, the birthday party, the boat, the missing boy, it's all about Toby. It's all about him!" I lean forward in my chair. "Can't you see, Ethan? My son is the key to all of this! He is the reason this is happening!"

And that's when it grabs me. It's a sudden jolt at first, and then it feels as if a giant trapdoor spider has leapt out, wrapped its legs around my head, and pulled me down into a barrel of ice water. The shock of which brings the day back to me like it's happening just now.

It's hot. English summers are often warm, but not always sunny, not like today. The sky is clear and gloriously blue. The windows are rolled down. The ocean breeze is fresh and heady with the smell of seaweed.

Toby is strapped into the passenger seat next to me.

"We're here. Are you excited?" I ask.

He nods, and I can tell by the big grin on his face that he's too excited for words. So, now might be a good time to ask my question. "So, um, listen, Daddy has a serious question to ask you."

"Uh oh."

"You haven't even heard it yet."

"Dad, you're not going to start talking about sex or something else embarrassing, are you?"

"What? No. But I do want to ask you an important question," I say in mock seriousness."

He turns to me, brown eyes squinting against the sun. "What's wrong?"

"Right now, in this very moment. Which of your parents is your favourite?"

"Oh, Dad," he complains, turning away from me and looking out of the window once more.

I laugh. "Come on, Toby. Just say the first thing that comes into your head. Just how you're feeling right now."

"You know you're not supposed to ask me that. Mummy doesn't think it's funny."

"Oh, I know, but it's just you and me here."

"You know I can tell her that you ex, exploited, a perfectly good father-son moment just to get me to say that you're the best parent."

I laugh, then find a parking space and pull into it. "Oh, well, I guess it was worth a try," I say in my best forlorn voice. "I'll just have to try some other time. Right after ice cream!" I declare with a grin.

"Yay!"

I'm about to get out of the car when he puts his little hand on my arm. "Dad?"

I stop and turn to him. "Yeah?"

"You're the best. But not better than Mummy, you're just the best dad in the world."

Tears instantly spring to my eyes.

"Oh no, I'm sorry, Daddy, I didn't mean to make you cry," he says.

"You do realise that they're happy tears, right?"

"I know," he says with a shrug, and then steps out of the car, but before he closes the door, he adds, "It's because I'm cute and I say cute things."

I just nod at the little man and I'm overwhelmed with love for him.

Seagulls greet us as we make our way to the back of the Volvo. It's old and has seen better days, but it's reliable and has seen us through some challenging times.

I open the boot and Toby retrieves the Galleon quadcopter as carefully as one would a ticking bomb.

"Okay, so, Toby, remember what we said. No flying that thing over people. It's why we're here early. As soon as it starts to get busy, you need to return to base. Okay?"

'Here' is a lookout point on the southern coast of England, where, after parking your car in what is pretty much a dirt field, and then making your way down a rocky path, you can reach what's left of the old pier – at the end of which are our favourite concession stands, featuring hot dogs and ice cream.

Toby sets the quadcopter, which is about the size of a large toaster, on the ground a few feet away from the car. He's already switched it on and the lights at its base flash red as it goes through its start-up procedure.

Ellie and I have been considering buying this thing for some time now, ever since the little man casually started leaving browser pages open on the family laptop. But, we've been putting it off because... well, it's quite expensive.

The Galleon is part of a new series of quadcopters that are designed to actually look like something, rather than a square thing with propellers on each corner.

In this case, it mimics an 18th Century Galleon, complete with sails, similar to the ones that fought in the battle of Trafalgar which, according to Toby, is one of Britain's greatest battles. It's when Nelson saw off both the French and Spanish naval forces, Ellie and I have been informed.

Yeah, my son loves history and boats – something he obviously gets from his grandfather – so when he saw this, well, it was the usual 'I'll never want anything for Christmas again' kind of plea.

And, to be fair to him, he worked for it. By that, I mean he contented himself with flying much cheaper models for nearly a year, and more than proved that he has a knack for piloting these things over lakes, parks, and general open spaces.

So, eventually, we took the plunge and opted for the best of the so-called fleet. An amphibious drone capable of conventional flight but featuring reverse thrust technology that swivels the propellers, enabling it both to fly and sail on water.

It is a thing of beauty – and I'm not just talking about the attention to detail, but about the thought that went into the aerodynamics of it, because, obviously, for a drone to fly as well as it does, it must comply with some basic aerodynamic rules. Flapping sails won't work. So, this thing has fins that are bent in such a way as to look like sails, but which are ultimately much sturdier.

Toby was in love the moment he unpacked it, and, if I'm perfectly honest, the kid in me still gets a kick out of seeing it do its thing.

A beep sounds, and then a loud buzzing sound fills the air. Seconds later, the ship takes to the sky in one rapid vertical ascent – the tiny British flag, the only organic part of it, flapping wildly behind it.

Toby holds the control box as I look up, cupping my eyes against the glare of the sun.

"Dad, I'm going to set it to 'follow mode' as we go down there. Watch this!"

There's a few seconds of concentration on his face as he taps the display. Then, "Look up and wave!"

I comply, and there's a shutter sound effect as he snaps pictures of us. We both pull faces, and he snaps a few more in quick succession; then, "Okay, let's go!"

"Are you sure that thing will…" But he isn't listening to me – he's already off, walking casually down the path.

"Come on!"

I obey my son and file in next to him.

"Look!" he says, holding up his hands and letting the control dangle from the lanyard around his neck. Sure enough, the drone is following us.

"Wow, that's so cool," I say, a grin spreading across my face.

"Wave!" he shouts. "I'm going to shoot video!" I comply, and there's a beep.

Then he yells and waves at the giant insect buzzing over us, "I LOVE MY DADDY!"

"Wait, that thing has sound, too?"

He looks at me and winks. "No, I just wanted you to know," he says casually, and walks off.

"Oh, you…" I call after him. He's a master manipulator. Just like his father, Ellie would say, if she were here, but she isn't because, well, it's a boy thing. Not that that would have bothered her, as we often do stuff as a family. No, she couldn't make it because David's launching a new game and things are a bit manic at the office.

We're at the pier now and, like an obedient pigeon, the drone is still following us.

"Dad, I'm recording the whole thing, and it's in HD. It's going to look awesome on the big TV later."

Our footsteps thump loudly now as we make our way over the weathered wood of the pier which, according to Toby, is over sixty years old, nearly a thousand feet long, fifty-three feet high, and recently declared one of the county's favourite attractions.

There's a strong breeze here, and yet, when I look up, that thing is gliding above us like it's on a track.

"So, the wind doesn't affect it then?"

"Nope. It's got GPS. That keeps it in the right place all the time, within a few feet."

"Cool," I say, gawking at it.

When I look ahead, I can see an elderly couple walking towards us. While, behind us, I can hear another pair of boots clunking against the wood.

There's quite a few people here already and I'm starting to get nervous about that thing flying above everyone. I've lost count of the articles I've read about the popularity of and rules associated with flying drones. There's no doubt in my mind that letting a ten-year-old pilot it over a public place is a definite no-no.

I don't want to say it, but I have to. "Toby, it's looking fairly busy." But he's walking about ten feet in front of me and yells, suddenly, "Look, Dad, three-sixty degrees!"

Almost instantly, the drone veers off. Seconds later, it starts encircling us like a sweeping helicopter getting a movie shot.

"So cool," Toby is breathing.

And it is. That's bloody amazing. But we're nearing the concession stands and there are even more people congregated here — about ten of them, standing at the kiosks or leaning on the metal railing and gazing down at the surf smashing on the rocks below.

"Okay, Toby…" But he isn't listening. "Toby!"

He finally turns to me. I gesture to the people and jerk my thumb in a downward motion.

"Oh, Dad," he complains. "Just a little longer?"

"No, not here. Bring it down," I say as discreetly as I can, because the last thing I want to do is draw attention to it. What I don't need is some clever dick getting in my face about it and ruining our day.

"Okay," Toby concedes. "I'll use the auto return to base features; that'll return it to the controller. Can we have ice cream now?"

"Sure," I say with a smile as I look up at the giant insect buzzing quietly above us.

"Return. To. Base," Toby declares, scowling at his screen. Then, he makes a show of tapping the button.

There's a beep, and a tinny female voice from the controller says, "Return to base initiated – 30 feet."

In that moment, there's vibration in my pocket. I glance at Toby, who's intently watching the drone slowly make its descent.

"25."

I pull the phone out of my pocket, glance at the display, and smile as I make my way towards one of the kiosks. "Hey, sexy," I say.

"Hey, handsome. What're you up to?"

"I'm out with my son. What about you?"

"Oh, you know, I'm here. Missing you."

"Yeah, how much?"

"Too much. I can't wait to see you tonight. Will you be able to get away?"

I glance at Toby. He's still waiting.

"20."

I pull a face. "I'm not sure about tonight. There's this thing I need to go to."

"Oh, but you promised."

"I know, but this is important; a friend of mine is launching this new product and, well, to him it's a big deal."

"Oh, no. But you'll come and see me after, right? I need to see you."

I glance at Toby.

"15."

"Oh please, pretty please. I'll make it worth your while."

"Oh yeah? How exactly do you plan on doing that?"

"Well, first, I'll pour us some drinks…"

"Go on." I look at Toby. He's still looking upward, but is scowling.

"10."

"Then, we'll sit on the bed …"

"9."

"… where I'll let you unbutton my blouse…"

"8."

Toby's moving towards the railing. Where's he going?

"…I'll unbutton your shirt …"

"7."

"Wait! No, Toby, no!""

"…then I'll trail my fingers down…"

"6 feet."

"TOBY! STOP!" *I drop my phone and run towards my son.*

"5."

He's clasping the handrail.

"4." *The drone is close. Slowly descending next to him, but it's going to miss the deck of the pier; it's going to plunge to the rocks below.*

"3."

He's climbed to the top of the handrail and is reaching for it as I reach for him.

"2."

"TOBY, NOOOOOO!"

"1."

He turns to me, a bewildered look on his face, his fingers inches from mine, and then he's gone.

"NOOOOOOOOOOOO! TOBY, NOOOOOOOOOOOO!"

ACCEPTANCE

Saturday. 3 weeks later.

So, now we know. I say 'we' because you found out at the same time I did.

Well, technically, you could say I already knew because I was there. I caused it. I'm the one responsible. But my mind chose to disassociate itself from that trauma, and it seems also from the rest of reality.

I suffered what is commonly referred to as a psychotic break. Where my 'break' means precisely that. I took a break from reality. I spent the good part of a month in a catatonic state, during which my mind attempted to process what had happened in the safest way it knew how. A bit like 'Safe Mode' in a computer program. During that time, it attempted to hide all the shitty stuff that happened in my life by burying it at the back of my mind while simultaneously generating an alternate reality... at least in my head.

The two weeks in my head were really two months in here. In therapy.

But it's only now that I can see the clues;

My unexplored childhood room at Dolce Vita.

Where I hid the memory of what really happened that day.

The missing boy and the ship I gifted him.

Toby and that thing.

My being implicated in the disappearance of the little boy.

The guilt and responsibility I feel for what happened that day.

No signal at the house.

Everybody getting a signal but me, indicative of my disconnection from reality.

The lack of photos of Toby on my phone.

These were both flaws as well as clues to my self-deception, yet I chose to continue to perpetuate the fantasy because reality was something I couldn't bear.

That's why, when I emerged from the revelation of what happened that day at the pier, I almost trashed Doctor Holmes' office and nearly kill him in the process. I wanted to. After all, he's the one who opened my eyes to this stuff. He's the one who brought me back to a reality I rejected by subjecting me to endless therapy sessions, as well as meds to suppress the delusions. *He* stopped me from seeing the things that aren't there. Like my little boy.

Ethan and I have talked about many things over the past few weeks. As you can imagine, most of what I said consisted of swear words. He, on the other hand, is on a bloody loop, spouting words like *acceptance* and *forgiveness*, *mourning*, *healing*, and all of that other bullshit, but at the end of the day, they're just words. They mean nothing in the real world. They don't help me to accept and forgive myself. How can I?

Yet, he still thinks that I'm ready. That it's time for me to deal with and accept what happened, without him.

Ready?

It just goes to show that he doesn't have the first clue about what it means to lose a child. A living, breathing, beautiful being that is of your own flesh and blood.

I'll never be ready.

I can never accept this. *But you can learn to live with it,* is his response. Learn to live? The man's on crack. How can anybody learn to live with the fact that they're responsible for the death of their own child?

And yet people do, is his response to that.

And yet, *I* want to punch him in the face every time he so much as suggests it. He so much as breathes the idea of me living without my boy.... I don't want to learn to live without him, because I don't want to accept that he's gone.

And yet, he is.

And despite that fact, he's cutting me loose today. That's right. Can you believe it? This will be our last session.

Of course, as is always the case with Doctor Ethan Holmes, there's still one last thing he wants to go through. One last angle. One other hornet's nest of shit he still wants to stir.

In this case, it's truth. One more truth before he sends me on my merry way. And for this one, he's even enlisted Ellie's help. Apparently, she'll be joining us at the end of this session for a little couple's counselling.

What do you think of that?

"Marco?"

"I think it's shit."

"What are we talking about?" he asks, calmly.

"That you're kicking me out of here at a time when I need you the most."

"Marco, we've talked about this."

"Yeah, we have. But you go out of your fucking way to make me confront this, you strip me of all protection, and then you kick me out there, butt naked?" I scowl at him, incredulously. "Who the fuck does that?"

He suppresses a sigh. "You know that isn't what I'm doing."

"Isn't it?"

"No, it isn't, and you know it isn't because we've discussed this. Bereavement isn't my area of expertise."

"Well, you seem to have done a pretty lousy job for the past few months, so why not carry on?"

He looks at me. "Do you truly believe that?"

"Yes I do," I say, jaw muscles flexing.

He shifts in his seat. "Marco. I know you're angry with me…"

"… too fucking right…"

"…because you feel that I am abandoning you, but you know that I am not. We've talked about this." His voice is calm and measured. "It's important to me that you and Ellie get the best possible support to help you deal with what has happened."

"And you think we're gonna get that from some stranger?"

"No. You are going to get that from a very capable colleague of mine who is going to give me regular updates. Come on, Marco." He's smiling. I'm not. I have my arms folded in front of me, nervously twitching my man-spread on what's left of the shitty chair.

Yeah, the chair. I can't believe that vases were smashed, furniture up-ended, diplomas and paintings swept from walls, and yet, this shitty thing still lives.

The memory of my destruction spree cools my temper like a cold shower and humbles me.

I look out of the window.

"It's going to be okay," he says.

"I'm sorry about what I did to your stuff," I respond.

He looks at me, the surprise clear on his face. Surprised because this is the first time I've said that, since I damaged and or scuffed much of the stuff in here.

He nods and smiles. "Thank you for saying that. I appreciate it. But it's okay. This place was due a refurbishment anyway. You see, as soon as I get rid of you, I have another batch of rich people I need to fleece to fund my extravagant existence." There's still a wry smile on his face.

"Have I ever mentioned how unprofessional you can be sometimes?" I ask.

"Yep. I believe you have."

Birds tweet noisily outside as we share silence, and I must have some kind of forlorn slash terrified look on my face because he repeats, sympathetically. "You *are* going to be okay, you know."

I focus on him and there's a lump in my throat. "There's nothing for me out there, Ethan,"

"You mean besides a life to live and a wife who adores you?"

"There's no life without him."

"That's your grief talking. You know it is. We've been over this. You're both still young – well, relatively." He smiles, then adds, seriously, "And while you'll never replace Toby, you can still start a family, forge a different life. And I know you don't necessarily want to hear it right now, but you need to understand that it isn't over, for either of you."

Tears well in my eyes. He's right, but at the same time I don't want to hear it. I still don't want him to talk about Toby like he isn't here. In fact, I've already conjured up a fantasy which, in case you're wondering, I know is exactly that. When I walk out of this place today, Ellie will be waiting for me and Toby will be standing next to her, holding her hand, and all of this. All of it will have been one of those shitty dreams.

"Where have you gone?" he's asking.

"I'm just thinking about the trip," I lie. "Just wondering if it really is the best thing for both of us right now."

"Well, you won't know until you try. I think it's the perfect change you both need, to breathe, get some perspective, and grieve properly, together."

He's talking about our leaving London.

We've decided to go and spend some time in the country. No, not with Ellie's parents. She's already spent nearly three months with them, and I think she's just about ready to murder them.

No, we're going to spend some time in Porthcove, of all places. Yes, the place does exist. As does my old man's will, in which he states very clearly that Dolce Vita is mine. Nobody has contested this. Why would they? They got everything else.

And it's okay. I'm fine with that. I'm just grateful he remembered me at all. No, not in an angst-ridden kind of way. I'm done with that because I am choosing to take the Doctor's advice. I am choosing to leave all of that shit in the past where it belongs. Just like I'm choosing to take with me the belief that he may not have been perfect, but he was the best father his own demons allowed him to be, and I'm going to take the best and leave it at that.

Of course, we don't know where we'll be staying yet, because we don't really know what we're going to find when we get there. And, despite everything that happened before, in my head, that is kind of exciting.

Ethan suggested it. He thinks that having a new, mutual, and collaborative focus will help us both. By that, he means us working on refurbishing Dolce Vita to a saleable condition, whatever that may be.

I think I want to sell. I don't know. We've just agreed to take one day at a time. And, for now, that's good enough for me.

Ellie's already contacted an estate agent to do a valuation for us. Sorry – a relator. Her name is Lucinda and she's one of those typically brash Southern Americans. The type that doesn't engage her brain before opening her mouth. I'm guessing that's probably why my wife likes her.

Ellie contacted Lucinda a while back, as soon as I found out that the old man had had a heart attack and had left me the house. Only, life got in the way. There were my so-called indiscretions, which the saint, otherwise known as my wife, forgave, on the understanding that we'd move away from London, back to where we first met. I agreed. And then, well... that day happened, and everything got cancelled, until now.

"Marco?"

"I'm just thinking about how different everything feels now," I say.

"How so?"

"Well, just thinking back on my life, a few months back. It's like none of that was real, as if I'm remembering the life of someone else."

"That's because you are. You were a completely different person back then. You had to be in order to get through the day. It was the only way you knew how to cope with everything that happened to you. The intimacy, your perception of love, the immense guilt you were carrying and yet suppressing, both for the things that happened in your past and now. It really is very important that you remember the work we've done here, Marco. Especially the part where we talk about culpability. Much of what happened wasn't your fault, including and especially what happened to Toby."

I shift in my chair for multiple reasons. I don't necessarily like him talking about it, and nor do I buy into the fact that it wasn't my being distracted on the fucking phone that led to my son…

"…I know you don't want to accept it. But I'm telling you now, if you really want to make this good, if you really want the future to be different from your past, then you need to accept and, most importantly, forgive not just those who wronged you, but yourself."

"Okay, now you're starting to sound like a Facebook poster."

He cocks his head. "Just because it might be a Facebook poster, doesn't make it any less true."

"You're an arsehole."

"Well, you know, I'm always interested in what you have to say."

He's smiling. This is our banter. And I'm going to miss it, and him, a lot.

His phone vibrates. "Ah, this could be Ellie," he says, reaching for it and then putting it to his ear.

"Yes? Oh, yeah. Yes, could see her through, please? Thanks." He disconnects the call and slips the phone back into his pocket.

"Should I be nervous?" I ask. My hands feel clammy.

"I don't know. Should you? Are you?"

"Actually, I am."

"Which is understandable. It's only ever been you and me in session."

"Yeah, and I'm not sure how I feel about…"

"… stop stalling, Marco."

"What?"

"You're stalling. You know why I want Ellie to join us. Deep inside, you know the truth, but, like most of the other things that brought you here in the first place, you're choosing to ignore it because you feel it's the right thing to do. That's because you're still struggling with the concept of functioning without your suit of guilt."

"Did I mention you were an arsehole?"

"Yeah, I think you did."

"Well, you're actually a dick!"

There's a knock on the door, and I look at it as I did that night. For some inexplicable reason, I'm scared. Like there's some other deep, crappy secret that I don't want to hear about, but this fucking guy insists I face.

He opens the door and there's Ellie. She looks beautiful. Her hair's in a ponytail and she looks youthful, nervous, yet tired. And I can't help but wonder if she's been sleeping, if her parents have been good to her.

The sight of her in this room once more, today of all days, lift my heart, and I realise just how bloody emotional I'm feeling. Something that would never have happened a few months back.

Thanks for nothing, Doc!

"Hey," I say, getting out of my seat.

"Hey," she responds, beaming an awkward smile as she takes in the room as if she's seeing it for the first time.

I kiss her on the cheek. We hug, tightly. And, as usual, her scent is an instant sedative.

The doctor is busy rearranging the room. He's pushes his chair over to my ugly one and replaces it with the desk chair.

Ellie perches herself on the seat and takes my hand.

"Ellie, thank you so much for joining us today," he says, like we're in church or something.

"Oh, it's no problem," she says with a smile and a reassuring smoothing of her hair.

"So, tell me. How have you been coping?"

"Oh, you know... One day at a time," she says, clearly putting on a brave face.

I squeeze her hand.

Ethan nods, sympathetically, and then asks, "How about the trip – are you all set?"

She nods enthusiastically, her ponytail bobbing up and down behind her. "I think so, but it doesn't feel real because I don't have much loaded in the car. Just a few things. Everything else is in storage until we know exactly where we're going to land."

"Are you excited?"

"I think so, yeah. It's both exciting and scary."

"Marco?"

"Am I excited?" I look up at Ellie. "I'm excited to have my wife back, yeah," I say, delicately lifting and kissing her hand. "Everything else... I'm scared shitless, mate!"

"And there it is," the doc says in mock disappointment. "Now, you two have been through an unimaginable amount of, and I'm going to use Marco's terminology here, shit. You've been through so much, in a few months, that most people don't endure in a lifetime. And, I can see that you're both nodding at that statement, but what I would really like is for you both to truly believe and understand it. Now, by 'understand', I mean I want you to appreciate just how much you've already endured as well as the inevitable challenges that still lie ahead. That means being kinder, gentler with yourselves, and each other. Recognising those things that you can change and accepting those things that you cannot. This is extremely important." The doctor's tone is serious, a bit like a parent talking to his children. And, like children, we're both paying attention. "Marco is a very good example of what I'm talking about, Ellie," he continues, looking at me.

I pull a face. Force a smile. "What did I do?"

"This whole thing happened, Marco, because of your refusal to *accept*," he says sternly.

"I don't know what you're talking about, mate," I joke, but the accompanying smile is awkward because I think he's making a point I don't yet understand.

"Yes, you do. It's one of the last things that you refuse to accept and are still blaming yourself for. That's why I asked Ellie here today, to help me explain to you that now is the time to stop."

"Well, maybe, Doctor, if you *explained* what you're going on about, I might be able to do something about it," I say, fake smile still on my face, but my back already up.

He nods. "Okay, but to do that, we're going to need to return to that day on the pier."

"Oh, hell fucking no, Ethan. We've done nothing but talk about this! I'm through talking about it. I mean, for crying out loud, on the one hand, you say consign the past to the past, but on the other, you insist on taking me back to places I don't want to be. I swear to God, you're a fucking sadist!" I shift in my chair, grinding my teeth.

"Have you finished?"

"Have you?" I look at him pointedly. Now I can feel Ellie squeezing my hand.

"I just want to ask you one question, Marco. Is that okay?"

"Do I have a choice?"

"Of course you do."

"Marco," Ellie says softly, blinking those blues at me.

Shit. "Go ahead. Ask me your stupid question," I say, waving at the man.

He clears his throat and asks, delicately, "Moments before the accident, you were talking on the phone; is that right?"

"You know I was," I say, irritated. I don't want to relive that with Ellie here. Arsehole!

"Who were you talking to?"

"What?"

"Who were you talking to?"

I squint at him. "You're a fucking piece of shit, do you know that?"

"Just, please answer my question."

"No, I'm not answering a stupid question you already have the answer to!"

"Why not?"

"Because I don't need to."

"Why?"

"Fuck you! Come on, Ell, let's get out of here," I say, moving to get up. "And to think I was feeling bad about this being our last session. Ell," I complain, because her hand is forcing me back into the chair.

"Marco?"

"Ell, let me up."

"Marco!" Ethan yells.

"What?" I snap.

"Look at your reaction. You haven't reacted like this in a while. Why do you think that is?"

"Um, I don't know, because you're pissing me the fuck off?" I ask.

"No, because you feel that you need to protect Ellie from an untruth."

I pull another face. "You've lost me."

"Please answer my question," he pushes.

"I told you…"

"I want you to answer my question."

"You know who I was talking to."

"Marco, just answer the man's question," Ellie interjects.

"No, I'm not, it's just a sick game to him. He already knows. You already know! Why he wants me to tell him who the fuck I was talking to is just some twisted thing he likes to do."

Ellie looks at me, at the doctor, and then back at me. Now it's her turn to look confused. "I don't understand. Why can't you just tell him that you were on the phone with me?"

I'm so busy glaring at the spectacled guy that I don't even hear Ellie at first, but then, as I absorb her words, I glance at her, back at him, and then double-take back to her. "What? What did you just say?"

She looks confused. "Why can't you just tell him that you were on the phone to me?"

"Because I wasn't on the phone to you," I mumble, grinding my teeth some more and shooting the bloke across from us another murderous scowl. I could quite cheerfully jump out of this chair, clamp my hands around his throat, and finish the job I started that day.

She frowns. "What are you talking about?"

I break my stare off with the therapist to look at my wife, and I can instantly feel my face relax. "Ellie, I wasn't on the phone to you when …" I can't finish my sentence because of the knot in my throat, the burning in my cheeks and the giant slab of shame pressing me down into my chair.

In all of the chaos, I don't think my wife and I have ever talked about this. We've never talked about the fact that I was whispering shit to some woman I can't even remember while my son… I can't do this!

"Why are you saying this?" she's asking.

"Because it's the truth, and I'm sorry! I'm so so sorry," I whisper as I feel the prick of tears.

"Is that what you've been telling yourself?" She asks, with a quiver in her voice.

"That's how it happened. If it wasn't for me…"

"… No, baby… no, no. That isn't how it happened," she interrupts. "Marco… Look at me." She turns to me in her chair and cups my face with her hands, "No, baby, that isn't what happened," she chants. Those blue eyes shimmering with her own tears. "It was me. I was... I was the one who called you."

I try to shake my head, but she's holding it firm so that I have no choice but to keep my eyes on her so that I will receive, understand, what she is saying. "It was me and you, *we* were talking on the phone."

"N-no. It isn't possible."

"It is, Marco," the doctor contributes. "You were both going to the launch that night. You planned to go as a family. You were role-playing on the phone as if you wouldn't be seeing each other, but you were all going, together."

"No, it isn't. I would remember. I would remember something like that," I protest.

"Yes, but only if you would allow yourself to, Marco. But you can't. You only know blame and shame. You blamed yourself for everything that happened to you as a child and you have been shaming yourself ever since. You know this. It's one of the reasons you have such a quick temper. You think that if you growl and attack, nobody is going to stay around long enough to see the truth, but someone did."

He looks at Ellie.

"Is this true?" I choke, following his gaze.

"Yes, baby." She trembles, tears streaking down her face.

"So, so, you heard when…"

"…Y-yes, baby. I did," she sobs, throwing her arms around me. We cling to each other as if our own lives depend on it.

And that's when the real tears come, and I'm not talking about gentle sobs, but the gut-wrenching ones that form deep in your chest. The kind of sobbing that tenses your skull and puts your whole body into a series of unstoppable convulsions for which there is no consolation, but only endurance strengthened by time.

We must stay that way for at least half an hour. Ethan says it's because we've commenced the process of exorcising everything we've been through, including my last failed attempt to replace truth with fantasy.

Apparently, it was easy for me to rewrite the reality of that phone call with the manifestation of guilt I was still experiencing over my infidelity. Even though Ellie had forgiven me and we had agreed to put everything behind us. Toby's death not only triggered my psychosis, but it changed everything – or, at least it did in my mind.

On the other hand, while it's all well and good to have an explanation for everything, one fact remains true; all of this happened because of me. No matter the reason. No matter how anybody tries to explain it.

But, I guess that's where the forgiveness comes in. If I really want to move on, I must forgive and accept the things over which I have no control.

Yeah, I mean, I'm thinking that, but still; it's easier said than done.

When we finally leave the building about an hour later, and I'm able venture beyond the iron gate, Ethan comes with us. To be perfectly honest, I struggle with the moment. For a variety of reasons, not least the fact that, despite my shitty treatment of him, this man has given my life back to me. Yeah, you could say that it's a bit worse for wear, but with time... who knows, eh?

Ellie squeezes Doctor Ethan Holmes so tight, I think she's seeking retribution for all the shit he's put me through, but she isn't. She also kisses him on the cheek and makes him promise to visit once we know where we'll be. Then, she agrees to sit in the passenger seat after I tell her that she needs to take a physical and metaphorical break from driving.

Then, I look at the man who's saved my life and he looks at me.

Fuck. My tongue just ran off again.

"You know, you actually do have lovely green eyes?" he helps out with a wink.

I laugh. "Have you any idea how incredibly inappropriate that was?"

"Absolutely. But this is your last day. You're no longer my patient. I'm allowed to say whatever I want."

"Yeah, like you ever held back."

I squint up into the sun. It feels good on my face. "It's a beautiful day," I say, as I search for the right thing to say. Then, after a few more seconds of breathing in the fresh air and listening to the bird chorus, I utter, "Ethan, I really want to say something profound, but I don't know how." I choke on the last words, finally looking at him.

"Shit, Marco. We haven't got that long. You need to get on the road."

I laugh. "You're almost as bad as David."

"Where do you think I get it from?"

I cock my head, curiously. "No, you two aren't...?"

He grins.

"You're bloody joking, right? You're a married man!"

"Happily. But, you know, over the past few months, David and I have talked a lot."

"Yeah?"

"Yes. Didn't I mention that?" he asks, feigning surprise.

"No, you didn't."

"Oh yes. He may not have been able to visit that often. Mostly, because I told him he wasn't allowed to, but your best friend checked in on you nearly every day."

Yep. My cheeks are burning again.

He gives me a reassuring smile, "See? I told you, you aren't alone out here." My face is probably glowing. I know he can see it, too, so he ploughs on "Of course, this means that if doesn't work out with my husband, David and I may start seeing more of each other…"

"No. Please tell me you're bloody joking."

"What do you mean?"

I glance at Ellie. She's buzzed her window down, has been listening to everything and is peeing herself with laughter.

"Oh, I see. Funny. Very funny," I say.

"What? You don't like that idea?"

"Hell bloody no. I already have those two ganging up on me; I don't need another joining the club. Shit – especially not you!"

We all laugh, and it's right now, in this very moment, that I allow myself to consider the notion that maybe, just maybe, we're going to be alright.

EPILOGUE

I'm still thinking about my time with Doctor Ethan Holmes when the text alert from my phone sounds loudly, bringing me back to the present.

We're inside a motorway Marks and Spencer. Ellie is already in the checkout line, carrying bottled water and a packet of boiled sweets. I'm mooching around and feeling like I need to buy something, but am disinterested in everything.

I pull the phone out of my pocket. There are two text messages. One from David, wishing us a safe journey and promising to visit us as soon as we let him know where we are, and the other is from the doctor. It contains just one word. "EΛT!"

I smile, grab a couple of sandwiches, some fruit, and join Ellie in line. She looks at my hands and then at me. "Doctor's orders," I say.

We pay for our goods and make our way silently towards the exit when, suddenly, Ellie drops the bag she's carrying and throws her hands to her mouth as her legs buckle beneath her. I rush forward to catch her fall and, in doing so, slam up against one of those coin-activated dinosaur rides.

The thing responds to my touch by greeting me with an overly excited American, Barney-like voice. *"Howdy, weary traveller, jump on and take a rest on my shoulders!"*

Toby used to love these things.

We're both sitting on the floor now, next to the ride that's bucking gently back and forth, lights flashing. The character laughing, *"Fun! Fun! Fun!"*

I slide an arm around my wife then pull her sobbing and quivering body into my chest.

People mill back and forth in front us, entering and exiting the building and going on to their lives as we sit here on the cold tiles. Most don't even see us. Some glance in our direction, others whisper, but none stop.

"I… I… miss him," Ellie garbles through sobs. "I miss him so much…"

"I know, baby. I know," I whisper, holding her close and stroking her hair while simultaneously wrestling with the wave of hopelessness that has engulfed me. My wife is in pain, and there is absolutely nothing I can do about it.

Nothing.

Why did this happen to her? Us. What did we do so wrong? I feel angry. Frustrated. Powerless. Hopeless.

"I'm sorry. I'm so so sorry," she says in between sniffs, shudders and gulps.

"Shh… you have nothing to be sorry about."

"I do," she says, pulling out of the embrace and looking up at me. Oh God, I wish I could take her pain away. "I do, Marc. I nearly gave up on you. I nearly let you go. I wanted to see it through, but it was hard. It was really hard. I just didn't think we'd ever get to the other side of this."

I smile affectionately. "Are you joking? You feel bad because you thought about giving up on me? Ellie, you're the only thing that kept me going through all of this and, fuck, I don't deserve you. I really don't. But, I'm bloody grateful I'm so bloody grateful to have you," I say, squeezing her close and planting delicate kisses in her hair.

"Sir, is everything okay?"

I look up to see a security guard peering down at us.

I can only imagine what we must look like, sitting on the dirty floor, "Um, we're fine," I say. "We're gonna be fine."

The words leave my mouth, but I have no idea if they're true. I mean, I want them to be true, of course I do, but I don't know if they ever will be.

Shit. Everything would be so much easier if all of this were untrue. If all of this were just another one of those dreams, where I'm going to wake up and find myself lying on the couch in our flat in London.

And it's now, in this very moment, that those two bloody words enter my head. I instantly squish them down, like moles with a mallet, but they pop up again. So, I smack them down once more.

No.

It takes us another five or so hours of road travel before we begin our descent into the hamlet of Porthcove, and I can tell you, it's probably one of the strangest feelings I've ever had. It's like going back to a childhood home, decades later. But then, I suppose I am. Everything's still here, but the perspective is completely different.

The high street looks nothing like how I imagined it. I mean, it's all here... But, the shop signs aren't painted, and nor are they all symmetrically aligned. The people who are roaming on and off the cobbled street, many of whom look like tourists, aren't wearing their best Sunday garb, but contemporary clothing – such as jeans, jumpers and trainers.

Nobody greets or smiles at our passing vehicle as I drive us off of the high street and down towards the harbour where a faded sign for Dolce Vita is hidden among a plethora of other road and general signs.

The bridge to the house is here, but it's over a brook and not a train track.

And the house itself looks nothing like an Italian villa. Far from it. It looks more like a small cottage made of natural grey stone. The picket fence isn't white, but weather-worn grey and broken in places.

It isn't more than five minutes since I pulled up outside of the house and killed the engine, before the black BMW crunches its way over the gravel to a stop behind us.

Out of the car, there emerges a diminutive, skinny looking lady in a red trouser suit who introduces herself as Lucinda Kaye. Oh well – at least I got part of it right.

Inside, the house is small, cosy, and much darker without the skylight and overhead balcony I imagined. They do not exist. Nor does the study, but there is a photography room. There's also a dining room that extends out to a small, but cute conservatory with views out to sea.

In the so-called den, there are a couple of two-seater couches and an armchair. Both look out onto a set of patio doors featuring more views of the sea. They're partially obscured by an overgrown hedgerow that surrounds the place. This, Lucinda recommends, we trim back to make the place feel brighter and airy.

In all, the estate agent doesn't stay longer than a couple of hours, since there isn't much for her to look at. She does say that the views are impressive and will no doubt add value, and that, with work, she's confident the place will actually fetch around one to one-point-five million, though she says she needs to take a closer look at the boundary plans to be able to give a definitive estimate.

Then, with a promise to be in touch soon, she climbs back into the BMW and leaves us.

The cottage has two small bedrooms upstairs. They're both a bit dusty, but it's nothing that a good clean and a fresh set of linen can't fix.

So, we decide to stay. Which means going out to get supplies, but first, we both realise we're famished to the point of feeling lightheaded. So, we decide to take our sandwiches down to the beach.

It's nippy outside, and foggy, but this doesn't deter us. We're both craving a stretch as well as the fresh ocean breeze after being cooped up in the car for so long.

So, hand in hand, we help each other down a rather precarious coastal path until we make it to the shingled shore where the fog has been burnt away by the sun in places, leaving patches of haze and winter sunshine.

There are a few people down here. Dog walkers, mostly.

And it feels odd being back on this stretch of beach. Odder still, when you add in the reality of what my mother tried to do to me here three decades ago. Yet, I remind myself that it is now just a blurry memory that belongs in the past. I replace it with the memory of my walk here with Ellie. Although, being here now, in this moment, I'm still struggling to convince myself that it never really happened, but that it was my subconscious, using the avatar of my wife, to try and help me process, heal, and eventually escape my self-delusion.

Jesus, you can go crazy just thinking about this stuff!

So, I distract myself by breaking the seal on a bottle of water and handing it to my wife. She looks at it like it's poison, but takes a dainty sip. I pull a face and she reluctantly drinks some more. Then, I take the bottle from her and replace it with a sandwich, which she promptly refuses before I insist that she needs to eat.

"It's my turn to take care of you," I say loudly, over the clash between fizzing surf and rattling pebbles.

"Um, it's going to take more than a sandwich and a bottle of water," she warns with a raised eyebrow and a smile.

"Baby steps, right?"

"Right." She smiles.

We kiss, and then I watch her slowly nibble at her sandwich as she gazes out across the water.

I love this woman, and I'm not saying that in a twee every day kind of way – I mean it in the sense that she is everything to me. I know it now. In fact, I think I'm much more aware of it now than I ever was before. Ultimately, the village, the house... they may all be different from how I imagined them, but there's always been one constant. Even then, in a whole artificial world, one thing remained true – my love, my attraction for this woman – and I know and truly believe that, no matter what, that will never change.

And it's now, in this tender moment, while what's left of my so-called guard is lowered, that I allow myself to flirt with those two words. The same two words that I've considered but resolved to ignore, since before we even left the institute.

What if?

God, I let myself savour them as an alcoholic does a sip of booze.

What if?

What if this was all another dimension of my delusion? What if all of this was just another one of those episodes, those dreams from which I can wake up and find myself in an alternate reality? What if? What if what is happening, right now, isn't?

Of course, I know I shouldn't be thinking like this, that I should not be indulging these thoughts, because to do so is to be playing with fire, to risk sending myself back into a whole new cycle... but *what if?*

Oh, this is crazy!

It's exactly what Ethan warned me against. If there is one thing he has warned me about, over and over again ever since my so-called emergence into the real world, is that it's important, vital, that I stay in the here and now, that I not be seduced into dwelling on anything other than what is happening to me in this very moment, in the present.

Because, *this* is my reality.

It's the very reason why he's prescribed those drugs to me, which I haven't taken yet because, well, with the travelling and everything... but what if, huh?

What if?

"Are you okay?" Ellie is asking.

"Yeah, I'm good," I say with a big smile as I glance ahead of us, where I catch sight of something. I almost miss it at first, but…there! Through the wisps of mist hanging over the shoreline, about ten yards away…

I cock my head to one side, as if I can see around the fog. Yeah! There! A little boy with sandy blonde hair, kneeling in the pebbles. He seems to be playing with something, but I can't tell what because he has his back to us.

From behind, no word of a lie, it looks just like him. So, I start walking forward. I start walking forward and wonder if this is a sign. Is this a sign? If I walk over there, will that boy turn around, and will I wake up from another weird dream?

Oh, God. Just the thought of that shines on me like a warm summer's day. Just imagine how happy Ellie would be. How happy we'd both be! Ecstatic!

"Marco?"

Ellie's calling to me, but I'm already a few steps ahead of her, moving fast.

"I'll be right back," I call over my shoulder. "I'm just going to check something."

"Check what? Marco?"

But, I'm not listening. I'm walking, staggering somewhat as my feet sink into the pebbles that click and suck at my boots.

"Toby?" I utter, squinting through the mist, but the boy doesn't turn. So I increase my pace. "Toby?"

I'm about fifteen feet away now.

"Toby?"

8 feet.

I've broken into a stilted jog. My breath fogging out in front of me. "Toby!"

The boy's shoulders stop moving. He heard me call his name. He recognised his name!

5 feet.

I scrunch to a halt. "Toby?" I utter as the boy shifts and slowly turns to look my way…

If you enjoyed

PSYCHOSIS

Please leave an Amazon review
so that others may enjoy it also.

If you can't wait for Tony Marturano's next thriller, sign up to the blog for the latest news, special chapter previews of future books and exclusive giveaways.

www.tonymarturano.com

ACKNOWLEDGEMENTS

As always, I'm so very grateful to everyone at a Different Angle, who have supported me throughout this book's journey, from manuscript to print. In particular, I'd like to thank those who have actively contributed to its realisation.

MY EDITOR
Jennifer Collins (for keeping me on the straight and narrow).

THE PSYCHOSIS FOCUS/READER'S GROUP
My heartfelt thanks to all members of the Psychosis reader's group, for giving so generously of their time and opinions!

(In no particular order)
Francesca Marturano-Pratt – Anna Pratt – Tamanda Flynn – Renee Owens – Lisa Hall – Rosa Littleton – Nicola Ramsbottom – Gill Mundin.

Special thanks to Anna Pratt who's always there when needed and to my number one fan – Francesca Marturano-Pratt.

YOU, THE READER
If you're reading this book, there's a good chance you bought it. I'm obviously very grateful for that. Thank you!
On the other hand, if you borrowed this book from somebody else. Even better! It means they thought it was good enough to pass on.

Thank you so much for taking the time.
Without you, my words would be but meaningless letters arranged on a page.

COMING SOON

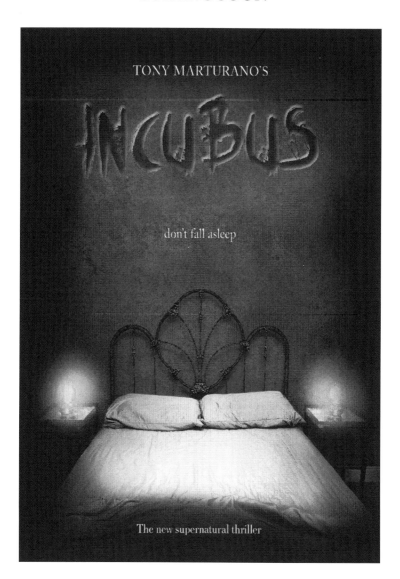

Printed in Great Britain
by Amazon

50538749R00243